THE HIGHGATE CEMETERY MURDER

IRINA SHAPIRO

Storm
PUBLISHING

To request permissions, contact the publisher at rights@stormpublishing.co

Ebook ISBN: 978-1-80508-177-7
Paperback ISBN: 978-1-80508-179-1

Cover design: Debbie Clement
Cover images: Trevillion, Shutterstock, Alamy

Published by Storm Publishing.
For further information, visit:
www.stormpublishing.co

ALSO BY IRINA SHAPIRO

A Tate and Bell Mystery

The Highgate Cemetery Murder

Wonderland Series

The Passage

Wonderland

Sins of Omission

The Queen's Gambit

Comes the Dawn

For Alex, Rebecca, and Andrew.
You are everything.

PROLOGUE

All Saints' Day

The silence was unnerving, the forbidding vaults and ancient monuments glistening with moisture after last night's rain. The trees, their brilliant autumn colors muted against the pewter smudge of the morning sky, looked for all the world like they were weeping for the dead. The cemetery was deserted, the paths muddy and unkempt.

Victor Tate bent his head into the gathering wind and planted his hand on his bowler to keep it from blowing off his head. He was both determined and reluctant to see to the morning's errand. It was only right that he should come today and lay flowers on Julia's grave, it being her birthday, but the memory of his clever, beautiful wife broke his heart all over again when weighed against the painful reminder of her untimely death nearly three years ago.

Julia would have been twenty-five today, a woman in her prime, possibly a mother, had the consumption not done its ugly work and devoured her from the inside, leaving behind nothing but a pitiful bag of bones too exhausted to keep fighting the ravaging illness. They'd had such a short time together, less than two years, but Victor had not remarried as everyone said he should. Perhaps he never would, not unless someone captured his heart the way Julia had. He didn't think it was likely to happen, but life was full of surprises, both good and bad, and he made every effort to keep an open mind and treat every day as if it were a blank page in the book that was life.

Victor's step slowed as he approached the lane where Julia was buried. He'd thought it'd get easier with time, but the lichen-covered gravestone aroused the usual feelings of guilt and shame. He knew he should come more often, clear away the wilted flowers and pull up the weeds that threatened to choke the monument, but he always found an excuse, unable to face the lonely spot without ruminating on the brevity and unfairness of life.

Victor looked around, his myopic vision turning the scene into a melancholy watercolor. Something in his surroundings didn't seem quite right. It looked like an angel on one of the gravestones was moving, its stone robe and marble tresses rippling in the wind. Victor fumbled for his spectacles, pulled them out of his pocket and put them on without taking his eyes off the terrifying seraph. The image crystallized, and Victor let out a strangled cry, dropping the poppies he'd brought to lay on Julia's grave and stepping on them in his distress.

A young woman hung on a marble cross like a Christian martyr, her wrists bound to the crossbar, her head tilted to the side. She wore nothing but a flowing chemise, the fabric whipping around her bare legs and hanging off her arms like broken wings. What appeared to be a human heart, held in place by a thin chain or a string, was suspended from the woman's neck, still oozing blood. The woman's eyes were partially open, as was her mouth, and Victor thought he heard a cry for help carried on the wind.

"I'm coming," he cried as he took off at a run. "Hold on."

Alerted by the sound of his voice, a figure materialized behind the cross. The man was about Victor's own age, late twenties. His bowler was pulled low over his eyes, and his caped greatcoat gave him the appearance of a bat about to take flight. For a moment, their eyes met, and both froze, immobilized by indecision and surprise. And then the man was moving, weaving between the stones before disappearing from Victor's view altogether, his dark shape swallowed by the unkempt greenery beyond the last row of graves. It was either follow the man or rescue the poor creature who had been so cruelly treated. The choice was obvious.

It took Victor several long moments to reach the cross, but he needn't have hurried. The blue gaze that looked down on him was not only fixed in death but tinged with red, as if the woman's eyes were glowing. The mouth he'd imagined to be frozen in a scream was slack, the lips bluish. The woman's flesh was as cold and white as the marble beneath her feet. She was dead, and probably had been for some time, but silent tears slid down her pale cheeks and dripped onto her feet. Victor stared up, paralyzed with terror. He'd heard it said that statues of the Virgin were sometimes seen to shed real tears, but he'd always dismissed the stories as fantastical tales of popish fervor. Above him, rainwater slid unnoticed down the amber leaves of an overhanging branch and dripped onto the young woman's immobile face, turning her from a grotesque corpse into a weeping angel.

Victor turned away and hastened toward the exit, desperate to get away from the terrifying spectacle.

ONE

All Saints' Day
Monday, November 1, 1858

Gemma Tate set aside her book and peered at the carriage clock on the mantel. It was past noon, and she'd have to leave in an hour to be on time for her shift. She had planned to have luncheon with her brother before she set off and Victor got down to his afternoon's work. His article was due by the end of the day, and he had yet to settle on the final version and pen a clean copy, devoid of all the crossed-out words and scribbled notes that only he could make out. Normally he expressed his thoughts with eloquence and grace, but Gemma knew he was worried about making a misstep and inviting ridicule from the editor. Mr. Lawrence was an unpleasant fellow who treated the journalists who reported to him with impatience and undisguised derision. Being new to the position, Victor had allowed his anxiety to get the better of him, even though Gemma had repeatedly assured him that his articles were nothing short of brilliant.

Springing to her feet, Gemma strode toward the window,

pulled aside the lace curtain, and gazed into the nearly empty street. An outmoded carriage rattled past, and a maidservant hurried down the street, a basket slung over her arm, but there was no sign of Victor. Gemma was irritated with herself for giving in to worry. Victor was a grown man and didn't need her to mother him, even if he was a touch absent-minded and sometimes forgot to eat if she didn't order him to leave his scribbling until later and join her for a meal. Perhaps he'd stayed at the cemetery longer than he'd intended to, or maybe he had decided to go directly to the offices of the *Daily Telegraph* and use one of the unoccupied desks to complete the article. Come to think of it, she didn't even know what the article was about. Victor had been unusually secretive and hadn't asked her opinion on the first draft as he normally did.

Well, she couldn't wait any longer, Gemma decided. She had to get ready, since she couldn't afford to be late. The omnibuses were meant to run to a schedule, but it was anyone's guess how long it would take one to come along, since their progress was frequently slowed by delivery wagons blocking the street, elegant carriages moving at a stately pace and stopping to allow the crossing sweeps to do their job, and pedestrians who crossed willy-nilly and forced the driver to slow down to avoid running them over.

Gemma hurriedly ate the soup she'd prepared for lunch, then rinsed the bowl and spoon and dried them on a tea towel. Ready to leave, she put on her coat and buttoned it against the wind, tied the ribbons of her bonnet beneath her chin, and grabbed her beaded reticule off the hall table. She opened the door and nearly collided with the meaty fist of the policeman who stood on the doorstep and had been about to knock. He was a burly fellow with florid skin and a flowing, graying moustache.

"I beg your pardon, ma'am," the policeman said.

Gemma noted that he wasn't one of the bobbies who

routinely patrolled the area. She'd never seen him before, and her heart squeezed with foreboding.

"Mrs. Tate, I presume?" the policeman said.

"Miss," Gemma corrected him.

"Constable Earnshaw," the man said. "May I come in?"

"That depends," Gemma replied, still hoping that his visit had nothing to do with her personally. "What is this about, Constable?"

"I don't think this is a conversation to be had on the doorstep, miss," Constable Earnshaw said, looking distinctly ill at ease.

Gemma stepped aside and let the man in, then directed him into the parlor. "Please," she said, indicating the settee. She took one of the matching armchairs and sat primly, her reticule in her lap. She realized that her hands were trembling, so she took a calming breath, drew herself up, and faced the policeman.

"What has happened, Constable Earnshaw?" she asked once she felt ready to hear the news.

"I'm sorry to inform you, ma'am, that Mr. Tate—your brother, I presume—met with an unfortunate accident. In the Strand," he added. "He was run over by an omnibus."

Gemma was on her feet in an instant. "My twin. What hospital was he taken to? I must go to him."

Constable Earnshaw looked at her with barely concealed pity. "I'm awful sorry, Miss Tate, but there was no call to take him to the hospital."

"Where is he?" Gemma repeated, her voice barely audible above the thudding of her heart.

"City mortuary."

"Are you sure it's Victor?" she cried, clinging to one last shred of hope. "Tate is not an uncommon name."

The constable nodded gravely. "Mr. Tate's colleague was passing at the time of the accident. He recognized the victim. But we do need you to formally identify the body. The man did say as you're Mr. Tate's next of kin. I hope you will permit me to accompany you, Miss Tate," Constable Earnshaw added. "The mortuary is no place for a lady on her own."

Gemma took a moment to compose herself, then faced the constable. "There's a service of a different nature I would beg of you, Constable Earnshaw."

"Name it."

"I am employed by Mr. Horace Gadd. I nurse his ailing mother, and I'm due at work at two o'clock. Might I impose on you to deliver a message to my employer?"

"Of course. And I'll be sure to explain the circumstances of your absence."

"I would be most grateful," Gemma choked out. She tried to speak again, but the words wouldn't come, and she had to clear her throat and swallow hard to ask the question that was uppermost in her mind. "Did Victor suffer, Constable?"

Constable Earnshaw looked even more wretched, the naked sympathy in his gaze all the answer she needed. "It wasn't a quick death, Miss Tate. And he did ramble some before losing consciousness."

"What did he say?"

"Something about an angel with marble hair and a bleeding heart. I expect he was delirious with pain."

"Yes," Gemma agreed. "I expect he was. Was he wearing his spectacles?" she asked. Victor was a careful man who normally chose to err on the side of caution. How had he ended up beneath the wheels of an omnibus? Or had he been trampled by the horses that pulled the unwieldy conveyance? "How?" Gemma whispered. "How did it happen?"

The constable shook his head. "I couldn't tell you, miss. The few passersby who heard his cry of alarm said he stumbled and fell just as the omnibus began to move. He was kicked in the head by the horses' hooves and then the wheels... did the rest."

"Dear God," Gemma whispered, horrified. "How he must have suffered."

"I think the kick to the head knocked him senseless," Constable Earnshaw hurried to reassure her.

"Might he have lived if help arrived in time?" Gemma asked.

"I doubt it," the constable said gently. "There's nothing anyone could have done for him. And I do wish you didn't have to see him like that, so if there's someone else that can undertake the identification..." He let the sentence trail off, but Gemma shook her head.

"There's no one. It was just the two of us and had been for some time."

"I'm ever so sorry, Miss Tate," Constable Earnshaw said with feeling. "I do hope you have friends who will see you through this difficult time."

"Not anymore," Gemma said under her breath. "Not anymore."

TWO

"Bell! Bell!"

The voice came from very far away, so Sebastian dismissed it, but it was more difficult to ignore the violent shaking that ensued, followed by a kick to his boot-clad ankle. The gossamer cloud of contentment Sebastian was floating on dissipated, and he began his descent to earth, a destination he'd been hoping to avoid for a few hours yet. His limbs felt leaden, and his brain muddled, the shards of memory and fragments of reason resurfacing and rearranging themselves into something spiky and hard that settled just beneath his breastbone. Thankfully, the sensation didn't last long, and the colorful shapes that swam before his closed lids merged into a surprisingly competent watercolor of a flower-filled meadow before another kick roused Sebastian from his stupor.

"Bell! Wake up, you daft sod," the voice boomed again. It sounded vaguely familiar.

Sebastian cracked open one eye and took a moment to examine his surroundings. The walls were painted dark red, and the embossed ceiling tiles that might have been pewter were darkened by years of smoke. Oriental lanterns affixed to the walls burned so low as to leave the room in near darkness, casting just enough light to make out the dark shapes that lay sprawled on wooden pallets and soiled mattresses. Their hair was matted, the eyes partially closed, the mouths slack, and limbs so limp as to appear boneless. And then there was the smell, a sweet, pungent haze that overlaid the more readily identifiable odors of unwashed bodies, wet wool, and a rather flowery eau de cologne that instantly identified Sebastian's unwelcome visitor. Sergeant Woodward. Sebastian forced open the second eye and turned to face the man.

"Bugger off."

"Get up," Woodward growled. "Lovell wants you."

"Leave me the hell alone."

"Well, this place resembles hell, and you're already alone, so I'd have to say you got your wish. But you have to come now, Sebastian."

"I'm not on duty," Sebastian muttered, his eyelids starting to flutter again.

"You are now. Get up, you witless cretin!" He kicked Sebastian again. Hard.

"Leave off, Woodward," Sebastian exclaimed, now really irritated but marginally more awake. "What's the great urgency?"

"A new case has come in."

"So?"

"So, Lovell said this one is yours."

"Why?" Sebastian demanded.

He forced himself to sit and face the exasperated sergeant, whose earnest face was screwed up in obvious disgust. Sergeant Woodward wasn't averse to a pint or six and saw nothing wrong with staggering home after relieving himself on a nearby wall or emptying his guts into the gutter, but he didn't hold with opium, especially if it was supplied by the Chinese, of whom he was deeply suspicious. To partake of their poison was an affront to his English soul and a sure sign of a weak character and propensity for disloyalty in the man who permitted himself to sink so low. Sebastian didn't blame the purveyor, only the addict.

Sergeant Woodward sighed with impatience. "Not my place to question Superintendent Lovell. He told me to find you. Don't force me to tell him where you spend your time."

"Quit threatening me," Sebastian replied, but there was no heat in his voice. Woodward was a good sort, and discreet when the situation called for it.

"Good God, Sebastian, have you been here all night?" Woodward asked as he hauled Sebastian to his feet. "Tidy yourself up and report to the super. I'll cover for you until then."

"Thank you, Albert," Sebastian said, and meant it. The brain fog was beginning to lift, and he recalled with painful clarity that no one else cared enough to either cover for him or worry about his well-being. Those days were long gone, and with them any desire to go home, not that he had a home. What he had was rented rooms in a soulless lodging house presided over by a prying widow who would gladly join him in his lonely bed if he so much as looked at her a moment too long.

"Don't mention it. You ought to be ashamed to hand your wages over to these Chinese scoundrels," Woodward hissed under his breath as Mr. Wu, the proprietor, glided past, his long, thin braid swaying against the black pajamas he usually wore, his slippered feet making no sound on the wooden floor.

"You're lucky Lovell doesn't know about this. He'd sack you on the spot. Pull yourself together, man," Woodward added harshly when Sebastian swayed on his feet and stepped into the sullen light of the autumn morning. He gulped rain-scented air until the last remnants of intoxication cleared and he was able to focus on the sergeant, who was watching him with a mixture of pity and disgust.

"It will get easier in time," Sergeant Woodward said as he

awkwardly patted Sebastian on the shoulder. "But you mustn't dull the pain, or it will never leave you, my friend."

Sebastian wanted to explain, to make Woodward understand that nothing blunted the razor-sharp edges of agony except for a few hours spent in an opium dream, but he kept silent. His pain was his own, as was the gnawing guilt that devoured him the way maggots feasted on a freshly buried corpse. Having been a policeman for nearly fifteen years, he saw death every day and in all its forms. Death by violence, by cold and hunger, by suicide, and by decree, the executions carried out before rowdy crowds that savored the spectacle and hoped the poor sod who was about to dance at the end of the rope would take a good, long time to die. Those deaths Sebastian could accept. They weren't his fault, not even when the condemned was hanged because Sebastian had hunted him down and had supplied the prosecutor with sufficient evidence to prove him guilty before judge and jury. There was only one death that had the power to crush his soul, but he wouldn't think of it now. He couldn't, not when he had to hurry home and change out of his rumpled clothes before he presented himself to Superintendent Lovell.

"Here," Sergeant Woodward said, and folded a few coins into Sebastian's hand. "Take a hansom. It'll be faster."

Sebastian accepted the coins and nodded. "Thank you."

"Thank me by crawling out of that dark hole you've been hiding in."

Sebastian nodded again. What could he say to someone who couldn't begin to understand just how deep that hole was?

THREE

Gemma clutched her reticule as if it had the power to anchor her as she awaited her turn. A middle-aged couple had arrived a few minutes before her to identify their son's remains. The young man had been pulled from the Thames only that morning and the fishy tang of river water and wet mud wafted into the waiting area and made Gemma nauseated. According to the mortuary attendant, there didn't appear to be signs of foul play, other than the theft of the man's purse, which was unavoidable if the body was recovered by one of the many boatmen who were always on the lookout for a floater. They thought it their due to seek compensation in whatever way possible, since no one would pay them for dragging the body ashore and summoning a constable.

The father's face was bone white, though he managed to retain control over his emotions, but the poor mother had fainted dead away when the sheet was pulled back and she came face to face with the bloated, reeking corpse that had been the son she loved. Smelling salts were fetched and administered, tea was brewed, and platitudes were offered. To his credit, Mr. Stubbs, who oversaw the identifications, had offered

Gemma a cup as well, but she had refused. She wanted to get this heartbreaking task over with so she could return home and grieve in private. She wasn't one to put her feelings on display, and she had no use for meaningless words of comfort. They wouldn't bring Victor back, nor would they ease her suffering or get her through the coming days.

Some small part of her still hoped that this was all a dreadful mistake and the man on the slab would be some other unfortunate victim, but she knew better. For all the criticism the police service routinely received, they got it right more often than not, and if Constable Earnshaw said that the person who occupied the table next to the suicide was Victor Tate, then chances were he was correct.

As she patiently waited for the grieving couple to take their leave, Gemma wondered if it was worse when a person died by choice. She supposed it was better for the individual who had taken their life, since at least they had exercised their will in that final moment of what had to be an unhappy existence, but it had to be more painful for those left behind. To know that their love wasn't enough to tether someone to this world had to hurt, but what Gemma was feeling was in no way better.

Victor had endured his share of pain, but he had been strong and determined, and he'd had so much living left to do. He'd been excited about his new position at the newspaper, and he had recently talked of writing a novel. Victor had been nervous about baring his soul to his readers, something he hadn't had to do when reporting on the news or writing an opinion piece based on research rather than one's own beliefs, but if he had seen it through, Gemma thought, his book would really have been something worth reading. Victor had been sensitive and observant, and capable of great compassion and understanding, his emotions rarely hindered by unshakable practicality the way Gemma's so often were. He would have created interesting and complex characters, not the mere caricatures that so often appeared in popular literature. Now he'd never tell his story, and she would never get to read it. In fact, this chapter of her life was over forever, only she'd had no idea that it would come to such an abrupt end on an ordinary autumn morning.

At last the hysterical woman was escorted out the door by her silent husband, and Mr. Stubbs approached Gemma, his expression apologetic.

"Thank you for waiting, Miss Tate. A regrettable delay, but the loss of a loved one can come as quite a shock, especially when the deceased was young and in robust health. I think you're made of sterner stuff," he added, taking in Gemma's rigid posture. "Not the sort to carry on in public."

"You're right on that score, Mr. Stubbs," Gemma replied. "Can we get on with it?"

"Of course. But if you feel unwell or would like that cup of tea after all, don't be afraid to say. All in a day's work," he said, giving her a rueful smile. "I've not been so hardened yet that I can't offer a bit of sympathy to someone who needs it."

"You're very kind, Mr. Stubbs," Gemma said. "Please, can you prepare my brother's remains."

"He's ready for you, my dear lady. Come this way, please. Oh, and you can go in, Mr. Ramsey," he said to the man who'd just arrived.

Mr. Ramsey nodded his thanks and preceded them into the room where a half-dozen corpses were laid out on narrow tables. Four were covered with grubby white sheets, one of those being the young man who had just been identified. Two were ready for viewing, the sheets pulled back to just below the shoulders. Mr. Ramsey stood next to the body of a woman; his mournful gaze fixed on the corpse, his head bowed. He took hold of the sheet and was about to pull it lower but hesitated with a glance at Gemma and Mr. Stubbs.

"I'll just wait until you're finished in here, Mr. Stubbs," he said.

"That would be advisable, Mr. Ramsey," Mr. Stubbs said, giving the man a hard look. "There's a lady present."

Gemma had seen plenty of corpses at the hospital in Scutari, and the ones she'd handled had looked considerably worse than the young woman on the slab, but just then she had eyes only for Victor. He occupied the slab closest to the wall, his face waxy, his eyes closed as if in sleep, his hair damp. Mr. Stubbs must have cleaned the blood from his face and hair, but Gemma could see remnants in his ear, and the collar of his shirt was brown with dried gore.

Gemma didn't ask Mr. Stubbs to pull the sheet lower. She didn't need to see the full extent of the damage, nor did she want to have to envision Victor's mangled remains for the rest of her days. The horse had kicked him in the back of the head, so his face had been miraculously spared, and she focused on that, taking off her glove and laying a hand on his cold cheek.

She'd promised herself that she wouldn't weep, but her vision blurred and she gripped the side of the table, afraid her legs would give out. Mr. Stubbs caught her under the elbow and remained at her side, steadying her, until she regained her composure.

"How badly was he hurt, Mr. Stubbs?" she whispered, her gaze going to the rust-colored stains on the sheet above Victor's abdomen.

"You don't want to know, Miss Tate. Please, trust me on that."

"He would have died in agony," Gemma whispered, her gaze still on Victor's face.

"Don't think on that now, Miss Tate. See how peaceful he looks? He was already past his suffering when he passed."

"He was always so careful," Gemma said under her breath.

"Miss Tate, if you will confirm that this is indeed Mr. Victor

Tate, then we can return to my office and complete the paperwork."

"It is," Gemma choked out. "This is Victor Tate."

Mr. Ramsey was watching her with sympathy, but she didn't return his gaze. Gemma had no time for anything but her own grief and couldn't think past leaving the mortuary. All she could focus on was the next breath, the next step, the next moment, the first in a lifetime of moments without Victor.

Mr. Stubbs escorted Gemma to his office, asked her to sign a statement of identification, and handed her a parcel containing Victor's personal effects. Gemma wasn't sure she could open it without breaking down, but she accepted it and nodded her thanks.

"If you require a recommendation, I would be happy to supply names of several reasonably priced undertakers, Miss Tate. The body will need to be collected within the next few days, you understand. There's just not enough room to keep them for long." Fresh cadavers were always coming in in a city where death stalked the populace, reaping indiscriminately whatever their station or age.

"I understand, Mr. Stubbs. I know a reputable undertaker," Gemma said. She fled the mortuary, the parcel containing Victor's possessions in her trembling hands.

FOUR

At home, Gemma hung up her coat and hat, set the parcel on the console table, and sank into a wingchair in the parlor, one of a pair she and Victor occupied every night as they read by the fire, or talked about their day or some news story that had caught Victor's attention. Already the house felt empty, the rooms echoing with loneliness.

Just that morning, as she and Victor had been having breakfast, she had become irritated with him for burying his nose in the paper when she longed for conversation. She'd offered to come to the cemetery, but Victor had decided to go alone. Gemma had understood his need for privacy and hadn't insisted. She hadn't really known Julia, since Gemma had answered Florence Nightingale's call and left for Crimea shortly after Victor and Julia had started courting. Gemma hadn't been there when they married or when Julia passed. Just like she hadn't been there when Victor died, bleeding out into the street, surrounded by gawking strangers.

Would he still be alive if she had insisted on accompanying him to Highgate? Or would Victor have died regardless, his fate finding him wherever he was because it was God's will?

Gemma shook her head, even though there was no one to see her. She didn't really believe that, not anymore. She'd seen too much willful ignorance, incompetence, and neglect during the war to believe that the slaughter of thousands was God's doing. Just as she didn't believe that Victor's accident had been anything more than a terrible misfortune brought about by a set of circumstances that could probably have been avoided had Victor done something differently.

Pouring herself a large medicinal brandy, Gemma took a gulp and huddled in the chair, her unseeing gaze fixed on the empty hearth, her fingers gripping the glass. Victor was gone and, no matter how long she cried or raged at the unfairness of his passing, she was now completely alone. She wasn't ready to consider the implications of this, not today, but, once Victor was laid to rest, difficult decisions would need to be made regarding her future.

After a time, some deep-seated need forced Gemma to set the glass aside and fetch the parcel Mr. Stubbs had given her. She wanted to hold Victor's things, to feel connected to him in a physical way one more time before turning her attention to the more immediate practicalities of death. She'd already stopped the clock, but she'd need to cover the mirror and hang a black bow on the door too, then take the mourning things out of the trunk. She hoped the gown was still serviceable, since she could ill afford to replace it when she had a funeral to pay for. Albright and Sons had offered a reasonable package for their parents' funerals, and Gemma hoped they would see her as a returning client and work with what she could afford. If not, she would be forced to seek a more affordable alternative.

Wiping away the tears that somehow wouldn't stop flowing, Gemma opened the parcel and shook the contents onto her lap. It was a meager collection. There was Victor's purse that held a few coins, the thin gold wedding band he'd still worn, the pocket watch that was now dented, and his notebook. Victor's spectacles weren't there—they must have been crushed—and his hat and coat must have been too badly damaged to be of any use and been disposed of too. Gemma set aside everything except the black notebook. Victor had always had it on him, along with a stub of a pencil. He'd used it to jot down notes for future articles, ideas for his novel, and unusual phrases that piqued his interest and which he was afraid to forget.

The notebook was three-quarters full, the pages covered in Victor's barely legible scrawl. Fresh tears blurred Gemma's vision as she leafed through the pages and recalled discussing some of the thoughts Victor had jotted down. He'd made notes everywhere, while sitting on a bench at the park, riding the omnibus, or even standing in line to buy a hot bun from a street vendor. Some things called for immediate recording before he became distracted and forgot that cutting witticism or fascinating fact. He also included descriptions of individuals he found striking or inexplicably off-putting, knowing he'd return to his notes when he began writing his novel and would want to introduce a character who would leave as much of an impression on the reader as the living person had left on him.

The brandy had taken effect by the time Gemma got to the final page. Her eyelids were drooping with fatigue, and her heart ached with longing for Victor's comforting presence, but she managed to rouse herself when she realized the notes were from this morning. Victor always dated his entries and the final entry had been made on November 1. "Highgate" was underlined twice, so hard that the lines had nearly torn the page, and the writing was sloppier than ever, especially toward the end. Gemma stared at the words and found herself reading them out loud as she deciphered the cramped writing.

Woman crucified in <u>Highgate</u>. Bleeding heart. Wearing undergarment. Crying tears of sorrow in death. Man in caped coat and bowler hat.

The next few words were difficult to make out, but Gemma thought they were: *Milky way and red streaks.*

And then, *I'm being followed.*

That last bit must have been written in haste when Victor had realized he was being trailed, but what on earth did the references to the Milky Way and the red streaks mean? She had heard of the Milky Way, of course, but couldn't imagine what it might have to do with the woman in Highgate. It hadn't even been dark when Victor had left for the cemetery, nor had it been so soon after sunrise that the sky would still be streaked with ribbons of red and pink. Besides, the sky had been overcast that morning, the sun hidden behind an impenetrable veil of gray and the air saturated with early morning mist. The notes had clearly meant something to Victor, and he'd jotted them down to remind himself of something important, but without further explanation the meaning was impossible to decipher.

Gemma set the notebook aside and stared at the silver-framed photograph on the mantel. It was a portrait of her and Victor, taken on their twenty-first birthday six years ago. They looked so young and hopeful, and so unprepared for what was to come: the deaths of their parents, the horrors of the Crimean War, and Julia's passing, of which Gemma had not learned until a letter from Victor had finally reached her several months after the siege of Sevastopol had been lifted, followed by Victor himself, who'd decided to join her in Crimea and report on the war. If he had been trying to outrun his grief, he hadn't succeeded, only heaped fresh pain on a heart already shattered by loss.

Feeling a bit unsteady, Gemma stood and reached for the photograph. They looked so alike. Everyone always commented on it. And why wouldn't they, being siblings? They'd both had chestnut hair that curled when Victor allowed his to grow too long between haircuts, pale green eyes, patrician noses, and high cheekbones, no doubt a gift from some long-forgotten ancestor on their mother's side, since their father's features had been decidedly blunter. The twins had both been of middling height, slim, and a little too direct for their own good, a trait they'd inherited from their father. At least that was what their mother had always said when they rushed in to express their opinions without considering the repercussions.

Gemma and Victor had always been close and almost uncannily attuned to each other's feelings. Maybe all twins shared such an emotional connection, but at times Gemma had thought it bordered on the psychic, not a term she would ever allow to pass her lips for fear of being thought ridiculous or eccentric. One didn't want to be mistaken for a spiritualist or, worse yet, a charlatan who claimed to have abilities that smacked of the profane. But a minuscule change in demeanor, a look, or a careless word had been enough to alert Gemma to what Victor was thinking, and the same had gone for him. He had discerned her thoughts before she'd verbalized them and had always taken her side in an argument, just as she had defended him before their parents when he was called upon to explain himself and justify his actions.

Their mother had been horrified by Gemma's desire to become a nurse, and she hadn't thought Victor's passion for writing would ensure a comfortable life and should ever be treated as anything other than a charming hobby. Their paths had been set out for them from a young age, and their mother had believed that they would unquestioningly do her bidding, particularly after the death of their father, which had put paid to adolescent pursuits.

It had been her parents' wish that Gemma marry Edgar Higgins, the son of their father's business partner in the haberdashery concern they had owned in Cheapside, and that Victor take over the business when their father passed. The twins, still in their late teens at the time, had considered this plan a fate worse than death. They had known little of death or how soon it would come to claim those they loved. The Higginses owned the shop outright now, and Edgar was married and father to three children. Gemma would have said that they were frightful brats, but her mother had taught her never to be uncharitable, so she kept that opinion to herself.

The proceeds from the sale of their half of the business had covered their living expenses while Victor tried valiantly to sell the pieces he'd written to anyone with a printing press. He had been offered a part-time position with the *Daily Telegraph* a few months back, and Gemma was earning a steady wage as a private nurse. Things had been looking up. Until today.

Gemma kissed the tips of her fingers and pressed them to Victor's face. Perhaps she was a little drunk on brandy or her brain was addled with grief, but she suddenly heard Victor's voice as clearly as if he were standing next to her.

It wasn't an accident, Gem.

FIVE

"Good of you to join us, Inspector Bell," Superintendent Lovell said as he glared at Sebastian, and gave him a once-over that clearly conveyed that he was less than impressed with Sebastian's crumpled appearance.

Unlike Sebastian, who was powerfully built, Superintendent Lovell was cadaverously thin, his narrow face and beaky nose underlined by a weak chin that was cleverly hidden beneath the pointed beard he'd worn for as long as anyone could remember. His light brown hair was brushed back and pomaded into place, bringing attention to a rapidly receding hairline, and his wire-rimmed spectacles magnified shrewd, if somewhat lashless, dark eyes.

The superintendent favored somber suits and stiffly starched white shirts paired with black silk ties. Some said that he resembled a university don, others that he had the sorrowful bearing of an undertaker, but appearances were deceiving, and to underestimate the superintendent was to make a grave error of judgment. Superintendent Lovell was neither high-handed nor melodramatic. He was intelligent, efficient, and entirely focused on results, unlike his predecessor, who had been soft-spoken and protective of the men but failed to instill either lasting respect or a desire to get the job done. Superintendent Mays had retired just over three years ago, and the commissioner, Sir David Hawkins, had brought in his own man, since Superintendent Mays had been appointed before his tenure and would not have been his first choice.

"Get yourself over to the city mortuary, Bell. A young woman was found in Highgate Cemetery, mounted on a cross like a bloody Christian martyr."

"She was nailed to the cross?" Sebastian asked. He didn't think life still had the power to shock him, but this got his undivided attention.

"No, tied. Probably some doxy that was snatched off the street."

"To what end?"

"Damned if I know. Could be an All Hallows' prank," Lovell said with disgust. "Went so far as to hang a bleeding heart around her neck. Disturbing in the extreme."

"A human heart?" Sebastian asked as he tried to envision what the superintendent was describing and succeeded all too well.

"Certainly appears that way."

"Are you suggesting that this was some sort of human sacrifice, sir?" Sebastian asked, all the while wondering if the heart had come from the woman's chest and if there was anything in the pre-Christian history of All Hallows' that referenced such barbarism.

"Best not to speculate until we know more, but once the papers get hold of the story—and it will no doubt make the evening edition—there'll be no getting away from it. We need to get ahead of this sordid tale. Find out who she was, cuff whoever has done for her, and provide me with an account of events that will explain what occurred in a manner that will bolster the reputation of the police service. No sense giving any more ammunition to those who see us as a waste of resources."

"In other words, squash the story, and do it quick," Sebastian summarized.

"If it's not too much trouble, Bell," Superintendent Lovell retorted sarcastically. "Or are you otherwise engaged at present? I can always give this case to Inspector Reece. He'll be happy to step in."

"I'm sure he will be," Bell replied, silently adding, *that worthless bootlicker.*

"Reece is a moron, but he gets things done," Lovell said, as if Sebastian had spoken aloud.

"By collaring innocent people for the crime," Sebastian argued.

Rumors that Inspector Reece sometimes planted evidence in order to get a conviction had been circulating for months, but Superintendent Lovell had yet to address them or reprimand Reece, who was distantly related to the Home Secretary and therefore virtually untouchable.

"Which is why I'm giving this one to you. I want the culprit behind bars and awaiting a well-publicized trial that will inevitably end in a trip to the gallows. If this depraved lunatic strikes again, there will be full-blown panic, and every prostitute in London will live in fear of conducting her business. Bad for the economy, Bell. And what's bad for the economy and for the gentlemen who enjoy a bit of night sport and have the ear of those in government is bad for the police service. Do I make myself understood?"

"You do, sir."

"Good. Well, what are you waiting for?" Lovell exclaimed when Sebastian failed to stand quickly enough. "And I expect to be updated regularly. You hear?"

"Yes, sir."

"I do declare, the criminals in this city are becoming more

creative with every passing year," Lovell grumbled under his breath as Sebastian walked to the door. "What's next, I ask you? A body swinging from the balcony at Buckingham Palace?"

Sebastian shut the door on Lovell's tirade and headed to the duty room, where Sergeant Woodward stood watching him from behind a polished counter.

"Who found the woman in Highgate?" Sebastian asked.

"Some journalist. He was near hysterical by the time he located a constable."

"Do we have his statement?"

"I'll have it to you as soon as Constable Bryant sets it down. He only just came back from Highgate before luncheon and made his report. I expect he's at the pub. Nothing gets between Bryant and his food."

"In that case, I'm off to the mortuary."

"Mr. Ramsey was dispatched to see to the corpse. She's probably on his table by now."

"Did anyone besides Constable Bryant examine the crime scene?"

Sergeant Woodward nodded. "Mr. Leslie of the London Cemetery Company was notified. He arrived shortly before the victim was taken down. I have his statement right here."

"Thank you."

Sebastian scanned the few lines of writing and returned the statement to Sergeant Woodward. "This tells me nothing."

"I gather there isn't much to tell, at least as far as the scene goes."

Sebastian nodded. "I'll speak to Ramsey first, before he sends her to the dead house."

"I do hope someone claims her remains," Sergeant Woodward said. "At least give the poor wretch a proper burial."

"She'll most likely end up in a pauper's grave," Sebastian replied. "Not too many doxies have anyone that's willing to shell out for a funeral."

Sergeant Woodward sighed. "I hear she was quite beautiful. And young. Probably one of those rustics that come up from the country, thinking the streets of London are paved with gold. Doesn't take long for them to find out what they must resort to in order to fill their bellies and pay for a roof over their heads."

Sebastian didn't bother to reply. He'd seen all too many women who had been beaten, disfigured, or left for dead by angry pimps, violent punters, and jealous rivals. He hoped this girl had already been dead by the time she was mounted on the cross; otherwise, it might have taken her a long time to die, and he would like to believe she'd been spared that at least.

SIX

Sebastian pulled out his watch and checked the time. Even if the surgeon had collected the remains from the mortuary, he might not begin the post-mortem immediately, and, even if he did, the dissection would take hours to finish. But the crime scene wouldn't wait, especially if it rained again, which it was threatening to do.

Before finding a cab, Sebastian stopped into Swann's Public House, a favorite with the men on account of its proximity to Scotland Yard. He found Constable Bryant at a table by the window. The constable stopped chewing when he saw Sebastian, and gestured to him to take a seat. Sebastian slid into a chair across from the constable and waited for him to swallow before asking his questions.

"The body in Highgate. What did you see, Constable?"

"Just the woman, guv. Beautiful, she were. Like an angel," the young constable said, his face going beet red.

Constable Bryant was flame-haired, ruddy-cheeked, and liberally freckled. The other constables teased him mercilessly on account of his violent blushing and crippling shyness, but he didn't seem to mind as long as the ribbing didn't run toward cruelty. His inherent shyness made him something of an outsider, and outsiders tended to be keen observers in Sebastian's experience.

"Why were you even near Highgate?" Sebastian asked, suddenly wondering how the case had come to the attention of Scotland Yard, which was clear across town, and so quickly.

"I live nearby."

"Isn't there a local station? Division S, if I'm not mistaken," Sebastian said.

Constable Bryant averted his gaze and tucked his head into his shoulders like a frightened tortoise. "There is," he muttered.

"So why did you not report it to them?" Sebastian asked, but he thought he could guess. "You didn't want to notify Division S because you figured that bringing this to the attention of Superintendent Lovell might have a positive effect on your prospects with the police service."

"Nothing wrong with having aspirations," Constable Bryant mumbled.

"Nothing at all, but sometimes expediency is paramount."

"She weren't going nowhere," Constable Bryant said. "And I thought the super would welcome a high-profile case."

"You were right there," Sebastian replied. The lad was cleverer than anyone gave him credit for. "Now, tell me exactly what happened."

"I were on my way to work, and this cove comes running, all wild-eyed like. Said there's a woman what's been crucified in the West Cemetery, and can I come. So I did."

"What exactly did he say, Constable?"

Constable Bryant's brows knitted in concentration, and he stared off into the middle distance as he tried to recall the particulars.

"It were hard to make sense of what he were saying, guv,"

the constable said at last. "It were all garbled like. He kept
saying she were crying, but he were sure she were dead." He
shrugged in obvious mystification. "And he kept going on about
a bleeding heart, like she were wearing it on the outside of her
body. I thought he were mad at first. Quite deranged."

"Was that all he said?"

"He said there was a man, but he'd run off."

"Description?" Sebastian prodded.

"That's where it got even more bizarre. He were spouting
something about a milky haze and black wings. I could hardly
understand what he were saying, he were so upset."

"Did you not attempt to clarify what he meant, Constable?"

"Like I said, he were all emotional and kept urging me to
hurry. I thought it were more important to get to the woman if
there were any chance she were still alive. I thought if she were
crying, then maybe..."

"So what happened when you arrived at the cemetery?"
Sebastian asked.

"By that time, a few people had spotted her and were
standing around gawking like it were a street performance. I
could hardly blame them. It were a sight to see, Inspector. She
were hanging there on the cross, a human heart around her
neck. If she weren't so beautiful, it'd be the stuff of nightmares,
but as it were, it brought to mind some biblical judgment. An
errant angel cast out from heaven," Constable Bryant said, his
gaze lifting heavenward as if he could see it all happening. "Like
Lucifer."

"Were you the one to take her down?"

Constable Bryant shook his head. "One of the gravediggers
had sent for the cemetery director, and he were there, clucking
like a hen what's about to lose its head." Constable Bryant
smiled at his own joke and continued. "Anyhow, Mr. Leslie—
that's the director—had already arranged for transport to the
city mortuary and had the gravediggers get her off the cross once

I got there. I caught a ride to the mortuary to save time, and to keep watch over the body, then ran the rest of the way."

"Did you see anything near the body, Constable?" Sebastian asked.

"Like what?"

"Anything at all."

Constable Bryant shrugged. "No. I looked around while they got her down, but I didn't see nothing odd. Just a rusty wheelbarrow, but no tracks. And it had rained in the night, so the wheels would have left a mark, 'specially if the wheelbarrow were weighed down with a body."

"What about footprints?"

"Can't see footprints on grass," Constable Bryant pointed out.

"What about on the path?"

"What with all the brouhaha, there were a dozen people gathered round by the time I had a chance to look."

"Do you have your notebook with you?"

The young man nodded and reached into his pocket, taking out his notebook and pencil.

"Draw me a map of exactly where the woman was found, or I'll waste an hour wandering about searching for the right grave. And write up your report as soon as you get back."

"I have it right here, sir," Constable Bryant said and pulled a folded sheet of paper from his breast pocket. "Wrote it all down while I were waiting for my food. But there won't be nothing in it as you haven't already heard."

Sebastian scanned the few lines Constable Bryant had written and handed the sheet back to the young man, who had drawn a crude map and passed it to Sebastian after tearing the page out of his notebook. He wore the virtuous expression of someone who was certain he'd done all he could, and was about to return to his pork pie when another thought occurred to Sebastian.

"Do you remember the name on the grave where the victim was found?"

The constable nodded eagerly. "Elizabeth Burrows. Beloved wife and mother. She were sixty-seven when she passed. Is that helpful at all, guv?"

"Not even remotely," Sebastian grumbled.

He had thought there was a chance that the grave was that of someone noteworthy and might offer a clue as to why it had been chosen, but perhaps whoever had mounted the body had simply looked for a cross that wasn't too high off the ground and could be easily accessed without needing a ladder to haul up the body. Even if the woman was slight, a dead weight was just that.

Constable Bryant looked crestfallen, so Sebastian hastened to reassure him. "Well done, Constable Bryant. I'll take it from here."

"I don't envy you, sir," the young man said. "This case is sure to be a corker."

"Superintendent Lovell thinks she was a doxy. A prank that went too far."

Constable Bryant shook his head. "She were no doxy, guv."

"And how would you know?"

"She were too..." It took the young man a moment to find the right word and, when he did, it wasn't overly helpful. "Lovely. And soft," he added, a dreamy expression coming over his plain features.

"Soft as in buxom? Were you admiring her bosom?" Sebastian exclaimed, outraged that the lad would ogle a dead woman. In their job, it was important to have respect for the dead.

Constable Bryant's color went from boiled beet to a particularly nasty shade of raw liver. "That's not how I meant it, sir."

"How did you mean it?"

"You could tell she were genteel. A lady," he added. "You

can always tell when a woman's been looked after, can't you? It shows."

"Yes, it does," Sebastian agreed. "Thank you, Constable."

"Just doing my job," Constable Bryant replied modestly.

Sebastian pushed to his feet, the folded map safely stowed in his pocket. As he left the tavern, he couldn't help but wonder if the constable's assessment of the victim was correct.

SEVEN

It took Sebastian over an hour to get to Highgate. The streets were thronged with carriages, omnibuses, and ponderous dray wagons loaded with casks of ale, mountains of vegetables, and animals, both alive and dead, on their way to butchers and slaughterhouses. Ragged crossing sweeps darted out before the finer carriages to clear away horseshit in the hope of earning a coin, and street vendors and costermongers offered everything from jellied eels to oranges and pitiful-looking posies. The traffic let up somewhat once they cleared London proper, but the dirt roads were narrow and rutted, and the hansom shuddered every time it rolled over a stone or sank into the mud, the conveyance tilting precariously to the side until it finally righted itself.

The cabbie dropped Sebastian off some distance from the cemetery's entrance on Swain's Lane, since the lane was congested with carriages of all shapes and sizes that formed a queue behind a glass-fronted hearse pulled by plumed black horses. The coffin inside was smothered in white lilies, and solemn-looking undertakers, black scarves trailing from their top hats, stood at attention as the mourners began to alight.

Someone important had undertaken their final journey, and the throng of mourners was about to descend on the cemetery. Sebastian hoped the plot or mausoleum where the recently departed was about to be interred was nowhere near the grave of Elizabeth Burrows. The scene had been trampled enough already, and anything of significance probably ground into the dirt.

Eager to get ahead of the funeral party, Sebastian slipped through the gates and went in search of the crime scene. Even with the map, it took him about a quarter of an hour to locate the right place, and, as Constable Bryant had said, there was nothing to see anyhow. The final resting place of Elizabeth Burrows, *Loving wife and mother*, did not show any signs of disturbance. The ropes that had held the dead woman in place had been severed and removed, there was no blood on the cross, at the base, or on the grass surrounding the grave, and there were no indentations in the ground that would suggest that a ladder had been used. In fact, no trace of the victim's presence remained save the numerous footprints left on the muddy path by curious onlookers.

Sebastian walked around, staring at the ground intently, but he didn't see anything aside from the wheelbarrow Constable Bryant had mentioned, abandoned some ten yards away. There were no tracks leading from the barrow to the cross or toward the wooden area beyond, so it hadn't been used to transport the body. In fact, there was nothing to suggest that the woman had been murdered at the cemetery, but if she had been killed elsewhere her killer would have to have brought her to this spot, which was a good way from the main entrance and could only be achieved by means of trespass. Despite the stone wall and the iron gates that were locked at night, body-snatchers regularly found their way into the cemetery, dug up fresh corpses, and melted into the night with their ill-gotten gains without being seen. There had to be alternative ways to get into the cemetery, either through the wall, over it, or beneath it. Or perhaps cemetery employees accepted bribes and left the gates unlocked, taking advantage of the ceaseless demand for fresh bodies, and benefitting from the brisk trade between the resurrection men and the anatomists, who were willing to pay any price for usable cadavers.

There wasn't much sense in looking for an access point, not before Sebastian had seen the victim and heard what the surgeon had to say about the manner of her death. He left the cemetery, found the cabstand and asked the cabbie to take him back to Westminster. He didn't believe in portents, but this investigation was not off to a good start, and only a few hours were left until the evening editions of the newspapers hit the streets. Once the story was out, the pressure to find the killer would truly be on.

EIGHT

An introspective, mild-mannered man in his early thirties, Colin Ramsey was often regarded as someone of no consequence by Sebastian's superiors, but he was clever and resourceful, and Sebastian admired his intelligence and trusted his instincts. They'd worked together on several cases, and Sebastian thought of the surgeon as a trusted friend. Colin Ramsey's cellar at the house in Blackfriars served not only as a makeshift mortuary but also as a classroom. He'd once confessed to Sebastian that, while he was in Edinburgh studying, he'd honed his skills on corpses stolen from cemeteries by body-snatchers, who operated in the city with impunity since the medical schools were desperate for subjects and turned a blind eye to the origin of the cadavers. The schools often accepted corpses that were in such an advanced state of decomposition that the students had to wear kerchiefs over their mouths and noses to avoid passing out from the smell.

Colin didn't have to resort to paying for stolen cadavers now that he was back in England, nor did he approve of desecrating a person's final resting place, but his partnership with the police afforded him a unique opportunity. He had a steady supply of cadavers that enabled him to take on private students. Those who wished to get ahead of their peers and weren't satisfied with watching surgeries performed from afar could attend the post-mortems and hone their own skills if the remains weren't likely to be claimed by a grieving family and could be used as a teaching tool before being consigned to a pauper's grave. Colin was able to make a comfortable living without having to accept a position at one of London's many hospitals, where he would be under the jurisdiction of more senior surgeons. Sebastian knew that their narrow-mindedness and refusal to implement new techniques, such as the use of ether and chloroform to spare the patient suffering, infuriated Colin and left him feeling helpless and hemmed in.

Sebastian found Colin at home, a leather apron with a bib tied around his waist. His mother, whose mind had been slipping since she had been widowed several years ago, giggled and waved to Sebastian absent-mindedly before a maidservant lured her to the parlor with the promise of tea. Sebastian braced himself as Colin turned toward the stairs. No matter how often the cellar was cleaned with carbolic, the pervasive smell of death clung to every surface and lingered in one's nose. Beneath the putrid stink of decay was another odor, the tang of despair, or perhaps Sebastian only imagined it because he associated despair with untimely death.

"So, you're the one who got this fascinating case," Colin said as he invited Sebastian to follow him into the cellar. "I was wondering whom Superintendent Lovell would assign."

"Seems I am the lucky winner."

Sebastian had a fairly good idea why Superintendent Lovell had hand-picked him to investigate this case. Solving it would preclude negative publicity and the inevitable calls for the Home Office to disendow the police service. Failing to solve it would give Lovell a reason to get rid of him, something the superintendent had been considering for months; he only needed a valid excuse for the paperwork and the men, who wouldn't take kindly to one of their own being dismissed. Sebastian was fairly sure that Lovell knew of his opium habit but had turned a blind eye thus far out of sympathy for Sebastian's loss. Still, no one's well of sympathy was bottomless, and Lovell was beginning to lose his patience. Sebastian's period of mourning was officially over, and the superintendent felt it was time he accepted his fate. Lovell had even hinted, in the broadest of terms, that Sebastian should think of remarrying, since it wasn't healthy for a man in his prime to remain alone for long.

Sebastian wasn't sure how he felt about getting the sack. A part of him would be deeply ashamed and angry with himself for allowing his reputation to deteriorate to such a degree that even the police wouldn't have him. But another part longed for new opportunities. He'd always wanted to see America, with its forests and plains and bustling cities. He could apply to the Pinkerton Detective Agency and become a private inquiry agent. He'd heard that the Pinkertons were well respected and handsomely compensated. It would be an exciting new chapter, especially since he'd never been further than Suffolk and had never set foot on a transatlantic liner. Besides, it wasn't as if there was anyone left to keep him in England. Everyone he had once loved was now beyond his reach. He was free as a bird, and as isolated as only a man surrounded by multitudes but completely alone in their midst could be.

The only arrangements he'd have to make would be for Gustav. He had inherited the cat from his German neighbor, who had died suddenly and left the poor creature trapped inside his rooms. Sebastian had been forced to break down the door to let Gustav out. There had been no one to claim Herr Schweiger's remains, so Sebastian had donated the body to science with the promise that, once Colin Ramsey was finished with it, he would see the man decently buried. Perhaps Ramsey would take Gustav. The cat could keep his mother company and hunt for mice.

Having come up with a possible solution to the very real possibility of imminent dismissal, Sebastian inhaled deeply, and instantly regretted such abandon since the stench grew more overpowering with every step. Still, if this case proved to be his undoing, he'd book the first passage out and go to Chicago. Now that he thought about it, he quite fancied becoming a Pinkerton and living in a place where nothing reminded him of Louisa.

NINE

The cellar was furnished with several cabinets, a narrow worktop to hold surgical instruments, and a wooden dissection table that had a hole at one end so the bucket beneath could collect the liquids that trickled down during a post-mortem. A small window set high into the wall was partially open, ventilating the space and bringing with it a hint of rain and the smell of decaying leaves that momentarily masked the pervasive odor that seemed to have seeped into the very walls.

A woman who appeared to be in her late teens and was dressed in a lace-trimmed chemise lay on her back, her abundant fair hair tumbling over the edge of the slab. Her eyes were closed, and, since there were no obvious signs of violence besides a few bloodstains on the fabric, it was easy to imagine that she was asleep and would wake, look around, and wonder what she was doing in this awful place. Sebastian almost wished that Colin would refuse to autopsy her and she would be buried as she had been in life, beautiful and whole.

"I'm afraid I haven't had time to work on her yet," Colin said as he approached the table. "Lovely, isn't she?" He ran his hand over the woman's hair, stroking it as if she could feel his gentle touch and be reassured by it.

Sebastian nodded, the present tense of the question not lost on him. He was glad that the young woman had not been assigned to the police surgeon, who treated every victim as if they were a side of beef and frequently poked fun at the deceased while working. Colin Ramsey had worked on dozens of corpses over the years and was no longer shocked by the ravages of death, but he still treated every cadaver with the utmost respect, never forgetting that they were living, breathing human beings before they had wound up on his dissecting table. Likewise, he attended every unclaimed victim's funeral to make certain that someone was there to bear witness and offer up a prayer for their soul. He never saw going as a chore, but as a privilege, and treated it as such.

"Can you give me a preliminary assessment?" Sebastian asked. "Might she have been a prostitute?"

Given what Constable Bryant had said and what Superintendent Lovell had suggested, it was important to start with that basic fact and work from there.

Colin sighed and shook his head sadly. "This woman was no prostitute. She's had a genteel upbringing and a comfortable life."

Sebastian agreed, based on what he could see so far, but he needed Colin to spell it out, if only to make sure they were in complete agreement. "How can you tell?"

Colin moved his hand down to the woman's face and gently cupped her cheek. "Her skin is supple and unblemished, her teeth well cared for, and her hands soft. Her hair is thick and lustrous. This is a young woman who enjoyed a varied and plentiful diet, the benefit of expert medical care, and a life of relative comfort."

"Could she have just arrived from the country?" Sebastian asked.

Farm girls were often wholesome and glowing with good health until, forced to live on the streets and sell their bodies to stay alive, the ravages of their new life took a toll and they began to look haggard and sallow, their stores melting away and their health deteriorating rapidly.

Colin shook his head again. "Country girls work from dawn till dusk. This woman has never worked a day in her life. And look here." He lifted her right hand and pointed to a groove on the fourth finger, then set the hand down and lifted the left hand. There was a similar groove on the third finger. "She wore rings, and her ears are pierced."

"Could have been cheap trinkets," Sebastian replied.

"I don't think so. Cheap trinkets tend to leave discoloration. This woman wore jewelry made of precious metals."

Sebastian shrugged, unconvinced. Many women wore jewelry. That fact in itself meant nothing. The other observations the surgeon had made were important, but the post-mortem would either prove or disprove them. There were plenty of prostitutes who resembled fine ladies and were pampered and spoiled by their employers to make them more appealing to a certain kind of man. Just because this woman had soft hands and had worn rings didn't mean she wasn't for sale.

"Her nails are torn. Any blood underneath?" Sebastian asked, moving on to more obvious details.

"Yes. I think she fought like hell, the poor love. Probably made it worse for herself."

"Was she raped?"

"Let's see," Colin said with a sigh.

It was clear that he was deeply disturbed by what he'd seen so far but was making an effort to remain professional. He reached for a pair of shears and cut the chemise down the middle, easing the fabric from beneath the body and handing it to Sebastian. The lawn felt soft and fine between his fingers, and the lace was neither yellowed nor mended in places. It was the only thing the woman wore, and it was impossible to tell anything from the garment other than that it was of fine quality and relatively new. Whatever jewelry she had worn was gone, and someone had disposed of her clothes and shoes. Given Colin's assessment of the victim's social standing, the woman would probably have been wearing an outer garment to keep her warm, unlike the poor women who could afford little more than a threadbare shawl to keep out the chill, but the cloak or cape was gone as well. The clothes might have been tossed in the river, or had most likely been sold to a shop dealing in second-hand clothes or to a rag-and-bone man. Either way, Sebastian doubted the items would ever be recovered, even if he knew precisely what they were looking for.

Now that the woman was unclothed she looked more like a corpse, or a statue. Her skin was pale as milk, her pink-tipped breasts full, and her legs long and shapely, but that was where the similarity to a work of art ended. The upper arms and thighs were covered in bruises, and the blond pubic hair was matted with dried blood that was also smeared on her inner thighs. A necklace of contusions encircled the slender throat.

Sebastian turned away when Colin pushed the legs apart and probed her nether regions. This woman, or more accurately girl, was still deserving of respect, whether she had been a whore or a duchess.

"You can turn around now, Inspector," Colin Ramsey called out. He didn't comment on Sebastian's need to look away.

"Well?"

"She was most definitely raped, possibly by more than one man, judging by the amount of bleeding and tearing. She was probably held down while her legs were forced apart. There are bruises on her inner thighs, her wrists, and her hips," Colin said. He looked disgusted and angry as he added, "This was a frenzied, vicious assault. And someone bit her breast."

"What?" Sebastian exclaimed. He'd missed that.

"Here," Ramsey said, pointing to the left breast. "Tooth marks around the nipple. Difficult to see unless you look closely."

"Post- or ante-mortem?"

"I think before."

"Cause of death?" Sebastian asked as he forced himself to tear his gaze away from the livid marks. Now that he'd seen them, he couldn't imagine how he'd missed them before.

The more he learned about this case the angrier he became, his blood boiling with a need to destroy those who'd done this. Rape wasn't uncommon, especially among the lower classes where the women didn't have the benefit of protection as they went about their lives, but this was something else entirely. Whoever had attacked this poor woman was no better than an animal—or a pack of animals, if there had been more than one assailant. This wasn't someone who was looking for sexual gratification. This was someone who wanted to inflict the maximum amount of pain and watch his victim suffer before she finally died.

"I have yet to open her up, but at first glance I'd say asphyxiation." Colin pointed to the angry bruises on the victim's neck. "She was strangled."

"I was told she wore a heart around her neck."

The woman's chest was clearly intact, so the heart had to belong to someone else, which, in a way, was even more disturbing.

"Yes." Colin walked over to a cabinet and extracted a jar that contained a heart, the disembodied organ floating in formaldehyde. "This is it. Mr. Stubbs had the presence of mind to preserve it."

"Is it human?" Sebastian asked as he peered at the pale pink gobbet.

"It resembles a human heart a great deal, but it's actually the heart of a pig."

"Really? I would have never guessed. So, what was the point of stringing it around her neck?" Sebastian asked.

"That I cannot tell you. I am not an expert on symbolism, but I reckon a pig's heart might be meant as an insult."

"Is the heart fresh?"

"Yes. The pig was probably slaughtered yesterday."

"And the chain?"

"Tin. It's over there," Colin said, pointing to a metal tray.

Sebastian sighed heavily, his gaze straying to the young woman, who was thankfully well past feeling pain.

"I've never seen anything like this," Colin said morosely. "Rape and murder yes, but the degree of violence and the presentation of the victim are quite disturbing. Someone put a lot of thought into this, Sebastian."

Sebastian nodded his agreement. "In my line of work I must retain a sense of professional detachment, otherwise I won't be able to remain objective, but after all these years I still find that some cases affect me more than others. This..." He gestured toward the woman and the disembodied heart. "This is appalling."

It was also heartbreaking, but as a policeman he wasn't supposed to admit to feeling anything beyond a desire to see justice done. It was important to remain stoic in the face of brutality, but Colin understood and would never judge him harshly. He laid a gentle hand on Sebastian's arm, his eyes warm with sympathy and understanding.

"If we are no longer able to feel compassion or horror at what has been done, then we have no business doing this job, Sebastian. We must hold fast to our own humanity in order to bring about justice for those who can no longer speak for themselves."

"I will find whoever did this," Sebastian said, to Colin, but his gaze was fixed on the woman, since in part he was speaking to her.

Especially if this is to be my last case with Scotland Yard, he added inwardly.

Colin nodded and gave Sebastian a pitying look. "Sebastian, you don't look at all well, if you don't mind me saying so. Why don't you get some food into you and return in two hours. I should be nearly finished with her by then."

Sebastian was about to protest, but saw the sense in what Colin had suggested. He hadn't eaten since yesterday, and nothing the surgeon discovered during the post-mortem would alter the facts, so there was no need for him to be present for the dissection.

"Thank you, Colin. I'll see you in a bit."

"Bring me back a steak and ale pie, will you? I haven't had time to eat." Colin reached into his pocket to extract a few coins, but Sebastian waved him away.

"It's on me. You just focus on our girl."

Colin raised a hand in acknowledgement, then reached for a scalpel, his attention already on his work.

Sebastian saw himself out and adjourned to a nearby chop-house, which was small but clean, and nearly empty at that quiet time between luncheon and dinner. He ordered a fillet of beef with roasted potatoes and a glass of claret and, as soon as the waiter left, rested his head against the back of the seat, closing his eyes for just a moment. He'd been in motion since Sergeant Woodward had come to find him that morning, and he was not only physically tired but emotionally wrung out and desperate for a quiet moment to organize his thoughts and try to put what he'd learned into perspective.

Regardless of what the post-mortem showed, he now knew that the nameless woman was a victim of a brutal rape that had culminated in strangulation, either intentional or accidental. Enraged as he was, he needed to put his personal feelings aside and focus on the details while they were still fresh in his mind, since that was the only way to understand something about the killer's frame of mind. Rather than leave the body where it fell, the perpetrators had decided to display the woman's corpse in a manner synonymous with Christian martyrdom and had adorned her body with a pig's heart. That, more than the rape and the murder, were the points Sebastian needed to focus on because those were the acts meant to send a message. But what was the message, and for whom was it meant?

Traditionally, the pig was thought of as a dirty animal that would eat anything, including other pigs and even human remains. To call someone a pig was to imply that they were the lowest of the low, which was why policemen were so often called pigs by the public, who resented their presence until they had need of them. Was the pig's heart meant as a taunt to the police? It seemed unlikely but couldn't be ruled out. Pickpockets and petty thieves were beginning to organize in the East End, and, although Sebastian hadn't heard of any similar cases, it wasn't beyond the realm of possibility that someone might get creative when it came to intimidation or retribution. If the woman on Colin Ramsey's table was some policeman's wife or daughter, any copper would think twice before venturing into areas controlled by the gangs.

The pig was also an animal shunned by the Jews, a number of whom had settled in London after fleeing persecution in their homelands, mostly in Eastern Europe and Holland. They tended to reside in the poorer areas of the city and earned their living through skilled craftsmanship, but were often forced to sell their products at lower prices in order to divert custom from their non-Jewish competitors, which could be cause for malcontent. Might the woman be Jewish, and could someone have desecrated her and mounted her on the cross as some sort of reference to the crucifixion?

That might account for the brutality and the desire to hurt her as badly as possible, Sebastian speculated. Antisemitism was at the heart of many a hate-fueled crime and would explain the presence of several assailants rather than just one man. Ganging up on an innocent victim guaranteed the desired result and absolved one of personal responsibility—but there was no irrefutable evidence to support this theory.

In truth, the whole thing was so bizarre, no fitting explanation sprang to mind. Sebastian could well understand why Superintendent Lovell hoped the woman was a prostitute and wanted to write her death off as a prank that had got out of hand, but Sebastian could think of no well-known Hallowe'en tradition that would lead to murder. It was the fashion to have jack-o'-lantern-lit parties and delight in the spookiness of Hallowe'en night, but the entertainments were mostly harmless. Gentlemen bobbed for apples, while young ladies played parlor games that usually centered on catching a glimpse of one's future husband in a mirror while alone in a darkened room. Louisa had told Sebastian about one such game, but the reflection she'd seen in the mirror when she was sixteen hadn't borne any resemblance to Sebastian and had been frightening enough to put her off trying again in later years.

She had told him a few other things as well, stories she'd learned from her Scottish nurse while her father had held a post in the Highlands. The nurse had filled Louisa's head with tales of witches and demons and had her convinced that the spirits and fairies parted the veil between this world and the next and walked the land on Samhain, as she had referred to All Hallows' Eve, sometimes seeking shelter in the crofters' cottages. There was something else Louisa had told him that Sebastian recalled only now. Offerings and sacrifices were made on Samhain to appease the pre-Christian gods and ensure that the supplicants would survive the long, cold winter, and sometimes, long ago, those sacrifices had been human. Sebastian was sure that somewhere in the wilds of Scotland there were those who still believed in the old ways and probably made some sort of offering to the gods of their ancestors, but he doubted the tributes were human.

Besides, this was modern-day London, and the particulars of the murder didn't bear out any one theory. At least not yet. Once his food arrived, Sebastian decided to put the case from his mind and refrain from further conjecture until he heard what the surgeon had to say. He also hoped that someone had reported the woman missing. If she was as well-bred as Colin seemed to think, then someone was sure to be alarmed by her disappearance and worried about her well-being. A well-to-do parent or husband was more likely to go to the police than an angry madam or a petty criminal who would prefer to avoid any undue attention from the law. Those individuals had their own code of conduct and meted out justice that didn't involve the police or the courts.

Identifying the victim would go a long way toward understanding what had happened to her, since at the moment she was a blank slate and no inferences could be drawn from her previous experiences. Sebastian hoped that, by tomorrow, they'd have a name.

TEN

By the time Sebastian returned to Colin Ramsey's house in Blackfriars, the penetrating light of the autumn afternoon had been replaced by the lengthening shadows of the approaching evening, and it had grown noticeably colder. Despite the oil lamp suspended from the ceiling, the greater part of the cellar was lost in shadow, the lamp casting just enough luminescence to spotlight the corpse, as if the woman were on stage.

Colin had finished the post-mortem and to Sebastian's great relief had already closed the body, albeit loosely, since he likely planned to open it up again. Several times Sebastian had arrived in the midst of a post-mortem and been confronted not only with various disembodied organs but with a chest cavity that gaped like a fresh carcass in a butcher's shop. He wasn't squeamish by nature, but the sight of such butchery disturbed him more than he cared to admit when the subject was human.

"Expecting your disciples?" Sebastian asked without judgment as he joined Colin by the slab. Every dead body offered a chance to learn, and Colin was a dedicated teacher, who provided his private students with an opportunity to further their education by doing, rather than watching from afar.

"Shame to let the opportunity go to waste," Colin replied. "There are several things I would like to point out to my students. Then we can discuss possible causes and implications."

Coming from anyone else that might have sounded hard-hearted, but Sebastian knew Colin Ramsey well enough to understand his motives. They were both deeply shaken by what had been done to this young woman, but at this stage the only service they could offer her was to find her killer and see him swing, and not to allow her death to be in vain. Every cadaver was an opportunity to learn and to teach. And, in turn, to save the lives of those who might otherwise perish.

"If you'd rather I didn't—" Colin began, sounding a tad flustered, but Sebastian forestalled him.

"It's all right, Colin. We both have a job to do," he said. "So, what can you tell me about her?" he asked, eager to discover if the surgeon had learned anything that might be of use to his investigation.

"She was in fairly good health. Slight scoliosis, but not something that would be readily visible to the untrained eye, and a somewhat enlarged heart."

"What does that mean?"

"Could have been due to irregular function of the thyroid, or perhaps she had elevated blood pressure. Impossible to tell now."

"Would that have killed her had she lived?" Sebastian asked.

"If she had high blood pressure it is possible that she might have died in childbirth. Something of a moot point now," Colin added sadly.

"Might she have borne a child?"

Colin shook his head. "I see no evidence of past pregnancy or childbirth. And she will never be a mother now."

"No," Sebastian agreed. "Anything else?"

"Her last meal was some sort of soup, possibly consommé, beef, potatoes, asparagus, and trifle."

"So dinner, then," Sebastian concluded. "Is that consistent with the time of death?"

"It was cold last night, and I have no way of knowing where she was kept after death occurred. Let us say that she died around midnight, but that's a rough estimate."

"Understood. And the method of murder? Do you stand by your earlier supposition?"

Sebastian's gaze slid to the nasty bruises on the woman's throat. If she had died by strangulation, then she had seen her attacker and had known what was coming, especially once he had subdued her and they had come face to face in the final moments of their struggle. Sebastian could only imagine the poor woman's helplessness and terror as she gazed into the eyes of the person who wanted her dead, since only one assailant could be responsible for choking her to death, even if there were others present.

"I do," Colin replied. "Based on the congestion and conjunctival hemorrhage commonly present in victims of manual strangulation, I can confidently say that she died by asphyxiation. And she didn't die easily," he went on. "Or quickly."

Sebastian sighed. "I didn't think she did, given what was done to her, but how can you tell from the post-mortem?"

Colin walked around the table and lifted the woman's foot. The sole was dirty and lacerated.

"I think she tried to run, but she was apprehended. And then there's this."

He gently turned the corpse over and showed Sebastian a large bruise between the shoulder blades.

"Someone hit her in the back?"

"Look closer. It's a boot print."

"A boot print?" Sebastian echoed, his anger mounting once

again despite his resolve to maintain professional detachment. Looking at the livid bruise, he got the distinct impression that whoever had done this had enjoyed playing with his victim, her fight for survival adding an extra layer of excitement to the depraved game.

Sebastian bent lower to examine the bruise. It was impossible to say anything about the shoe other than that it was large, the man's foot bigger than either Sebastian's or Colin's. Sebastian squinted in the poor light as he tried to make out a pattern of hobnails, but the skin was so mottled it was impossible to tell whether the boot had belonged to a gentleman or a workman.

"I think she fought, tried to run, but someone took her down and then stepped on her back, hard, to hold her down," Colin explained. "Her face must have been pressed against the floor or the ground. She has scratches on her temple and her ear, just here."

Sebastian hadn't noticed the scratches before, as they had been obscured by the victim's hair. Now they were clearly visible, since the hair had been pulled back and tied with a string to keep it out of Colin's way.

"Any other marks?" Sebastian asked.

"There's bruising consistent with a struggle, and there's blood on the back of her skull."

The woman was still on her stomach, and Colin parted the hair at the back of her head to show Sebastian.

"Is her skull fractured?"

"No, but her scalp is badly lacerated, and there's grit trapped inside the wounds."

"What do you reckon?" Sebastian asked as he touched the abrasions on the woman's head, his touch feather-light, as if she could still feel pain.

"If I had to guess—and don't quote me on this—I'd say that whoever strangled her had her either on the floor or up against the wall and hit her head against the stone to subdue her. I don't believe the death was the accidental result of a struggle. Her attacker wanted to inflict as much suffering as possible before she died." Colin laid his hand on the woman's shoulder, almost as if he hoped to comfort her. "What sort of monster...?" His voice trailed away as he stared at the ugly bruise, then lifted his gaze to Sebastian.

"This feels very personal," Sebastian said. "A manic attack motivated by strong feeling."

"Yes, I agree," Colin said. "I think whoever strangled her was raging, his bloodlust only assuaged by death. So even if there were several people present, the one who killed her had to be the instigator."

"Not necessarily," Sebastian replied. "But he was definitely the one that lost control."

"Something about this woman undid him," Colin agreed. "It wasn't enough to hurt her. He must have wanted to see the light go out of her eyes."

Sebastian nodded. "It was the only thing that brought him peace."

If Colin was surprised by Sebastian's observation he didn't comment. Instead he said, "There's something else I'd like to show you. I don't believe this would be admissible in a court of law, but it might be of some help to you."

"What is it?" Sebastian asked.

Colin turned the body over once again and wrapped his hands around her neck. "What do you see?"

"I see you pretending to strangle someone who's already dead," Sebastian replied.

"Besides that, or have all powers of observation deserted you?" Colin asked with a humorless chuckle.

Sebastian looked closer. Even in the dim light, he could see that the bruises extended beyond Colin's elegant hands.

"She was strangled with something wide, like a scarf or a leather strap? That would mean that her attacker was most likely behind her." Sebastian shook his head. "That doesn't seem to support what we know so far."

"You're half right. She was strangled with something wide, but not by a strap. It's not as obvious at the front, but if you examine the back of the neck, you can see finger marks, just here. The killer had large hands that encircled her whole neck."

Colin removed his own hands and showed Sebastian the back of the woman's neck, where eight oval contusions formed a pattern that would correspond with fingers. Having finished, he turned the body over to lie on its back.

"He wasn't behind her. They were face to face at the moment of death. The killer fractured the victim's larynx and broke the hyoid bone," Colin added, pointing to a spot just below the woman's chin and correctly assuming that Sebastian might not be familiar with the Latin terms. "Her voice box is crushed."

Sebastian nodded. He couldn't trust himself to speak, his fury at what had been done to this unfortunate girl choking the breath from him and dragging his mind back to his own loss, his own pain. He took a moment to collect himself, then turned to Colin. "Can I have a light?" he asked.

Colin lit one more lamp and held it aloft, illuminating the woman's face. Sebastian fitted his own hands around the neck, nodded when they failed to cover the bruising, then moved on to the feet. He examined one foot, then the other, and used his nail to scrape at one of the deeper lacerations.

"What are you thinking?" Colin asked.

"There's grit, but no soil, so she was kept inside, but the floor was made of stone that was perhaps uneven."

"Could be any cellar or warehouse in London," Colin remarked.

"Could be," Sebastian agreed.

"Any theories?" Colin asked when Sebastian failed to continue.

"I was just thinking. There are no traces of soil or grass on her feet. She had to have been undressed and already dead by the time the killer brought her to Highgate, since her feet never touched the ground."

"She may have been alive," Colin argued. "Let us suppose that the killer lured her to Highgate, maybe for an assignation. Perhaps it was an All Hallows' prank, as Lovell suggested. Placing her trust in him, the victim came willingly, but then once they got there something changed. Perhaps he'd been expecting more than she was willing to give. Or maybe she became frightened, wanted to leave, and they rowed. He tried to force her, and she fought, but he overcame her resistance. It's possible that he bashed her head against a gravestone to subdue her, which would explain the grit, then raped her and, unable to stop, strangled her, possibly during sexual congress. Not wanting the victim to be identified, he removed her clothes and mounted her on the cross to confuse the police."

Sebastian considered Ramsey's suggestion. "On the whole, it fits, but there are too many holes in that theory."

"Such as?"

"You said that she died around midnight, but the journalist saw the man by the body closer to nine a.m."

"Maybe the person he saw wasn't the killer but a visitor to the cemetery, who realized that he might be blamed for the murder and decided to make himself scarce," Ramsey replied.

Sebastian shook his head. "Even if she came to Highgate willingly, you yourself said that given the extent of her internal injuries there was probably more than one assailant, and, although the killer was clearly a strong man, it would take more than one person to get her up on that cross. One to hold her, and one to get the ties in place. And she would have to have been undressed for the boot print to register so clearly on her back. If she fought and tried to run, there would be dirt and grass on her feet and in her hair, since she was clearly brought down while still alive, and her chemise would be covered in dirt. There would also be more dirt on her face, since she would have thrashed."

Colin opened his mouth to refute Sebastian's suggestion, but Sebastian held up one finger to forestall him. "The killer would have to have brought rope and a pig's heart, so a romantic tryst doesn't seem likely, does it?"

"Perhaps it was all part of the prank," Colin suggested. "There may have been several people involved, and maybe they had planned to desecrate someone's grave."

"Perhaps," Sebastian conceded. He could see how the details could be made to fit the narrative in a way that made sense, but his instinct refused to accept this explanation. It didn't feel right. "Is there any way to tell if she was foreign?" he asked.

"An immigrant, you mean? Not without hearing her speak. The only thing that would give her away is an accent, since her features and coloring are common to this part of the world."

"How much would you say she weighs?" Sebastian asked, his mind moving on to other possibilities.

"Between eight and nine stone," Colin Ramsey replied. "Why do you ask?"

"I doubt the killer carried her across London. If she wasn't murdered at Highgate, he would have needed a conveyance to transport the body. I don't see any dirt or straw in her hair, so I don't think it was a wagon."

"A hansom?" Colin asked, his expression thoughtful. "It would be awfully brazen to move a dead body in a cab, unless the driver was handsomely paid for his silence."

"Given the severity of the attack and the possibility that there were a number of people involved, someone must have seen something," Sebastian insisted.

"But would they be willing to talk?"

"Not if they feared they'd be the next to hang on a cross," Sebastian replied.

"It seems you have your work cut out for you, old friend," Colin said, his eyes warm with sympathy.

"I will find out who did this to her," Sebastian ground out. "I owe her that."

Colin was about to reply when the bell jangled upstairs. "My students are here."

"I'll leave you to it, then. Do let me know if you think of anything that might be pertinent to the case," Sebastian said as the two men walked up the stairs and approached the front door.

"I will," Colin promised, but his attention was already on the three young men waiting on his doorstep.

Sebastian tipped his hat to the men and walked away, resolutely ignoring the newsboy's cry as he hawked the evening edition. It seemed the story was already in the papers.

ELEVEN

Sebastian had always loved dusk, that liminal hour between light and dark when the ugliness so prevalent during the daylight hours was swallowed by the shadows, and the purpling sky glowed with stars in a way he could only describe as magical. It was at dusk that he was sometimes able to forget, for just a moment, what his life had become and recapture that feeling of wonder, until reality reasserted itself and he was right back where he'd started. Tonight, he couldn't manage even a moment of peace. The face of the beautiful young woman was seared into his brain, and his mind was teeming with questions as he traversed Westminster.

Lights were coming on in the windows, and the shop-keepers were preparing to lock up for the night. Clerks disgorged by their places of business were heading home, their caped coats and black hats making them look like a colony of bats fleeing a dark cave. The shopgirls were more colorful in their bonnets and crinolines, a different sort of flock altogether, but they looked as downtrodden as the men, their shoulders hunched with fatigue, their faces set in lines of tension. Sebastian hoped that they had someone waiting for them with a hot meal and a kind word.

As tired humanity flowed around him, he decided there was no point in returning to Scotland Yard. He had nothing to report, and, if the woman had been identified, Lovell would have sent word to Colin Ramsey, knowing that Sebastian would make his way there at some point during the day. He needed time to consider and formulate a plan, which, at this stage, was easier said than done. The revelation that the woman came from a well-to-do family had changed his perspective on the case, but he still had nothing concrete to go on. People were often reluctant to involve the police. The common people didn't think they would be taken seriously and given the same treatment as the gentry, and the gentry held off for as long as possible, mindful of the scandal that might ensue once word got out. It was a shame to think the nameless woman's family was worried about her reputation when she was already beyond such worldly cares.

Sebastian inhaled deeply and fixed his gaze on the rising moon as he considered what he knew. The victim had dined lavishly before being taken or lured to the place where she had been raped and murdered, and it was highly unlikely that she had eaten such a meal alone. She was hardly more than a child, so it stood to reason that she had sat down to dinner with her family, or her husband, if she had married young. Aside from the bruises sustained during the attack, her skin was soft and unblemished, her body well cared for. This was a young woman who'd been well-treated and sheltered from the harsh realities of life, a woman who would have enjoyed a comfortable and happy existence had her future not been stolen from her, her life extinguished well before her time, in a manner that was unusually savage.

A woman not so different from Louisa, a cruel little voice reminded him, but Sebastian forced himself to ignore the visceral stab of pain and directed his thoughts back to the case.

The victim's clothes and shoes were missing but, if the chemise was anything to go by, they would have been fashionable and of fine quality. Likewise, if she had been wearing jewelry, it'd be worth a few bob, and the items might have been sold or kept as a souvenir. Either way, they weren't likely to be recovered, so it was more prudent to focus on the sequence of events.

If the woman had died around midnight, as Colin had surmised, and the man seen at Highgate had been the one to mount her on the cross, then the body had been kept somewhere until the early hours. This could be for one of two reasons. Either the man hadn't wanted to transport a corpse at night because he might be too conspicuous when fewer people were abroad, or he had been afraid that the body would be snatched by grave-robbers before it was discovered. The latter made more sense, especially if the killer had access to a carriage. It seemed he'd wanted to ensure that his handiwork was seen, and there had to be a reason the body had been displayed in such a dramatic manner.

Sebastian wished he knew more of the man who was seen near the body, but it seemed that Constable Bryant hadn't been able to get anything useful from the near-hysterical witness. Even something as basic as the man's height and build would be helpful in trying to tie him to the murder or serve to rule him out. If the man was slight, chances were he wasn't the one to brutalize the girl, but he could have been an accomplice or a procurer of the necessary supplies, like the binds and the heart. It resembled the human organ enough to be mistaken for one, and perhaps that had been the point. Maybe the pig and all the associations the animal brought to mind didn't figure into this, but then why hang it around the victim's neck? Surely there was some hidden meaning. Could it be a reference to the killer's own heart? Had the woman broken or stolen his heart, and now it belonged to her? Was it possible that she had been the killer's sweetheart or wife? Or maybe she had ended an affair with her lover, who had retaliated by inflicting such violence on her. Some men couldn't handle rejection, be they husband or admirer. They didn't usually rape and murder the object of their affections, but it wasn't unheard of.

Crimes of passion were just that, a moment of insanity, the killer succumbing to their deepest, darkest desires and taking out their love or hatred on the one person who had the power to stoke them. The physical injuries pointed to more than one man, but perhaps the attack had been so frenzied and prolonged that he had hurt the victim more than one would expect of only one perpetrator. And would such a strong man be able to crucify the victim on his own? Sebastian thought that was possible. The man might have carried the body through the cemetery until he spotted a monument that suited his purpose. The base of the cross on Elizabeth Burrows' grave was not as high as some of the others Sebastian had seen, which was probably why it had been chosen. The killer had then held the woman against the monument with one hand and managed to tie a wrist to the crossbar with the other. That would require strength and dexterity, but it could be done. And perhaps he had returned with the heart later, having procured it specifically for the purpose.

On the other hand, there could have been more than one assailant, which would rule out a spur-of-the-moment crime of passion brought about by something the victim might have said or done to anger her attacker. If two or more men had set out to rape and strangle the woman then the assault might have been planned, the victim either randomly chosen or intentionally selected for a particular reason. It would be much easier for two people to carry the body, then mount it on the cross, and use the heart, tin chain, and rope if the items had been prepared in advance and were ready to be deployed. And if the attack was premeditated, then the motive would be entirely different and even more heartless than an act of sudden violence brought on by loss of temper.

There was no way to test any of these theories without identifying the victim. First thing tomorrow, Sebastian would check with the Yard, then, if there was nothing, he would visit every other division in London to see if someone had reported the woman missing. Even if she had been murdered by her husband, her lover, or a random lunatic, who chose her simply because she happened to be in the wrong place at the wrong time or had fit a particular feminine ideal, she was young enough to have living parents or siblings. Given her social status, she had to have had a maid, possibly even an entire staff at her disposal. Someone out there, in the dark metropolis that spread before him, had to have realized that she was gone, and, with the story already in the papers, perhaps they would wonder if the nameless victim was their daughter, sister, wife, or mistress. And once Sebastian had a name, he could begin to identify possible suspects.

He also intended to speak to the man who'd come upon the victim. The man might have shared everything he knew, but sometimes a well-phrased question could jog a person's memory and shake loose some hitherto forgotten or overlooked detail, especially once the person had calmed down and had time to reflect on what they had seen. Or perhaps the scoundrel had shared all the details in the article he'd written for his newspaper. No wonder the story had broken so quickly. Perhaps the journalist had already monetized the victim's death and was even now gloating at making the front page.

By the time Sebastian arrived at home, he had the outline of a strategy and was surprised to realize that he felt something he hadn't experienced in a long while—lack of apathy. The anger he felt had lit a fire in his belly and reminded him why he had decided to become a policeman in the first place—a need to protect and defend. Superintendent Lovell was well within his rights if he decided to dismiss him, but even if this was to be his last case with the Yard he'd do everything in his power to solve this case.

"Would you care for some supper, Inspector?" Mrs. Poole asked as she came out to greet him. "It's boiled beef tonight."

"Thank you, Mrs. Poole, but I've eaten," Sebastian replied, glad he'd splurged on a hearty meal earlier. Mrs. Poole's boiled beef was cold, dry, and bland, and settled in the stomach like a brick at the bottom of a river.

"Kedgeree for breakfast," Mrs. Poole announced, looking at Sebastian as if she expected applause.

"Looking forward to it," Sebastian replied, and hurried up the stairs before she could ask him about his day or, worse yet, the case.

As a rule, respectable women did not read anything beyond the society pages, the news being either too distressing or too complicated for them to absorb, but Mrs. Poole sent out Hank, the boy she employed to help with the heavier chores, every morning and evening to purchase a copy of the *Daily Telegraph*. Hank also bought the weekly edition of the *Illustrated London News* and every new penny dreadful. Mrs. Poole devoured the stories and picked over the details, seeming to relish the tragedy and pain that befell others and pumping Sebastian for information when she thought he might have access to the investigation. He was always polite but kept her at arm's length, and had never shared anything of his personal history. As far as Mrs. Poole knew, Sebastian was a confirmed bachelor who had little interest in settling down. Had she suspected anything different, he was sure his tenancy would have to come to an end, since she saw every unmarried man under the age of seventy as a potential husband and let it be known that she would consider any reasonable proposal.

When he let himself in, the darkness in his rooms felt almost solid, the only sign of life Gustav, who was curled in a wingchair by the cold hearth but jumped down and attempted to weave himself around Sebastian's ankles as he went to light the gas lamps. Sebastian noted the *gift* Gustav had left for him and wrapped what was left of the mouse the cat had feasted on in an old newspaper and tossed it into a rubbish bin to be disposed of tomorrow, while resolutely ignoring the siren call of the whisky. To drink until he fell into a deep, dreamless sleep would be his chosen method of spending the evening, but he had to be sharp tomorrow morning, and it wouldn't do to show up reeking of spirits.

Instead, Sebastian settled at the writing desk situated between the two windows in the tiny sitting room. He pulled out a fresh sheet of paper, opened the bottle of ink, and dipped his pen. No one was coming to rescue him, so it was high time he saved himself and considered his future. Putting pen to paper, Sebastian wrote the greeting and inwardly congratulated himself on taking this first, monumental step toward applying to the Pinkertons. Unsure how to phrase his inquiry, he decided that he'd have one small drink to steady his nerves. After all, it had been a trying day, and he felt emotionally raw and physically drained. Having finished the drink, he poured another and sank into the wingchair. He'd finish the letter to Mr. Pinkerton before he went to bed and post it first thing tomorrow.

TWELVE

Tuesday, November 2

Gemma spent a sleepless night, her thoughts fragmenting and rearranging themselves endlessly like the colorful bits of glass inside a kaleidoscope. The bright chips were memories of Victor, her love for him, her faith in his unwavering support, and the cold comfort of knowing that he was now with his beloved Julia. The darker pieces that overshadowed the light were her grief, her anger, and her growing suspicion.

I'm being followed.

Gemma couldn't let go of the idea that Victor had been pushed under the wheels of that omnibus, and she wouldn't be able to rest until she discovered the truth.

Rising early, she made a cup of tea and forced herself to eat a bit of bread. It would soak up the bile that soured her stomach and made her feel ill. As she ate her solitary breakfast, she reflected that this was the first time in her life that she had ever spent the night completely alone. There had always been someone, from her parents, servants, and Victor when she had been a child, to other nurses and patients when she had been in Scutari or on a ship to and from Crimea. It was sobering to realize that this had been the first night of many and that she would probably spend the rest of her life on her own.

Unable to finish the bread, she gave up on breakfast, and carried the cup and plate into the kitchen and rinsed them before returning to the bedroom. She opened the trunk at the foot of the bed and pulled out the outmoded mourning attire that lay neatly folded beneath the spare woolen blanket and the gowns she wore during the summer months. The gown made of black crape fit surprisingly well. She'd been unbecomingly thin when she'd returned from Crimea, but she'd filled out since then and was back to her normal weight, an achievement she owed to Victor and his love of food. The day he received his first wage from the newspaper, Victor had taken her to a cozy restaurant he'd found, and had insisted they order champagne. He had been so proud and hopeful.

Gemma smiled dolefully at the memory, then roused herself before examining the black bonnet and short wool cape that she'd worn after her mother had died. They would do for now, but she might have to dye one of her older gowns black, since she didn't have enough to wear for the duration of the mourning period. The black crape bow was at the bottom of the trunk, and Gemma hung it on the door. She didn't expect any visitors or condolence calls, but etiquette had to be observed. She was about to leave when she remembered Victor's notebook and slid it into her reticule. It was the only proof she had, and she hoped that whoever she spoke to would recognize the significance of Victor's final entry.

When she arrived at Scotland Yard, Gemma was met by a friendly desk sergeant. He had neatly parted and oiled hair and a waxed moustache, the ends of which tipped upward when he smiled. He looked quite smart in his uniform too, and for some reason that made Gemma feel more hopeful about the upcoming interview.

"Good morning, madam. How can I help?" the sergeant asked cheerily. He probably thought she'd lost her lapdog or wanted to report a troublesome neighbor.

"I would like to speak to a detective, please."

"In regard to?"

"I believe my brother was murdered," Gemma said, and lifted her chin defiantly.

"I see," the sergeant said. "Constable Daley, see if Inspector Cotton is free to speak to this lady," he called out to a passing constable who looked no older than eighteen and still sported adolescent spots on his pasty skin.

"Yes, sir."

Constable Daley returned a few moments later. "If you'd follow me, madam, Inspector Cotton will see you now."

The constable escorted Gemma to a small office that held two desks, one of them unoccupied but clearly in use. Perhaps the other detective was out on a case and Inspector Cotton was awaiting a new assignment. The man didn't bother to stand when she walked in. Instead, he leaned back in his chair, appraising her as if she were a horse he was considering purchasing. He had to be in his fifties, and showed clear signs of unhealthy living. There were bags under his eyes, the skin discolored and loose, and webs of broken capillaries in his nose and cheeks. The buttons on the tweed vest that matched his suit strained against the bulk of the man's belly, and the collar of his shirt was yellowed and limp from lack of starch. This was someone who not only enjoyed his food and drink but paid little attention to his appearance; Gemma could see a bit of dried egg on his waistcoat and mucousy snot in the unkempt moustache that obscured his upper lip. She detested slovenliness and was sorely disappointed by her first impression of the man.

"Do sit down, Mrs....?"

"Miss Tate," Gemma replied crisply, and accepted the proffered seat.

"So, what can I do for you, *Miss* Tate?"

Inspector Cotton emphasized her unmarried state, which didn't bode well. It was difficult enough for a married woman to get taken seriously, but an unmarried woman was treated no better than an orphaned child who lacked a father to tell them what to think and how to behave. Without a man to guide her in her thinking or accompany her on such an important errand, she would be lucky if the detective even heard her out.

"My brother, Victor Tate, died yesterday when he was crushed by the wheels of an omnibus." Gemma's voice quavered, but she continued, desperate to get her story out before she was dismissed. "Victor was a journalist and always carried his notebook. He made some notes shortly before he died, and I have reason to think that he was murdered."

She went to unclasp her reticule, but the man made a dismissive gesture with his tobacco-stained hand. "Miss Tate, I heard about the accident. Your brother stumbled and fell. You have my sympathy," he added with the air of a man who was anything but sympathetic.

"Inspector, my brother was the one to discover the dead woman in Highgate. He saw someone near the victim and believed he was being followed."

"As a journalist, he no doubt had a vivid imagination."

"He didn't imagine the woman mounted on the cross. It's all right there in the notebook, and the story is in the papers," Gemma insisted. "If you would only allow me to show you."

"An unfortunate coincidence. Nothing more. No doubt your brother was distracted by the morning's events and wasn't paying attention to where he was going."

"Inspector—" Gemma began, but Inspector Cotton cut her off.

"Miss Tate, we are very busy with real cases and can't afford to waste time on conspiracies imagined by grieving young women. Now, I can see that you're distraught," he said, moderating his tone somewhat, when he saw Gemma's outrage. "Losing someone you love is one of the hardest things to bear, but making up a murderous plot to explain away a terrible accident will not bring you peace. Only time can do that."

"Inspector, I must insist," Gemma tried again, but the man had said all he was going to say on the subject.

"And I *must insist*, miss, that you kindly remove yourself from the premises before I see fit to charge you."

"Charge me with what, exactly?" Gemma demanded. She hadn't expected a warm welcome, but the man was downright hostile and dismissive.

"Charge you with wasting police time."

"Police time?" Gemma cried. "You don't look very busy to me, so perhaps you're the one who's wasting the time you're being paid for."

She regretted the words as soon as they were out of her mouth, but the damage was done. Inspector Cotton turned puce with rage.

"Get out," he roared, to the astonishment of a constable who happened to be passing the open door. "Now!"

Gemma pushed back the chair hard enough to scrape the floorboards, and felt a childish sense of vindication when Inspector Cotton winced. "Good day to you, sir. You haven't heard the last of this."

"Oh, I think I have. Constable," Inspector Cotton called. "Escort this woman outside and tell the desk sergeant that she's barred from reentering the building."

The constable's eyebrows lifted comically, but Gemma wasn't laughing. This buffoon of a man had just ruined her only chance of discovering what had really happened to Victor. She supposed she could try one of the other divisions, but suspected she wouldn't fare any better. Unless proof of a crime smacked someone in the face, they weren't likely to acknowledge it. The constable took Gemma by the elbow and steered her toward the vestibule.

"I'm sorry, ma'am," he said quietly. "Inspector Cotton can be a bit..." He seemed to be searching for the right word, so Gemma supplied a few of her own.

"Lazy? Boorish? Incompetent?"

"Eh, I was going to say impatient," the constable replied. "But all those fit," he added in a conspiratorial whisper. "Wouldn't want him investigating my loved one's death, I can tell you that. Couldn't detect his own arse with both hands."

The constable blushed furiously when he realized just how inappropriate a comment he'd made, especially when speaking to a woman, but Gemma smiled at him gratefully.

"Who would you recommend I speak to, Constable?" she asked.

"I'm not in a position to recommend anyone. Perhaps you should try hiring a private investigator."

I can't afford a private investigator, Gemma thought, but didn't say so to the constable, who was now holding the door open for her.

"Good morning, ma'am," he said, and closed the door the moment she was through.

Tears blurred Gemma's vision, but she didn't bother to stop walking as she opened her reticule and fumbled for a handkerchief. The collision nearly knocked her off her feet, and she would have fallen on her backside had the man not grabbed her just in time and steadied her.

"I am so sorry," he exclaimed. "Are you all right?"

"Eh, yes, I think so," Gemma replied. He was still holding on to her, his gaze sympathetic as he took in her swimming eyes and trembling hands.

"Miss Tate, is it not?"

Gemma blinked and looked up at him, but he was a stranger to her. "I'm sorry, but have we met?"

"Not formally, no, but I saw you yesterday. At the mortuary."

Now she remembered. He was the man who'd come to claim the body of the fair-haired young woman.

"Are you bereaved as well, sir?" Gemma asked, even though he hadn't looked grief-stricken yesterday.

"No. I'm a surgeon. Colin Ramsey, at your service," the man said, and bowed awkwardly.

"It's good to meet you, Mr. Ramsey."

Gemma would have walked away, but Colin Ramsey still had his hand on her elbow. He looked down at her and smiled shyly. "Miss Tate, you seem upset, and I have yet to have my breakfast. Might I interest you in a cup of tea? There's a pleasant tearoom a few streets over. Perhaps you can tell me what has distressed you so. I might be able to help."

"I doubt it," Gemma replied.

She wasn't in the habit of accepting invitations from strange men but, if she were honest, she felt too shaken to go home and spend the rest of the day staring at the four walls of the parlor, wondering whether she might have succeeded in convincing Inspector Cotton to take the case if she had only managed to control her temper. She needed someone to talk to, and maybe this man could offer useful advice. He was on his way to Scotland Yard, so perhaps he could help her find someone who'd actually listen to her version of events.

"All right," Gemma said. "And thank you, Mr. Ramsey."

"Not at all. You'll be doing me a great favor by keeping me company."

They talked of trivialities on the way to the tearoom, then surrendered their coats and Mr. Ramsey's hat and settled at a table in the corner, looking for all the world like two people who knew each other well and were comfortable in each other's presence.

THIRTEEN

Colin Ramsey ordered crumpets with butter and strawberry preserves, and tea, while Gemma settled for coffee. She couldn't eat even if she wanted to, but she was fading fast after her sleepless night and knew from previous experience that coffee would revive her. Now that they were face to face and the subject of the weather had been exhausted, her stomach was in knots, and she had to work hard to keep the tears at bay. It was always easier to maintain control when people were brusque; when they were kind it made one feel more vulnerable somehow.

"I am happy to share," Colin Ramsey said when the hot crumpets were brought to the table.

"Thank you, but I'm really not hungry. Enjoy your breakfast, Mr. Ramsey."

Colin Ramsey buttered a crumpet and spread the preserves but didn't take a bite. Instead he set the crumpet on his plate and fixed Gemma with his knowing gaze. "Miss Tate, we can simply enjoy each other's company for a half-hour and go our separate ways, if that is what you wish, or you can tell me what upset you so, and I will do whatever is in my power to try to help."

Gemma nodded. She was tempted to hide behind small talk, which was safe and would help to pass the time, but this was her one chance to get someone who had access to Scotland Yard on her side. She took a fortifying sip of coffee, swallowed the bitter brew, and told Colin Ramsey about her suspicions.

"Do you also think I'm deluded, Mr. Ramsey?" she asked once she had finished, when he failed to say anything.

Colin Ramsey looked thoughtful, then shook his head. "If your brother had met with an accident on any other day, then I would say that perhaps your suspicions were the result of grief and a desire to assign blame, but, given that he was the person who came upon the woman in Highgate and saw who might have been her killer, I think your concerns are perfectly valid."

"So you believe that he was being followed?"

"I believe that he believed it. Perhaps he was trying to get away from the person who had caused him concern, or perhaps his death wasn't an accident at all, and he was deliberately silenced."

"He was in the wrong place at the wrong time," Gemma said miserably.

"It would certainly seem so."

"But he told the constable everything he knew. What was the point of killing him after he'd made his statement?"

"Perhaps the individual realized that your brother worked for a newspaper and thought it best to avoid the sort of publicity an article could generate."

Gemma nodded. "Or a likeness."

"Likeness?"

"Victor could have asked one of the illustrators to draw a likeness of the man he had seen. Perhaps it would have led to an arrest."

"Perhaps," Colin Ramsey replied. "A drawing is certainly more effective than a verbal description." He absent-mindedly stirred his tea, even though he hadn't added sugar. "Miss Tate, how committed are you to finding out what happened to your brother?"

"One hundred percent," Gemma replied without hesitation.

"It could be a dangerous undertaking."

"I realize that, but I won't be able to rest until I know what really happened."

"Would it make you feel better to know for certain that your brother was murdered?"

"Yes."

"Why, if you don't mind me asking?"

"Because I simply can't believe that Victor would be careless enough to walk under the wheels of an omnibus. It's not such an easy thing to do, is it? Even if he had stumbled, he could have righted himself, fallen against the side of the conveyance, or landed on the pavement. He might have even collided with a horse's rump, but I can't see how he would have become trapped between the horses and the wheels. And he must have done, judging by his injuries."

"I see what you mean," Colin Ramsey replied. "The timing would have to be just right for the victim to fall between the horses' front and back legs and find himself on the ground just as the wheels rolled forth."

"Precisely," Gemma said, gratified that he saw her point.

"So it is your theory that someone waited until just the right moment before pushing Victor off the curb?"

"It is." Gemma took a deep breath and asked the question that had been on her mind since the Highgate Cemetery victim had first been mentioned. "Mr. Ramsey, can you tell me about the woman's injuries? What was the cause of death?"

"Miss Tate, I really don't think—" he began, but Gemma forestalled him.

"I have seen horrors beyond your darkest imagining while

nursing in Crimea. Some men were so mangled, they no longer resembled human beings. Nothing you say will shock me, Mr. Ramsey. I assure you."

"Be that as it may, I am not at liberty to discuss the results of the post-mortem."

"You said you would help," Gemma reproached him.

"I did, and I will." Colin Ramsey took a sip of tea and set the cup in its saucer. "I was on my way to Scotland Yard to deliver the post-mortem report. If you give me your address, I will leave a message for Inspector Bell to call on you at his earliest convenience."

"If he's anything like Inspector Cotton, don't bother," Gemma said. She didn't mean to sound rude, but she was disappointed and felt let down.

"He is nothing like Inspector Cotton," Colin Ramsey said, and Gemma could tell from the smile that tugged at the corners of his mouth that he was personally acquainted with Inspector Bell and genuinely liked the man. "Inspector Bell is intelligent and, what I believe is even more important in a policeman, intuitive. He will see the connection that Inspector Cotton failed to make. Or refused to make, I should say. Cotton is lazy and doesn't hold women in high regard, particularly when they challenge his authority, but Inspector Bell sees the entire person, not just the limitations of their sex."

"Well, that's something, I suppose," Gemma grumbled.

"Inspector Bell is a good man, Miss Tate. A caring man. He will help."

"Thank you," Gemma said. Hearing the inspector described in such a flattering way gave her a tiny shred of hope. "I will call at the undertaker to discuss the funeral arrangements, but then I will be at home for the remainder of the day. Tomorrow I will go to work."

Colin Ramsey scribbled down Gemma's address in a small

book he'd pulled from his pocket, then looked up at her with an expression of concern. "Are you sure you're ready to return to work, Miss Tate? Perhaps you should take a few days to come to terms with your loss."

"It will take considerably longer than a few days to come to terms with Victor's death, Mr. Ramsey. Keeping busy is the best way to deal with grief."

Gemma chose not to add that she couldn't afford to remain at home, not even while in mourning. She wasn't the sort of person to court pity, nor did she wish to discuss her financial situation with a virtual stranger.

Colin Ramsey smiled. "I take your point, Miss Tate. I prefer to keep busy as well."

"Have you recently lost someone?" Gemma asked.

He nodded. "My father. He passed three years ago now, but I still miss him. And, sadly, my mother is unwell."

"Unwell how?" Gemma asked, the nurse in her stepping to the forefront.

"She's in reasonable health physically. It's her mind that's been affected," Colin Ramsey said sadly. "My mother was always a clever, capable woman, but now she forgets things and sometimes seems to disappear into the past. There are times when she thinks I'm my father, and other times when she believes I'm still a little boy. I no longer feel safe to leave her on her own."

"Are there any other symptoms? Has your mother suffered a stroke, perhaps?"

Gemma belatedly realized that she was probably overstepping her bounds. Colin Ramsey was a doctor, even though he wasn't addressed as such. She always thought it was terribly unfair that surgeons were not permitted to use the title and had to be referred to as mister, even though they understood considerably more about the workings of the human body than the physicians who obtained their knowledge from medical texts and thought themselves vastly superior to men they considered to be no better than butchers. In all fairness, some of them were butchers, but there were those who believed in furthering their knowledge and trying out new methods and did their utmost to save every patient who came before them. Gemma had a feeling that Colin Ramsey was one of those progressive surgeons, and if he was, he most certainly did not need her to diagnose his mother; but he didn't appear offended.

"I don't believe Mother has suffered a stroke, Miss Tate. I see none of the symptoms of physical impairment that usually accompany such an event. I think my father's death affected her so deeply that she wasn't able to fully recover. Grief addled her mind."

"Miss Nightingale once called it a softening of the brain," Gemma said. "How old is your mother, Mr. Ramsey?"

"Sixty-two. She had me rather late in life. She was nearly thirty," he confided.

"Sixty-two is not so very old. Perhaps you're right and the trauma caused the onset of the symptoms."

Colin Ramsey sighed. "Unfortunately, the passage of time has not lessened the symptoms. If anything, she's getting worse."

"Is there someone to help you?" Gemma asked.

"I employ a maid. Mabel. She cooks and cleans and looks after Mother while I work. She's a kind girl," Colin Ramsey added. "I trust her."

"It helps to have someone you can trust."

He grinned. "Mabel refuses to go down into the cellar, where I perform the post-mortems. I have to clean that room myself."

"Can't say I blame her," Gemma said, and smiled for the first time since Victor's death. "I wouldn't relish cleaning up after a post-mortem either."

"It is rather gruesome, I suppose, but needs must. Without a post-mortem, the police are often working blind."

"Don't tell them that," Gemma replied. "They think they know it all."

"Policing and medicine are inextricably linked, if you ask me. Medicine can function without the police, but the police cannot function without the insight of medicine." Colin Ramsey looked at Gemma eagerly. "So, you knew Florence Nightingale."

"I learned so much from her, and not just about nursing."

"Yes, I can well imagine that. A formidable woman, by all accounts."

"Strong, determined, compassionate, and very brave," Gemma said. To her mind, *formidable* had a negative connotation and an implication that the woman in question was hard, inflexible, and uncaring. Florence Nightingale was none of those things, but few were interested in getting to know the real woman. They preferred to think of her as the symbol of perseverance and strength she had become, an unexpected hero of a misguided war.

"I wager she would have made an excellent doctor."

"You think women can be doctors, Mr. Ramsey?"

"I think women can be anything, given the chance. Even police detectives."

"Now you're just humoring me," Gemma said, and picked up her reticule. "I thank you for the coffee, but I really should be going."

Colin Ramsey sprang to his feet as Gemma stood. "I'm very sorry for your loss, Miss Tate, and I do hope we meet again soon. You can be sure I will pass on the message to Inspector Bell." He looked at her shyly. "Would it be all right, do you think, if I called on you sometime—to inquire about the investigation?" he hastened to add.

Gemma's initial instinct was to say no. It would hardly be appropriate, but she had few friends in this city, and this man had been so kind to her. "Yes, Mr. Ramsey. It would be all right," she said, and having wished him a good morning took her leave.

FOURTEEN

Sebastian set out after an early breakfast and spent the morning in pursuit of a name. No reports of a missing woman had come in to Scotland Yard, so he proceeded to call on ten of the seventeen divisions, but came away with nothing. Everyone had heard of the Highgate Angel, as the woman was now being referred to, but no one had any inkling who she might be.

Sebastian entered the duty room at Scotland Yard just after noon and was instantly hailed by Sergeant Woodward.

"Lovell wants you. And you'd better get in there right quick," Sergeant Woodward said with an amused grin.

His amiable disposition and good humor were a welcome change from the duty sergeants Sebastian had been questioning all morning. One would think that the other divisions would offer a fellow policeman every cooperation, but they guarded their patches jealously and saw no reason to help, since it would be Scotland Yard in the papers if Sebastian solved the case, and not their station.

"What's his mood like?" Sebastian asked.

"Like a mad dog that wants to tear out your throat."

"Excellent," Sebastian replied sarcastically.

"Forewarned is forearmed."

"Unless I can put down said dog, the warning does me little good."

"Someone's going to get it. Better you than me," Sergeant Woodward said with a sly grin. "You can take him with one arm tied behind your back."

"In the boxing ring, maybe. In here, I'm not so sure."

Sebastian strode down the corridor toward the superintendent's office and knocked on the door.

"Come."

"I was told you wanted to see me, Superintendent," Sebastian said, not bothering with the niceties.

"Shut the door and sit down, Bell." The super did look angry, but there was something else in his dark gaze. Fear perhaps. Or foreboding.

"What's happened, sir?"

"What's happened?" Superintendent Lovell shot back. "I'll tell you what's happened. While you were Lord knows where, lollygagging the morning away, a certain personage paid me a visit."

"And who might that be, sir?" Sebastian asked.

The superintendent clearly wasn't interested in his excuse for coming in so late and wasn't aware that he'd stopped in early that morning to check with Sergeant Woodward whether there were any developments in the case.

"Alastair Seaborne, Viscount Dalton. Heard of him, have you?"

"In passing," Sebastian admitted, although he couldn't remember in what context he'd heard the name. "What did he want?"

Superintendent Lovell yanked open the top drawer of his desk and withdrew a cabinet card. It depicted a fair-haired young woman of about seventeen, her light eyes wide with wonderment, her high-necked gown prim and virginal. She wore diamond and pearl studs in her dainty ears, and Sebastian could just glimpse a diamond and pearl ring on the fourth finger of her right hand. His heart nearly stopped beating when he understood the significance of the portrait.

"Is it her, Bell?" Lovell demanded, his voice intentionally low. "Is the chit from Highgate the Honorable Miss Adelaide Seaborne, daughter of Viscount Dalton and granddaughter of the Earl of bloody Caledon?"

"Yes."

"Is there any doubt, Bell?" Sebastian could detect a note of pleading in the superintendent's voice. He'd rather the woman from Highgate were anyone but Adelaide Seaborne, but miracles were not in Sebastian's remit.

"No, sir. It's most definitely her."

"Lord preserve us," Lovell moaned.

"What does the viscount think happened to his daughter?" Sebastian asked.

"He said that his daughter is missing and asked that I keep the inquiry into her disappearance quiet. He doesn't want her name bandied about in the papers, for obvious reasons."

"Has he *seen* the papers?"

"I would assume that he has, but there is nothing to connect Adelaide Seaborne to the woman in Highgate at present, and I would like to keep it that way."

"Did the viscount provide any details as to his daughter's disappearance?" Sebastian asked.

He was grateful to have a name, but that was just the start. The more information he had to go on, the better. If he were allowed to remain on the case. Now that Lovell knew who the victim was, he might want to assign someone else, a detective he thought might fare better when dealing with someone of Viscount Dalton's stature. Someone like Edwin Reece, whose sycophantic fascination with the aristocracy could for once work in his favor.

"The viscount said that the girl's lady's maid raised the alarm on Monday morning."

"It's Tuesday afternoon," Sebastian pointed out.

"I can only assume that the family hoped the girl would turn up."

"Does the viscount have any idea where she might have gone?" Sebastian asked, but he already knew that all his questions would go unanswered. At this stage, the viscount was concerned with protecting his daughter's reputation and would share as little as possible of what had taken place before Adelaide's disappearance, expecting the police to find the girl and bring her home with the minimum amount of fuss. Perhaps the viscount feared that his daughter had run off to Gretna Green to be married and wanted her brought back; but, if that were the case, time would be of the essence and surely the man would have come to the police before now? Adelaide Seaborne would have been wedded and bedded by now if she'd left on All Hallows' Eve and had actually made it as far as Scotland. So maybe a quickie wedding wasn't the viscount's overwhelming concern. He had to have some idea of what his daughter had been up to, since a lady of Adelaide Seaborne's social standing wasn't likely to become a random victim. She would be guarded day and night, and never, ever leave the house unaccompanied.

"I want you to call on the viscount and break the news. Gently, Bell," Superintendent Lovell added, as if Sebastian were some sort of simpleton and had no concept of grief.

"Yes, sir. I will need to question the family."

"You will question the family if and when they're ready, and not a moment sooner."

"Yes, sir," Sebastian replied, even though he had no intention of obeying the directive.

"And for the love of God, Bell, don't tell the viscount that his daughter has been autopsied. With any luck, he'll never have cause to find out."

Bell stared at the superintendent in astonishment. "How do you imagine he might not find out that a post-mortem has been carried out?"

"Individuals of his station do not lay out their dead at home," the superintendent said haughtily. "An undertaker will collect the body and prepare it for viewing. A high-necked gown will hide all manner of sins. And if luck is on our side, the undertaker will see the wisdom of keeping mum on the subject."

"And if he doesn't?"

"I'll explain to the viscount that you had ordered it without my say-so."

"Very wise of you, sir," Sebastian replied caustically.

"Now you listen to me. The stakes just got considerably higher. If we fail to apprehend Adelaide Seaborne's killer, heads will roll. Let's do ourselves a favor and solve this case before the executioner reaches for his axe."

"Yes, sir."

"How do you intend to proceed?" Lovell asked, giving Sebastian the gimlet eye. He needed to make certain Sebastian didn't disobey his orders.

"I will start with the servants," Sebastian said. "Particularly the lady's maid who reported her mistress missing. And then anyone else who had dealings with Adelaide."

"Good. There's little that servants don't know." Lovell nodded approvingly.

"And then I would like to interview the victim's family," Sebastian added. "When they are ready."

"Remember your place when questioning your betters."

"I wouldn't dare forget, sir," Sebastian replied.

"And remember not to stare."

"How do you mean?"

"I mean that you show respect. And deference. No need to nail anyone to the wall with that penetrating glare of yours."

"Should I tug at my forelock, sir?"

"Don't get smart with me, boy."

"No, sir."

"Now, get out there and do our job." Lovell pulled out his pocket watch and flipped open the cover. "It's just gone noon. I expect a report by six."

"Understood," Sebastian replied, and cursed himself for not finishing his letter to the Pinkertons last night. If Superintendent Lovell no longer had faith in him, he would seize any opportunity to dismiss Sebastian, so it was imperative that he have a plan B. He'd be sure to post the letter tomorrow, just in case, but he would do his damnedest to solve the case now that he knew who the victim was. He had to do it for Adelaide, not for Lovell.

FIFTEEN

Gemma anxiously glanced toward the clock, and was reminded once again that she had stopped it last night out of respect for Victor. She stood, fetched Victor's notebook, then sat down again and turned to the page marked November 1. The paper was already dogeared from constant handling. Having reread the last entry for what seemed like the hundredth time, she finally admitted that there were no more clues to find. Victor had said all he could and would have filled in the blanks had he lived. He'd likely never imagined that this was to be his final message, or his last day. He would have been confident that he'd lose the tail once he got off the omnibus and entered the offices of the *Telegraph*. And he would have set his thoughts and impressions down on paper, and might have written the article that would make the front page.

Gemma set the notebook aside and stood again, unable to sit still. She walked to the window, peering at the church clock just visible in the distance. She had been back for less than an hour, but it felt like an age, and her emotions had run the gamut from melancholy to anger to overwhelming grief and then back to anger and impatience. The more she thought about it, the more she believed that Victor's death had not been accidental. Even if he was frightened, he would never have become careless. That simply wasn't his nature. If Victor fell, it was because he was pushed, but there was nothing Gemma could do to prove it, not on her own. But she couldn't sit there and wait for some man to hear her out. She had to do something.

Having come to a decision, Gemma turned on her heel and strode into the entryway, ready to head over to the offices of the *Daily Telegraph*. She would say that she'd come to collect Victor's belongings, which would give her an excuse to find out which colleague had witnessed the accident and question him about Victor's final moments. Anything he told her would be helpful—but if she left the house, she would risk missing Inspector Bell. Just now, he was her best chance of finding out what really happened, and he wasn't likely to come back if she wasn't at home when he called. Desperate as she was for answers, she had to be sensible, and patient, which was the hardest thing to do.

Sighing resignedly, Gemma set down the bonnet she had been about to put on and returned to the parlor, where she sank into a chair once again, worn out by the feeling of helplessness and the overwhelming need to do something useful. She sprang to her feet again moments later when there was a knock at the door. Assuming it was Inspector Bell, Gemma rushed to answer the door, her heart racing with anxiety. She hoped the man would be competent, and kind. She didn't think she could open up to someone who treated her like a feeble-minded female, not when she felt so fragile already, but she didn't imagine Inspector Bell could be worse than Inspector Cotton.

Instead of a detective, Gemma was surprised to find her employer waiting on the doorstep. Mr. Gadd was in his early forties, a stout man with deep-set brown eyes and wavy black hair that was gently threaded with gray. As far as Gemma knew, he had never married. He still lived in the family home, his mother his only companion.

"Mr. Gadd," Gemma said, doing her best not to show surprise.

"I do hope I'm not intruding," Mr. Gadd said, and smiled in an ingratiating manner.

"Not at all. Please, come in."

Gemma took Mr. Gadd's coat, gloves, and hat, and stuck his walking stick into the umbrella stand by the door. She then invited him into the parlor, where he took a seat across from her and met her gaze shyly.

"I'm very sorry for your loss, Miss Tate. I apologize for dropping in uninvited, and I won't take much of your time, but what I have to say is best said in person."

"Oh?" Gemma felt a pang of unease but reminded herself that she had no reason to fear anything Mr. Gadd had to tell her. She had spent countless hours in his home, and he had never been anything less than courteous and helpful. He wouldn't choose this moment to say anything unkind.

"Miss Tate, I don't mean to be indelicate, but I can't help but acknowledge that your situation has unexpectedly changed and that you might have some concerns regarding the future."

Gemma nodded. She couldn't deny the truth of what Mr. Gadd was saying, but his observation still made her intensely uncomfortable. Victor had been gone all of a day, and she wasn't ready to discuss her plans for the future. But it was more likely that Mr. Gadd was there for his own benefit, so Gemma rushed to put his mind to rest.

"Mr. Gadd, I assure you, there's no cause for concern. I mean to continue working. Nothing will change as far as our arrangement goes."

"And to that end, I would like to make you a proposal, Miss Tate," Mr. Gadd replied, looking unaccountably smug.

For one awful moment, Gemma thought that he meant to

propose marriage, but then she realized she was being utterly ridiculous. Even if Mr. Gadd harbored feelings toward her, she didn't think he would be callous enough to make her an offer of marriage the day after her brother had died. A period of mourning had to be observed, if only for propriety's sake, and he would wait to make any declaration until she was officially out of mourning. When Gemma failed to respond, Mr. Gadd continued.

"Life is not easy for a woman on her own. Putting aside the financial burden of maintaining a residence and covering one's personal expenses, there's also the question of safety. I propose that you give up this house and move in with Mother and me. There's plenty of room, and you will have the freedom to come and go as you please without having to worry about money."

"Mr. Gadd—" Gemma began, but he raised a hand to cut her off.

"I would not expect you to work any additional hours or garnish your wages in lieu of room and board, Miss Tate. I'm simply offering a practical solution."

"That's very generous, but I couldn't possibly accept," Gemma said.

Mr. Gadd nodded his understanding. "You think it would be improper for us to cohabit, but plenty of nurses accept live-in positions and fare quite well. I assure you, I mean you no harm. In fact, I'm quite fond of you," he added, his face turning a tell-tale shade of pink. "I only want to help."

Gemma took a steadying breath and offered what she hoped was a smile of gratitude rather than a grimace of discomfiture. "Mr. Gadd, I thank you for your thoughtful offer, and you're right, a live-in position would probably work best given the situation, but I'm simply not ready to make any long-term decisions just now."

"Of course. I completely understand, and I wouldn't expect you to give me an answer right away. Think about it and let me know whenever you feel ready. In the meantime, please don't feel you have to return to work right away. I will pay you for the time regardless."

"How will you manage?" Gemma asked, relieved that the conversation had moved on to more practical matters.

The sort of tasks she performed for Mrs. Gadd could not be undertaken by a man and, as far as she knew, Mr. Gadd had no female relatives. The maidservant used the time when Gemma was with Mrs. Gadd to see to household chores and couldn't possibly be expected to take on the care of the invalid full-time.

"I have engaged the services of a widowed lady who came highly recommended. She is not a nurse, at least not in the same sense as you are, but she will help me look after Mother until you feel ready to return. I think we can manage for a week or two."

"Thank you, Mr. Gadd. That's very kind."

"Not at all, Miss Tate," Mr. Gadd said as he pushed to his feet. "I hope it's not too presumptuous of me to say that I consider us to be friends. Please, feel free to call on me if you need anything, and do let me know when the funeral is to be. I would like to pay my respects."

"Thank you. I will," Gemma said, and walked Mr. Gadd to the door.

She felt an immense sense of relief when he left and she was once again on her own.

SIXTEEN

Viscount Dalton and his family lived in a sprawling mansion in Park Lane. The house sat well back from the street and was surrounded by wrought-iron railings and manicured lawns. Built in the neo-Palladian style, it boasted a portico worthy of a Roman temple, complete with a peaked roof, massive columns, and a flight of steps wide enough to accommodate a dozen people standing shoulder to shoulder. Stone urns replete with aglaonema graced the stone balustrade. Sebastian noted with grim satisfaction that the name of the plant just came to him, and inwardly thanked his mother for her keen interest in all things green and for forcing him to help her in the garden when he was a boy. As a policeman, knowing something of botany came in surprisingly handy.

The ornamental wrought-iron gates were shut, presumably because the family wasn't at home to visitors, so Sebastian found a back gate and took himself to the tradesmen's entrance. To present himself at the front door would be an affront and start his inquiries off on the wrong foot, and he had no desire to offend, not when he needed the butler's cooperation.

"Can I help you?" a liveried footman asked when he opened

the door. He was a fine specimen, tall and well formed, a testament to the high standards of the household.

"Inspector Bell of Scotland Yard to see Viscount Dalton."

"As if," the footman scoffed.

"Let him in," an authoritative voice called from somewhere to the footman's right.

The chastised footman stepped aside and allowed Sebastian to enter. He ignored the footman and the curious bootboy, whose blue eyes were as wide as saucers at the mention of Scotland Yard, and addressed himself to the butler, who was tall and thin and stood erect as if on parade. He had neatly brushed gray hair and a clean-shaven face, and his hooded dark eyes studied Sebastian with practiced indifference. In Sebastian's experience, butlers were a breed unto themselves, but some were more helpful than others. This man had the look of someone who'd rather face cannon fire than assist the police.

"Your name, sir," Sebastian said when the man failed to introduce himself.

"Lewis."

"Take me to the viscount, Mr. Lewis," Sebastian said.

"What's your business with his lordship?" the butler asked.

So, he is going to play games, Sebastian thought as he bristled with irritation. This wasn't the first time he'd come to tell a family that their loved one was dead, but delivering such difficult news never became easier, nor did one become immune to the grief and shock that followed. Sebastian would have preferred to speak to the viscount without engaging in a battle of wills with the butler, who had to know that the viscount had sought the help of the police and was awaiting news of his daughter, but a showdown seemed inevitable.

"As you are well aware, Mr. Lewis, the Honorable Miss Seaborne has been missing since Sunday night. His lordship paid a visit to Scotland Yard this morning to make a report to that effect. I am here with an update. Now, kindly announce me to his lordship."

Since Adelaide Seaborne wasn't with him, the butler correctly assumed that it wasn't good news. "Is she—" Lewis couldn't finish the question, but Sebastian saw genuine emotion in the man's face.

"I need to speak to the viscount," he reiterated. He wasn't about to tell the butler first and have the household learn of Adelaide's death before her parents.

"Wait here," the butler said, all emotion now under rigid control. "I will inform his lordship you're here and inquire if this might be a convenient time for him to speak to you."

Sebastian bit back the retort that sprang to his lips and gave a curt nod. Antagonizing the butler would serve no purpose other than to impede the investigation. Not having been offered a seat, he remained standing, and took in his surroundings. He could see at least a dozen servants, all going about their tasks in subdued silence, presumably because he was there. The cook and her minions were preparing luncheon for the family, what he assumed to be a lady's maid was mending a lace collar, and the bootboy had returned to a bench in the corridor and was polishing a pair of riding boots. A woman with an authoritative air, presumably the housekeeper, swept past and gave Sebastian a flinty look, while the footman he'd seen earlier and his counterpart were getting ready to serve lunch. The house was not decked out for mourning, which meant that Viscount Dalton still hoped for a happy reunion. Sebastian's news would devastate the family and the staff, since, regardless of their feelings toward their young mistress, they would be affected by a death in the family.

Lewis returned and gestured for Sebastian to follow. They exited through the green baize door that led into the house proper and crossed a tiled floor that was polished to a mirror shine, toward the drawing room. Sebastian registered that it was a beautiful, expensively furnished room, but the majority of his attention was focused on the viscount, who stood before the glowing hearth, his gaze on the silver-framed photograph on the mantel. From where Sebastian stood, he thought it was a family portrait.

"Inspector Bell of Scotland Yard, my lord," Lewis announced.

Sebastian entered behind him and bowed from the neck. "My lord."

Viscount Dalton was around fifty and had the distinguished air of someone who'd led a life of comfort and privilege. He was tall and barrel-chested, his gently silvered dark hair neatly pomaded, and his pale blue eyes clouded with worry. His dark gray suit was fashionably cut and of the highest-quality broadcloth. He wore a maroon puff tie studded with a diamond pin and a waistcoat of matching maroon silk, the pattern picked out in silver thread. The viscount cut an imposing figure and had the bearing of a man used to getting his way in all things.

He gestured toward a studded leather wingchair before the hearth and invited Sebastian to sit, taking the chair opposite and crossing his legs. Sebastian was grateful not to be left standing before him like an errant boy.

"I take it you've been charged with finding my daughter," Viscount Dalton said. "Is there any news?"

"I'm very sorry, my lord, but I'm afraid it falls to me to be the bearer of bad news."

"What are you saying, man?" the viscount barked.

Sebastian wished he didn't have to spell it out, but he had little choice. "Your daughter's body was discovered in Highgate Cemetery on Monday morning."

"My daughter's *body*?" the viscount choked out. "You mean that sordid story in the papers is about my Addie?"

"I'm very sorry, sir."

The viscount blanched, his hands gripping the armrests of

the chair so hard his knuckles turned white. He bowed his head, and Sebastian thought he was crying, so he remained perfectly still, giving the man the space he needed to take in the news. They sat in silence for a few minutes, the viscount making no sound but clearly in the grip of strong emotion. When he looked up, his eyes were red-rimmed and glittering with tears. He wore an expression Sebastian had seen so many times before, and not so long ago on himself—shock, utter disbelief, and the realization that something infinitely precious had been lost and life would never be the same again, this agonizing pain a lifelong companion one hadn't yet known this morning but would walk with for the rest of one's days. No amount of wealth and privilege could insulate Viscount Dalton from pain and loss, and it was clear to Sebastian that despite the man's valiant effort to gain control of his emotions he had been shaken to the core, his heart shattered at the news of his daughter's death.

"Are you certain it's her?" Viscount Dalton asked once he trusted himself to speak once again, and Sebastian was forced to extinguish the tiny flame of hope that had flared in the man's heart.

"I am. The woman we found is the woman in the photograph you left with Superintendent Lovell. I have personally seen both," Sebastian added, in case the viscount wasn't inclined to accept his word. "You will, of course, be asked to identify your daughter conclusively. I'm deeply sorry for your loss, my lord," he said again.

"Thank you," the viscount replied quietly. "How did she die?"

His voice shook and his hand trembled slightly on the armrest of his chair. He clearly realized it would be unbearably painful, but he had to know what happened. The newly bereaved had that in common. They were desperate for every morsel of information, even though the images those details conjured up usually tore them to bits. Still, learning what had happened was a way to remain connected to their loved one, the agony of those first few moments preferable to the numbness that followed once the immediate demands of death were satisfied and they were left to deal with their pain on their own.

"She was strangled," Sebastian said softly.

Technically, strangulation had been the cause of death, and Sebastian saw no immediate need to tell this heartbroken man that his daughter had been raped and had fought valiantly for her life before the breath had been choked out of her. No father needed to suffer such torment.

The viscount's hand flew to his mouth, seemingly to stifle a cry of horror. "Do you think it was quick?" he asked at last, desperate to hear that his daughter hadn't suffered.

"I'm sure it was," Sebastian reassured him.

"Where is she? Where's my Addie?"

"She was taken to the city mortuary," Sebastian replied. That was also true, to a point.

"I will have Ellery and Mason Undertakers collect her remains tomorrow. Mr. Ellery has met my daughter on several occasions and will be able to identify her. I can't bear to see her there, in that place," the viscount said hoarsely. "I will wait until she's been laid out and brought home."

He clearly wasn't strong enough to see his daughter among the dead, her body bruised and battered, her eyes glazed. He would prefer to pretend she was sleeping, snug in her satin-lined coffin and pretty in her favorite gown, with no signs of brutality to mar his last memory of her.

"As you wish, sir." Sebastian hoped Colin Ramsey had returned the body to the mortuary forthwith, instead of sending it to the dead house. A message had been sent advising him to deliver the remains to the mortuary before the family's undertaker presented himself to collect the body. The dead house was for the poor wretches who had no one who had cared for them in life and now had no one to honor them in death.

"My lord, I know your loss is intensely painful and you would probably prefer to be left alone, but it's vital to the investigation that I learn as much as I can before the trail goes cold. If I could ask you a few questions."

Sebastian was disregarding Superintendent Lovell's directive, but this was the time to learn what he could, while the viscount was off balance and might answer truthfully. Once the horror of his daughter's death fully sank in, he'd turn his attention to safeguarding what was left of her reputation for the sake of the family. Any father would want to see his daughter's killer brought to justice, but Sebastian couldn't begin to understand who'd wish for Adelaide Seaborne's death without first understanding something of her life.

Viscount Dalton took a deep breath, as if steeling himself for what was to come, then nodded. "You may ask what you wish, Inspector. I will do whatever I can to help with your investigation. It won't bring my Addie back, but I need to know that her tormentor was brought to justice."

"Tell me about your daughter, my lord," Sebastian invited.

The viscount smiled sadly. "She was a delight from the day she was born. Absolutely perfect, and very spirited."

Sebastian noted the spirited part. That was another way to say that Adelaide had been rebellious and difficult to control. Could it be the girl's high spirits that had led to this tragedy?

"What happened wasn't her fault," Viscount Dalton snapped, and, for one mad moment, Sebastian wondered if he'd spoken aloud.

"No, sir," he was quick to agree.

"Addie was kidnapped and murdered by some lunatic."

"When was the last time you saw your daughter, my lord?"

"I saw her at dinner on Sunday night."

"Who was present? Was it just the family?" Sebastian asked.

"It was myself, my wife, and Adelaide. My son dined at his club."

"And what did you have, if you don't mind me asking?"

Viscount Dalton seemed surprised by the question but answered without hesitation. "There was consommé, roast beef with potatoes, asparagus, and trifle. It was Addie's favorite sweet."

The description of the meal tallied with what Colin had said and served as confirmation that the dinner had been Adelaide's final meal.

"Thank you, my lord. And how did your daughter seem at dinner?"

Sebastian had no idea how to refer to the daughter of a viscount. He knew she was the Honorable Miss Seaborne, but how did that translate into everyday speech? Miss Seaborne? Her ladyship? Just plain Adelaide? No, he couldn't risk calling her by her Christian name for fear of causing offense, even if her father had referred to her as Addie. He'd go with Miss Seaborne and see if he earned himself a reprimand.

"She was in a bit of a sulk."

"May I ask why?"

The viscount sighed. "My daughter came out last year."

"Came out, sir?" Sebastian asked.

"Was presented to society. It was her first Season."

"And how old was she at the time of her coming out?" Sebastian asked.

"Seventeen. Oh, she took London by storm," Viscount Dalton said, his gaze warming at the cherished memory. "The most beautiful young lady at any gathering. And one of the wealthiest," he added, an edge of derision creeping into his voice. "Even if she were plain, she would have garnered attention."

"I take it there were a number of suitors?" Sebastian asked carefully. Now they were getting somewhere, and it seemed to help the viscount to reminisce about his daughter as she had been—beautiful, spirited, and on the brink of a glittering future.

"Of course. Dozens."

"And did Miss Seaborne favor any of them?"

"She did favor a few. One in particular. Mr. David Parker."

"Mister?"

The viscount nodded. "Yes. And American to boot. Naturally, I wouldn't have it, and I told her as much when she asked if he might be permitted to call. 'Absolutely not, my girl,' was my reply. It was bad enough that Parker wasn't of noble lineage, but American? Never."

"Might this Mr. Parker have taken the rejection badly?"

Viscount Dalton shook his head. "I don't know that he was rejected, Inspector. I have reason to believe that Adelaide was still stringing him along."

"What makes you say that?"

"The disagreement we had on Sunday night. Adelaide had several noble suitors, but I had settled on Oliver Mayhew, the 4th Marquis of Penrith. A fine man with an impeccable lineage, a sizeable fortune of his own, and a sterling reputation. In fact, an announcement of Adelaide's engagement to Lord Mayhew was imminent. Sunday night, I told Adelaide that the notice would run in *The Times* this week. Adelaide asked me to wait."

"Was Miss Seaborne not happy with the arrangement?"

Viscount Dalton glared at him. "If you're asking if my daughter was in love with her future husband, then the answer is no. She liked him well enough, but she had notions."

"What sort of notions, my lord?"

"The sort of notions impressionable young girls get after reading romantic novels and imagining that they should swoon with longing at the sight of their intended."

"I take it Miss Seaborne wasn't swooning over Lord Mayhew?"

"She was enamored of Mr. Parker."

Sebastian drew in a sharp breath. This was where he had to tread very carefully. "My lord, is it at all possible that Miss Seaborne had intended to run away?"

"With Parker, you mean?" the viscount snapped. Sebastian nodded. "And he strangled her in a cemetery?"

"Perhaps Miss Seaborne had changed her mind and an argument ensued," Sebastian suggested.

Viscount Dalton shook his head. "Parker might not be my choice of son-in-law, but he's a decent man, and I think he genuinely cared for Addie. If she had agreed to a secret marriage—and I don't believe my daughter would ever do that—I trust that Parker would have brought her home if she changed her mind."

"Why do you believe Miss Seaborne would never agree?" Sebastian asked carefully.

The viscount scoffed. "Addie was headstrong and at times argumentative, but she was also practical. She would not wish to be cut off from her family or her life in London, and she would be if she married Parker. Besides, she knew she wouldn't get a penny from me," he added. "Not if she married against my wishes."

"Would that matter to Mr. Parker?"

"Probably not. He had no need of Addie's portion, but Addie would be hurt by it. At least her pride would be."

"And was there anyone else Miss Seaborne might have formed an attachment to prior to Mr. Parker?"

"Why should that matter?"

"Perhaps someone held a grudge or thought that if he forced Miss Seaborne into marriage, you would have no choice but to accept him and hand over the dowry."

"Don't be ridiculous. No one would dare to force Addie."

Clearly someone had, and the result had been tragic. Sebastian took a moment to gather his thoughts. This careful dance he had to perform was exhausting, but he could hardly ask his questions outright, his lordship's feelings be damned. Adelaide Seaborne might have rejected a dozen men. Perhaps she'd done so gently, with a view to their masculine pride, or she could have been a coquette and strung them along before ruthlessly dashing their hopes. Most men would accept her refusal with quiet fortitude, but there were always those who, once a seed of resentment was planted in them, allowed it to take root and grow until the anger and humiliation overwhelmed them. It was also possible that Adelaide had been conducting an affair rather than a flirtation. Given what had befallen her, there was no way to tell if she had been a virgin before that night. Perhaps the jilted party was even a husband of whom her father knew nothing. Sebastian would be sure to bring that up with Adelaide's lady's maid. She was bound to know if her mistress had been hiding something.

"There was someone before Parker," the viscount said. "Adam Langton."

"And who is he?"

"He's the son of Baron Yates."

"I take it he wasn't up to scratch either?"

The viscount shot Sebastian a look of annoyance. "No, he wasn't. Fine-looking fellow, I'll grant him that, but his reputation precedes him."

"What does he stand accused of?"

"Gambling, mainly. He is a man who needs a wealthy wife if he hopes to maintain his position in society, and my daughter was not going to be the one to bankroll him. Fortune hunters were always a concern since Addie would be bringing a considerable dowry to the union."

"Did Mr. Langton propose to Miss Seaborne?"

"He never got that far. He asked for my blessing. Naturally, I refused."

"Might he have been angry enough to consider some form of retaliation?"

"You mean was he angry enough to strangle my daughter and dump her body in Highgate Cemetery? I doubt it. He very quickly moved on to Lady Darby's daughter. The girl is plain and overweight, so Lady Darby was persuaded to overlook Langton's love of the gaming tables in order to get the girl suitably wed. They were married last month and left for their wedding trip immediately afterwards."

Sebastian was just about to ask another question when a well-dressed young man entered the drawing room. The familial resemblance was unmistakable. He had to be in his late twenties, at least ten years older than Adelaide, and was a younger, handsomer, fitter version of his father. Adelaide must have taken after her mother, since she bore little resemblance to either man.

"Do excuse me, Father. When I heard there was an inspector from Scotland Yard, I wondered if there might be news."

"My son, George," the viscount said, his gaze on his son.

Sebastian rose to his feet to greet the man, but George paid him no mind, his attention on his father.

"Is Addie all right?" George asked. "Do they know where she's gone?"

"Addie is dead, Georgie. Murdered." The viscount's voice caught, but he managed to retain control of his feelings. Now that the initial shock had worn off, he seemed determined to get the interview over with without giving in to his emotions. The grief Sebastian had witnessed earlier had been reined in, replaced no doubt by a need to see Adelaide's killer apprehended and hanged.

George went white to the roots of his hair and clenched his hands into fists. Sebastian thought the young man might go for him, deciding that to kill the messenger was better than doing nothing at all. Then all the fight went out of him, and he collapsed onto the settee. His eyes glittered with tears and his bottom lip trembled as he tried to get hold of his emotions.

"George," his father warned him.

George nodded his understanding. Giving in to grief in front of an underling was not acceptable behavior. The family would grieve in private, away from the prying eyes of both the servants and the police.

George resolutely squared his shoulders, raised his chin, and addressed Sebastian. "Inspector, Addie was the most beautiful, tender-hearted girl you could ever hope to meet. She was also a complete innocent and saw the best in everyone, be they her social equal or a beggar in the street. I can't begin to imagine what she must have endured." He drew a quivering breath. "Please, find whoever did this. I know it won't bring Addie back, but knowing justice was served will at least grant us some peace."

"I intend to," Sebastian replied, feeling affirmation was needed even if he was in no position to make promises. Not every case was solved, and not every killer was brought to justice. "If I might ask you a few questions, sir."

"Of course," George said. "Anything I can do to help."

Sebastian wished he could interview George Seaborne in private and make the most of his obvious vulnerability and grief, but the viscount made no move to leave, and Sebastian could hardly evict him from his own drawing room.

"When was the last time you saw your sister, Mr. Seaborne?"

"Sunday afternoon. We all went to church, then had Sunday lunch together. After lunch, Addie and I went for a walk in Hyde Park. It was a fine day, and I thought she could use a bit of company. We were back in time for tea. Then I went out."

"Where did you go?" Sebastian asked conversationally.

"I visited a lady of my acquaintance," George said, casting

an embarrassed look in his father's direction, "then met a friend for dinner at my club. Afterwards, I adjourned to Peter White's house with a few others and played billiards."

"What time did you return home?"

George looked down at his folded hands. "I didn't get in until about ten the following morning. I'm afraid I had too much to drink and wound up spending the night in Peter's guest room. It was when I got home that I discovered Addie was missing."

"Did your sister confide in you, Mr. Seaborne? Was she frightened of anyone or had she perhaps thought someone was watching her?" Sebastian asked. He noticed that the viscount was looking at his son intently, perhaps wondering the same thing.

George Seaborne shook his head. "Not that I know of. Addie was in good spirits when we went for our walk. She told me about a book she was reading, then asked for my advice."

"Advice on what?" the viscount demanded.

George shot his father a sidelong glance, and the viscount gave him an almost imperceptible nod, giving him permission to speak. When a child was dead, family squabbles could not remain private, even if they had no bearing on the case.

"Addie wished to talk about her engagement to Lord Mayhew and her feelings for Mr. Parker."

"And what did you advise, Mr. Seaborne?" Sebastian asked.

George sighed deeply and turned to the viscount. "I'm sorry, Father."

"Just be truthful, George," Viscount Dalton replied. He appeared resigned to whatever George was about to share.

"I advised her not to rush into an engagement with Lord Mayhew. I thought Father might come around to the idea of Mr. Parker."

"Did you, indeed?" the viscount exclaimed, clearly

surprised by his son's admission. "And what gave you the right to undermine me in such an underhanded way?"

"Addie wasn't happy, Father. And the only thing you had against Mr. Parker was his nationality. Had he been British, you would have at least considered his suit."

"He is a commoner," Viscount Dalton barked.

"Yes, he is, but is that really that much of an impediment? It seems to me you take no issue with commoners when it suits your own ends."

A look of naked resentment passed between father and son, and Sebastian filed it away, to be examined later. This argument seemed to stem from something in their mutual past, and he had yet to determine if it had anything to do with Adelaide's death.

"Mr. Seaborne," Sebastian asked, drawing the young man's attention back to him, "did Miss Seaborne tell you of any plans to go out on Sunday night?"

George shook his head vehemently. "No. In fact, she said that she was going to have an early night."

Sebastian didn't have any more questions to put to the men, but he needed to speak to the women, who tended to be more observant, especially where young ladies were concerned.

"May I speak to Viscountess Dalton?" he asked.

"Absolutely not. My wife is already distraught. I can't imagine what this news will do to her," the viscount said, and Sebastian felt immense relief that he didn't have to tell Adelaide's mother what had been done to her.

"Did Miss Seaborne have any other siblings?"

"No, it was just us two," George said with feeling. He angrily wiped away a tear that had begun to slide down his cheek.

"May I be permitted to question the staff?" Sebastian asked.

Viscount Dalton nodded. "Speak to Lewis. He will arrange it." The viscount stood and yanked the bell-pull. A few moments later, Lewis appeared in the doorway and his gaze passed from the viscount to George Seaborne and then bored into Sebastian.

"Lewis, Inspector Bell would like to speak to the staff. Allow him the use of your pantry. I'd like his inquiries to be kept private."

"Yes, my lord."

"And Lewis," he added when the butler turned to leave.

"Yes, my lord?"

"We are a house in mourning."

Lewis's shock was obvious, and his face crumbled like overcooked pastry, but he immediately collected himself and nodded curtly. "Yes, my lord. I'm deeply sorry for your loss. I will see to everything."

"Thank you, Lewis."

Sebastian stood and followed the butler out the door. He had learned more than he had expected, and hoped that the servants would be even more forthcoming.

SEVENTEEN

"I would like to start with Miss Seaborne's lady's maid," Sebastian said as soon as they were through the baize door.

"The female servants are the province of the housekeeper," Lewis replied.

"Mr. Lewis, I'm not interested in either the hierarchy of the household or whatever power struggles you indulge in below stairs. I would like to speak to Miss Seaborne's lady's maid. Please see to it. Unless you are unable to coordinate your efforts with the housekeeper and would like me to return upstairs and make my request to his lordship?"

Lewis leveled at him a look that was pure venom but inclined his head marginally. "As you wish."

"Thank you, Mr. Lewis," Sebastian replied politely. "Where might I conduct the interview?"

"Through here," Lewis replied, and showed Sebastian to the butler's pantry. "I will bring Jones to you."

Miss Jones was in her mid to late twenties. She was short and plump, her round face dominated by a snub nose liberally sprinkled with freckles. Her blue eyes were huge, and she practically vibrated with anxiety. She lowered herself into the cane chair across from Lewis's desk, which Sebastian now occupied, and clasped her hands in her lap.

"Is it true?" she cried. "I heard Mr. Lewis tell Mrs. Henshall that Miss Adelaide is dead."

"Yes, I'm afraid it's true, Miss Jones," Sebastian replied softly.

"And Miss Adelaide was the one they wrote about in the papers? I don't read the papers myself, mind, but I heard the grooms talking about it at breakfast. They said a body was found in Highgate, on a cross. Mr. Lewis told them to be quiet. He said it wasn't an appropriate subject of conversation for the servants' hall, but everyone heard them."

"Yes, Miss Seaborne's body was found in Highgate," Sebastian replied. "This is a murder inquiry, Miss Jones."

"Lord preserve us," Miss Jones moaned as the magnitude of what had happened began to sink in. "What will become of me?" she whispered.

"I expect you'll find out soon enough," Sebastian said. He felt sympathy for the woman, but there was nothing he could do to help. If her services were no longer required, she would find herself without a job. "Now, I must ask you a few questions."

"Of course. Anything I can do."

"How long have you been a lady's maid to Miss Seaborne?"

"Two years now."

"And do you look after the viscountess as well?"

"No, Inspector. Her ladyship has her own maid."

"What was Miss Seaborne like?" Sebastian asked.

Miss Jones inhaled sharply and bit back whatever it was she really wanted to say. "She was lovely."

Sebastian could understand the woman's reluctance to speak ill of her mistress, especially now that she was deceased, but he needed to know the truth. "Miss Jones, the greatest service you can still perform for your mistress is to help me catch her killer. You have my word that anything you say to me will be held in the strictest confidence."

"In a house such as this, nothing is ever private, Inspector Bell," Miss Jones replied.

"I'm not part of this house, and I do not report back to anyone other than the superintendent of Scotland Yard. Now, what was Miss Seaborne really like?"

Miss Jones sighed heavily, then checked that the door was firmly shut and turned back to Sebastian. "She was a right little baggage, if you must know."

"In what way?"

"She always had to have her own way, and she wasn't above making threats."

"What sort of threats?"

"She threatened to have me sacked if I didn't do what she said."

"Would she really have had you sacked, or was it just an empty threat to keep you in line?"

"I wouldn't know, Inspector. I was too afraid to lose my position, so I did anything she asked."

"And did that involve delivering secret messages or covering for her with her parents?"

Miss Jones nodded.

"Whom did you deliver messages to?"

"Mr. Parker, at his hotel. And I had to accompany her when they met."

"How often did they meet?"

"At least once a week," Miss Jones replied. Now that she had taken the step of talking about her mistress, she would answer any question Sebastian put to her, and he meant to learn as much as he could from the one person who'd known Adelaide's habits intimately.

"Did Miss Seaborne ever quarrel with Mr. Parker?" Sebastian asked.

"Not that I saw."

"Do you know if they made plans to elope?"

Miss Jones shook her head. "Miss Adelaide would never do that."

"Why not?"

"Because she didn't want a sordid little ceremony in some Scottish village, that's why. She wanted a grand affair that would be the talk of London. A stunning gown, orange blossoms in her hair, a lavish celebration, and a bridegroom her father could be proud of. For all her willfulness, she wanted her papa's approval."

"Did Miss Seaborne ever go up to Mr. Parker's room?"

"No," Miss Jones said without a moment's hesitation.

"Did she ever meet any other men in secret?"

"What other men?" Miss Jones asked, surprised by the question.

"The footmen are rather good-looking."

Miss Jones scoffed. "Miss Adelaide wasn't the sort to moon over footmen, and they wouldn't dare look at her or speak out of turn. His lordship would have Lewis sack them without a character before they could ask what happened."

Sebastian nodded. A picture of Adelaide Seaborne was beginning to form in his mind. A beautiful, spoiled, haughty young woman who, although eager to play at being in love and partial to romantic intrigue, wouldn't risk throwing her comfortable life away to marry a man her father didn't approve of.

"Miss Jones, when was the last time you saw Miss Seaborne?"

"Miss Adelaide dined with her parents on Sunday evening, then retired to her bedroom."

"Clearly, she did not remain in her bedroom, so someone must have seen her leave," Sebastian pointed out.

The maid's gaze shifted to her hands, and she nodded miserably.

"You saw her go out?"

Miss Jones nodded. "She begged me not to tell."

"Where did she go?"

"She wouldn't say."

"Whom did she go with?" Sebastian pressed.

"I don't know, Inspector, but she seemed very excited. I think it had something to do with All Hallows' Eve. His lordship would not approve if he knew. That's why she didn't tell anyone."

"What made you think it had something to do with All Hallows' Eve?"

"She was talking about it earlier, while I was helping her dress for dinner. She said that on All Hallows' Eve, the veil between the world of the living and the world of the dead was parted and it was possible to contact the dead."

"Was there someone she had hoped to contact?"

"I don't know. She never said."

"Had Miss Seaborne expressed an interest in spiritualism before Sunday night?" Sebastian asked.

Miss Jones shrugged. "Not in any real sense. She was just curious about what happens after one dies. I suppose now she knows," she added morbidly.

"So, was it a séance she was going to?" Sebastian asked.

"How else would you contact the dead, unless it was some heathen ritual?" Miss Jones snapped.

"Would Miss Adelaide participate in a heathen ritual?"

"She was brazen enough to do anything," the maid said. "She thought she was invincible."

Sebastian could see the envy in the woman's face. She would never know such freedom. But then the envy was replaced by horror as Miss Jones must have recalled that her mistress was dead.

"Is it my fault what happened to her?" Miss Jones asked, her eyes filling with tears.

"No. You have no reason to reproach yourself."

"But if I had said," she persisted.

"Sounds to me like Miss Adelaide would have done what she wanted to do regardless."

"She would have," Miss Jones agreed. "Oh, I just knew something awful was going to happen," she muttered as she wrung her hands in her lap.

"How did you know, Miss Jones?"

"A bird flew into a closed window last week. Dropped dead onto the drawing room windowsill. And it was black," Miss Jones whispered. "Everyone knows that's a bad omen. A harbinger of death. I just didn't think it'd be Miss Adelaide that died. I thought for sure it'd be someone else." She began to cry, and Sebastian gave the weeping maid a few moments to compose herself, then continued.

"Who did you think was going to die?" he asked.

"I hoped it'd be Mr. Ahmad," Miss Jones said. Sebastian couldn't help but notice that she kept her voice very low.

"And who is Mr. Ahmad?" he asked, lowering his own voice.

Miss Jones looked toward the door again, as if the mysterious Mr. Ahmad was about to burst in brandishing a cutlass, then, satisfied that the door was still firmly shut, turned back to Sebastian.

"He's his lordship's valet. He's a Mussulman." Miss Jones nearly choked on the word and swallowed hard before continuing. "His lordship brought him over from India. He likes Mr. Ahmad and won't hear a bad word said about him."

"But you don't like him," Sebastian said, and gave Miss Jones a smile of encouragement meant to reassure her that she was speaking to a kindred spirit.

Miss Jones drew in a sharp breath and leaned forward. "He looks like the Devil himself and holds with all those heathen beliefs," she exclaimed. "And who'd expect anything different with him coming from such a wild, unchristian place? He doesn't belong here. What his lordship needs is a proper English valet to look after him. Someone who understands the needs of a gentleman."

"Has Mr. Ahmad ever said or done anything that would be deemed threatening?" Sebastian asked.

"Well, no, but I don't talk to him, do I? I've got nothing to say to the likes of him."

"How does he get on with the rest of the household?"

"Much as you'd expect. They give him a wide berth. He used to take his meals in the servants' hall, but now he takes a tray in his room, since no one will speak to him. A small victory for the rest of us," Miss Jones added spitefully.

"And Miss Adelaide? Did she ever speak to Mr. Ahmad?"

"Not that I saw, but that doesn't mean he couldn't have harmed her."

"Harmed her how?" Sebastian asked.

Miss Jones glanced toward the door again. "Mr. Lewis says that people like Mr. Ahmad can influence someone's mind without even trying. They poison the well. That's why his lordship feels bound to him and won't see him off, because he's in Mr. Ahmad's thrall. And now Miss Adelaide is dead."

Sebastian sighed with exasperation. This wasn't the first time he'd come up against ignorance and unfounded prejudice, and it wouldn't be the last, but he needed to meet this Mr. Ahmad and judge for himself.

"Why did you think Mr. Ahmad might die? Is he ill?"

"He refused supper on Sunday night. Cook said so. I thought maybe he felt unwell." Miss Jones sighed with disappointment. "But he seemed right as rain on Monday morning."

"What time did you see Mr. Ahmad on Monday?"

"I can't remember. I had more pressing worries on my mind by then, didn't I?" Miss Jones replied waspishly.

"Is there anyone of Miss Adelaide's acquaintance that might have invited her to a séance?" Sebastian asked.

"I'm sure I don't know, Inspector."

"Did Miss Adelaide leave on foot?"

Miss Jones pressed her lips together, then let out her breath in a gush. "I saw a carriage waiting outside the gates. She got inside."

"What time was this?" Sebastian asked.

"Approximately half past nine."

"Was there anything notable about the carriage? A crest, perhaps?"

"It was dark, and I didn't see anything resembling a crest. It wasn't a hansom, though; I can tell you that."

"Did you see the coachman?"

"Just a dark shape. Wore a slouch hat and caped coat."

Which told Sebastian nothing of either the man or his passenger. Most coachmen wore something similar, especially on a cold night.

"Why did you wait so long to raise the alarm?" Sebastian asked. If Miss Jones had known that Adelaide Seaborne had gone out, she would have realized that she hadn't returned long before the following morning.

Miss Jones's eyes filled again. "She ran me ragged, Inspector. Changed three times before she finally sneaked off. I waited up for her, but I was tired and fell asleep on the chaise. I was in a panic when I woke. It was near eight o'clock in the morning, and her bed wasn't slept in."

"Did you tell anyone that Miss Adelaide had gone out when you reported her missing?"

Miss Jones looked like she was going to be ill. "I'd have got the sack on the spot if I admitted that I knew. I said I never saw her leave."

"How did she leave? I presume Mr. Lewis locks up for the night."

"I reckon she went out through the conservatory. That's what I would do if I wanted to get away unseen. May I go now, Inspector? I told you everything I know," Miss Jones pleaded.

Sebastian thought that Miss Jones had probably snuck out at some point, maybe to meet a man or simply to escape the confines of the house for a short while. No doubt she thought she'd be sacked as soon as Sebastian reported back to the housekeeper, and feared for her future.

"Yes, you may go, Miss Jones."

She stood but didn't immediately leave. "You gave me your word," she reminded him.

"You have nothing to fear from me," Sebastian replied, but his mind was already on the next interview. "Please tell Mr. Lewis I'd like to speak to Mr. Ahmad."

Miss Jones nodded and yanked open the door, only to come face to face with the butler, who'd either just approached the pantry at that very moment or had been there the whole time. Miss Jones gave a little cry of alarm and fled.

"You need to leave now," Lewis said without preamble.

"I'm not finished questioning the staff," Sebastian replied.

"His lordship would like to hold a memorial for Miss Adelaide. All the servants are expected to attend."

"Mr. Lewis—" Sebastian began, but the butler cut across him.

"You may return tomorrow, Inspector. Both the family and the staff alike are in shock. Allow them a few hours of private contemplation. I will ensure you have access to whomever you wish tomorrow. Does ten o'clock suit?"

"It will have to. Good day to you."

"Good day, Inspector. Do leave by the servants' entrance."

"Of course."

Sebastian left the Park Lane residence and headed to Bethnal Green to speak to Miss Tate. The message Colin Ramsey had left with the duty sergeant that morning was frustratingly vague, asking only that Sebastian call on Miss Tate at his earliest convenience. It sounded as if the lady had something relevant to impart in regard to the death of the journalist who'd been on the scene, which was the first Sebastian had heard of it. It'd be remiss of him not to hear her out, even though Sergeant Woodward had assured him that Victor Tate's death was an accident and in no way related to the Highgate murder case. Still, Sebastian wished Colin had been just a little bit more specific, but he'd probably been pressed for time. If he hurried, Sebastian would have just enough time to call on Miss Tate before returning to Scotland Yard to update Superintendent Lovell on his progress.

EIGHTEEN

When she opened the door, Sebastian thought at first that the woman in black crape was the housekeeper, but immediately reconsidered. Her manner was anything but subservient and her gaze entirely too direct. She was a handsome woman in that forthright way some women had, although they were usually older and more often than not widowed. Having to navigate life on one's own, especially if there were children to care for and not enough money to alleviate constant worry, always left its mark.

"Inspector Bell to see Miss Tate," Sebastian announced, just in case he had got it wrong and she was a servant after all.

The woman smiled and opened the door wider. "Please, come in, Inspector. I'm Gemma Tate. I've been expecting you," she added eagerly, and Sebastian could see how much his visit meant to her.

Miss Tate took his coat and hat, then invited him into the parlor. It was a small room, with well-used furniture and a worn carpet, but it was tasteful and welcoming. A fire burned in the grate, but the room was chilly since Miss Tate was obviously conserving coal. Judging by the silence, there didn't appear to be anyone else in the house.

"If you prefer it, we can speak in a more public setting," Sebastian said, in case she was uneasy about entertaining a man in her home without the benefit of a chaperone.

Miss Tate's mouth quirked with amusement. "If I can't trust a policeman, whom can I trust?" she asked pointedly. "Besides, my reputation is not uppermost in my mind just now. Do sit down, Inspector. Would you care for tea?"

"I don't want to put you to any trouble," Sebastian said, and hoped she would ignore him. He was gasping for a cup of tea and starving to boot. He hadn't eaten since breakfast, and his stomach was growling with hunger. He wouldn't have objected to a dollop of whisky in the tea either, since he was beginning to feel jittery without the crutch of opium and alcohol to get him through the day.

"It's no trouble. I was about to have some myself."

"In that case, I would love some tea," Sebastian replied.

"I won't be a moment," Miss Tate said. "The kettle's just boiled."

She left Sebastian on his own and hurried to the kitchen. Inquisitive by both nature and occupation, Sebastian couldn't forgo the opportunity to learn something of Miss Tate, so he stood and walked over to the mantel. Three photographs in modest pewter frames were on display, and they told a story. The first was of a middle-aged couple who had to be Gemma Tate's parents. They were the very picture of genteel respectability. Mr. Tate was probably in some sort of trade, but he didn't have the staid look of a clerk about him. If Sebastian had to guess, he'd say the man was a shopkeeper. There was an air of bonhomie about him, the sort men cultivated when attempting to court repeat custom. Mrs. Tate looked like an older, slightly stouter version of her daughter, her expression open and trusting.

The second was of Gemma and her brother, their youthful faces solemn yet somehow filled with joy and hope. They had to be very close in age, since it was impossible to say who was older. Their demeanor spoke of casual intimacy and a lifetime of shared confidences and private jokes.

The third photograph was of a group of women who, judging by their caps and identical white pinafore aprons, had to be nurses. Gemma Tate was fourth from the right in the bottom row, her feet right above the inscription at the bottom. Scutari 1854.

So, she was a nurse. That explained the air of quiet competence and lack of fear at being alone with him. Sebastian couldn't help but wonder how Miss Tate had fared since returning from Crimea. The brave women who'd followed Florence Nightingale had served their purpose, as far as the country was concerned, and were now regarded with suspicion and, at times, harsh judgment. After all, what sort of young woman left the protection of her family and sailed to a foreign land where she would be surrounded by lonely, frightened men day and night? There were those who said that the nurses were women of questionable moral character, while others came straight out with it and called them whores.

Miss Tate, who must have been in her early twenties when the war began, did not strike Sebastian as a woman of loose morals, but who knew what she'd got up to in Crimea? Being surrounded by suffering and death made one question one's values and plans for the future and seize whatever happiness one could, but, given the lady's unmarried status, whatever companionship she had found, if any, had not led to a permanent arrangement.

Upon hearing Miss Tate's footsteps, Sebastian quickly resumed his seat, and smiled when she walked in bearing the tea tray. He was overjoyed to see several slices of cake and a plate of tea sandwiches. Miss Tate set the tray down on the low table and looked up.

"How do you take your tea, Inspector?"

"Milk, two sugars."

She poured him a cup, then made one for herself, adding just a splash of milk before pouring the tea.

"Please, help yourself," Miss Tate said. "I expect you had no time to eat this afternoon."

"How did you know?" Sebastian asked.

"I can always tell when someone is hungry."

Sebastian took a slice of walnut cake, while Miss Tate helped herself to a tiny sandwich.

"I haven't eaten either. To be honest, I hate eating alone, so I tend to avoid it, but I suppose I will have to get used to it. I have many solitary meals ahead of me now."

"I'm very sorry for your loss, Miss Tate."

"Thank you. Did Mr. Ramsey fill you in?"

"He implied that your brother's death has something to do with the case I'm investigating, but I think you had better tell me yourself. Mr. Ramsey's note was very brief."

Sebastian applied himself to the tea and cake while Miss Tate told him of her suspicions. The cake was a bit stale, but he didn't suppose her mind was on baking. Her account, however, was most intriguing. What were the chances that the only eyewitness to the disposal of Adelaide Seaborne's body would die in an accident mere hours after reporting what he had seen? And there was the entry in the notebook, the words written in Victor Tate's own hand. It was, of course, possible that Victor Tate had imagined that he was being followed. He had been understandably upset, and the bit about the Milky Way sounded just this side of sane. Perhaps he'd spotted something odd in the sky and had interpreted it as some sort of omen. Everything else fit with what Sebastian already knew.

"Was your brother interested in astronomy?" Sebastian asked.

"Not particularly."

"So you have no idea what he might be referring to when he mentions the Milky Way?"

"No. But he thought he was being followed and then died shortly after. Will you tell me that I'm just a fanciful woman whose judgment is clouded by grief?" Miss Tate asked pointedly.

"I agree with your theory that the two deaths are probably connected."

"Does that mean you will help me?" Miss Tate asked, leaning forward in her eagerness.

"Unless I want to lose my position, I must investigate the woman's murder first."

"Because of the way she was found?"

"That's only part of it," Sebastian replied. He wasn't ready to share the identity of the victim, not before he had a chance to speak to Superintendent Lovell and find out how he meant to handle the press.

"How did she die, Inspector? Please, tell me," Miss Tate implored. She must have noticed his hesitation. "I'll find out soon enough anyway. It's sure to be in the papers tomorrow."

Sebastian was in no doubt that she would purchase a newspaper and read it. Miss Tate was not a woman bound by convention. "She was strangled," he said at last.

"Was she interfered with?" Miss Tate asked without any hint of embarrassment.

"Yes."

"The poor woman," Miss Tate said with feeling. "How cruelly she must have suffered."

She looked to him for confirmation, and he nodded. He couldn't bring himself to lie to her. "Her death was not an easy one."

"Do you believe she was a random victim, someone who happened to be in the wrong place at the wrong time?" Miss Tate asked.

"Victims are rarely random, Miss Tate."

"Are you suggesting that they get what's coming to them, Inspector?" Miss Tate challenged him. He could see he'd upset her.

"Not at all. I'm only saying that there's usually a reason someone is targeted, and until we work out that reason we are unable to solve the crime."

"And you think that this poor woman gave someone motive to do what they did?" Miss Tate bristled. "Surely nothing warrants such savagery."

"I do. I would be willing to bet everything I own that nothing about this crime is random and that the morbid display of the body was not only intentional but well thought out."

"And what does the display suggest?" Miss Tate asked. She was clearly disturbed by Sebastian's grim view, and was probably worried that she might be next, given what had happened to her brother.

"The display suggests that this was a very personal attack, meant not only to wound but to humiliate."

"Humiliate the victim?" Miss Tate echoed, tilting her head to the side like a curious bird.

"Or her family."

"Do you know who her people are?"

Sebastian had schooled himself to never give more information than was strictly necessary, but something about this woman invited confidences, and he found himself, against his better judgment, telling her the truth. He didn't think she was the sort to gossip and, like it or not, she was now involved.

"The victim is the Honorable Miss Adelaide Seaborne, daughter of Viscount Dalton and granddaughter to an earl."

Miss Tate looked shocked, then said, "That would explain it, I suppose."

"Explain what?"

"Why Victor had to die. Had this woman been a street-walker or a servant, the killer wouldn't be so concerned with protecting his identity."

"Miss Tate, I assure you that we investigate every unlawful killing, be it of a duchess or a scullery maid."

"That's not quite what I meant, Inspector."

"Would you care to enlighten me?"

"The person Victor saw must have been afraid that he would be recognized, so it stands to reason that he's well known."

"That's an interesting theory, and one I will have to explore."

"Let me help you," Miss Tate offered.

"How can you help me?" Sebastian asked and tried to hide the smile that was tugging at his lips.

"That depends on how you can help me," Miss Tate replied without missing a beat.

Sebastian waited for her to elaborate. She was a curious woman, intelligent and obviously very determined.

"If you will supply me with the name of the colleague who identified Victor and the identity of the omnibus driver, then I will speak to them in your stead."

Sebastian balked at the idea. Determination didn't always go hand in hand with good sense, but Miss Tate appeared to be perfectly serious. She was waiting for him to reply, her gaze eager and her hand trembling ever so slightly as she held her teacup.

"Miss Tate, the need to understand what happened is completely natural. It's part of the grieving process, but I'm afraid I cannot allow you to get involved in the investigation," Sebastian said, his tone mild, yet firm.

"I'm not asking to be involved, Inspector Bell. I simply wish to speak to the men who were there when Victor died. Perhaps they saw something. Or someone."

"I'm sorry, but I simply can't permit it."

"Permit it?" Miss Tate cried. "I don't need your permission to speak to someone. I'm not employed by Scotland Yard, and you are hardly in a position to tell me what to do. In fact, I mean to go to the offices of the *Telegraph* first thing tomorrow morning."

Sebastian nodded, acknowledging his mistake. Miss Tate wasn't the sort of woman to be ordered about. If he hoped to sway her, he had to appeal to her intellect and sense of propriety.

"Do forgive me, Miss Tate. It wasn't my intention to censor you in any way. You are correct. I can't stop you from pursuing your own investigation, but surely you realize that questioning witnesses will put you in danger. I was only thinking of your safety."

"I will be perfectly safe," Miss Tate countered.

"If you truly believe that your brother was murdered, then poking into the manner of his death will draw unwanted attention, and not only from his killer."

"What on earth do you mean?"

"Should a potential employer get wind of your involvement, they might think twice about offering you a position."

Sebastian hated to add to her anxiety about the future but what he was saying was true, and Miss Tate knew it. Any whiff of scandal could cost her dearly, both personally and professionally.

"Are you suggesting that my reputation will be tarnished?" Miss Tate replied. She clearly hadn't considered the possibility and Sebastian was gratified to note that he'd hit a nerve.

"Is that a risk you're willing to take?" he pressed.

"I'm not, Inspector, which is why I won't question anyone," she replied with a small smile.

"So how do you propose to obtain the information you seek?"

"By playing the grieving sister. And as far as my safety goes, I can look after myself."

"Can you?" Sebastian asked, and tried in vain to suppress another rogue grin. The woman had spirit and cunning, qualities he admired in either sex.

Miss Tate smiled back. "No doubt you already know that I was a nurse in Crimea. You wouldn't be much of a detective if you didn't take a look around while I was in the kitchen." Her amusement was replaced by a look of deep sadness. "When you spend years surrounded by lonely, frightened, sometimes desperate men, you have to learn to see to your own safety. It wasn't only Sevastopol that was under siege, Inspector."

Sebastian nodded. He could imagine how the patients might form an attachment to the women who nursed them and how the able-bodied men would see the nurses as being there for the taking because they were not under the protection of husbands or male relatives.

"Did your parents not object to you going out to Crimea?" he asked, his gaze traveling to the respectable-looking couple in the photo.

"My father passed away several years before the war. However, my mother was vehemently opposed to the idea of me becoming a nurse. I would have respected her wishes and remained at home, but she died a few months before I left for Crimea. So you see, there was no one left to object."

"I'm sorry," Sebastian said.

Miss Tate inclined her head in acknowledgement, then continued. "Victor eventually joined me in Crimea. He reported on the war."

"It must have been comforting to have him near."

"He wasn't always near, but it did make me feel less alone to know that he was there." Miss Tate took a sip of tea, then set down her cup, her expression quizzical as she studied Sebastian. "Why did you become a policeman, Inspector Bell?"

The question took Sebastian by surprise. No one had ever asked him that, not even Louisa. She had simply accepted his occupation, just as she would have had if he'd been a clerk or a shopkeeper.

"Because I hated farming," he quipped.

"Were your parents farmers?"

He nodded. "I grew up on a farm in Suffolk."

Miss Tate didn't say anything, but her inquiring gaze demanded a more detailed answer. Sebastian didn't really want to talk about his past, but Miss Tate had been forthcoming with him. It would be churlish to refuse to answer.

"My father was born to be a farmer. He loved the land, the animals, the changing of the seasons, and the certain knowledge that he would do exactly the same thing every day of his life in exactly the same order," Sebastian began.

"And that very knowledge made you feel like you were drowning," Miss Tate said, surprising him with the astuteness of her observation. Surely he wasn't that transparent, but perhaps she had felt something similar herself. Why else would she have wanted to become a nurse? After all, a well-bred young lady from what appeared to be a good home would have only one aspiration—to marry a suitable man and produce a family.

"Yes, it did," Sebastian admitted. "I would have liked to join the army, but I didn't have the means to purchase a commission and I wouldn't have made a good foot soldier. I'm not keen on following orders," he confessed.

"I would have never guessed," Miss Tate replied, a small smile tugging at the corners of her mouth.

"Joining the police service appealed to my sense of fair play and made me feel like I was making a real difference where it was most needed."

"And you enjoyed the danger and the unpredictability policing brought into your previously well-ordered life," Miss Tate summarized with a knowing nod. "How old were you when you joined the police service?"

"I started out as a constable at eighteen and was promoted to detective by the time I was twenty-five."

"Your work must be extremely rewarding," Miss Tate observed.

"Sometimes it is, and at other times I question the police's ability to make inroads into curbing the activities of London's criminal element. There are so few of us and so many who willingly break the law and take what they want without any thought for those they hurt. We must prioritize certain cases, since we don't have the manpower to investigate every case at once."

Sebastian belatedly realized that he shouldn't have admitted to being short-handed; he'd played directly into Miss Tate's plans. She gave him a searching look.

"Will you get me those names, Inspector Bell? I can't see the harm in simply speaking to the men in question."

Sebastian tilted his head and considered the woman before him. She studied him back, her determination to get her way evident in her direct gaze. If he refused, she would proceed on her own. If he agreed, he might retain a modicum of control over her actions and benefit from the information she gathered without investing time he didn't have. And as much as he hated to admit it, she had a point. There was nothing odd about a grieving sister asking questions about her brother's final moments, and the people she spoke to might be more forthcoming when speaking to a woman.

"Only if you promise not to do anything foolish," he said at last.

"What would constitute foolish in this case?" Miss Tate asked. She seemed to find his concern amusing.

"Voicing your suspicions. Asking pointed questions. And not being aware of your immediate surroundings."

Miss Tate waved a dismissive hand. "Get me the names and allow me to prove my mettle, Inspector."

Sebastian let out a resigned sigh. "All right. I will send someone round with the names tomorrow morning."

"Excellent. Shall we meet tomorrow evening to discuss my findings?"

"I'm not sure what time I will finish for the day," Sebastian replied, already looking forward to discussing the case with Miss Tate.

"No matter. Come when you're able."

"Till tomorrow, then, Miss Tate," Sebastian said as he pushed to his feet. "And thank you for the tea."

"Till tomorrow. And best of luck with your inquiries, Inspector Bell."

NINETEEN

There was still tea in the pot, so Gemma refreshed her cup and reached for the last sandwich. This would have to sustain her until tomorrow morning, since she had no plans to make supper. She'd meant it when she'd said she hated eating alone, and there wasn't much in the larder anyhow. She'd have to go to the shops tomorrow. And she'd have to start thinking about the future. She had set aside the funds for the funeral and the rent was paid through the end of the month, but she would need to leave then. She couldn't afford the house on her own, nor did she wish to stay.

On the face of it, Mr. Gadd's offer was an attractive one. Mrs. Gadd had suffered a stroke just over a year ago and, although she required help with basic tasks, her overall health had not suffered drastically, and she was likely to live for years yet. The position would provide Gemma with a comfortable home, meals, and a steady income, which she could put away until she was ready to leave Mr. Gadd's employ. But the idea of living in Mr. Gadd's house gave her pause. He was a kind man, but he was also a 42-year-old bachelor who might easily give in to romantic ideas and maybe even act on them.

Gemma had been around enough men to recognize when someone found her attractive, and Mr. Gadd didn't bother to hide his admiring looks or a desire to spend time in her company under the pretense of sitting with his mother. Gemma did not find Mr. Gadd the least bit appealing and tried to avoid those uncomfortable moments when Mrs. Gadd fell asleep and it was just the two of them, the intimacy forced by the setting encouraging Mr. Gadd to engage her in an awkward tête-à-tête.

Despite the financial benefits, it would be unwise to open herself to a situation that could quickly become intolerable, since the barest amount of encouragement on her part might lead to a proposal. Not only would she find herself trapped in a loveless marriage if she accepted, but as Mr. Gadd's wife Gemma would be expected to care for her mother-in-law for the rest of her days, not a task she relished since it was bound to become more demanding as the years went by. No, she would have to refuse Mr. Gadd's offer and hope that he didn't dismiss her on the spot.

The most logical step would be to find work in an infirmary or a hospital, since she could volunteer for extra shifts and maybe even receive meals as part of her compensation, but the thought of working in a hospital again made her stomach clench with apprehension. She never wanted to set foot in such a place again, not because she no longer wished to help people but because she had lost faith in the institutions she had once respected. In Scutari, she had worked without thinking, since stopping to analyze what was happening around her would probably have addled her wits. She had never seen such senseless slaughter or such stubborn refusal to acknowledge mistakes, both in military strategy and in the treatment of patients. Cartloads of bodies left the hospital every day, bloodied, mangled corpses of young men who'd given their lives for nothing and could probably have been saved if they had received adequate care and timely medical intervention.

In a London hospital, around forty percent of patients died of post-operative infection. In Scutari, it had probably been closer to eighty. And now that the nurses were back and Florence Nightingale was revered as the only true hero to emerge from Crimea, the all-male doctors refused to hire experienced nurses or, if they did, relegated them to cleaning, changing bandages, and taking out bedpans. The doctors refused to take any advice, make any improvements, or even treat the nurses with the respect they deserved. The nurses were viewed with suspicion and branded immoral by the very men they had tried to save and by their wives and mothers, who had no idea what to make of the returning nurses and did their utmost to put them in their place.

Gemma thought the doctors felt threatened by the brave women who not only had experience of emergency surgery and post-operative care but had survived conditions beyond all imagining. She would never again take for granted a clean bed, a hot bath, or even a room that didn't reek of human ordure and wasn't overrun with rats. In her mind's eye, she could still see the vile creatures gnawing on the limbs of patients who were too weak to swat them away and hear their incessant squeaking as they scurried about in the dark. Not that the situation was all that much better in London.

The summer had been an absolute nightmare, the miasma coming off the Thames so thick and pungent it had been nearly impossible to draw breath without choking. At last, plans were being considered for redirecting the waste that flowed into the Thames via interconnecting sewers, but it would take years for the system to be put in place. In the meantime, the Great Stink, as it had been named, had finally receded with the arrival of the cooler weather, but the outbreaks of cholera caused by raw sewage had taken their toll, especially on the poor, who couldn't hide behind stout walls or decamp to the country, where they could breathe fresh air and eat uncontaminated food.

Gemma supposed, now that she had no one left to stay for, she could find a situation in the country if she wished. There was no shortage of families looking for an experienced nurse to take care of a loved one, and they would be offering a live-in position. It was something to consider, but she wasn't ready to make any big decisions when she was so emotional and still reeling with shock. She needed to understand what had happened to Victor in order to lay him to rest.

Inspector Bell would help. She was sure of it. She liked the man and thought that perhaps he had liked her too. Not in any silly romantic sense but in that quiet masculine way that reassured her that he thought her competent and, hopefully, intelligent. Gemma thought he must be good at his job. He had to be if he had been entrusted with such a high-profile case.

He was attractive too, Gemma acknowledged as she set down her empty cup. She wasn't impressed with dandies, whom she found ridiculous and effete. She liked men who looked the part and were handsome in a classic, solid way. Inspector Bell's features were pleasing, if a bit stern. His eyes were the color of brandy, and she liked that he wore his dark blond hair a little long and natural. She despised hair oil and pomade almost as much as she hated beards and moustaches. Being a nurse, she found them unsanitary, and couldn't help but look for signs that would confirm the presence of lice. A smooth face was vastly preferable, as was a generous mouth that smiled easily, the humor reaching the eyes and making them twinkle, as they had when Inspector Bell permitted himself a smile.

Gemma shook her head in dismay when she realized which way her thoughts were heading.

"You've been alone too long, my girl," she said out loud, and sighed heavily.

She was twenty-seven years old, and her chances of getting married were practically non-existent, unless she encouraged Mr. Gadd. Not because she couldn't attract the attention of a man but because, more often than not, she didn't want the attention she had unwittingly captured. She wasn't the sort of woman who could be a meek, subservient wife, occupied with the comfort of her husband and careful not to let an opposing view slip from her lips. And if she ever permitted herself to speak freely, any man, even the bravest of the species, would run a mile from a woman who considered herself his equal. If she were ever to marry, it would have to be to someone who saw her as a partner, not a domestic servant who was also expected to satisfy his needs without any regard for her own, and she was fairly sure a man like that had yet to be born.

Even Victor had chosen a wife who'd put him first, and he would have been happy in his marriage had Julia not become ill. Victor had been a man who'd needed looking after and would have remarried in time. Gemma was sure of it. He would have always looked after his sister, but she would have been nothing more than a tolerated sister-in-law, or a beloved aunt. She would never have had a life of her own. Gemma didn't mind spinsterhood, but she had longed for children and that she would never have them was her only regret.

Perhaps one day, if she achieved financial security, she would take a child from an orphanage and raise it as her own. An unmarried woman might not be considered a suitable guardian, but she'd find a way around such unreasonable prejudice. There were so many unwanted children. Surely she'd manage to find one, if not in an orphanage then maybe on the street. The thought lessened her loneliness somewhat as she cleared away the tea things, then returned to the parlor and watched the fire as it died out. She'd be warm enough under the eiderdown. There was no need to waste any more precious coal tonight.

TWENTY

Sebastian would have liked nothing more than to go home and enjoy a very large whisky, or better yet spend a few hours lost in an opium dream, but he couldn't give in to the urge, not when he was working a case. And this case bothered the hell out of him, even more now that he'd heard what Gemma Tate had to say. Victor Tate's death added an unexpected layer of complexity to the investigation, since it was entirely possible that he had been the second victim of this brutal crime.

Sebastian was convinced that the only way to prove that would be to uncover what happened to Adelaide Seaborne. He didn't like to admit, even to himself, that he would rather investigate a stabbing or a beating anytime. Those crimes he could comprehend. This case made the hairs on the back of his neck stand to attention with the wrongness of it. Everything about it had been staged: the victim, the bleeding heart, the faux crucifixion. Someone had put a lot of thought into this and had wanted him to come to certain conclusions, only all those conclusions would be wrong because they were meant to distract him from the truth, and therefore the killer.

Several colleagues he could think of would kill for this case.

It would focus attention on them like a lighthouse spotlight on an incoming ship and give them an opportunity to make themselves known to the press, and in turn to those they hoped to impress into allowing them to move up the career ladder. They wanted to be admired by the public and feared by the criminal element. Solving this case would send a clear message. *If I can solve this puzzle, I can solve anything. I'm someone to be reckoned with.* But they might be disappointed. This case was a trap, meant to lead the self-satisfied detective right into the massive fiasco that would haunt them for the rest of their lives.

All detectives had a list of cases they had failed to resolve, but this one would never let them go because it would make them feel small, and stupid, and ashamed. This was going to be the investigation they were remembered by, even if they managed to solve every case thereafter. And this was why Lovell had given it to Sebastian. Lovell wanted to distance himself from Sebastian's failure and feed him to the sharks that would circle if he failed to cuff the culprit. This was his last chance, and he had to unravel this mystery if he hoped to walk away from Scotland Yard with something left of his professional reputation, which was in tatters already because of what had happened to Louisa.

The only way to work this investigation was to rely on solid policework, and that meant interviewing the two men Adelaide Seaborne had been romantically involved with, either of whom might have snapped and murdered her in a jealous rage. By tomorrow, the identity of the victim would hit the streets, so now was the time to catch the suspects unawares and observe their reactions to the news. Even if someone was a consummate actor or completely devoid of a soul and incapable of remorse, they still gave something away when confronted with news of their victim's demise. In place of shock and grief, it was either momentary nervousness, a spark of pride at their handiwork, or at times annoyance at being singled out. The time to question

Lord Mayhew and David Parker was now, tonight, so Lovell would have to wait. As a policeman himself, he would understand the need to prioritize.

David Parker could have lost his temper because Adelaide had told him she had agreed to marry Lord Mayhew. And Lord Mayhew might have found himself humiliated if he had discovered that his intended was infatuated with someone else and had sampled love's delights with the man she longed for. What complicated matters was that both men were wealthy enough to pay someone to teach Adelaide Seaborne a lesson and keep their noses clean in the process, so the only thing Sebastian would have to go on was his gut instinct, which was a bit rusty these days.

Taking his notebook out of his pocket, Sebastian verified the addresses he'd obtained from Lewis and strode toward the nearest cabstand. He'd start with Lord Mayhew and hope he found the man at home.

TWENTY-ONE

Lord Mayhew's residence was in Charles Street, which was a fashionable address but couldn't rival the grandeur of Park Lane. The house was a four-storied stucco structure with a classical portico, wrought-iron railings, and tall sash windows. The panes of glass sparkled, the paint gleamed, and the doorstep was so cleanly swept, Sebastian wondered if anyone was permitted to use the front entrance. He didn't bother to go round the back and search for the servants' entrance, instead using the polished doorknocker to announce his presence.

An urbane major-domo opened the door and was about to send Sebastian packing when Sebastian produced his warrant card, his credentials and presence clearly taking the man by surprise.

"Inspector Bell to see Lord Mayhew," Sebastian announced.

"What is the nature of your business, Inspector?" the major-domo asked.

"The nature of my business is confidential."

"Wait here," the man said, once he had permitted Sebastian into the foyer and hastily shut the door. Nosy neighbors were to be found in every neighborhood, and Lord Mayhew clearly valued his privacy, or at least his butler did.

"Your name?" Sebastian asked before the man went in search of his master.

"Keating."

It always irritated Sebastian when servants failed to give their full name. It was as if their very identity had been stolen from them, their entire being reduced to one word, like a dog that didn't warrant more than a single moniker when addressed.

"I'll take your things, Inspector," Keating intoned when he returned. He held out his hand for Sebastian's coat and hat, then directed him toward the door on the right, which led to a well-appointed room decorated in shades of sea green and cream.

A man of about thirty sat in a comfortable chair by the fire, an open book in his lap. His dark hair was neatly trimmed, his dark eyes were almond-shaped and accented by heavy brows, and his pencil moustache crawled like a caterpillar between a prominent nose and a thin upper lip. Oliver Mayhew didn't bother to stand, but Sebastian could see that he was of slim build and not very tall. He was in his shirtsleeves and wore black trousers, a silver and black waistcoat, and a black silk cravat. He gave the impression of someone who was keenly aware of current fashion and fastidious in his dress, even when at home and on his own.

Lord Mayhew did not invite Sebastian to sit down. Instead, he cocked his head to the side, studied him for a moment, probably to unnerve him and remind him of his lowly status, then finally invited him to state his business.

"A young woman was found dead in Highgate Cemetery on All Saints' Day, my lord," Sebastian began.

"What is that to me, Inspector?"

"The victim was identified as Miss Adelaide Seaborne," Sebastian said, his gaze never leaving the man's face. What he saw there was shock, disbelief, denial, and sorrow. He caught no trace of fear nor any attempt at masking the feelings that came naturally.

"Sit down," Lord Mayhew said gruffly. "Excuse me, I need a moment."

He stood, walked over to the window, and looked out over the gaslit street. His shoulders were tense, and his head bowed slightly as he pulled a handkerchief from his pocket and dabbed at his eyes. Sebastian watched and waited. There was no call to interrupt. The man would come back soon enough, and the calmer he was the more likely he'd be to answer Sebastian's questions.

Turning away from the window at last, Lord Mayhew pushed the handkerchief back into the pocket of his well-tailored trousers and resumed his seat.

"Tell me everything," he said.

Sebastian relayed the pertinent details, all the while taking in Oliver Mayhew's every expression and exclamation of outrage.

"I don't understand," Mayhew cried after he'd finished. "Who would do such a thing?"

"That's what I'm tasked with finding out, my lord," Sebastian replied calmly. "When was the last time you saw Miss Seaborne?"

"I saw her on Saturday. We attended a musical recital, followed by supper. Adelaide's parents were present as well."

"And how was Miss Seaborne when you saw her?"

"She enjoyed the performance and conversed animatedly with her supper companions," Lord Mayhew replied. "I did not hear what they spoke about since I was seated some way away from Miss Seaborne."

"What was performed?" Sebastian asked.

Lord Mayhew seemed surprised by the question but answered readily enough. "It was a selection of arias from

Handel's most notable operas: *Floridante, Rodelinda,* and *Scipione*. I am not a fan of Handel myself, but Viscount Dalton had invited me, and it was an opportunity to spend an evening in the company of Miss Seaborne."

"When were you to marry?" Sebastian asked.

"I had hoped to marry this year, but Miss Seaborne said she would prefer a June wedding."

"Do you think she was stalling for time?"

"Probably. I would be a fool to believe that I was her heart's desire."

"Why did you want to marry her, then?" Sebastian asked.

Lord Mayhew smirked. "Because she was beautiful, accomplished, and handsomely dowered."

"Was her portion a deciding factor?"

"No, but marrying an heiress never hurts." Lord Mayhew exhaled loudly. "I really did admire her, Inspector. She was a lovely girl, and I think we could have been happy together."

"But your engagement had yet to be announced," Sebastian reminded him.

"A mere formality. I wasn't overly concerned about the delay."

"Was there anyone who might have wanted to harm Miss Seaborne? A jealous suitor, perhaps?" Sebastian prompted.

"Miss Seaborne had several ardent admirers, but I doubt any of them would resort to such brutality. It's just the way of things, isn't it? Someone gets accepted, and someone gets rejected."

"Not everyone is as philosophical as you are, my lord."

"No, I don't suppose they are, but when it comes to society marriages deep feelings are rarely engaged. It's a mutually beneficial arrangement that either leads to genuine affection or to a union of convenience where both parties find whatever happiness they can outside the marriage."

"And what of Mr. Parker? Are you acquainted with him?"

"The American?" Lord Mayhew asked. "What of him?"

"I hear Miss Seaborne was quite taken with him."

"Was she? I wasn't aware."

Lord Mayhew was clearly lying, but Sebastian thought it was more to save face than because he held any real grudge toward the American. David Parker had never really stood a chance, so there was no point in Oliver Mayhew becoming overly emotional about a suitor who would return to his native country in a matter of weeks and become a distant memory, at least for him.

"Where were you Sunday night into Monday morning?" Sebastian asked.

"I attended church with my mother and uncle, then joined them for luncheon. My mother wasn't feeling well. She succumbs to bouts of melancholia brought about by the death of my younger sister. So I offered to stay a while. My presence always cheers her up. We played piquet, had a light supper at eight, and then Mother retired. My uncle and I headed to Brooks around ten and remained at the club until well past one. We played whist, and at least a dozen members can vouch for my whereabouts. I dropped Uncle Giles at home at about two a.m. and returned home. I woke around eleven on Monday, which every member of my staff can confirm."

"Does your mother reside with your uncle?" Sebastian asked, just for the sake of clarity.

"Yes. My mother and her brother always got on, and now that they're both widowed they are grateful for the company."

"I see. Thank you for your assistance, my lord."

"I trust my name will not be bandied about in the press in relation to Miss Seaborne's murder," Lord Mayhew said.

"Was anyone besides your families aware of your impending engagement?"

"Not that I know of."

"Then I don't expect it will be."

Lord Mayhew nodded. "One never wants one's name connected to a scandal."

"No, my lord."

"I will wish you good evening, then, Inspector Bell."

"And to you, sir."

Sebastian wasn't about to take Mayhew's word for his whereabouts. He'd have to check with Brooks just to rule the man out as a suspect, but he couldn't see Oliver Mayhew resorting to rape and murder. He just didn't seem the sort to give in to his passions or to soil his clean, well-manicured hands. His earlier display of emotion had been more shock than grief for the young woman he had planned to marry. Sebastian had no doubt that Lord Mayhew would be married by June. One wealthy, aristocratic bride was as good as another.

When Keating brought his things, Sebastian asked, "What time did his lordship come home on Sunday night?"

The man's expression did not change. "He returned around two a.m. and went directly to bed."

"How did he seem?"

"Inebriated."

"And his clothes?" Sebastian asked.

"Reeking of cigar smoke but otherwise clean. Why do you ask?"

"No reason," Sebastian replied, and took his leave.

TWENTY-TWO

Sebastian didn't have to go far to conduct his next interview, since David Parker had taken up residence at Brown's Hotel in Mayfair. The clerk wouldn't allow Sebastian upstairs but grudgingly sent a bellboy to inform Mr. Parker that he had a visitor and even offered the use of a small private parlor. It was meant to look like a solicitous gesture but was probably intended to keep Sebastian out of the path of the guests. The presence of the police on the premises never boded well.

David Parker arrived a few minutes later and immediately offered Sebastian his hand in greeting. "Inspector, how do you do?"

"I'm well, thank you."

"How can I help?" David Parker asked as he settled into a club chair across from Sebastian. "I'm going to order a drink. Can I get you anything?"

"Whisky," Sebastian said, despite his better judgment.

David Parker signaled to a waiter who hovered near the door. "Two whiskies, my good man. And make them doubles," he added.

Sebastian could see why Adelaide Seaborne had found

David Parker more to her liking. He was tall, broad-shouldered, and handsome, with thick, curling dark hair that was brushed back from a high forehead, sky-blue eyes, and heroic bone structure. He was also amiable and did not appear as class-conscious as his British counterparts. His hands were large and muscular, the hands of a man who wasn't averse to a bit of heavy lifting, and his face was unfashionably tanned.

He also had to be not only wealthy but well connected. To stay at Brown's Hotel for several months cost a pretty penny, and the man had to have been invited to gatherings reserved for members of the *ton* in order to have met the lovely Adelaide and have remained in her social sphere long enough to form an attachment.

The waiter brought their drinks, set them on a conveniently placed table, and withdrew.

"Cheers," David Parker said, and took a healthy swallow.

Sebastian took a sip of his whisky and set the glass back down with some reluctance. He couldn't afford anything this good on a policeman's wage and would have liked to savor the treat.

"So, why do you wish to speak to me?" David Parker asked once the formalities were out of the way.

"The body of a young woman was discovered in Highgate Cemetery on Monday morning."

"Yes, it was in the papers," David Parker said. "An awful thing to have happened, but do you believe she was someone I might have crossed paths with?"

"The victim was identified as Miss Adelaide Seaborne."

David Parker's reaction was immediate and probably genuine. His eyes filled with tears, and his hand shook so violently, he spilled a bit of whisky on his trousers.

"Dammit," he cried, and reached for a serviette to dab at the stain. "Are you quite certain it's Addie?"

The use of the pet name wasn't lost on Sebastian, especially when Lord Mayhew had referred to his future wife only as Miss Seaborne.

"Yes, we are certain."

"My God, what a tragedy. What happened? How did Addie come to be there?"

Sebastian relayed the facts he considered germane, all the while watching David Parker closely. He wept openly, seemingly unashamed to put his feelings on display, and Sebastian couldn't help but warm to him.

"I don't understand," David muttered. "Who would do such a thing? Addie was such a lovely girl, and so generous of spirit." He dabbed at his eyes and blew his nose noisily. "She was always well chaperoned. How did she come to be out alone?"

"It seems she sneaked out to attend a séance."

"I can believe that."

"Really? Had she expressed an interest in the occult?"

"No, but she was curious about the mechanics of such gatherings. She thought that most mediums were charlatans and was convinced that she could spot their tricks if she got to see them up close."

"And had she ever attended a séance before?" Sebastian asked.

David Parker smiled sadly. "No, but she wanted to, in the name of research, you understand. Of course, her parents would never allow it, and rightly so."

"And what do you think of spiritualism, Mr. Parker?" Sebastian asked, wondering if David Parker might have planned to attend the same séance.

"I think it's nonsense and these fraudsters are exploiting the bereaved."

"Have you ever been to a séance?"

"No, I have not, but my mother has hosted a few. She fancies herself a mystic. And before you ask, she's a true believer."

"Mr. Parker, you've been in London for some time now. What is your purpose in being here?" Sebastian asked.

David Parker smiled wistfully. "My father is a self-made man, Inspector. He never had the benefit of a good education or the perks that come with great wealth. He thought I should go off on a Grand Tour before joining him in the family business."

"And what is the family business?"

"My father has his fingers in many pies. Coal mines in Wyoming, shares in two railroad lines, and even prospecting claims in Montana. I am his only son, and he wants to give me all the things he never had."

"Does not a Grand Tour imply that you actually tour?" Sebastian asked.

"It does. I started out in Italy, spent a few weeks in Greece, and then made my way to Germany, where I met Lord Sutter, who invited me to come to London. He's a very agreeable fellow, and we've become fast friends."

"So, you arrived in London, were introduced into society by Lord Sutter, and decided to stay?"

"I was only going to stay a few weeks, a month at most. Then I met Addie, and my plans changed."

"Did you ever meet Miss Seaborne in private?" Sebastian asked.

David Parker had the decency to look ashamed. "I have to admit that I did. We devised ways to meet and saw each other at least once a week."

"Where did you meet?"

"In Hyde Park, at the British Museum, at a tearoom Addie liked. I even endeavored to rent a cottage in Somerset when her family visited Bath for a few weeks in the summer."

"So, you admit that you met with the young lady in secret?"

"We were always adequately chaperoned."

"By whom?"

"Her maid, Miss Jones."

"Miss Jones was afraid to lose her place. She would keep your secrets no matter what you got up to," Sebastian said. "Were you and Miss Seaborne ever intimate?"

Sebastian had hoped to catch David Parker off guard, but the question did not seem to surprise him.

"I'm not a cad, Inspector Bell. My intentions towards Adelaide were completely honorable."

"Yet you were sneaking about behind her father's back."

"I won't lie; I was prepared to defy her father and would have married Addie in secret if she had agreed, but I would never do anything to dishonor her."

"But she wouldn't agree to a secret wedding?" Sebastian asked.

"Addie cared for me, but she wasn't nearly as flighty as she pretended to be. She wanted to marry for love, but she also wanted a place in society and all the things that came with such a position. She had no desire to move to the Wild West, as she called it."

"Were you hoping to change her mind?"

"Yes and no."

"Which one is it?" Sebastian asked.

"I had hoped that her feelings for me would prevail, but I didn't want her to be unhappy. I cannot remain in England. I must return home and take my place in the family business. If Addie wasn't prepared to share my life, then I would accept my disappointment and eventually find someone else."

"It is my understanding that Miss Seaborne was to marry Lord Mayhew. The announcement was imminent. Did she tell you of her plans?"

"Yes."

"And how did you feel about her decision?"

"I won't lie, Inspector. I was hurt, but I also understood her reasons."

"Yet you still pursued her."

"I told her I would remain in London a little while longer but would return home in time for Christmas. She said she needed time to be sure. I don't think she liked Oliver Mayhew, not in any real sense."

"Mr. Parker, where were you on Sunday night into Monday morning?"

"I was here. I never went out. Lord Sutter did invite me to join him at this club, but I wasn't in the mood and spent the evening alone. I did come down to dinner, and had breakfast brought to me at eight a.m. The staff can confirm my alibi."

"Do you think you need an alibi?" Sebastian asked, but couldn't help a small smile. He liked David Parker and was inclined to believe him.

"You clearly think I do, or you wouldn't be here."

Sebastian inclined his head in agreement.

"Do you think it would be okay if I called on Addie's parents to offer my condolences?" David Parker asked.

Sebastian thought *okay* an odd word, but he was familiar with this incomprehensible American term from reading about the Pinkertons in an American newspaper he'd found at a crime scene in Wapping a few months ago. An agent had been quoted as saying that he was okay after being shot in the course of apprehending a wanted murderess. He had also boasted about receiving a reward, the sum so substantial it was more than okay.

"Perhaps you should write first," Sebastian said. "I'm not sure they're receiving."

"Thank you. I will remain in London until after the funeral, should you need to speak to me again. After that, I will return home."

"Very good, Mr. Parker. I wish you a good night."

Sebastian tossed back the rest of the whisky and left David Parker to his thoughts. He verified his alibi with the front desk and spoke to the manager, who confirmed that Mr. Parker took his breakfast at eight every morning and had been there to greet the waiter on Monday. He had not left the premises until well after ten.

Feeling less than satisfied with the progress of the investigation, Sebastian returned to Scotland Yard. Lovell would be gone for the day, but he needed to speak to Sergeant Woodward.

"Good evening, Inspector," Sergeant Woodward said when Sebastian walked in. "You've missed Lovell. He left more than an hour ago."

"I need you to send someone to Brooks to check Oliver Mayhew's alibi for Sunday night."

"Meadows is still here. He can stop in on his way home."

"Is there a file on Victor Tate?" Sebastian asked.

"There's no official file, since his death was an accident, but Constable Earnshaw, who was called to the scene, did write up a report."

"Do you still have it?"

Sergeant Woodward shrugged. "I threw it away. Here, let me have a look," he offered. "The bin hasn't been emptied yet." He ducked beneath his desk, pulled out the wastepaper basket, and rummaged through the rubbish. "Ah, here it is."

He handed Sebastian a sheet of paper that had been wadded into a ball and looked like it had been chewed by some toothless animal.

"I'm going to take this," Sebastian said.

"Be my guest. We've got no use for it." Sergeant Woodward gave Sebastian an inquisitive look. "Get anything on the Highgate lovely?"

"Not as much as I'd like, but it's early days yet."

"Your days will be numbered if you don't collar someone for the crime, and soon," Sergeant Woodward said. "Lovell is champing at the bit to make an arrest."

"I'm sure he is, but I can hardly arrest someone without enough evidence to support the accusation," Sebastian replied.

"There are some who might not have that particular problem," the sergeant replied.

Sebastian nodded. "The day I resort to planting evidence on some poor sod just to make an arrest is the day I leave the police service."

"Just make sure it doesn't leave you," Sergeant Woodward warned. "I'm not the only one who knows where to find you these days."

"Thank you for the warning, Sergeant. Have a good evening," Sebastian replied sharply.

Sergeant Woodward was a good man and a solid copper, but it didn't take much to loosen his tongue and, if he joined a few of the lads for a drink after his shift, anything Sebastian told him would make the rounds by tomorrow morning. He only hoped Sergeant Woodward would forget about Sebastian's interest in Victor Tate. He had no desire to explain himself to Lovell, at least not yet.

He stuffed the paper into his pocket and walked out into the night.

TWENTY-THREE

Wednesday, November 3

Sebastian threw the empty whisky bottle a baleful look, then searched the desk drawer for a packet of headache powder. He didn't find it, so he headed to the dining room for breakfast, hoping against hope that Mrs. Poole would not be in a chatty mood and would leave him to eat in peace. Luck was on his side, and she retreated to the kitchen as soon as she delivered his plate to the table. Sebastian had coffee, which was an additional charge, two fried eggs, a slice of ham, and buttered bread. The coffee relieved the headache somewhat, but his hands trembled as he buttoned his coat, and he nearly dropped his key when he tried to fit it into the lock of his room.

The chemist shop was already open, so Sebastian purchased a bottle of Smith & Ward's Tonic, which was usually prescribed for hysterical women and contained enough laudanum to quell the shaking and give him a temporary sense of well-being. If he used it sparingly, it would get him through the next few days. He opened the bottle outside the shop, took a swig, and stowed it in the pocket of his coat.

Feeling marginally better, Sebastian first stopped by Division H, which wasn't too far away, and asked to see Constable Haze. He'd met Daniel Haze during another investigation, and the young bobby had made an impression on him. He was an intelligent, earnest man who longed to make his mark and was always willing to lend a hand to a fellow policeman. Daniel was just about to head out on patrol, so Sebastian had caught him just in time.

"Constable, would you mind doing me a favor?" Sebastian asked as he followed Daniel Haze outside.

"If I can," Constable Haze replied cautiously. Sebastian liked that about him. He never committed to anything before finding out exactly what was expected of him.

"Would you be able to deliver a message to Bethnal Green?"

"Of course, Inspector. I can take it right over."

Sebastian took out a folded sheet of paper and handed it to Daniel. "It's for Miss Gemma Tate. The address is written just here."

Daniel Haze smiled knowingly. "Is this personal business, Inspector?"

"It's to do with a case I'm investigating. You might have seen it in the papers. The body in Highgate."

"You're working the Highgate murder?" Constable Haze exclaimed, his eyes widening with barely suppressed excitement. "The Highgate Angel. That's what the papers are calling her."

"There's nothing angelic about a murder, Constable," Sebastian said reproachfully.

"I do wish I could transfer to Scotland Yard," Constable Haze said wistfully. "I would dearly love to become a detective."

"There's plenty of crime right here in Whitechapel. If you do the legwork, you'll eventually move up the ranks. There's always room for advancement."

"That's the plan, sir," Constable Haze answered with a hopeful grin. "Inspector by thirty."

"You seem awfully chipper this morning," Sebastian said, smiling back at the eager young man.

Daniel's cheeks went a subtle shade of pink. "I'm to be a father, sir. In the spring."

"My congratulations to you and your wife."

"Sarah," Daniel supplied. "My wife's name is Sarah."

"Sarah. I'll remember that in the future."

Constable Haze was still smiling. "I'll see that Miss Tate gets this, Inspector Bell."

"Thank you. I appreciate your assistance."

"Don't mention it. Just put in a good word for me if the situation calls for it." Constable Haze tipped his hat and walked off, a jolly spring in his step.

Sebastian arrived in Park Lane a few minutes before ten. Even though he was expected, Lewis did not look overly pleased to see him, but few people were. A detective in one's home never boded well. Sebastian hoped that the viscount was not an early riser and would not require the services of his valet until Sebastian had had an opportunity to interview the man.

"I'll begin with Mr. Ahmad," Sebastian told Lewis, who had reluctantly surrendered his pantry once again.

"What could you possibly want with the viscount's valet?" Lewis grumbled.

"I have some questions to put to him," Sebastian replied, giving nothing away. He didn't owe Lewis an explanation.

"As you wish," the butler said curtly. "I'll send him in."

Sebastian wasn't quite sure what he had expected. Perhaps a man in native dress wearing a turban and a ceremonial dagger, but then he realized he was thinking of the Sikhs, a few of whom he'd seen at the London docks. Mr. Ahmad wore a well-cut suit, a black tie, and shoes polished to a shine. He had to be close to forty and had the bearing of an ex-soldier. His skin was a warm brown and his eyes a cold black. Sebastian could see why Miss Jones found him intimidating, but there was no hint of malice in Mr. Ahmad's bearing, only forbearance.

"Please, sit down, Mr. Ahmad." Sebastian flipped open his notebook. "Can I have your full name?"

"Fadil Ehsan Ahmad. How can I be of service to you, Inspector?" the valet asked in slightly accented English. Not for the first time, Sebastian wondered how he'd come to be in the viscount's employ.

"How long have you worked for the viscount?" he asked.

"Nearly five years now."

"And how did you meet?"

"We met aboard a ship to England. I was a lascar, employed by the East India Company. His lordship's valet had taken ill, and I was tasked with looking after his needs. Once we arrived in England, he offered me a position in his household."

"What became of his own valet?" Sebastian asked.

"Sadly, he died during the voyage and was given a burial at sea."

"Do you like living in England?" Sebastian asked.

It had to be difficult for someone like Fadil Ahmad to put down roots, since most Englishmen shared Miss Jones's sentiments and were wary of anyone foreign. That sort of emotional isolation would make for a lonely existence and foster resentment, especially if the individual was treated with undisguised hostility by the rest of the staff and didn't have anyone they felt close to outside the household.

"It has its advantages," the valet said with a one-shouldered shrug.

"And how do you get on with the rest of the staff, Mr. Ahmad?"

"Inspector, am I being accused of something?"

"No, you're not."

"Then why are you asking me these questions?"

"Did you have any dealings with Miss Seaborne?" Sebastian asked, preferring to avoid Mr. Ahmad's question for the moment.

"Not really."

"Did you ever discuss religion or the customs of your countrymen?"

"Yes, we frequently enjoyed a spirited chat over tea," Mr. Ahmad replied, the bitterness in his tone impossible to miss.

"Mr. Ahmad, Miss Seaborne is dead," Sebastian reminded him. "This is not the time for sarcasm."

"No, it isn't," Mr. Ahmad agreed. "Miss Seaborne occasionally asked questions about India. She said she hoped to see it someday. She was curious by nature and liked to be shocked. I think it gave her something of a thrill."

"And were your stories shocking?"

"Most things are shocking to a sheltered English lady, Inspector, even though London is as much of a jungle as some of the wildest parts of India."

"Why do you say that?" Sebastian asked, genuinely interested.

"Because the natural order is for the strong to feed on the weak. One doesn't have to be in a jungle to see that principle at work."

"You are right there," Sebastian replied, and wondered where Mr. Ahmad saw himself in this hierarchy. He certainly wasn't a weakling, but he could hardly claim a position of power when he was despised by the other servants. His only source of support was the viscount, who could easily withdraw his favor if he felt that the valet's presence in the household was causing discord among the rest of the staff.

Mr. Ahmad cocked his head to the side and studied Sebastian for a moment. "I ask again, Inspector. Why are you directing your questions to me when Miss Seaborne was murdered far from this house?"

"The heart of a pig was found hanging around Miss Seaborne's neck," Sebastian said. Mr. Ahmad's shock was evident. "I see that means something to you."

The man pinned Sebastian with a narrowed stare. "Evidently, it means something to you as well."

"Countless murders occur in this city, but most of them are simple, vicious, often unpremeditated acts of violence. The killers don't usually bother to display the corpse or shroud the act in layers of symbolism."

"And you think the heart is symbolic of something?" Mr. Ahmad asked carefully.

"I think you of all people would see how it could be."

The valet nodded. "Yes, I can. There have been a number of attacks on Muslim sailors who've settled in London. Their doors and windows have been smeared with pig's blood. In one instance, a pig's entrails were strewn around a Jewish-owned butcher shop in Whitechapel, where some of those sailors buy their meat, since the dietary restrictions are similar and the shop is not contaminated by pork. But what would any of that have to do with Miss Seaborne?"

"I don't know, but, seeing as there is a Muslim retainer in the household, I thought it prudent to discover where things stand. Incidentally, does the cook cater to your dietary restrictions?"

Mr. Ahmad chuckled mirthlessly. "She would prefer not to, but his lordship requested early on that I not be served pork or anything that has come in contact with unclean meat. If the family and the servants are having pork, then I will limit myself to eating vegetables or a boiled egg."

"So, that's another thing that sets you apart," Sebastian said.

Mr. Ahmad let out a heavy sigh. "Inspector Bell, as you might imagine, I'm not very popular with the other members of staff, so I keep to myself when not attending to his lordship's needs. However, I still don't see what any of this has to do with Miss Seaborne's death."

"Bear with me, Mr. Ahmad," Sebastian said. He wasn't sure how any of this was relevant either but thought it important to understand how Mr. Ahmad fit into the household and Adelaide Seaborne's life. "Do you have any friends in London?"

"Are you asking if I associate with my countrymen?"

"I am."

"I do have several acquaintances whom I see on my afternoons off. They have never met Miss Seaborne, nor have they been the target of an attack, if that's what you're thinking."

"How do they earn their living?"

"One is a cook. His employer, a major in the Cavalry, had developed a taste for ethnic dishes while serving in India, and when the major returned home he brought my friend with him. There's also an English cook, but they get on fairly well. The other friend is in charge of his master's stables."

"And are they happy here?" Sebastian inquired.

"If you're asking me if they would be happier in India, the answer is no. We all have things we long to get away from. For some of us, that means crossing the ocean and living in a foreign land."

Sebastian nodded. He could well understand the desire to cross an ocean to get away from one's pain. "Do you know of anyone who was intentionally targeted, Mr. Ahmad?"

"Several men were attacked a few weeks back. I don't know them personally, but people talk."

"May I have their names, please?" Sebastian asked.

"I would have to ask what you plan to do with the information."

"I mean them no harm. I simply wish to ask if they know who is behind these attacks."

"Do you honestly think that the pig's heart around a

viscount's daughter's neck is somehow connected to the Indian lascars who chose to remain in England for reasons of their own?"

"I think the pig's heart was a message. At this stage, I don't know for whom."

Mr. Ahmad inclined his head. "All right, Inspector. I will tell you, and I hope that you are a man of your word and will not make life difficult for people who are only trying to survive."

"I give you my word that they will not be harassed in any way, at least not by me."

The valet nodded. "Saeed Mahmoud and his two brothers work at Munk's Tannery in the Rookery of St. Giles. They have been targeted. More than once, I might add."

"Do you know why?" Sebastian asked.

"Because they are easy targets and there are those who believe they're taking jobs meant for Englishmen." Mr. Ahmad looked disgusted. "Not many Englishmen care to do the work the Mahmouds do, but they still resent their presence."

"What sort of work do they do?"

"Liming," Mr. Ahmad replied.

"What does that entail?"

"Let's just say it's not a very pleasant occupation, nor is it well paid."

Sebastian made another note, then looked up. "Where were you on Sunday night, Mr. Ahmad? It has come to my attention that you didn't want supper."

"I get my afternoon off on Sundays, since his lordship doesn't have need of me after he gets home from church. I went to visit my friend, the cook, and he treated me to a wonderful meal. I returned by seven o'clock and went up to my room. I didn't eat because I was still full. Mr. Lewis saw me go up."

"Thank you, Mr. Ahmad. You're free to go."

Mr. Ahmad stood and left the pantry without saying another word.

"Who else do you wish to speak to?" Lewis asked once he saw the valet leave. Sebastian had the uncomfortable feeling that the butler was intentionally keeping close in order to listen in on the conversations.

"You," Sebastian replied, and felt a glint of satisfaction at the surprise on the butler's face.

TWENTY-FOUR

Lewis looked furious when Sebastian invited him to take the guest chair in his own office, since he considered a policeman to be socially inferior to his own exalted status, but Sebastian didn't budge. Such was life. Sometimes positions were reversed and the people one looked down upon suddenly gained the upper hand. Sebastian flipped his notebook to a clean page and looked up at the butler.

"What do you wish to know?" Lewis demanded, his desire to get the interview over with evident.

"As a rule, a butler knows everything that goes on within a household."

"So does the housekeeper," Lewis replied.

"I'll speak to her as well. Tell me, Mr. Lewis, did Miss Seaborne sneak out often?"

Lewis's face registered shock. "Sneak out?"

"Yes. Did she leave the house at night without telling anyone?"

"No. Her ladyship kept a tight rein on her daughter."

"Why is that?"

Lewis didn't reply.

"Mr. Lewis, why did Lady Dalton feel she had to keep a tight rein on her daughter?"

"Why do you think?" Lewis sneered. "Because she was a comely young woman with a large fortune and limited experience of men. If debauched, she would be ruined, her chances of making an advantageous match forever destroyed."

"And do you think Miss Seaborne sneaked out to see a man?"

"This is the first I've heard of Miss Adelaide sneaking out, so I really couldn't say."

"Who could?"

"Maybe Elsie. She's the downstairs maid. She might have seen something, since Miss Adelaide wouldn't have left by the front door."

"I'll speak to Elsie next, then," Sebastian said. "Is there anyone in the household who resents Mr. Ahmad's presence more than the others?"

Lewis was clearly surprised by the question but answered nonetheless. "Everyone resents him in equal measure."

"Because?" Sebastian pressed.

"Because he's foreign. People who go into service to earn their bread live in fear of ending up in the workhouse if they're dismissed."

"What does that have to do with Mr. Ahmad?"

"If the master can bring in one foreign person, he can bring in another, and another, and pay them less to do the same job. The others simply fear for their positions and their future. It's really nothing personal. Mr. Ahmad is a decent sort," he added grudgingly.

"How do you know? Do you ever talk to him?" Sebastian asked.

"Not as such, but I can take measure of a man, and he's well-mannered and educated. To be frank, I don't know why he'd even want to be a valet. I'm certain he could find a better position back in India."

"I'm sure he has his reasons," Sebastian replied.

"Perhaps he can't go back," Lewis offered, his sneer implying that the valet might have something to hide.

"Perhaps not. Did the viscount ever express an interest in hiring more foreign servants?"

Lewis pressed his lips into a thin line of disapproval before finally answering. "He was considering hiring a new groom. He said these Indian fellows were good with horses."

"How would that affect the grooms already employed by the viscount?" Sebastian asked.

"Well, there's no need for three, so one would have to go, I suppose."

"Did the grooms know this might happen?"

"No. I was the only one who knew, and I didn't tell anyone. No sense stirring up trouble in the household."

"Mr. Lewis, were all the servants accounted for on Sunday night?" Sebastian asked.

"What are you suggesting?"

"I'm suggesting that someone who works in this house might have murdered Miss Seaborne."

"Why on earth would they?" Lewis exclaimed. His surprise seemed genuine.

"There are two good-looking young footmen whose affections might have been trifled with. And there are two grooms who might be in danger of losing their place. It's not impossible that they would follow Miss Seaborne when she left the house."

"And they would murder her and hang a pig's heart around her neck? I think you're reaching, Inspector," Lewis said, his disdain for Sebastian obvious.

"Perhaps the heart was meant to point a finger at Mr. Ahmad."

"I know you associate with the dregs of society in your line of work, Inspector Bell, but everyone who works in this house is decent and hard-working. I locked up for the night early on Sunday, and I can personally vouch for all the male servants. They never left."

"Do the grooms not sleep in the stable?" Sebastian asked.

"It's too cold to bed down in the stable. The grooms share a room in the men's corridor, and they were both accounted for."

"They might have left using the same door as Miss Seaborne," Sebastian said, "and returned without you realizing. Surely you sleep, Mr. Lewis."

Lewis shook his head. "I lock the door to the men's quarters at night so, unless they have a duplicate key, they can't leave."

"You lock them in?" Sebastian echoed. It was his turn to be surprised.

"Mrs. Henshall locks the women in as well."

"To what end?"

"When you have two dozen men and women who spend their days in the same house, Inspector, attachments form and inappropriate relationships often ensue. After a parlormaid got with child by a footman last year, Mrs. Henshall and I decided that nothing of that sort would occur again, not on our watch."

"I see. What happened to the two of them?" Sebastian asked, suddenly wondering if there might be a grudge of a different sort to consider.

"The pair of them were dismissed without a character. Normally, when such a thing happens, the troublesome young woman finds herself in the workhouse and the man takes whatever employment he can find, but this story had a happy ending," Lewis said derisively. "The couple married and left London. They now live near Leeds."

"Are you certain?"

"I am. Mary, the other parlormaid, is the young woman's sister, and they write to each other regularly."

"What are their names?" Sebastian asked.

"Percival and Anne Rowley."

Sebastian jotted the names down in case he might have need of them and asked one final question. "Is there anyone in this house who might have held a grudge against Miss Seaborne?"

Lewis's expression was one of quiet sincerity. "No one, Inspector. Miss Adelaide was well liked."

"Thank you. I'll speak to Elsie now."

TWENTY-FIVE

Elsie was about the same age as Adelaide Seaborne. She was also fair and blue-eyed and had an hourglass figure that no doubt didn't go unnoticed by the male staff. Sebastian imagined she would have been the toast of London society had her circumstances been different. She sat rigidly upright, her hands clasped in her lap as she studied Sebastian. She must have liked what she saw, because she smiled coyly.

"How can I help, Inspector?"

"If you wanted to sneak out at night, how would you do it, Elsie?" Sebastian asked, cutting straight to the chase.

"I would go out through the conservatory. There's a door the gardener uses when he comes inside to see to the plants."

"And is that door kept locked?"

"The gardener has his own key, but it can be unlocked from the inside. No one would notice if it were left open for a few hours."

"Have you ever seen Miss Seaborne go into the conservatory in the evening?"

"She weren't interested in plants," Elsie said with a knowing smirk.

"That's not what I asked."

"I saw her sneak out once," Elsie admitted. "I didn't tell no one and then fretted all night that if anything were to happen to her, I'd be blamed on account of keeping quiet."

"And now something has happened," Sebastian pointed out.

"It weren't my fault."

"Elsie, did you see Miss Seaborne leave the house on All Hallows' Eve?"

Elsie nodded.

"What was she wearing?"

"She were wearing a velvet cloak over her gown."

"Was she wearing a hat or a bonnet?"

"The hood were up," Elsie replied.

"How did she seem?"

"Giddy. She probably thought it were a grand old lark."

"So she didn't appear to be frightened?"

"Not at all."

"Is there anyone in the house who might have assisted in her escape?"

"I don't think so, Inspector. They're all too afraid of losing their place, and Mrs. Henshall and Mr. Lewis are not the sort to offer second chances."

"What about Miss Jones? Might she have been in on it with Miss Seaborne?"

"Never," Elsie said with a shake of her head. "Timid as a mouse, that one. She'd never do anything to compromise herself."

"What if she were threatened?"

"Who by?" Elsie asked. The possibility had clearly never occurred to her.

"By Miss Seaborne. It seems she wasn't above such manipulation."

"I wouldn't know nothing about that. Miss Jones is not one for sharing confidences." Elsie looked sullen. "Look, Inspector, I don't know nothing else. May I go now? I have work to be getting on with."

"Just a few more questions, Elsie. Did you ever see anyone else go out through the conservatory door?"

"Like who?"

"Like one of the footmen, perhaps."

Elsie shook her head. "No, never. And I'd know if someone went out and came back in. There'd be dirt on the floor."

"What about when Miss Seaborne went out? Was there dirt?"

"I cleaned it up before anyone saw. But there was no dirt come Monday morning. She never came back," Elsie said sadly. "Should I have told?" Her eyes were huge with fear and regret.

"From what I have heard, Miss Seaborne would have found another way to get where she was going," Sebastian replied.

"That's true," Elsie said, clearly reassured. "She didn't like anyone telling her what to do."

"Elsie, was Miss Seaborne friendly with any of the male servants?"

Elsie's mouth fell open. "You think she were carrying on with someone in this house?"

"It's important to rule out the possibility."

"No, not her. She weren't the sort. I don't think she ever really saw any of us. We were part of the furniture."

"What about Mr. Ahmad? Did Miss Seaborne see him as part of the furniture as well?"

Elsie made a show of thinking. "I think she were curious about him, on account of him being foreign. I saw them talking in the library once, when I went to sweep out the hearth."

"And how did they seem?"

Elsie shrugged. "Miss Adelaide seemed coy, and Mr. Ahmad looked like he'd rather be anywhere else, truth be told. He looked cornered."

"Thank you, Elsie," Sebastian said. "You may go."

"You're welcome. My afternoon off is every other Thursday," Elsie added, that playful look creeping into her eyes again. "And I'm not averse to showing a gentleman that's courting me a bit of affection."

"I'll keep that in mind," Sebastian said, and smiled at her. He had no intention of courting Elsie, no matter how pretty or willing she was, but she might prove useful yet, and he saw no reason to reject her outright.

"If you would ask Mrs. Henshall to come in," he called after her.

The housekeeper was a formidable woman in her mid to late thirties. Her hair was neatly pulled back beneath a black lace cap, and her bearing was that of a duchess. She sat across from Sebastian, her slanted green eyes watching him like a cat's. Sebastian didn't think she'd appreciate being questioned, but she would probably lap up a bit of respect, so he tried a different tack.

"Mrs. Henshall, as the housekeeper you know everything that goes on, both above and below stairs. Is there anything you feel I should know as I go about my investigation?"

Mrs. Henshall looked surprised, since she had no doubt expected to be interrogated, and took a moment to consider the question.

She sighed. "Most well-bred young ladies will do their father's bidding regardless of their own feelings, but Miss Adelaide was headstrong, and passionate."

She said the last bit with as much distaste as she would permit herself. To be passionate was a most undesirable quality in a woman of breeding, and any emotion besides that of wishing to please the men in her life had to be stamped out.

"What are you suggesting, Mrs. Henshall?" Sebastian asked.

"If you give someone enough rope, they'll hang themselves, Inspector."

"Are you saying that what happened to Miss Seaborne was her own fault?"

"Wasn't it? Modest, obedient girls don't find themselves hanging on a cross in a cemetery wearing nothing but their unmentionables. If his lordship had taken a firmer hand, she'd already be married and well on her way to giving her husband an heir."

"Was there anyone Miss Seaborne did not get on with in the household? Anyone she would have liked to see get the sack?" Sebastian asked.

Mrs. Henshall scoffed. "She didn't care enough one way or the other. As long as there was someone to see to her needs, she was content."

"What about Mr. Ahmad? I am told Miss Seaborne liked to converse with him."

Mrs. Henshall shook her head in obvious disapproval. "She made him uncomfortable. She was always cornering him and asking him questions. I think she enjoyed the power it gave her, since he couldn't very well refuse to speak to her."

"Were there any other men in the household that Miss Seaborne singled out?"

"She was very fond of Mr. George. Thick as thieves they were, despite the age difference. He's grieving something awful, the poor man."

"Thank you, Mrs. Henshall. That's very insightful. Do let me know if you think of anything else."

The housekeeper inclined her head in acknowledgement of her service and sailed out of the butler's pantry. Sebastian leaned back in the chair and sighed. He hadn't heard anything that would lead him to believe that what had befallen Adelaide Seaborne had originated in the house. Whatever had led to her death had happened after she left on Sunday night, and he would give much to discover where she had been headed and who had been waiting for her in the carriage.

Just as he stepped into the corridor, Sebastian came face to face with Lewis. The butler still looked angry, but now there was a note of wariness in his gaze.

"Anyone else you wish to speak to, Inspector?" he asked tartly.

It was nearly time for lunch, and some of the servants would be too busy to speak to Sebastian until the family was finished with their meal, at which point it would be time for the servants' dinner. Given that most of them had been up since dawn and hadn't eaten in hours, they wouldn't appreciate being denied a chance to rest and eat.

"Not at the moment, Mr. Lewis."

"Then I will show you out."

"I remember the way," Sebastian replied, and walked toward the door.

He breathed deeply when he stepped outside, glad to be free of the oppressive atmosphere of the house. The air smelled of loamy earth, decaying leaves, and smoke from the chimney pots on the roof. There was also the barely perceptible tang of straw and horseflesh, since Sebastian stood downwind from the stables located behind the house. The smell was oddly comforting, and he briefly recalled the horses on his parents' farm when he was a boy.

As he began to walk in the direction of Piccadilly, Sebastian reflected that, although being a policeman was a dangerous and often thankless job, he would never trade places with a domestic servant. To spend one's entire life catering to someone's whims, living by their rules, and dreaming of those two free afternoons per month had to be a fate worse than death, but of course, there were much worse alternatives, and death didn't always come quickly enough to save one from years of physical and emotional suffering.

TWENTY-SIX

Armed with the note Constable Haze had delivered, Gemma decided to start with the offices of the *Daily Telegraph*, since it would take some time to locate the omnibus depot and probably even longer to find the driver in question. The colleague who had identified Victor was Jacob Harrow, a well-respected correspondent whose features often strayed into the journalist's own opinion as much as they reported current events. He had a way of tapping into the readers' discontent, a talent that garnered him not only numerous fans but approval from the newspaper's editors, who appeared to care more about the publication's circulation than the reporting of unbiased news. Of course, the only person Gemma had been able to share her opinion with was Victor, since she could hardly admit to reading the papers or, worse yet, having an opinion on the articles. She had met Jacob Harrow once and would have been happy not to renew the acquaintance, but in this instance she had little choice.

Even though she had little money to waste, Gemma decided to splurge on a hansom and instructed the cabbie to take her to the Strand. When she entered the offices of the *Daily Telegraph*, she was greeted by nearly impenetrable cigar smoke, the scratching of nibs on paper, and harassed-looking men who had a deadline to meet. No one paid her much mind, so she asked the nearest man to point her in the direction of Mr. Harrow's desk.

"It's over there, but I doubt he'll see you," the reporter replied with a sneer. "You've no business here, madam."

"I have every business," Gemma replied.

She squared her shoulders and marched toward Jacob Harrow's desk, doing her best to ignore the curious stares and amused grins of the men, who no doubt expected to see her evicted from the premises at any moment. Jacob Harrow's dark head was bent over an article he was writing, his fingers stained with ink and a glowing cheroot dangling from the corner of his mouth.

Gemma coughed politely, and tried to look demure when he finally looked up. His gaze was distracted, his mind still on whatever he was working on, but once he recognized her the cheroot fell from his mouth, landed on the article, and promptly set the sheet on fire, forcing Mr. Harrow to put out the flame with his bare hands. Once he was sure his desk was not about to be engulfed by an inferno, he fixed Gemma with an inquiring look.

"Miss Tate, what are you doing here?" he asked.

"I am here to see you, Mr. Harrow," Gemma replied, moderating her tone so that her statement sounded less like a demand and more like a desperate request.

This man, who had called himself a friend, had witnessed Victor's death and had not even had the decency to call on her. And now he had the gall to look surprised, as if she had done something improper by coming to find him. Well, perhaps she had, but that was hardly the point. She needed information, and she was going to obtain it in any way she could.

"I only need a few moments of your time."

Jacob Harrow stubbed out what was left of his cheroot and

stood. Everyone was watching, some covertly, others with obvious interest. They didn't know who Gemma was, but it was apparent from the general reaction that few women ever set foot in this smelly, chaotic room, where unkempt men spun stories that gripped the public and often shaped the opinions of others with a mere turn of phrase.

"This way," Mr. Harrow said, and escorted Gemma to a small room furnished with four leather armchairs grouped around a low table. "We conduct interviews in here," he said as he closed the door behind them.

It was a relief to shut out the noise and the stench of the main room, and Gemma settled into a chair and set her reticule in her lap. Jacob Harrow sat across from her, tilted his head, crossed his feet at the ankles, and looked at her expectantly.

"Mr. Harrow, I apologize for accosting you at your place of business, but I need to know how Victor died."

Jacob Harrow exhaled loudly. "Miss Tate—Gemma—please let this go and remember Victor as he was."

Gemma shook her head. "I have tried to do that, but I need to hear about his final moments."

"And I'm trying to spare you the pain of having to imagine them," Jacob Harrow replied. "Please believe me when I say that I only have your best interests at heart."

"Mr. Harrow, please give me the credit for knowing my own mind," Gemma said. "Understanding what happened will help me come to terms with my grief."

"All right," Jacob Harrow said with the air of a man who felt greatly put upon. "What do you wish to know?"

"Did you witness the accident?"

"I did."

"Did Victor stumble, as they said?"

"I really couldn't say. I was some distance away. I saw Victor alight from the omnibus and walk forward. A few moments later, I heard the screams of the passersby and came running. Several people were kneeling beside Victor. They tried to offer assistance, but there was little they could do."

"Was Victor still alive at that point?" Gemma asked, her breath catching in her throat.

Jacob Harrow gave her a pitying look. "He was, but just barely."

"Did he say anything?"

"He whispered your name," Jacob Harrow admitted. "And then he muttered something about a fallen angel. I believe he was referring to Adelaide Seaborne."

Gemma didn't have to feign grief in order to get him to open up. Tears rolled down her cheeks as she imagined the pain and confusion Victor must have endured in those final moments. Death came for everyone, and, when all was said and done, every person did their dying alone, but it helped to have a loved one near, and to offer and receive those final messages of love and support that meant so much to both the dying and the bereaved.

Jacob Harrow handed Gemma his handkerchief, and she dabbed at her eyes before asking her final question. "Would Victor have lived had he received medical assistance at once?"

"I don't believe so. He was too badly hurt."

"Thank you for your honesty, Mr. Harrow."

"Miss Tate, will you be all right?" Jacob Harrow asked. "Victor did say it was just the two of you since the death of your parents."

"Yes, thank you. I will be just fine."

"If there's anything you require—"

"I don't," Gemma replied firmly. There was something duplicitous about the man, and she wanted nothing from him, save information.

"When is the funeral to be? I would like to pay my respects."

"I will be sure to let you know," Gemma replied.

"Will Victor be laid to rest next to his wife?"

"Yes. That's what he would have wanted."

"I will be there. And I really am sorry for your loss, Gemma."

"I never gave you leave to address me by my Christian name, Mr. Harrow," Gemma said as she stood to leave.

"Then please accept my apologies. I didn't mean to cause offense. I will see you at the funeral, Miss Tate."

"Good day, Mr. Harrow."

Gemma left the room and walked between the rows of desks toward the exit. She needed to get outside. This place oppressed her, just like the men in it, their hungry gazes scouting for a story, their pens setting down words that either belittled or magnified other people's pain depending on the angle of their story. No doubt they thought she was Jacob Harrow's paramour and would poke fun at her the moment she left.

The last desk in the row was unoccupied at present, but last night's edition of the *Daily Telegraph* lay open next to an ashtray that contained a smoking cigar. The headline screamed:

HELL'S ANGEL

The byline below read: By Jacob Harrow.

Gemma grabbed the newspaper, folded it, and stuffed it beneath her arm, to the obvious surprise of the man who occupied the desk opposite. He glared at her as if she were a thief, but she didn't care. She needed to know what Jacob Harrow had written about the murder, and Victor's sad part in it.

TWENTY-SEVEN

Outside, Gemma hurried toward the omnibus stop down the street. Several people stood waiting, one well-dressed gentleman checking his watch and tutting impatiently to no one in particular.

A newsboy occupied the corner, his young face animated as he bellowed, "Murder in Highgate. New details come to light. Read all about it." He took a deep breath and continued. "Latest penny dreadful for sale. Gruesome tale of bloody revenge. Get your copy before supplies run out."

The child was no older than eight, but he seemed to have a natural knack for salesmanship, and the papers went fast, nearly every man that passed stopping to purchase either a copy of the newspaper or a penny dreadful. Or both.

"Pardon me, but when is the next omnibus due?" Gemma asked the woman closest to her. She was middle-aged and very stout and wore a bonnet of black crape with a quilling of white silk that surrounded her round face like an old-fashioned ruff.

"'Bout twenty minutes ago, love," the woman said. She sounded dispirited. "They're never on time. When it comes, it comes. Just have to be patient."

"Thank you," Gemma replied.

It was cold and had begun to drizzle, the moisture coating Gemma's face and her woolen cape. She would have liked to take cover but couldn't afford to leave her post. Inspector Bell had provided her with a name but not any suggestions on how to find the man. The depot was likely located somewhere on the outskirts of London and would be both difficult and expensive to get to and from. Gemma thought there was an easier way, but her plan required patience.

It had to have been another quarter of an hour at least before the omnibus finally rolled into view, the tired horses ambling along as if they were on their last legs. As the conveyance came to a stop and the waiting passengers boarded, Gemma called out to the driver.

"Pardon me, sir, but are you acquainted with Mr. Otis Best?"

"Sure am," the man replied.

"Where can I find him? Is there a depot he reports to after his shift?"

The man shook his head. "Don't bother with the depot, miss. There's no telling when Otis will get there."

"So how do I find him?" Gemma asked as the man made ready to move on.

"Just wait. He should be driving the next omnibus."

"And how long will that take?" Gemma called after him. The man shrugged and turned his attention to guiding the horses back into traffic.

Taking refuge under a bookshop awning, Gemma tried to block out the shrill voice of the newsboy and huddled deeper into her cape, grateful that her mourning bonnet had a wide brim and protected her somewhat from the wind. She would have gladly gone inside and perused some of the newly arrived volumes, but didn't dare leave for fear of missing her chance to speak to Otis Best. The chill wind tugged at her bonnet and found its way beneath her cape, and her face felt clammy and numb, but Gemma ignored the cold. Desperate for something to do while she waited, she read the article Jacob Harrow had written, then offered the newspaper to a beggar who shuffled past. He probably didn't know his letters, but he could use the paper for more practical purposes when the need arose.

By the time the omnibus finally appeared, Gemma's feet were half-frozen and her cheeks were stinging with cold. The driver was an older man dressed in a mangy sheepskin coat and a brown slouch hat with a wide brim. His wooly muttonchops were streaked with gray, and his moustache obscured his mouth almost entirely, but his clean-shaven chin was as pink as that of a newborn babe. Dark eyes peered from between folds of sagging skin, and his bushy eyebrows were drawn together in irritation.

As soon as the omnibus came to a full stop, Gemma hurried toward the stop and called out to the driver. "Are you Mr. Best?"

He looked taken aback but nodded.

"Mr. Best, I urgently need to speak to you."

"I'm behind schedule as is," the man replied gruffly. "'Fraid I can't linger, ma'am."

It was obvious he had no wish to speak to her, so Gemma made a spur-of-the-moment decision.

"Then I will come with you," she exclaimed, and scrambled onto the bench, settling next to Best, who looked at her as if she had just sprouted a pair of horns and called herself the Devil. Scruffy as the man was, Gemma's proximity to the horses' backsides was even more alarming, and she drew back, afraid the horses would do something unspeakable and splatter her shoes.

"Ye can't be 'ere," Otis Best exclaimed. "'Gainst regulations, this is."

"The sooner you tell me what I want to know, the sooner you'll be shot of me."

"Shot of ye?" the man echoed. "Are ye mad, woman?"

"Not mad. Determined."

"What's this 'bout, then?"

He gave Gemma a sidelong glance, and she wondered if he was thinking how to best remove her, but the passengers were all aboard and were calling to the driver to get a move on. The men seated on the top deck were eyeing Gemma with interest, and someone at the back called out, "Just look at her. Bold as brass."

"I only need to ask the driver a question," Gemma replied politely, turning around to see who was yelling at her.

Another voice chimed in. "Off with ye, ye nosy baggage. Or ye'll soon find yerself on yer arse in the mud. Or worse."

Gemma ignored the threat and turned to the driver. "Mr. Best, the man that was trampled the other day was my brother. Please, I only want to ask you a few questions."

"Ask, then. Don't know if I'm of a mind to answer," the driver replied gruffly, then shot Gemma a sideways glance. "I'm sorry for yer loss, miss."

Gemma thought she caught a whiff of spirits on the man's breath and wondered if he was inebriated, but he appeared sober enough to answer her questions and to handle the plodding horses, which looked old and docile.

"What happened? Did he stumble?" Gemma asked, doing her best to heed Inspector Bell's warning and not ask the man outright if Victor had been pushed.

The driver shrugged. "Don't know, do I? There were a carriage gainin' fast on me left, so I were distracted-like. Didn't turn round till I 'eard 'im scream," he added apologetically.

Gemma flinched as if she had been physically struck when she realized that these were the very wheels that had crushed Victor and the horses that had trampled him. The breath caught in her throat, and she felt momentarily untethered, her mind unable to formulate the next question and put it into words.

Noticing her reaction to his words, the driver's expression softened, and Gemma thought she saw a glimmer of genuine sympathy in his eyes. He may not be at fault, but a man had been crushed to death before his eyes. That had to leave a mark.

"Best ye don't think on it too much, miss," Otis Best said. "No good will come of it. Consider it a mercy ye weren't 'ere when it 'appened. There's some things ye can never unsee," he added under his breath.

Gemma nodded and forced her attention away from the wheels. Her time was limited, so she had better ask her questions before they reached the next stop.

"Did you see anyone coming towards the man who died?" she asked, swallowing back the tears that threatened to choke her, then realized that this was just the sort of question Inspector Bell had warned her about asking.

"No," the driver replied.

"Did anyone try to help?"

Otis Best shrugged. "I were too busy trying to keep the 'orses from bolting to pay much mind to the injured cove."

The man probably knew nothing, and even if he did he wasn't going to tell her, Gemma realized. Telling tales not only lost jobs but sometimes cost lives, and it was entirely possible that he was drunk at the time of the accident and would draw attention to his own negligence by revealing the details.

The driver suddenly turned to her, his shaggy eyebrows lifting and his lips pulling back to reveal tobacco-stained teeth as he seemed to recall something. "Yeah, I remember now. There were one fellow as come to yer brother's aid immediate-like. I noticed 'im on account of 'is eye."

"What was wrong with his eye?" Gemma asked.

"Cloudy, it was," Otis Best said and seemed to shudder with the recollection. "The cove stared up at me, for just a moment-like, and it frightened me something awful."

"And his other eye?"

"Black as night. Never seen nothin' like it. I reckon 'e were blind in one eye."

"How peculiar," Gemma said.

"I seen old people 'ave eyes like that, but never just the one."

"And was he the only one who tried to help?" Gemma asked, wondering if the man with the strange eyes was the last person Victor had seen before he passed and if he had been kind.

The driver turned to Gemma, his gaze imploring her to listen to reason. "Let it go, miss. There ain't nothin' anyone could'a done for yer brother. I'm sorry to 'ave to say it so blunt-like, but 'e were a goner as soon as 'e fell. It were a mercy 'e died quick. Cling to that if ye need something to 'old on to."

"Can you tell me anything more about the man with the cloudy eye?" Gemma asked, ignoring the well-meant advice. "Surely you must have noticed something."

"Young, well dressed."

"Anything else?"

"What else is there?" Otis Best asked.

"Did you hear him speak?" Gemma asked.

The driver considered the question. "Yeah, I s'pose I did."

"How did he sound?"

"Posh. Like a gentleman."

"Were there any red marks on his face?" she asked, recalling Victor's entry.

"Not on 'is face, no, but 'e did have scratches on 'is neck. 'Bove 'is cravat."

Gemma opened her mouth to ask another question, but the driver maneuvered the horses toward the next stop and pulled on the reins.

"Ye get off now, ye hear? I've nothin' more to tell ye."

Gemma nodded, and carefully climbed off the bench.

The rain was coming down in earnest now, and she shiv-

ered violently. Rainwater found its way between the collar of
the cape and her skin and trickled down her back, and her skirt
was soaked. Another few minutes out in the open and her feet
would be wet as well. Seeing an approaching hansom, Gemma
raised her hand and called, "Please, sir. Stop."

The driver pulled over, and she climbed into the cab,
grateful to get out of the lashing rain.

"Where to, madam?" the driver called from his elevated
perch at the back.

Gemma gave him her address in Bethnal Green and leaned
back against the cracked leather seat. She'd go home, take an
umbrella and her shopping basket, then dash to the shops in
Bethnal Green New Road. Once back, she would await the
arrival of Inspector Bell, probably with a large medicinal brandy
close to hand.

TWENTY-EIGHT

Sebastian's first stop after leaving Park Lane was at Ellery and Mason Undertakers. Mr. Ellery was able to confirm that Adelaide Seaborne's remains had been collected from the mortuary and the funeral would take place Wednesday next, with Miss Seaborne being laid to rest in the family mausoleum. Until then, she would lie in repose at the house, where all those wishing could say their final goodbye.

"Mr. Ellery, the family is not to know that Miss Seaborne was autopsied as part of the investigation into her death," Sebastian said sternly.

"I quite understand, Inspector," Mr. Ellery said. He was a wisp of a man who was beginning to resemble his deceased clients in both color and facial expression, which seemed to be frozen in lines of agreeable servitude.

Satisfied, Sebastian was just about to leave when Mr. Mason stepped out of his office.

"We do not answer to the police, Inspector Bell," he said, having overheard Sebastian's request. Mr. Mason was an imposing man and clearly in charge. "I think the viscount would like to know what was done to his daughter without his express permission."

Sebastian stared the man down, giving him a moment to consider the ramifications, before speaking. "Mr. Mason, do you imagine that the family will continue to use your services if you inform them that Miss Seaborne was carved up by a Scottish-trained surgeon in his cellar while half a dozen students hungrily ogled her more intimate areas? There's nothing they can do to punish the police, not if they hope to keep the matter private, but they will punish you for causing them unnecessary pain."

Mr. Mason paled visibly, too much a man of business not to realize that Sebastian had a very valid point.

"I strongly suggest that you use your considerable skill to disguise any evidence of a post-mortem. I'm sure a high-necked gown or perhaps a lace fichu will do the job nicely. There's no need to cause the family any additional suffering. Are we agreed, Mr. Mason?"

Mr. Mason gave a curt nod. "Since you put it that way, I think that's probably the wisest course of action."

"I'm glad you see sense. Good day to you both," Sebastian said, and departed before Mr. Mason could try to extort payment for his silence.

Having seen to one unsavory task, Sebastian braced himself for the next. The St. Giles Rookery was one of the worst slums in London, a rat-infested, disease-ridden midden heap populated by whores, pimps, cutthroats, and the unfortunates who were too poor to ever hope for anything better. Had Sebastian still been in uniform, he wouldn't be likely to get out alive or still in one piece since the criminals and paupers alike blamed the coppers for all their ills. Likewise, few visitors walked away with their possessions intact. Sebastian took the coins out of his pocket and deposited them inside his boot. No self-respecting thief would allow him to get away with his pockets unpicked, but hopefully no one would try to rip the boots from his feet. The plan was to get in, question the Mahmoud brothers, and get out before dusk settled on London, not that the rookery was any safer during the daylight hours.

Sebastian turned up the collar of his coat and pulled his hat lower. There was little chance of someone recognizing him, but the dodgier he looked the better his chances of leaving alive. He strode down alleyways so dingy and narrow that light barely penetrated the gloom, the refuse-heaped streets fronted by dilapidated houses with broken windows, doors hanging askew on broken hinges, and crumbling steps. Some windows were covered with tatty sheets, but he could still hear the mewling of hungry babies and the vicious rows between the occupants, occasionally followed by the sounds of blows and muffled crying. Children, dressed in rags despite the cold, darted past like frightened mice, always on the lookout for unsuspecting strangers to rob.

The ground beneath Sebastian's feet was slimy with rotting vegetables, human and animal waste, and smelly mud. Several women ranging from fairly young to way past their prime called out to him, offering their services. A fair-haired girl no older than nine offered to pleasure him for a tuppence, while a boy who looked just like her but a little younger slipped his hand into Sebastian's pocket. To his disappointment, he came away empty-handed and uttered a word no child should know under his breath.

"Do you know Munk's Tannery?" Sebastian asked the girl.

"Two streets over," she replied, now indifferent to him.

Sebastian hurried on, following the awful smell of lime and dead animals. The tannery was a ramshackle structure with slatted walls, a muddy yard filled with vats of Lord-only-knew-what, and grim-faced men and women who were focused on their tasks. A squat man with a filthy apron tied around his ample waist and a cap pulled low over his eyes spat through a gap in his teeth and called out to Sebastian.

"Oi! What ye want 'ere?"

"I'm looking for the Mahmouds."

"Feck off."

"I only need to speak to them for a few minutes."

"Oh, yeah? It'll cost ye, governor," the fat man replied. He was either Munk himself or an overseer who delighted in wielding his limited power. He did have meaty fists, though, and Sebastian was sure that he used them liberally and often.

"How much?" Sebastian inquired.

"That's a fine coat," the man said.

"Like it would fit you," Sebastian scoffed.

The man glared at him. "Price just gone up."

"You're not getting my coat."

"Your boots, then. They's about my size."

"Try again," Sebastian replied, anger bubbling inside him.

"Seems ye don't 'ave much to offer."

"I'll give you my hat. It'll make you look even more handsome than you already are."

"Ye think?" the man replied with a smirk. "Give it 'ere."

Sebastian handed over his hat, which he'd acquired quite recently and was rather fond of, and the overseer called out to two men who were using long poles to stir something inside a stinking vat of lime. The third brother had to be doing something else.

"Hey, Moody," he called out to the older of the two men. "Someone actually wants to talk to ye. Two minutes or I dock yer wages."

"I want to speak to all the Mahmouds," Sebastian said. There was no way he could interview three men in two minutes.

"Two minutes," the overseer reiterated.

The older man approached Sebastian and looked at him with obvious mistrust. He was slightly built and wore tattered, soiled clothes, and shoes that were held together with rags. "What do you want?" he asked.

"I'm Inspector Bell of Scotland Yard," Sebastian said, keeping his voice low. "What's your full name?"

"Ibrahim Mahmoud."

"I need to ask you a few questions."

"What about?"

"I heard you've been harassed," Sebastian said.

"What of it?" the man asked with a shrug.

"Can you tell me what happened?"

"Why are you interested?"

"For a case I'm investigating," Sebastian replied.

"So, you are not going to do anything to help us."

"I'll see what I can do."

Ibrahim Mahmoud laughed mirthlessly. "Pardon me if I don't hold my breath."

"Mr. Mahmoud, you have nothing to lose by telling me," Sebastian said.

"Don't I? You think this conversation will go unnoticed?"

"No, but we are already speaking, so you may as well tell me."

"Someone threw pig's blood on our doorstep," the man replied. He sounded tired and resigned to dealing with unwarranted hatred.

"Is that it?"

"No."

"What else, then?"

"My brothers were pelted with pig shit. They want to drive us out. Take our jobs, such as they are."

"Who is the ringleader?" Sebastian asked.

"If I tell you, he'll kill us."

"Give me a hint."

"There's a gang that runs the rookery," Ibrahim said. "They're behind it."

"Have they ever harassed your women?"

"We don't have women."

"All right, have they ever gone after anyone else?"

"How should I know?" Ibrahim asked. "Look, I don't have anything more to tell you, and I have to get back to work. I can't afford to lose any pay. It's a pittance as is."

"Why does the boss keep you on if everyone wants you out?" Sebastian asked.

"Because he pays us less. He can do that because we're 'unchristian swine'," Ibrahim Mahmoud said bitterly. It was obvious that he'd heard the phrase a number of times.

The man walked away, his shoulders hunched against an invisible enemy. His younger brother didn't even look up from his work, probably too afraid to draw attention to himself. The overseer wasn't watching the Mahmouds, though. His gaze was on Sebastian, and his free hand was balled into a fist.

Sebastian approached the overseer and met his narrowed gaze. "What do you know of the gang that runs St. Giles?"

"I know I've got nothin' to tell ye."

"I am an inspector with Scotland Yard," Sebastian warned him, and snatched his hat from the man's meaty paw. "I can have this place razed to the ground."

"We're not afraid of rozzers round 'ere," the overseer replied with a smirk. "They's afraid of us."

Sebastian saw the arc of the man's arm out of the corner of his eye but didn't have enough time to jump out of the way. A closed fist slammed into the side of his head, and the world tilted. A dense silence descended on him, his reflexes as slow as if he were underwater, his vision dimming at the corners and shrinking to narrow tunnels of muted light.

Sebastian stumbled and nearly fell but managed to keep his balance. If his feet went out from under him, he'd be completely helpless, unable to get back on his feet as he slipped in the muck. Still, he seemed to lack the coordination to fight back, and a wave of nausea threatened to overwhelm him as he gulped the fetid air and knew with unwavering certainty that he would wind up in one of those vats if he didn't run.

The glint of a knife was all it took to bring Sebastian to his senses, and suddenly he was fully alert, his muscles throbbing with renewed energy, his survival instinct kicking in when his mind had yet to fully catch up. He took off, cutting through a dank alley to get to the other side as soon as an opportunity presented itself. There was no way the fat man could keep up with him, but there were younger, fitter men now after him, the pounding of their feet alerting Sebastian to their number. There had to be at least half a dozen, and if they caught him they'd end him, and they wouldn't be quick about it. Most predators liked to play with their kill before putting it out of its misery. It helped to satisfy the bloodlust that came upon men when they smelled victory.

Taking back the hat had been a stupid move, Sebastian admitted to himself as he bolted down a narrow street, but he really liked it, and he couldn't allow that bully to intimidate him. Besides, it was better that the thugs who were after him saw Sebastian as the target of their rage rather than the Mahmouds, but he was certain that another racist attack against the brothers was imminent, and it was his fault. He'd endangered them, and for that he was sorry, but there really was nothing he could do to improve their lot.

The pounding of feet grew closer, and Sebastian tapped into the last reserves of his strength to run faster. The only reason they hadn't caught up to him yet was because they had lost a few precious moments grabbing clubs and arming themselves with knives. The men were gaining on him, hurling abuse that seemed to bounce off the stone walls and roar in his ears. Sebastian hurled himself into a passing wagon as soon as he reached a major thoroughfare and yelled, "Drive, man!" before pulling up a moth-eaten blanket to cover himself. The wool was worn so thin he could see right through it.

The farmer who was driving the wagon must have seen the mob emerge from the mouth of the alley and realized he'd get a beating if he failed to get out of their way. He brought the whip down on the horse's rump, and the animal bolted, spurred on by pain and the instinctual need to avoid another blow. Given the amount of traffic, the men could have easily caught up with the wagon if they had realized Sebastian was hidden in the wagon bed, but they looked around helplessly, wondering where their prey had gone. Their profanity-laced diatribe faded into the distance, and the motion of the wagon and the ability to lie still afforded Sebastian the chance to catch his breath and acknowledge just how close he'd come to disaster.

"You can get out now," the farmer said once they were several streets away. "No one is after you."

"You saved my life," Sebastian said as he threw off the blanket and sat up. His coat was covered in straw and his hat had come off when he'd jumped in, but he was unharmed.

"Yeah, I reckon you owe me," the man said.

Sebastian removed his boot, took out several coins, and passed them to the driver. "I reckon I do," he agreed.

"Thank you kindly," the driver said as he examined the denominations. "I'll drink a pint to your continued good health."

"Can you take me a bit further?" Sebastian asked.

The farmer gave a nod, and Sebastian sank back onto the wagon bed.

He could hardly call on Miss Tate in the state he was in. He'd have to change out of his mud-spattered trousers, brush down his coat and hat, and wipe the muck from his boots before he set foot on her clean carpet. Mrs. Poole would have a thing or two to say if she saw him, but he hoped to get upstairs without encountering his landlady or Hank, who'd be sure to rat him out.

TWENTY-NINE

An hour later, and presentable once again, Sebastian took a hansom to Bethnal Green. The rain had stopped hours ago, and the sky was clear. A lemon-colored band of heavenly light stretched between the rooftops and the deepening blue of the approaching evening. The air smelled fresh and clean, and, as the carriage moved along at a good clip, all Sebastian could see was the beauty that so often eluded him. Perhaps it was his brush with danger, or the dose of tonic he had permitted himself before leaving the house, but he felt almost at peace, a sensation that was so rare it made him catch his breath. Moments like this reminded him that it was possible to move forward and, if he only waited long enough, maybe life would have meaning once again.

When Miss Tate let him in, Sebastian couldn't help but inhale deeply. She smelled of lavender soap and something faintly floral, but that wasn't what his nose had instantly reacted to. The heavenly aroma of meat made his stomach lurch with hunger. Once again, he hadn't had a chance to eat. He'd purchased jellied eels from a street vendor just before he set off for St. Giles, but that was hours ago. He was starving and hoped

Mrs. Poole would keep supper for him if he didn't get back in time. She refused to serve her lodgers after eight o'clock but still charged them for the meal.

"Do come in, Inspector," Miss Tate said as Sebastian handed over his coat and hat. "Have you eaten?"

Sebastian wondered if this was a trick question, then decided to answer truthfully. "No, I haven't had time."

"Well, that's rather fortunate, since I was hoping you would join me for an early dinner. I made mutton stew, and there's apple charlotte for after." She looked a bit embarrassed and hastened to add, "If we're going to be in this together, I think it's only natural that we should break bread together."

"*Are* we in this together?" Sebastian asked, surprised that Miss Tate seemed to view their association as some sort of part-nership.

"Well, of course we are," Miss Tate replied, clearly equally surprised that he didn't.

"Miss Tate," Sebastian began gently. "You are not part of this investigation."

Miss Tate looked as if he had just slapped her but quickly recovered her composure and jutted out her chin, her shoulders squaring defiantly in the process.

"Since I have some things to share with you, and I hope you have something to share with me, then I would argue that I *am* part of the investigation. And it's always more pleasant to converse over a meal, wouldn't you agree, Inspector?"

Sebastian sighed inwardly. He didn't want to encourage her in the unreasonable assumption that she was now his partner, but Miss Tate had something to tell him, and he wanted to hear it. And she had been kind enough to invite him to share her meal when she was clearly worried about her financial situa-tion. He could hardly throw her hospitality back in her face by continuing to dress her down.

"Yes, I would," he said at last, not quite sure if he was

agreeing that it was more pleasant to talk over a meal or that she was indeed a part of the investigation.

"Then please make yourself comfortable in the dining room."

The table was set for two, and Sebastian wondered if he had just taken Victor Tate's seat. It might hurt Miss Tate to see him there, or maybe it would bring her comfort not to have to dine alone, since she had specifically told him how much she disliked it. Miss Tate brought out a plate of thickly sliced bread and a bowl of buttered peas, then returned to the kitchen and came back with a covered dish containing the stew. It smelled even better up close, and Sebastian's mouth watered.

"May I serve you?" Miss Tate asked.

"Please."

She gave him a generous helping, then took a smaller portion for herself and added some peas to the side of her plate.

"May I pour you a glass?" Sebastian asked when her gaze settled on the bottle of wine.

"Yes, please," Miss Tate replied politely. "Victor was very fond of his claret. There are several bottles left."

Sebastian poured them both wine and set the half-empty bottle down before helping himself to a slice of bread. If anyone saw them like this, they would think they were a courting couple, or perhaps a somewhat awkward married pair who didn't have much to say to each other. He hoped the wine and the food would help in that regard.

"This is delicious," he said after swallowing the first bite. "Somehow, I didn't take you for a cook."

"Well, since Victor and I couldn't afford to hire someone to cook for us, it fell to me. I can competently make several simple dishes, but anything more elaborate ends in disaster."

"Miss Tate, what did you learn today?" Sebastian asked after they had been eating in silence for several minutes and she had not broached the topic of the investigation.

"More than I expected."

That surprised him. "Please, tell me."

Miss Tate set down her cutlery and looked at him in a way that tugged at his heart. Today had been difficult for her, that was obvious, and she was still reeling.

"First, I saw Mr. Harrow. He didn't tell me anything useful about the accident, but I did discover that his article about the Highgate murder made the front page of Tuesday's morning edition. And I read it," she said quietly.

"Was there something in the article that stood out to you?" Sebastian didn't know Gemma Tate well, but he knew her enough to realize that she wouldn't have brought it up without a good reason.

"Jacob Harrow seemed to know an awful lot for someone who wasn't present at the scene. And he referred to the victim by name when speaking to me."

"Did he? Did he name her in the article?"

Sebastian hadn't bothered to read the papers, since they tended to focus on the more lurid details in order to increase their circulation. Their morbid speculation was of no use to him, and he found that the tone often implied that the victim was at fault, which made him feel angry and helpless on behalf of the bereaved. And if Adelaide Seaborne had been named, Lovell would be spitting nails; losing the ability to control the release of information meant that he would have to deal with Viscount Dalton's fury.

"He did not name her outright in the article, but he did imply that the victim was of noble birth," Miss Tate said. "How would he have known that?"

"He wouldn't," Sebastian said. "She had not yet been identified at the time the paper would have gone to print. Was there anything else you noticed?"

"Not in the article, but I found the driver of the omnibus, Otis Best." Miss Tate sounded triumphant, so Sebastian laid down his knife and fork and gave her his undivided attention. "He said that he didn't see Victor fall, but he unwittingly provided proof that Victor was murdered."

"By doing what?" Sebastian asked, sitting up straighter at this pronouncement.

"Mr. Best said that a man had come to Victor's aid. I think it more likely that he simply wanted to make certain that Victor was beyond help and he could safely leave."

"What man? And how is coming to someone's aid proof of murder?"

"Mr. Best said that the man had one cloudy eye. The way he described it, it sounded like a cataract. But the other eye was normal. We thought that Victor had written 'Milky Way,' but I think what he had actually written was 'milky eye.' Such a defect is extremely rare and not easily concealed. Once Victor had seen the man's face, he would be able to recognize him again, if only based on that one trait. The driver also said that the man had scratches on his neck, and Victor had alluded to red streaks," Miss Tate announced triumphantly. "He wasn't talking about an astronomical event but the man he'd seen at Highgate Cemetery."

"Well, I'll be buggered," Sebastian said under his breath. Unfortunately, Miss Tate heard him and looked quite shocked. "My apologies," he hurried to add.

She smiled. "I've heard worse. But do you agree that this is significant, Inspector?"

Sebastian nodded. Victor Tate might have lived a long and healthy life had the man at the cemetery been blessed with normal eyes, even if Victor had noticed scratches on his neck. The scratches would heal in a few days, and no one would be the wiser if the man wore a scarf or a high cravat that covered the affected area. Although neither circumstance conclusively proved that the man had murdered Victor Tate, it did point to the likelihood that the same man had been present at both

Highgate Cemetery and the Strand at the time of Victor Tate's accident, which supported Victor's supposition that he had been followed. It was very possible that he had been murdered to keep the man's identity safe.

"Is it common to get a cataract in one eye?" Sebastian asked. He'd never heard of such a thing.

"I suppose anything is possible, but the driver said the man was young, so I would think cataracts unlikely," Miss Tate replied. "Perhaps the defect is a result of an injury. There was one patient at Scutari whose face was damaged by shrapnel. A piece got in his eye. Before the injury, both eyes had been blue, but the eye that took the shrapnel turned nearly black, since the shrapnel seemed to tear the pupil and distort it until it overtook the iris almost entirely."

"Was the man blinded in that eye?"

"Yes. There was no way to restore his vision."

"Poor chap," Sebastian said with feeling.

"At least he survived. Many others didn't."

"So our man could have been born with this defect, or he might have come by it accidentally," Sebastian mused.

"A defect like that would certainly set him apart," Miss Tate said. "At least we're civilized enough not to view it as a mark of Satan or some other form of devilry. But anyone born with a defect is always marked for judgment. There was one patient who had two different-colored eyes. One as blue as the summer sky, the other brown. It was extremely disconcerting, especially since he had rather a contrary nature and was scrupulously polite one minute and hurling insults the next. It was as if two separate personalities were warring inside him. The other nurses gave him a wide berth and said he was possessed. I think the head injury he'd suffered had unbalanced his behavior and caused him to lose control."

"Did he improve?" Sebastian asked.

Miss Tate shook her head. "He died of a hemorrhage."

"When I was a boy, I saw a child my age perform in a freak show. He or she—it was hard to tell—wore a loincloth, and its entire body was covered in hair. The man who kept it caged swore that the child was born to a human mother who'd been attacked by an ape, and he made the child act like a monkey. Everyone laughed and clapped, and I started to cry and asked my father to take me home."

"People can be very cruel, can't they?" Miss Tate said. "Sometimes even to their own children. The child's parents probably sold it to the freak show, either to spare themselves lifelong embarrassment or to monetize their child's rare condition."

"Probably both," Sebastian said. "I've often wondered what became of that child."

Miss Tate sighed. "As long as people are willing to pay to ridicule and taunt the poor creature, it will be forced to perform its trick."

"I expect you're right."

"More stew?" Miss Tate asked with forced cheerfulness.

Sebastian would have happily accepted another helping, but that would be selfish. Miss Tate could have the remainder of the stew tomorrow. She was clearly making small economies, since the room was chilly, only a few pieces of coal burning in the grate.

"Thank you, no."

"What about you, Inspector? What have you discovered?" Miss Tate asked, giving him a look that clearly implied that she hadn't forgotten their earlier disagreement.

"Nothing conclusive. Adelaide Seaborne sneaked out on All Hallows' Eve. Her maid thought she might be going to a séance. A black carriage waited for her outside the gates, but it bore no crest or any identifying markings."

"Was Adelaide Seaborne interested in spiritualism?" Gemma asked.

"I don't believe so. Based on what those who knew her said, she saw it as a bit of harmless fun and possibly a way to humiliate the medium by exposing their methods."

Miss Tate looked thoughtful. "I suppose a séance would seem amusing to a flippant young girl, but most people who attend such gatherings take them quite seriously and would be deeply offended by anyone who belittled their feelings."

"Have you ever been?" Sebastian asked. He couldn't see practical, efficient Miss Tate buying into all that nonsense, but people had many facets, especially when unbalanced by grief.

Miss Tate smiled ruefully. "Yes, once. I went with my mother after my father died."

"And what did you think?"

"I thought it a cruel, thoughtless parlor trick intended to prey on people who are heartbroken and desperate. I almost said as much, but my mother seemed to feel more at peace afterwards, so I held my tongue. Besides, no one likes to feel like they've been hoodwinked." Miss Tate fixed Sebastian with an inquisitive stare. "What about you, Inspector? Have you ever attended a séance?"

"No, I haven't."

But he had thought about it. In the days after Louisa's death he had wondered if he might be able to make contact. There was so much he needed to say, but he knew he couldn't do it. For one, he didn't really believe it was possible to speak to the dead, and for another, he couldn't bear to face Louisa, especially in a room full of strangers. In the end, he ended up pouring out his heart to her grave and hoped that if she was out there somewhere she'd hear him, and maybe forgive him.

"Was that all you were able to discover?" Miss Tate asked when the silence had stretched between them for too long. She seemed disappointed with Sebastian's lack of progress.

"Viscount Dalton's valet is an Indian Muslim," Sebastian said. He was curious what Miss Tate might make of that.

"Mr. Ahmad looked after the viscount on the voyage to England and has remained in his employ."

"Why is that important?" Miss Tate asked.

"People who are of the Islamic persuasion don't eat pork and consider the pig to be an unclean animal."

"Like the Jews," Miss Tate said.

"Yes. There have been a number of attacks on Muslim sailors who've settled in London. Pig blood and entrails were used to desecrate their homes or persons."

"But what does that have to do with Adelaide Seaborne?"

"I thought the pig's heart might be a warning to the viscount or a ploy to implicate the valet, but I have yet to find proof to support this theory. The members of the viscount's household openly resent the valet's presence, but, as far as I can tell, no one has threatened him with violence or has accused him of any wrongdoing."

"Do you know who's responsible for the other attacks?" Miss Tate asked.

"A few of the attacks were carried out by a gang in St. Giles, but I don't see why they would target the daughter of a viscount. Their attacks are more immediate and appear to be motivated by a desire to ridicule and intimidate."

"Perhaps the pig's heart was simply meant to insult and had nothing whatsoever to do with religion," Miss Tate suggested.

"Yes, I think you might be right. Whoever killed Adelaide Seaborne wished to desecrate her remains."

"So, what now?" Miss Tate asked. "What do we do?"

"*You* do nothing. I won't have you involving yourself, Miss Tate. I thought we were clear on this point."

"So I am supposed to pretend that my brother's death was an unfortunate accident again?" Miss Tate challenged him.

"Yes, that is precisely what you should do. Whoever pushed Victor under the wheels of the omnibus isn't taking any chances, so, if his killer realizes that you now know of the connection, he might decide to seek you out."

"And how would he realize that I know?" Miss Tate countered.

"How is not really the point."

"What is the point then?"

Sebastian sighed with ill-concealed exasperation. "Miss Tate, you're a sensible woman. Please don't pretend to misunderstand me. If the killer felt no compunction about pushing your brother beneath the wheels of an omnibus, think of what he might do to you."

He didn't want to spell it out for her or remind her what had been done to Adelaide Seaborne, but he would if she persisted in this foolishness. As much as he admired her determination and bravery, he feared them as well. Gemma Tate clearly didn't understand how precarious her position would be if her interest became apparent, more so because she was a woman. Sebastian genuinely worried for her safety and hoped that he had impressed that on her.

Miss Tate looked set to argue but must have seen something in his unyielding gaze and the firm set of his jaw that brought the point home. She nodded, albeit with obvious reluctance. "All right. I will do nothing. And you? What will you do?"

"Do you still have the newspaper?" Sebastian asked.

"No, I gave it away."

"No matter. I will have a chat with Mr. Harrow and ask how he came by the information."

"And?" Miss Tate asked. "Surely there's something else you can attempt."

"I prefer not to share my hunches until I've had a chance to test them out."

"You shared your theory about attacks on Muslim sailors," Miss Tate pointed out.

"Yes, because it came to nothing."

"Can't you give me a hint?"

"No," Sebastian replied with a smile.

"Because you think I will act on the information?"

"I think no such thing," Sebastian replied smoothly. "Because you gave me your word and I know you will honor your promise."

"Touché, Inspector. I'll get the pudding, then," Miss Tate said, and stood.

"May I help you clear away the dishes?"

"If you don't object to doing women's work," Miss Tate replied.

"I always helped my wife."

The words tumbled from his lips before he had a chance to stop himself, and he was grateful when Gemma didn't question him. She simply nodded and picked up the dish with the remaining stew. Sebastian collected their plates and cutlery and brought them into the kitchen, carefully putting them in the sink.

It was only once the charlotte had been cut and served and the tea poured that Gemma asked the question that had clearly been on her mind.

"How long has it been, Inspector?"

He didn't bother to ask what she was referring to, since he'd seen her steal a glance at his ring finger. "Nearly three years."

"I'm sorry."

"Thank you."

"Did you love her?"

That question took Sabastian unawares, and he choked up, finding himself unable to answer. He nodded mutely and hoped that Miss Tate would drop the subject, but it seemed she wished to know the details. It had to be the nurse in her.

"Did your wife die in childbirth?"

A part of Sebastian wanted to say yes and move on to safer topics, but something about this woman demanded the truth, and he couldn't bring himself to lie to her. It had been a long time since he'd spoken to anyone of Louisa. Longer still since he had admitted to the manner of her death and his part in it. It was like ripping open a slow-healing wound, knowing all the while that it would not only bleed but cause unbearable pain also. But the pain was always there, and some days it threatened to overwhelm him. If not for the opium, he might have taken his life by now, but the poppy dreams brought Louisa back to him, if only for a short while, and it was knowing that she would want him to go on that kept him walking when he crossed a bridge or stopped him from falling when he stood on a platform as a train chugged into the station. It was also the fear that he would forfeit his chance of meeting her in the afterlife. He had to live out whatever time he was given. Only then would they be reunited, never to be parted again.

"Louisa did not die in childbirth," Sebastian said quietly. "She was murdered, and our unborn child was torn from her womb."

Miss Tate's hand flew to her mouth, her eyes huge with shock. "Do you know who—?" she began, and Sebastian nodded.

"There were these two brothers, the Teagues. They were master cracksmen and came from the West Country in search of richer pickings. No safe was an obstacle for those two. After a two-year investigation, I was finally able to arrest Philip Teague, but his brother got away. My testimony sent Philip to the gallows."

The pity in Miss Tate's eyes was enough to break him, but he continued. Now that he had started, he needed to get it out. "That day, at the hanging, Jim Teague swore that he'd get his revenge, but I was fool enough to think he'd seek it against me, and I was prepared. What I wasn't prepared for was that he'd take it out on the one person I loved most in the world. He broke into our house a few weeks after his brother's execution, stabbed Louisa, slashed open her stomach and pulled out her womb and entrails, and wrote his name on the wall, using her blood. Colin Ramsey thought she was still alive when Teague left her. She'd managed to crawl towards the door, but no one heard her cry for help. She bled out in the corridor."

"Oh, I'm so sorry, Inspector," Miss Tate whispered. "Did you ever bring him in? Were you able to get justice for Louisa?"

"No," Sebastian said. "Jim Teague left London."

That was all the truth Sebastian could handle. He couldn't bring himself to tell Gemma Tate that he'd spent weeks obsessively tracking Jim Teague. He couldn't eat, or sleep, or return to the house he'd shared with Louisa, and often woke in a doorway or on a bench, cold and stiff, and unable to remember what day it was. He'd stalked the streets, until one night he had seen Teague coming out of a tavern near Aldgate. Sebastian had hit him over the head with a cudgel he carried, then carted his body outside the gates, taking him to the spot where the city's nightsoil men emptied their wagons of heaving piles of shit. Jim Teague had begged for his life when he came to, but nothing he said would have bought him another day on this earth. Sebastian had cut him open from heart to groin but made sure he was still alive when he tossed him on top of the stinking pile and watched as his entrails slid from his body, his lifeblood pouring from his abdominal cavity. Sebastian had stood there until Jim Teague breathed his last, then used one of the shovels to heap nightsoil over the body. There would be no Christian burial for Jim Teague, and no one to mourn his death. Ashes to ashes, dust to dust, and shit to shit.

Sebastian had thought that avenging Louisa and their baby would bring him some peace, but committing murder had made him feel even worse. That was when he'd first sampled the pipe, needing to escape from his anger and guilt, even for just a few moments. He'd lost days, sometimes weeks, as he lay in a semiconscious stupor on soiled pallets that reeked of other men's desperation. Eventually he had crawled back to the land of the living, but the damage had been done, and he had to live with his demons until it was his turn to bleed into the earth.

"Was there anyone to offer you comfort?" Miss Tate asked. She was watching him intently, and Sebastian suspected that she realized he hadn't told her the whole story.

Sebastian shook his head. "My parents died of typhoid fever before we married, and Louisa's family wanted nothing to do with me. They blamed me, and rightly so."

"With Victor gone, I'm completely alone," Miss Tate said flatly. "My employer, Mr. Gadd, offered me a live-in position, but I don't believe I will take it."

Sebastian didn't want to pry into her reasons, but, given the look of distaste that passed over Miss Tate's features, he could guess why she didn't see the offer as a promising opportunity.

"I can offer you Gustav," he said. "He is surprisingly good company."

"Excuse me?" Miss Tate stared at him, uncomprehending.

"Gustav is my cat. Well, he's not really mine. He belonged to a neighbor who died a few months ago. I thought he could keep you company. And he's very good at catching mice. He leaves me offerings nearly every day."

"Thank you, Inspector, but I don't think I want a cat just now. Why do you want to get rid of him if he's such a proficient hunter?"

"I think he deserves a better home than I can offer him."

"You rescued him, did you not?"

"Yes."

"Then you're bound to each other for eternity."

"If I would have known that then, I would have let someone else save him," Sebastian said, and belatedly realized that Miss Tate had been joking.

"I don't think I will be able to take a cat where I'm going," she said.

"Where are you going?"

"I will have to give up this house by the end of the month. I will find a respectable boarding house that will allow me to live within my means."

"I'm sorry," Sebastian said.

"Don't be. I have no wish to remain here by myself. It's too sad. At least in a boarding house, I will have some company. Perhaps I'll make new friends."

"I hope that you do."

There didn't seem much more left to say, so Sebastian thanked Miss Tate for the meal and wished her a good night.

"Will you keep me apprised of any developments?" Miss Tate asked as she walked him to the door and handed him his coat and hat.

"I will, but only if you keep your promise not to involve yourself any further. Miss Tate, I will have your word," Sebastian added with as much authority as he could muster when Miss Tate failed to respond in the affirmative.

She nodded resignedly. "You have my word, Inspector."

Sebastian would have liked nothing more than to go home, but it was still early enough that he could catch Superintendent Lovell at his desk, and he owed his superior a progress report. Lovell would not take kindly to not being kept informed.

Finding an empty cab, Sebastian climbed in and headed across town to Scotland Yard, wishing not for the first time that policemen had ready transportation at their disposal. As the conveyance rolled down the darkened streets, the clip-clop of hooves beating a rhythm and a soupy fog wrapping its gauzy fingers around the watchful city, Sebastian's mind couldn't help but return to the worst day of his life, and for a second he was tempted to tell the cabbie to take him to Mr. Wu's opium den instead. But unless he made a conscious decision to stop, he would remain in the thrall of opium forever. It wasn't the oblivion he would miss, but Louisa. It was only when he was nearly insensible, his body limp like a rag doll's and his mind free of its constraints, that he felt her near. Sometimes he even saw her face and felt her cool hand on his brow, and for those few moments of bliss he would have remained an addict forever, but Louisa wouldn't want that for him.

Sebastian's vision blurred as the cab passed very near to where they used to live, the foggy alley a murky portal to their shared past. He never got to say goodbye, not properly, had never told Louisa just how much he loved her, and had never held his son in his arms. Colin Ramsey had not permitted him anywhere near the body and had had Constables Meadows and Earnshaw restrain Sebastian until Louisa's remains were taken away. At least Louisa and the baby were together. That knowledge brought him comfort. They would sleep in eternal peace, blessedly beyond earthly pain and forever out of his reach as long as he still drew breath. He didn't think he'd ever love another woman or want to create another family, but, once this case was closed, he'd have to brave the unforgiving consequences of opium withdrawal and try to reclaim what was left of his life. He was through feeling sorry for himself, and, whether he went to America or decided to remain in England, he would do so a sober man.

THIRTY

After Inspector Bell left, Gemma locked the door, secured the windows, and applied herself to washing the dishes. She used the pump to pour water into a basin, then added hot water from the kettle to dissolve the grease. She worked mechanically, her mind on their conversation. Inspector Bell had been surprisingly forthcoming, but Gemma had the impression that sharing confidences didn't come naturally to him. She thought that perhaps he had needed to talk about his wife and had chosen Gemma because, once this case was over, they would never see each other again and there would be no painful reminders of shared intimacy. And she had been a nurse too long not to notice the symptoms of compromised health. There was the pallor, the slightly dilated pupils, the barely-there tremor in the man's hands. She didn't think it fair to jump to conclusions, but she thought that perhaps Inspector Bell had a tendency to overindulge in spirits, or possibly a fondness for opium.

Before the war, she would have judged him harshly, but now she could understand only too well. The desire for oblivion, no matter how short-lived, was a consequence of great stress, the mind's need to circumvent past tragedy in order to continue to function. Now that she understood the depth of Inspector Bell's grief, she felt only sympathy and understanding. If she didn't pride herself on stringent self-control, she might have happily joined him in his vice. Several hours of blessed insensibility would be most welcome at a time when she felt so frightened and alone. Since Victor's death she'd seen several men on the street who resembled him, making her heart leap into her mouth and her hands shake with agitation. Her mind reminded her that these random people couldn't be Victor, but the way they tilted their head, or walked, or pushed their spectacles up their nose to keep them from sliding down were unbearably painful.

Victor was gone and would soon be buried. Gemma hadn't bothered to order black-rimmed funeral invitations. There was no one to invite. She still had a few friends among the nurses who had come back from Crimea, but they were no longer close, and, although she would have given anything to have Miss Nightingale's support on what would be one of the hardest days of Gemma's life, she didn't think it right to impose on her mentor. No, it would be just Gemma, the vicar, a handful of mourners, and the casket containing her brother's remains. At least he would sleep next to Julia, something that in life he hadn't been able to do for too long.

Having finished with the dishes, Gemma retreated to the parlor and poured herself a large brandy. She might not have turned to opium just yet, but she was well on her way to drowning her sorrows.

THIRTY-ONE

Thursday, November 4

Sebastian inwardly cursed himself for a weakling. He'd missed Superintendent Lovell by mere minutes last night, but he had been just in time to join Sergeant Woodward and Constable Meadows for a pint, his earlier resolve to give up his vices forgotten, or at least postponed. He'd had no reason to hurry home, nor had he relished the thought of spending the rest of the evening alone, going over his conversation with Miss Tate and working on his newfound sobriety. It had been a long while since he'd enjoyed the company of his fellow officers and he'd needed a reason to stay a while longer before returning to his lonely room, so he'd matched them pint for pint.

This morning he had a splitting headache, and the light that streamed through the office window behind Lovell's head sliced into his eyes like a scalpel cutting into tender flesh. Sebastian made a supreme effort to focus his attention on the superintendent, who was in full flow and would need to indulge in a few more minutes of righteous indignation before he finally ran out of steam and was prepared to deal with the facts as they were presented to him.

"This is it? This is what you bring me?" Lovell demanded. "A man with a milky eye and a scratch on his neck? What am I to do with that, Bell? And what is this poppycock about attacks on Muslims? What on earth would that have to do with the daughter of such an esteemed personage?"

"It was important to rule it out, sir," Sebastian ventured.

"And have you ruled it out?"

"Until I can explain the significance of the pig's heart, I will not call myself satisfied."

"Satisfied?" Lovell bellowed. "Do you know who is not satisfied? The commissioner. And Alastair Seaborne. He expects an accounting at two p.m. From me," the superintendent barked, and waved a sheet of paper, presumably a summons from the viscount.

"I would be happy to go in your stead, sir. I have yet to speak to the viscountess."

"And what makes you think the lady will speak to you?" Lovell demanded.

"If she loved her daughter and wishes to see her killer brought to justice, then she will," Sebastian replied calmly.

"Sometimes I don't know whether to applaud your pigheadedness or to chastise you for it. Perhaps you're not suited to investigating anything that doesn't involve the hoi polloi or the scoundrels whose degeneracy is better suited to brothels and gaming hells."

"I hate to point this out, sir, but the brothels and gaming hells are heaving with—how did you put it—esteemed personages, as you well know. Wealth and breeding and depravity are not mutually exclusive."

"Don't speak to me of depravity, Bell. I know how you spend your wages, and God help me if you ever darken my door while under the influence. Get a grip on yourself, man."

"Yes, sir."

Lovell's gaze softened now that his anger had blown out. "I know you're still grieving, Sebastian, even though the official period of mourning is over. And I would be happy to tell you again that it wasn't your fault, and you mustn't blame yourself, but I know you won't listen. Take the time you need to mourn your loss, but don't lose yourself in the process. You're too good a detective and too intelligent a man to give in to such turpitude."

"Yes, sir," Sebastian muttered.

"I cannot continue to make excuses for you."

"No, sir."

"You either come up to scratch or you're out."

"Yes, sir," Sebastian replied, wishing only to be set free so he could continue with the investigation.

Investigating the deaths of people he'd never known in life was just work. He cared about the victims, wanted to see justice done, but there was no need to carefully guard his heart since those involved had no power to break it. The victims had others to mourn them. All he had to do was give the loved ones closure so that they could begin to grieve. And although there was a prescribed period of mourning based on the closeness of the relationship, no one could put a timeline on sorrow.

"May I go now, sir?"

Lovell made a dismissive gesture. "And don't forget to see the viscount at two."

"No, sir."

Free at last, Sebastian left the superintendent's office, walked around the corner, and followed the corridor until he reached the last door on the right. Inspector Ransome was composing a report, his dark head bent over his work. He'd just made an arrest and had dispatched the accused to Coldbath Fields Prison to await trial.

"Bell, what can I do for you?" John Ransome asked, his eyes

alight with curiosity. "Word is you're making a spectacular hash of the Highgate murder investigation."

"Have you been assigned to another case yet, Ransome?" Sebastian asked, ignoring the jibe. Ransome was a good sort, and a lot more intelligent than Lovell gave him credit for.

"Not yet, but I'm sure something will come in shortly. Always does."

"Can you do me a favor?"

"Depends on what it is," Ransome replied with a grin. "If you're after a mug of tea, make it yourself. You might even get a bun if you hurry."

"I don't want tea. I need someone to check the archives."

"For what?"

"Two things. Violent crimes against women on All Hallows' Eve, and anything involving a pig."

"A pig?"

"A pig, or any part of a pig."

"Does slapping someone with a sausage count?" Ransome quipped. "Because there are a few of those."

"No."

"And what constitutes a violent crime against a woman? You'll need to be more specific. A man can beat his wife to death, but most magistrates would judge him to be within his rights if he was sufficiently provoked, so that's out. And do whores count?"

"I'm looking for something out of the ordinary. Not a few slaps or a rough punter, but something that just doesn't sit right."

Ransome looked intrigued but shook his head and chuckled at the request. "All right, but if something interesting comes in, I'm gone."

"Fair enough. Just leave whatever you find on my desk."

"I'm actually glad I didn't get the Highgate case," Ransome said as he leaned back in his chair, clearly eager for a chat. "Too much at stake. If you get a solve, Lovell will take the credit. If you fail to make an arrest, you'll probably get the sack. Someone always needs to take the blame where the upper crust is involved, and it won't be Lovell or Commissioner Hawkins, you can be sure of that. They didn't get where they are by putting their own heads on the chopping block. What are you going to do if Lovell dismisses you?"

"I have a few options," Sebastian replied.

"I hope one of those options is not the workhouse. You do have something put by, don't you, Bell?" Ransome asked. "Of course, he might just demote you to constable, so you'll still get a living wage."

"Can happen to any of us," Sebastian replied noncommittally.

John Ransome smiled slyly, and his eyes twinkled with something almost devilish. "There's more than one way to get ahead."

"Oh?"

"Can't tell you yet, old boy. It's still in the works, but do make sure you have a plan in case things don't go as expected."

"I'll be fine, but I thank you for your concern. Now, find me those files."

"You owe me one, Bell."

"I'm good for it," Sebastian replied, and walked away. He had several hours until he was due to present himself in Park Lane, plenty of time to visit the offices of the *Daily Telegraph*.

The sun had retreated behind fluffy clouds, and the air was brisk and smelled of the hot pies that were arranged on a tray slung around a street vendor's neck, coal fires, hot cider, and the tang of the river. Sebastian's headache had dissipated somewhat, and he enjoyed the walk and wondered what Miss Tate was doing to occupy her time. Perhaps she was already searching for new lodgings, or maybe she would wait until after the funeral.

The newspaper office was a hive of activity: people calling out to each other, cigars smoldering in overflowing ashtrays, and the smell of wet ink overlaying the smoky air. There was always a sense of urgency in a newsroom, the sort that Scotland Yard never seemed to achieve, even though their business was life and death, whereas the newspapers only reported on issues that affected others. Jacob Harrow looked less than pleased to see Sebastian and tried to fob him off by claiming that he had constraints on his time. Sebastian dismissed his excuses.

"This is a murder inquiry, Mr. Harrow. I don't have the luxury of time and will not work on your schedule. Now, you can speak to me here, or we can have this conversation in a more formal setting."

Harrow's cheeks reddened with embarrassment, since several colleagues were within hearing distance of the exchange.

"As you wish, Inspector," he said, and led Sebastian toward a room that faced the back of the building. It was small and utilitarian, not the room Miss Tate had described, but it didn't matter. Sebastian wasn't there to be treated as a guest. He needed his questions answered, and then he'd be on his way.

"What do you wish to ask me, Inspector?" Jacob Harrow asked.

Sebastian leaned back in his chair and studied the man. Miss Tate had not commented on the man's character, but he had the impression that she didn't like Jacob Harrow. He could see why. There was something reptilian about the man, his gaze slithering over Sebastian as if he wanted to swallow him whole. Sebastian met many people in his line of work and had learned early on that every person was a lock that needed the right key. He thought Jacob Harrow was driven by self-interest, so it would be to that self-interest that Sebastian would appeal.

"Mr. Harrow, let's not waste each other's time unnecessarily," Sebastian began.

"Just now, it's only my time that's being wasted," the journalist retorted.

"Which is why I'm willing to make this worth your while."

"Oh?"

"A scoop in exchange for information."

"Do you have a scoop worth trading, Inspector?" Harrow asked, licking his lips in anticipation of a story.

"I have a theory about the murder that needs bearing out. Help me fill in the blanks, and you will have your story."

Jacob Harrow was visibly disappointed. "Whatever your theory, I'm almost certain it's wrong."

"How can you be so sure?"

"Because you're not the only source that's available to me," Harrow boasted.

"Is that how you knew the identity of the Highgate Cemetery victim before the police?"

Harrow pursed his lips and refused to answer, his gaze boring into Sebastian with ill-disguised mistrust.

"How is it that you happened to be present at the scene of Victor Tate's accident?" Sebastian asked. He preferred to keep his cards close to his chest until he was ready to share anything.

"I was on my way to work. Surely you occasionally run into other policemen when approaching Scotland Yard."

"I do, but most of them manage to live through the day."

"Lucky for them."

"Did you see what happened?" Sebastian asked.

"Why are you asking me about Victor? I thought you were here to talk about the 'Angel.'"

"In due course," Sebastian replied. "Did you see Victor Tate fall?"

"From a distance. I didn't see exactly what happened. I assumed he'd stumbled. Victor was frequently lost in thought. He might have simply tripped as a result of not paying attention."

"Was anyone next to him when he fell?"

"I really couldn't say."

"And when you reached the scene of the accident, was there anyone trying to help him?"

"There were several people, but it was too late. He was too gravely injured to bother with a doctor. He died a few moments later."

"Did you happen to notice a man with a milky eye who had scratches on his neck?" Sebastian asked. He was watching Harrow intently, and it paid off. The reaction was momentary. A brief widening of the eyes, a shifting of the gaze away from Sebastian's face, a hand going to the knot in his tie. Probably a nervous gesture.

"No, I didn't."

"Are you certain?" Sebastian pressed.

"It all happened so quickly."

"Mr. Harrow, I think we had better continue this conversation at Scotland Yard."

"On what grounds?" Harrow demanded angrily.

"On the grounds of you lying to me."

"What makes you think I'm lying?"

"You're not the only one that relies on other sources. Shall we?" Sebastian asked as he made to rise.

"All right, all right," Jacob Harrow said, holding up his hands in a gesture of surrender. "There was a man that fits that description."

"Who is he, Mr. Harrow?"

"How should I know?" Jacob Harrow's tone bordered on belligerent, and Sebastian welcomed his hostility. It meant that he was on the right track.

"If you didn't know, then you wouldn't bother to deny his presence at the scene."

"You're like a dog with a bone, aren't you!" Harrow exclaimed. A flush was spreading up his neck, and his gaze kept sliding toward the door. Sebastian was in no doubt that Jacob Harrow longed to escape this closed room and get away from the interrogation.

"Obstruction is a crime, Mr. Harrow," Sebastian reminded him.

"His name is Thomas Wright. His father is Jonathan Wright."

"The MP?"

"The very one," Jacob Harrow confirmed.

"So why wouldn't you just tell me that?" Sebastian demanded.

Harrow looked away, his gaze fixed on something beyond the window. His leg shook nervously, and he was drumming a tattoo on the arm of the chair.

"Jonathan Wright is one of your sources," Sebastian concluded. "And you don't want the relationship to sour."

"I have to earn a living, Inspector. If Mr. Wright discovers that I set you on the trail of his son, who happens to be a friend, he might choose another journalist to confide in."

"I see. And do you have reason to suspect that Thomas Wright was not there by accident?"

"I don't know, but he didn't acknowledge our acquaintance, which leads me to believe that he preferred to remain anonymous. Thomas fled as soon as Victor Tate breathed his last."

"Do you happen to know where Thomas Wright lives?"

"No, but you can probably find out at his club. It's the Oxford and Cambridge Club in Pall Mall."

"Are you a member?"

"I didn't have the privilege of attending such a prestigious college. His father mentioned it. He's a member as well."

"Thank you, Mr. Harrow," Sebastian said, and pushed to his feet.

"Now, give me that scoop you promised," Harrow

demanded. He was visibly relieved that the interview was over, and his mind appeared to be on his next journalistic coup.

Sebastian shook his head. "I'd rather give a helping hand to someone who's more willing to return the favor."

"You bastard," Jacob Harrow hissed. "You will live to regret toying with me. You can be sure of that."

"Good day, Mr. Harrow," Sebastian said, and left.

THIRTY-TWO

The Oxford and Cambridge Club was housed in an imposing Greek Revival-style building in Pall Mall. It boasted unblemished white walls, Corinthian columns, wrought-iron railings, and friezes above the sash windows of the top floor that probably depicted some heroic scenes but were difficult to make out when looking up from the street. Sebastian imagined that the rooms within were expensively and comfortably furnished and that the dining room served old favorites as well as some newfangled dishes for its more adventurous members. He'd never get to find out, since he'd never get past the door.

The retainer manning the front desk was an older man, dressed like a butler and just as righteous. His lip curled and his nostrils flared as soon as Sebastian entered the vestibule, and he actually emerged from behind his desk and stood in front of Sebastian, barring his way.

"Members only, I'm afraid," the man said, his tone gratingly nasal.

Sebastian held up his warrant card. "Inspector Bell of Scotland Yard. And you are?"

"Alfred Barrington."

"Mr. Barrington, I would like to speak to one of your members. Mr. Thomas Wright."

"Mr. Wright is not in attendance at present."

"Perhaps I should check for myself," Sebastian replied.

"That is quite out of the question, Inspector," Mr. Barrington bristled. "I can assure you that Mr. Wright has not visited us in several days."

He was still blocking the way, and Sebastian wondered if the man would really go so far as to tackle him if he tried to get past. There seemed little point in resorting to an altercation. There were other ways to discover what he needed, and they were just as effective. If there was anything he'd learned from his years in the police service, it was that the upper classes and those who served them would go to great lengths to avoid anything that might result in unpleasantness or any hint of scandal, and would be willing to give the police whatever they needed as long as it got them to leave quietly.

Likewise, the higher-ups in the police did not wish to irritate those who had the power to destroy them and tended to tread carefully when dealing with persons and institutions wielding both personal and political power. Any number of people within the walls of the club had the ability to make Lovell's and in turn the commissioner's life a misery, and they wouldn't thank Sebastian for bringing trouble to their door.

"Since Mr. Wright is not here, I'd like to ask *you* a few questions, Mr. Barrington," Sebastian said in what he hoped was a placatory tone.

"And I will answer them to the best of my ability, but I cannot allow you to come inside."

"I understand," Sebastian conceded. The man took a step backward, but he would no doubt pounce if Sebastian attempted to get past him. "When was the last time you remember seeing Thomas Wright?" Sebastian asked.

"I can't recall."

"Perhaps you fail to recall that you saw him today."

"He is not here, Inspector Bell."

"Is that the sign-in book?" Sebastian asked, spotting a leather volume resting on a scrolled lectern near Mr. Barrington's desk.

"You cannot look at that. The names of the members are private."

Mr. Barrington did his best to look down his nose at Sebastian, but that was difficult to do when the person one was trying to insult was a head taller. Sebastian decided that he'd wasted enough time on pleasantries. It was time to remind the gatekeeper what would happen if he refused to cooperate.

"Mr. Barrington," Sebastian said smoothly, "I can return with a dozen constables and invade this fine oasis of snobbery, searching every nook and cranny until I find what I'm looking for. Or you can allow me to quietly look at that book and provide me with Mr. Wright's address. He need never know you were the one to hand it over."

Mr. Barrington looked like he was going to be ill, but, having considered his options, he nodded curtly. He was clever enough to know when he was beaten and to opt for the least public solution. "Fine, you win, but you can't look at the book here. You might be seen."

"I would be happy to relocate to a more private area."

"Follow me," Mr. Barrington hissed, and escorted Sebastian to a small office off the vestibule, the sign-in book under his arm. He slapped the book on the desk, then turned to a row of filing cabinets set against the back wall. Sebastian wasn't invited to sit, but he made himself comfortable, nonetheless, and opened the book to the current date.

There were only about a dozen names, and none of them were Wright. He then went backward, scanning each page for Thomas Wright's name. Mr. Barrington had been telling the truth when he said that Thomas Wright had not visited the club in the past few days. His name did not appear until Sebastian got to October 31, and the time of his arrival was identical to the person whose name was before his. It would seem they had arrived together and left within a few minutes of each other.

"This gentleman here," Sebastian said, pointing to the name above Wright's. "Did he accompany Mr. Wright, or did they just happen to walk in at the same time?"

"The gentlemen arrived together. They're close friends and often dine together," Mr. Barrington hurried to confirm, most likely believing that he was giving Thomas Wright an alibi.

"Is it normally just the two of them?"

"Not always. They're part of a bigger group. Most of our members know each other from their university days, hence the purpose of the club," he added spitefully. To his mind, a policeman couldn't possibly be university educated or under-stand the bonds of brotherhood.

Sebastian didn't bother to disabuse him of his prejudices. Instead, he turned his attention back to the register and leafed through the month of October, making a note of Wright's comings and goings.

"Do you have that address for me, Mr. Barrington?" he asked once he was finished.

The man consulted the list he'd taken out of a cabinet, found the entry he was looking for, and copied out the address. Sebastian was tempted to ask to see the full list of members, but changed his mind. At this moment he had what he needed, and there was no point in antagonizing the man further. He could always come back if the situation called for it. Sebastian pock-eted the address while Mr. Barrington snatched up the sign-in register and held it to his chest as if it were a holy relic.

"I trust we won't be seeing you again, Inspector."

"You may trust no such thing, Mr. Barrington. Thank you for your assistance."

Sebastian slipped the sheet of paper into his pocket, tipped his hat to Mr. Barrington, and left the club. Once outside, he had a decision to make. He could head to Wright's home, but he had no reinforcements, no cuffs, and, if anything happened to him, no one would know where he had gone or what he had discovered. Confronting Wright unprepared would be foolish in the extreme. Instead, Sebastian decided to return to the Yard.

"Back so soon?" Sergeant Woodward asked when Sebastian entered the building.

Sebastian placed the paper with the address on the counter. "I need Thomas Wright, who resides at this address, to be picked up and brought in for questioning. I should be back around four."

"What are we to do with him in the meantime?"

"Put him in the cells. I seriously doubt he'll be going home once I'm done with him."

"Is this the cove who's done for Miss Seaborne?" Woodward asked, clearly awed. "Lovell will hand you a promotion and a hefty pay rise if you bring in the killer in under a week."

"Let's not count our chickens before they hatch, Sergeant," Sebastian replied. "Right now, Wright is a suspect. Whether I have enough to charge him remains to be seen. And I don't want the press to hear about this."

Sergeant Woodward tapped the side of his nose. "Understood. Those double-dealing newshounds won't hear a word from me."

"Has Constable Meadows confirmed Lord Mayhew's alibi?"

"He has. Mayhew is accounted for. Is he an acquaintance of our Mr. Wright?" Sergeant Woodward asked.

"I believe he is," Sebastian replied. He made a gesture of farewell as he headed out to Park Lane.

THIRTY-THREE

Feeling unreasonably defiant after his visit to the gentlemen's club, Sebastian presented himself at the Seabornes' front entrance. The double door was adorned with black crape bows, and the curtains in all the ground-floor windows were drawn, making them look like closed eyes. From the outside, the manor had an air of abandonment, as if everyone had suddenly left, but that was often the feeling one got from a house in mourning.

Sebastian was gratified by the apparent shock on Lewis's face when a footman, who now wore a black armband, answered the door and invited Sebastian into the foyer.

"Tradesmen call at the back," Lewis reminded Sebastian as he strode toward him.

"I'm not a tradesman, and the viscount is expecting me," Sebastian snapped.

"The viscount is expecting Superintendent Lovell."

"He's unavailable at present. Are you going to announce me, or should we quibble a while longer?"

"You're insolent, sir," Lewis snapped.

"So I've been told," Sebastian said, and handed his coat and hat to a passing maidservant.

She was dressed in black in observance of Adelaide Seaborne's passing. She hurried off without meeting Sebastian's gaze. Inside, the house had the sorrowful air of a home that had lost its heart, the clock on the drawing room mantel silent and the mirrors swathed in black. A salver containing several black-bordered envelopes held condolence cards, and the vase that had held a colorful arrangement of flowers on his first visit now stood empty and resembled a bucket.

"Viscount Dalton will see you now," Lewis announced when he returned, and bid Sebastian follow him.

This time, the viscount was in his study, a well-appointed room with an intricately carved mahogany desk, chairs uphol-stered in butter-yellow damask, and bookshelves filled with well-thumbed volumes. Several silver-framed photographs were arranged on the mantel, an oil painting of a pleasant country scene hung on the wall, and yellow damask curtains with ties of gold braid framed the tall windows that overlooked the still-green lawn. The carriage clock on the mantel stood silent, and the man behind the desk was dressed in mourning attire, his eyes shadowed by grief and obvious fatigue.

"I was told the superintendent is unavailable to speak to me," the viscount said warily.

Sebastian thought that the viscount had tried to rouse himself to anger but, now that the reality of his daughter's death had sunk in, what Sebastian saw before him was a husk of a man, his innards gutted by loss and pain. Not all parents loved their children, but this man had obviously cherished his daughter and would never fully recover from her untimely passing.

"Superintendent Lovell thought it best if you hear the news from the man who's actually investigating the case."

"Did he, indeed? Well, let's hear what you have to say, Inspector." The viscount gestured toward a chair, and Sebastian settled across from him. "What have you learned?"

"Miss Seaborne left this house, most likely by way of the conservatory, after dinner on Sunday to attend an All Hallows' Eve séance. A carriage was seen waiting for her by the gates. It is my belief that she knew the person who'd come to collect her and got into the carriage willingly."

"And then?" the viscount asked. He didn't seem overly surprised by his daughter's antics.

"She was taken somewhere, where she was murdered."

"You don't believe Addie was killed at the cemetery?"

"I saw nothing at the scene to support that assumption. It had rained that night, but Miss Seaborne's hair and chemise were dry when she was discovered. I believe she was brought to the cemetery just before opening time."

"Because the killer wanted her to be found."

"It would seem so. Is there anyone who bears you a grudge, my lord?" Sebastian asked.

"Enough of a grudge to murder my daughter?" the viscount asked, his disgust glaringly obvious. "No one I know is that depraved, Inspector."

"But is there anyone who comes to mind?" Sebastian pressed.

Viscount Dalton shook his head. "I have always done my best to be good to those around me, be they a gentleman or a servant. And I've tried to turn the other cheek when people have wronged me. I can't think of a single person who'd bear me such malice."

"What about your son? Might someone have wanted to revenge themselves on Mr. Seaborne?"

"George is a good man, Inspector. He has a close-knit group of friends, and he has always been a respectful and obedient son. He has never involved himself in a relationship with either an unwilling or a married woman, and I wholeheartedly approve of his choice of bride. There's nothing in our family history that would warrant an attack on Adelaide."

"Might Mr. Seaborne have resented the portion you had settled on Miss Seaborne?" Sebastian asked carefully. It was an incendiary question, but it needed to be asked.

The viscount shot Sebastian a sharp look but kept his anger under control. "I consulted George before settling on a sum, since he would be the one to administer the annual payment once I'm gone, and he wholeheartedly agreed with the amount I proposed. You can verify this with my solicitor, since he was present for the conversation, should my word on the matter not be sufficient." The viscount's gaze became searching. "What about David Parker and Oliver Mayhew? Could my daughter have become a pawn in a rivalry for her affections?"

"Unless either man paid someone to kidnap and murder your daughter, they're in the clear. And frankly, I can't see why they would resort to such savagery. To kill someone in a fit of passion is one thing, but to plan such a vicious and elaborate attack is something else entirely and seems completely at odds with the relationship these men had with Miss Seaborne and what I have observed of their natures."

"So you have nothing," the viscount said. His shoulders seemed to droop even lower as he sagged in his massive chair.

"I am exploring several possibilities and would like to ask you a few more questions, if you would bear with me for a few more minutes."

"All you do is ask questions," the viscount grumbled.

"That's the job, my lord. I ask questions until the answers begin to make sense and arrange themselves into a discernable pattern."

Viscount Dalton made a vague gesture with his hand. "Ask what you will, Inspector. At this juncture, I have nothing but time."

"Do you have any other children?"

George Seaborne had stated that he didn't have any siblings

besides Adelaide, but that didn't mean that his father didn't have children George didn't know about. Titled men were known to sire children on their mistresses and sometimes even on members of the household staff. Such an illegitimate child might, as they often did, nurse a deep resentment not only toward their father but toward their legal heir, and might wish to seek retribution.

"I do not have any other children," the viscount stated flatly.

"Are you certain?"

"Yes, I'm certain. Why should that matter? Did you think Addie was murdered by a disgruntled by-blow?"

"It's not impossible. And I need to make certain that your remaining heir is not in danger."

"George can take care of himself. He frequents a gymnasium, and meets with a fencing instructor twice a week."

"I'm glad to hear that," Sebastian said. "Why do you employ Mr. Ahmad as your valet?"

"What relevance does that have to Addie's death?" the viscount demanded. It was obvious that the question had taken him by surprise, as it was meant to.

"I thought that the pig's heart strung around Miss Seaborne's neck might have something to do with the killer's animosity toward either Jews or the followers of Islam."

"That's absurd," the viscount exclaimed, having clearly come to the end of his patience. "If this is the focus of your investigation I'm going to request that you're taken off the case, since you're clearly blundering in the dark. Surely Superintendent Lovell can find a more capable man, one who can separate the wheat from the chaff and concentrate on the facts, instead of these random suppositions that not only lead nowhere but waste precious time, giving my daughter's killer a chance to cover his tracks." The viscount's face had turned an angry red, and his eyes blazed with determination. This part of the investigation was the one thing he could still control, and he seemed firm in his resolve to have Sebastian replaced.

Sebastian could understand how Viscount Dalton felt and had seen this sort of reaction many times before. The man was angry, frustrated, and riddled with guilt, incessantly going over every decision he had undertaken and every mistake he might have made that had led to this outcome. He needed to feel that he was doing something to apprehend his daughter's killer, even if that meant meddling in the investigation and abusing his position.

Sebastian moderated his tone and addressed the aggrieved man. "My lord, I understand how painful this is for you, and, of course, it is your prerogative to have me removed from the case, but any detective worth his salt will ask the same questions if he hopes to get to the truth."

"Will he?" the viscount challenged him.

"He will, unless he decides to fit someone for the crime and closes the investigation, in which case the person who murdered your daughter will remain at large, free to enjoy his life without fear of discovery. If you bear with me, you have my word that I will get to the bottom of this."

"I would like to believe that, Inspector Bell, but your insinuations border on impertinent and your conspiracy theories are quite fantastical. First you accuse me of siring murderous bastards, and now you think my daughter was part of some misguided plot against non-Christians?"

Despite the unfairness of the accusation, Sebastian bit back the retort that sprang to his lips. No man or woman liked to be confronted with their indiscretions, especially by someone they considered socially inferior, nor could they bear to think that something they had done had resulted in the death of their child. The viscount was clinging to the last vestiges of control, desperate to protect his privacy and peace of mind, but questions had to be asked and secrets had to be revealed if they hoped to learn the truth.

"Impertinent as it might seem, it would be remiss of me not to explore every angle, if only to rule out the possibility and whittle down the list of suspects. And as for the plot against non-Christians, it would sound far-fetched if this house didn't have a connection to Islam, however tenuous it may be."

The viscount inclined his head in what could be acquiescence, but Sebastian had to be certain.

"Do I have leave to continue, my lord?" he asked.

"You are abrasive and dogged in your manner, Inspector Bell, but perhaps these qualities are necessary in your profession. You may continue, and I will answer your questions, for Addie's sake."

"Thank you, sir," Sebastian said, relieved that he wasn't about to be tossed out on his ear, particularly since he was about to annoy the viscount further. "May I?"

He stood and walked toward an occasional table situated in a cozy alcove furnished with comfortable armchairs, picked up the book that rested on the table and returned to his seat. The viscount paled.

Sebastian opened the book, scanned the first few pages, then closed it and set it on the desk. "This is a very beautiful edition."

"Do you even know what it is?" the viscount demanded furiously.

"It's the Qur'an, translated into English by Alexander Ross."

"How do you know who translated it? Have you seen it before?"

"It says so on the flyleaf. Are you a follower of Islam, my lord?"

"I have not converted, no. The Qur'an was a gift from a

friend who studied Islam while serving in India and embraced some of its practices. I confess, I find it fascinating, and I have enjoyed several engrossing discussions with Mr. Ahmad. I thought that reading certain passages might bring me comfort; that's the reason you found the Qur'an on display."

"You still haven't told me why you decided to employ an Indian lascar when there's no shortage of well-trained English valets," Sebastian reminded him.

"Is that a crime, Inspector?"

"No, but it is unusual. Mr. Ahmad told me that your valet became ill on the return voyage. You could have easily replaced him once you arrived at home."

"Yes, I could have, but I had developed a rapport with Mr. Ahmad and thought he deserved a chance at a better life."

"And is this a better life?"

"I think so, but he had always been free to leave. I would have paid for his passage back to India if he had expressed a desire to return home. It was my understanding that he had nothing to go back to."

"What were you doing in India, my lord?" Sebastian asked.

"I went to see my brother," Viscount Dalton said. "Robert was wounded during the Second Anglo-Burmese War. He was in a hospital in Prome, then was transferred to Fort William in Kolkata. I had hoped to persuade him to resign his commission and come home."

"Where is he now?"

"Robert died in 1854. Of a snakebite, of all things."

"I'm sorry," Sebastian said.

"So am I. I miss him. Still, I don't see what all these questions have to do with my daughter's death. It's hardly a felony to take an interest in other faiths or to employ a non-English valet."

"I thought that perhaps there was someone who was aware

of your interest in the Islamic faith and wanted to send you a message."

"Like who?" The viscount looked troubled, and his gaze kept straying to the volume on his desk.

"Someone who finds it objectionable. I'm sure you realize the other members of your staff want nothing to do with Mr. Ahmad."

The viscount looked genuinely surprised. "No, I didn't know that. He's never said."

"No, I don't expect he has, but he's treated like a pariah below stairs."

"The poor man," Viscount Dalton said.

"It can't be easy to be despised in one's own home," Sebastian agreed.

"I'll have a word with Lewis," the viscount said. "Such an attitude won't be tolerated under my roof."

Sebastian nodded. It wasn't his place to interfere in the running of the viscount's household or to address the worries and complaints of his employees. Perhaps a conversation with Lewis would help to reassure the staff that their livelihood wasn't in danger, or perhaps their dislike had nothing to do with fear of losing their positions. Some prejudices ran deep and would not be easily rooted out, especially if the viscount's interest in Islam was common knowledge among the staff.

"Have you discussed your interest in the Muslim faith with anyone in your household?"

"No one besides Mr. Ahmad. It's not the sort of thing I would share with the servants, and my wife and children were never interested in theological discussions."

"Did Miss Seaborne get on with Mr. Ahmad?"

"Their paths rarely crossed, Inspector."

"Yet I understand they had several conversations about India."

"So what? Addie was a curious girl. She had dreams of traveling the world."

"And your son? How does he feel about Mr. Ahmad?"

The viscount shrugged. "They don't have much to do with each other."

"Does Mr. Seaborne have his own valet?"

"He does. Peterson."

Sebastian made a note of the name and moved on. "And is there anyone outside your household who knows of your interest in the Islamic faith?"

The viscount hesitated, but his need to understand what happened to his daughter obviously prevailed, and he answered, albeit reluctantly. "Only my friend Jonathan Wright. It was he that gifted me this beautiful volume."

"Jonathan Wright?" Sebastian echoed. The name cropping up again couldn't be a coincidence, but he had yet to understand how the information fit with what he already knew.

"Yes. Jonathan and I have known each other for decades," the viscount replied. "We met at Eton."

"And is it common knowledge that Mr. Wright has immersed himself in the study of Islam?"

"It is not, and what I tell you is never to leave this room. Is that clear, Inspector?"

"Crystal," Sebastian replied. "Unless the information is relevant to the case, in which instance I will have little choice."

The viscount sighed with impatience. "Jonathan's interest in the Islamic faith has nothing whatsoever to do with your investigation, Inspector Bell, but it could impede his political career. He keeps his views on the subject private, since there are those who would use the information against him and paint him as someone who could not be trusted to uphold cherished English values."

"But surely the members of his household are aware,"

Sebastian said, wondering all the while if it was possible to keep one's faith entirely private.

"I don't believe so. All they know is that pork causes Jonathan indigestion, and he won't have it served at table. He has also given up alcohol, which is hardly a crime. Jonathan Wright attends church regularly with his family, as do I."

"I see," Sebastian said. "Might someone have noticed your Qur'an when they paid a social call?"

"I don't normally receive visitors in the study. This room is solely for my own use. Even members of my family rarely come here. You're grasping at straws, Inspector, and won't find the connection you're searching for in this house."

Sebastian inclined his head in acknowledgement of the rebuke, but he did not agree. A house this size had a staff that numbered in the dozens and, even though the viscount might not take them into account, every one of those below stairs knew more than he gave them credit for, including what their master kept in his study and what he discussed with his valet. When one had a staff, nothing was truly private, and the servants' fear of being replaced was very real and valid, as well as their suspicion of anyone who adhered to a different set of beliefs.

"I would like to speak to Lady Dalton."

"My wife hasn't left her bed, and I won't have you disturbing her in her grief," the viscount snapped.

"My lord, no one knows a young woman's heart like her mother. Perhaps her ladyship knows something that can help us find Miss Seaborne's killer."

"I very much doubt it."

"Still, I must insist," Sebastian said. He knew he was pushing his luck, but it was imperative that he speak to the viscountess.

Viscount Dalton walked to the door and yanked on the bellpull. "Lewis, get Merrick and ask her to help her ladyship to the sitting room. Inspector Bell wishes to speak with her."

Lewis shot Sebastian a filthy look. "Yes, my lord. Right away, my lord."

"You may wait in the foyer," the viscount said. "I have said everything I wish to say to you, Inspector."

"Thank you. I am grateful for your assistance, my lord."

The viscount nodded, then grabbed the Qur'an off the desk and shoved it into a drawer, which he locked.

THIRTY-FOUR

Sebastian was left to stand in the foyer for over half an hour before he was finally invited to follow Merrick, her ladyship's lady's maid, to the viscountess's private sitting room. It was a lovely, feminine room, decorated in dusty rose and gold, and overlooked the rose garden, which was still dotted by several autumnal blooms. The viscountess wore a loose garment in a deep shade of plum and reclined on a velvet chaise positioned near the hearth. Despite the heat from the fire her legs were covered with a woolen rug, and she shivered visibly, making the delicate lace at her throat quiver like a disturbed spiderweb.

"Good afternoon, my lady," Sebastian said when she failed to look at him.

Viscountess Dalton inclined her head marginally. She didn't invite him to sit, but it would make for an awkward conversation if he had to tower over her.

"May I sit, your ladyship?"

"Yes," she replied wearily.

Sebastian moved a chair closer to the chaise and seated himself. The woman before him was pale and had dark circles beneath her eyes, her skin almost translucent in the light of the fire. Unlike her husband, who despite his grief still managed to maintain his bluster, the viscountess looked like a limp doll, a woman so broken no amount of time would heal her. She had the same fair hair as her daughter, and her agonized gaze sliced through Sebastian's heart. What struck him was how young she was. She couldn't be more than thirty-five, which meant that George Seaborne could not possibly be her son.

"I'm deeply sorry for your loss, my lady," Sebastian said.

"Thank you." Lady Dalton's voice was so weak, Sebastian could barely hear her.

"I won't detain you for long. I only need to ask a few questions."

"I don't know if I can go on without her," Lady Dalton whispered. "Addie was..." She paused as she searched for the right word. "A light in the darkness," the viscountess said at last. "Addie was all that was good in my life."

"Then help me find whoever did this," Sebastian said.

"I will tell you whatever I know, but it's not much. If I had known..."

Her eyes filled with tears and the maid was instantly at her side, handing her mistress a lace-trimmed handkerchief and asking if she might like a dose of a restorative tonic to calm her nerves. Sebastian was acutely aware of what such a tonic contained, and hoped he would get to ask his questions before the woman became insensible.

"When was the last time you saw your daughter, my lady?" he asked gently.

"At dinner, on Sunday. She said she had a headache and retired to her room immediately afterwards."

"Did you suspect that she had plans to leave the house?"

The viscountess shook her head. "I thought she wished to go to her room because she had quarreled with her father."

Since Sebastian was already aware of the reason for the disagreement, he decided not to press the viscountess on the details. Given her fragile state, her ability to cooperate wouldn't last long, and he hoped to learn something he might have hitherto missed.

"My lady, did you support your daughter's wish to marry Mr. Parker?"

The viscountess smiled sadly. "I did not, but I could understand Addie's feelings for Mr. Parker only too well. I was young and impressionable myself once, but I quickly learned that love and desire burn out, particularly once the man in question is no longer forbidden fruit but one's husband. I tried to explain that to Addie and to assure her that in time she would see the wisdom of marrying a man whose position in society would guarantee her a life of comfort and respectability, but she wasn't ready to listen." The viscountess sighed heavily. "When I wouldn't intervene with Alastair, Addie found a champion in George. He encouraged her to stand up to her father and hold out for love."

"Did Mr. Seaborne think his lordship would eventually relent?"

"George knew Alastair doted on Addie. He thought that perhaps he would take her happiness into account."

Sebastian nodded. Clearly Adelaide's happiness was not as desirable as a man with the right pedigree.

"Did you approve of Mr. Seaborne's involvement?" Sebastian asked. Meddling would be the more appropriate word, but Sebastian had to be careful not to cause offense.

He was surprised when a spark of anger flared in the viscountess's pale eyes. "It didn't much matter if I approved. George would do as he saw fit, even if his advice would cause nothing but harm. If not for his encouragement, Addie might still be alive."

Having realized that she had perhaps revealed too much of her true feelings, Lady Dalton made a dismissive gesture with her hand. "Young men always think they know best," she said.

"They don't have the benefit of experience." She sighed shakily. "George is devastated. He probably blames himself for what happened."

"Why would he do that?" Sebastian asked.

"Because he encouraged Addie's bad behavior. I wager he was the one who told her how to get out without getting caught, never imagining that she would make use of the information."

"My lady, is there anyone you can think of who would have invited Adelaide to a séance?"

The viscountess shook her head. "No one of our acquaintance is interested in such things. Besides, Addie was more interested in the living, maybe because she had never lost anyone that truly mattered to her."

Sensing a dead end to the conversation, Sebastian decided to change tack. "I take it Mr. Seaborne is not your son?"

"No. George's mother died when he was ten. I married the viscount a year later and raised him as my own."

"And Mr. Seaborne and his sister were always close?"

"Addie looked up to George and always eagerly anticipated his visits when he was at Eton and Cambridge. Of course, like most young men, George had little time to spare for a sister who was nearly eleven years his junior. He teased her mercilessly, but sometimes he invited her along when he went for a ride in Rotten Row. Addie was an accomplished horsewoman. I think he was proud of her."

"And was Mr. Seaborne previously married?" Sebastian asked. George Seaborne still lived at home, but if Adelaide was eighteen now then George was twenty-nine, an age when most men had been married at least once and might have one or more children.

"George recently became engaged. Of course, now we'll be planning a funeral instead of a wedding."

That didn't really answer Sebastian's question, but the viscountess covered her face with her hands, clearly no longer able to keep her despair at bay. Her shoulders quaked and she keened like a wounded animal, her pain so visceral it tore at Sebastian's soul. He left the viscountess to the ministrations of her maid and backed out of the room without disturbing the weeping woman any further.

"If that will be all, Inspector," Lewis said when Sebastian returned downstairs.

"I'd like to speak to Peterson."

"Why?" Lewis demanded.

Sebastian didn't bother to answer. He didn't owe the butler an explanation.

Lewis sighed heavily, as if Sebastian had asked for something quite unreasonable. "You may speak to him in my pantry."

"Very well," Sebastian replied, and followed Lewis through the green baize door once again.

THIRTY-FIVE

Peterson was precisely what Sebastian had expected of George Seaborne's valet. He was in his early thirties, with neatly oiled fair hair, shrewd gray eyes, and a lip that seemed to curl with derision when they were introduced. He sat in the cane guest chair, crossed his legs, and folded his hands primly in his lap, then met Sebastian's gaze and smiled slyly.

"How can I help you, Inspector?"

"What time did George Seaborne go out on All Hallows' Eve?"

"Around five. He had plans to dine at his club."

Sebastian noted that Peterson did not mention that George had plans to see his mistress and gave him credit for being loyal, even if George Seaborne himself had no qualms about admitting to a dalliance despite his impending marriage.

"And what time did he return?" Sebastian asked. He had George Seaborne's account of his whereabouts, but he wanted to verify the information with his valet.

"I really couldn't tell you." Peterson's lip curled again, and he shrugged with indifference, all the while watching Sebastian as if the valet were a cat toying with a mouse. Sebastian felt a stab of anger toward the man. All too often he had to question individuals who felt that a policeman was beneath them, but he wasn't about to let this slippery character get the best of him. He would have an account of George Seaborne's movements even if he had to browbeat his valet.

"Mr. Peterson, if you find that answering a few questions in regard to your employer's sister's murder is too much of an imposition, perhaps we should continue this conversation at Scotland Yard. I have no doubt that being questioned in connection with a murder will do wonders for any future employment opportunities. Or will Mr. Seaborne be taking you with him when he leaves this house?"

Peterson's reaction was immediate. He blanched, his eyes widened with obvious shock, and Sebastian knew he'd struck a nerve. The valet was worried about his future, since he was technically employed by the viscount and might not be invited to work for George Seaborne once he married.

"I will have the truth, Mr. Peterson," Sebastian said.

The valet shifted uncomfortably in his seat, and Sebastian could almost see the cogs turning in his head as he considered the possibilities. The drooping of the shoulders and the look of resignation was either a ruse or the valet's realization that it was in his interests to tell the truth.

"He didn't come in until around ten the following morning," Peterson said, a shifty look passing over his face.

"You needn't worry, Mr. Peterson. I already knew that," Sebastian said, letting the man off the hook. Peterson looked relieved, having no doubt thought that admitting that George Seaborne had been out all night would put him in the frame for murder.

"And what time were you summoned on Monday?" Sebastian asked.

"Close to one."

"What did you do then?"

"I wished Mr. Seaborne a good afternoon, inquired about his plans for the day so that I would know which clothes to lay out, and took away the clothes he'd worn the night before. They were in a heap on the floor."

"What was the condition of Mr. Seaborne's clothing?"

Peterson seemed surprised by the question. "How do you mean?"

"Were his clothes soiled?"

"No more than usual. I sent his shirt, cravat, and undergarments to the laundry, then brushed his coat and polished the shoes."

"Have the items been laundered?" Sebastian asked.

"Yes. They were returned that evening."

"How did your employer seem when he woke?"

"He was hung over," Peterson replied. "He said he had a devil of a headache and asked for a highland fling."

"A what?"

"It's a Scots cure for a hangover. Corn flour mixed with warm buttermilk and seasoned with salt and pepper. Mr. Seaborne says it works a treat. Never tried it myself."

"And did it help?"

"He appeared to be feeling better and had plans to go to the gymnasium later in the afternoon, but then he found out that Miss Seaborne was missing." For the first time since entering the room, Peterson showed some genuine feeling. His gaze softened, and his mouth drooped. "She was lovely, Miss Seaborne."

"Mr. Peterson, how do you get on with his lordship's valet?" Sebastian asked.

"I don't. Can't abide the man."

"For what reason?"

"Do I need a reason? Just don't like him."

"Did Mr. Seaborne ever say anything to you about Mr. Ahmad?"

Peterson's gaze slid away from Sebastian, and he shifted in the chair again.

"Mr. Peterson, what did Mr. Seaborne say about Mr. Ahmad?"

"He said that Ahmad thinks all noble Englishmen are lazy and stupid and all Englishwomen are trollops who will sell themselves to the highest bidder."

"Did you ever see Mr. Ahmad treat anyone in a disrespectful manner, particularly the women?"

Peterson shook his head. "Look, I might not like the fellow, but if I'm honest I've never seen him put a foot wrong. He never so much as looks at the women, and he never makes any untoward comments, like the other lads do when they think no one can hear them. It's like he's not even human."

Sebastian nodded. This was getting him nowhere. "Did you see Miss Seaborne on Sunday evening?"

"No. I went up to my room after dinner and read until I went to sleep. Mr. Lewis can vouch for me."

"And what if George Seaborne had returned during the night and had need of your services?" Sebastian asked. "Would you not be locked in with the rest of the male staff?"

Peterson shook his head. "Mr. Seaborne would wake Lewis when he returned, and Lewis would come and get me."

"So, the door to the men's corridor remained locked all night?"

"As far as I know."

"Thank you, Mr. Peterson," Sebastian said. "Do let me know if you happen to remember anything else."

"Will you tell Mr. Seaborne you spoke to me?" Peterson asked.

"I don't report to Mr. Seaborne."

Peterson's relief was obvious. "I really am sorry she's dead," he said as he stood to leave. "Miss Adelaide didn't deserve what happened to her."

"No, she didn't," Sebastian agreed.

Having finished with the valet, he decided it was time he returned to Scotland Yard.

THIRTY-SIX

Sebastian had expected to find Thomas Wright in custody when he returned to Scotland Yard, but Sergeant Woodward was quick to dash his hopes.

"The constables didn't find him at home. They lay in wait for more than two hours, but Wright never showed his face. What will you have me do?"

"He may have gone to his parents' house, but I would rather not involve his father just yet. Have them try again early tomorrow morning. That's the one time of day when you can usually find a gentleman at home."

Sergeant Woodward nodded. "I will get Meadows and Bryant onto it. By the by, Ransome wants to see you."

Sebastian was about to reply when a well-dressed gentleman in a caped coat and a beaver hat entered the duty room, and the sergeant's attention was instantly diverted. Leaving him to take down the man's complaint, Sebastian went in search of John Ransome, who was enjoying a cup of tea and a biscuit in the common room.

"You wanted to see me?" Sebastian asked.

"Hm," Ransome replied, his mouth still full. He swallowed,

gulped down the remainder of his tea, and gestured for Sebastian to follow him to his office.

"What have you found?" Sebastian asked as he unbuttoned his coat and pulled up a chair, setting his hat on his knee.

"I found three cases that may be relevant because of the date, but there were two other incidents that might fit the bill," Ransome said. "Both in 1855."

"Tell me about those first," Sebastian invited.

"The first victim, Shelly Gibbons, said that she was grabbed off the street on Midsummer Night and raped by a group of men. This happened near Shadwell Dock and the woman was beaten and left in an alleyway. The complaint was never followed up."

"Why not?"

"The constable who took the report wrote 'prostitute' at the bottom and underlined it twice. Probably thought she got what was coming to her."

"Who was it?" Sebastian demanded. He'd be sure to have a quiet word when he got hold of the man.

"There's no signature."

"And lucky for him too because that sort of attitude should not go unpunished," Sebastian ground out.

He thought he knew who the constable might have been and wished he could teach the man a thing or two about compassion and kindness, but the policeman in question was no longer with Scotland Yard. He'd been stabbed several times while trying to break up a fight between two sailors and although still alive was unable to work.

"What about the second incident?" Sebastian asked.

"The second complaint was made by one Saoirse Byrne, a maidservant, who claimed that she was viciously abused by a dozen men."

"Where?"

"Vauxhall Gardens."

"Is there anything else in the report?"

Ransome shook his head warily. "There's some hogwash about pagan rituals. She claimed there was some significance to the date."

"Which was?"

"The first of August."

"How badly was she hurt?" Sebastian demanded.

"Badly enough, I reckon, if she'd screwed up the courage to involve the police."

"Was the complaint investigated?" Sebastian asked, but he already knew the answer.

"What do you think?" Ransome asked with an eloquent roll of his eyes. "An Irish maid comes blathering about some ritual nonsense but can't provide any additional information on the perpetrators? I expect she was sent home with a flea in her ear."

"Do we have an address or the name of her employer?" Sebastian asked.

"Mrs. Harriet Smith of Bethnal Green."

"That's it?" Sebastian demanded. Was he supposed to go knocking on doors in the hope that he'd find Mrs. Smith and her maid?

"Afraid so."

"Unbelievable," Sebastian muttered under his breath. "What about the three cases you think relevant? I certainly hope there's something more to go on."

"Not as such," Ransome replied. "The first was logged on the first of November 1855. A prostitute by the name of Hetty Cooper said that she was taken hostage and raped by a group of masked men. In a church," he added with obvious relish.

"Was her claim ever investigated?" Sebastian asked.

Ransome held up one sheet of paper. "Nothing beyond taking her statement was ever done. I expect Inspector Cotton, who was the one to speak to her, figured she was so thoroughly pickled in gin she'd imagined the whole thing."

"Does it say where she was taken from?"

"She was near Covent Garden, on the lookout for custom, when she was approached by a young gentleman. That's all that's on file."

"Damn Cotton," Sebastian swore.

"Good thing he's retiring. The man is a disgrace," Ransome agreed. "Couldn't find hops in a brewery."

"What about the other two?"

"A body of a young woman was found in Kensal Green Cemetery on the first of November the following year. She had been raped and strangled. The only reason she was even found was probably because the body was dumped after daybreak. Had she been left there at night, she would have wound up on some surgeon's dissecting table."

"Do we have a name for her?"

"Amelia Paine. Her disappearance was reported by her mother the same day the body was discovered. Amelia was nineteen and worked at a milliner's shop. Mrs. Paine said that Amelia was a very careful girl and would never have gone off with someone she didn't know. She believed her daughter had been taken by force."

"Was she?"

"There were no signs of struggle. The surgeon who performed the post-mortem said he smelled spirits on her and thought she might have been insensible at the time of the assault. I hope for her sake that she was," Ransome added.

"Was anyone ever charged?" Sebastian asked.

Ransome shook his head. "There wasn't much to go on."

"And the third?"

"Last year."

"First of November?" Sebastian asked.

"You got it in one. Another prostitute. The complaint was made by her madam, who was very put out by someone damaging her property. She said the girl was badly hurt and frightened out of her wits. She kept saying she had seen the Devil."

"Who took the statement?"

"Inspector Reece."

"Did he bother to follow up?"

"He did, but it doesn't seem as if he did anything beyond that. Reece doesn't bother to get up in the morning unless he can lick some lordling's arse, so, unless the complaint was filed by a man of substance whose favorite whore had suddenly become unavailable, he'd not be likely to care."

Sebastian swore under his breath. "It's no wonder the people don't trust the police when you have such incompetents investigating serious crimes."

"I think Lovell is too busy playing at politics to run the Yard properly," Ransome said quietly. "What this place needs is new blood. A young, ambitious man to revamp our image."

"I think you're right," Sebastian agreed.

"Ever think of throwing your hat in?"

"No. You?"

"I would if I thought I had a good chance." Ransome had that smirk again that told Sebastian he was up to something, but he ignored him. Lovell wasn't going anywhere just yet, so the whole thing was a moot point.

"Do we have a name for the third woman?"

"Polly Lawrence. The concerned citizen that reported the case was Lucille Moore of Madame Lucille's," Ransome added sarcastically.

"That's rather an exclusive establishment, if I have my brothels straight," Sebastian said.

"Indeed it is."

Ransome produced a copy of the *Swell's Night Guide Through the Metropolis*. It was several years out of date but still an eye-opening document when it came to London's brothels and other gentlemanly pursuits. "Says here that one must obtain an introduction to Madame Lucille in order to gain entrance, but getting a friend to vouch for one is well worth the effort since Lucille's girls are beyond compare."

"Does it say anything about Polly Lawrence?" Sebastian asked. The guide frequently listed prostitutes by name and waxed poetic about their most noteworthy attributes.

Ransome ran his finger down the list of honorable mentions. "Ah, here we go. 'A freshly picked bloom.'"

"What's that supposed to mean?" Sebastian growled.

"Probably means that she was only recently deflowered and well worth the price Madame Lucille was charging."

"What year was the guide printed?"

"1846."

"Her bloom must have faded somewhat by 1857."

"I've never been to Madame Lucille's myself, not having friends who could provide me with an introduction," Ransome quipped, "but I would venture to guess that, if a harlot is well cared for, her working life should last longer than a decade. Besides, establishments like Madame Lucille's get them young. She could have been all of twelve in 1846."

"Yes, that's a valid point. Do we have addresses for Hetty Cooper and Mrs. Paine?" Sebastian asked.

"Yes." Ransome reached for a clean sheet of paper and copied them out. "What are you thinking?"

"It could be that the only thing these cases have in common is the date. Plenty of women get beaten, raped, and killed on other days of the year. Two were prostitutes, one of them a common streetwalker and the other a valued commodity. The third was a respectable shopgirl."

"I doubt they're connected," Ransome said.

"I won't know unless I speak to the surviving victims. Does the file mention who performed the post-mortem on Amelia Paine?"

"Mr. Harding. Last I heard, he'd moved to Somerset with his new bride."

"Then I will start with the two prostitutes. Hopefully they're still with us. Thank you, John."

"You owe me a pint," John Ransome reminded him.

"I'll owe you considerably more than that if I find a connection."

Sebastian left Ransome's office and headed toward the main entrance.

"Inspector Bell, this lady is here to see you," Sergeant Woodward said when Sebastian reached the duty room. Woodward glared at the woman in a manner that suggested that this wasn't their first meeting.

Sebastian was surprised to find Gemma Tate standing before the desk, her haunted gaze fixing on him as if she were drowning and only he could save her.

"Miss Tate, are you all right?" Sebastian asked as he approached her. "Did something happen?"

Like the viscount, Miss Tate looked considerably worse today than she had the last time he'd seen her. Her skin had a grayish hue, and her expression was one of utter bewilderment. Her eyes misted over, and, rather than have to comfort her in the duty room, Sebastian took her by the arm and guided her through the door.

"Where are you taking me?" Miss Tate asked as he propelled her down the street.

"I'm taking you for a drink."

She looked like she was about to protest, then clearly saw the wisdom of his suggestion and meekly ambled along. Sebastian took her only as far as the nearest public house, and maneuvered her through the door and toward a table in the corner. He went to the bar and ordered a pint for himself and a half-pint of cider for Miss Tate. She looked a sorry figure when he turned to bring the drinks to the table. Her shoulders were hunched, her head bowed, and her hands clasped on the table.

"I'm sorry," Miss Tate said as soon as he set the cider before her. "I shouldn't have come. I know you're very busy. I didn't even realize where I was heading until I found myself in front of the building."

"It's quite all right, Miss Tate. Tell me what happened."

Miss Tate took a sip of her cider and set the glass on the table with a shaking hand. "I was all right. I was coping," she said, her gaze searching out his eyes. "I tried to keep myself occupied, but it's difficult in the evenings. The silence..." Her voice trailed off.

"I know," Sebastian said. He was all too familiar with the evenings, when the silence weighed so heavily on him the only thing he could do was drink until he could no longer remain upright.

"It's like a solid thing, isn't it?" Miss Tate said. "It presses down until the weight becomes unbearable and you think you will collapse beneath it. I know you understand," she said, watching him intently.

"I do."

"I keep telling myself that it will get easier—with each passing day, the weight will get a little lighter, a little easier to carry—but then I had to prepare Victor's things for the burial." A tear slid down her cheek, and he could see the pain in her eyes. "I think that's when it truly hit me. I will never see him again or hear his voice. I will never have anyone in my life who loves me so freely or who shares my memories of a time and of the people who are no longer with us. I never felt so alone as I did at that moment." She choked on her words and took a gulp of cider, spilling a little down the front of her cape.

Sebastian reached across the table and covered her hand with his own. "How can I help?"

"Let me help *you*. Please. Assign me a task, no matter how

trivial. Perhaps I can speak to Adelaide Seaborne's lady's maid or find a way to approach the housekeeper. Servants always know more than they are saying, and I would hardly be in danger."

Sebastian shook his head, dismayed by Miss Tate's request. At least she had come to him first rather than acting on her own, which was something. She was a woman of her word.

"You are not to go anywhere near the family or the servants, Miss Tate. Besides, I have already interviewed the maid and the housekeeper, and I don't believe they have anything more to add."

"There must be something I can do," Miss Tate pleaded.

Sebastian could understand her desperation. It wasn't so long ago that he'd felt the same; he understood the value of taking action and knew how difficult it was to do nothing. But he couldn't allow Gemma Tate to endanger herself. Until he understood what he was dealing with, it was his responsibility to keep her safe. Gemma did not appear to fit the type, but Sebastian would never forgive himself if she became the next victim. To torment a woman like her would bring some depraved thug great pleasure and serve to send a message Sebastian did not care to receive.

"I need you to be patient. I will call on you as soon as I learn anything relevant," Sebastian promised, but it seemed Miss Tate wasn't ready to give up.

"Did you find the man with the milky eye?" she asked.

"I found out who he is and where he lives, but he may have done a runner."

"So he's lost to us?" Miss Tate asked.

"Not lost, as such. Misplaced," Sebastian said, and saw a hint of a smile touch her lips.

"Do you have any other leads?"

"I was actually on my way to interview ladies of the evening," Sebastian confessed.

"Why?"

"Several women were abducted and assaulted on All Hallows' Eve. One didn't survive, but I'm hopeful that the other two might be able to shed some light."

"Only two?"

Sebastian sighed wearily. "There was also an Irish maidservant, Saoirse Byrne, who made a complaint that might or might not be relevant since the assault did not happen on All Hallows' Eve, but the constable who spoke to her never got a proper address. All we have is the name of her employer. Mrs. Harriet Smith. Much good it does me. At least the maidservant survived the attack, so that's something I suppose."

"And the one who didn't survive?"

"She worked in a milliner's shop. Her mother was the one who reported her missing. She said her daughter was a respectable girl who'd never go off with someone she didn't know, but the post-mortem showed no signs of struggle."

"Do you think she went willingly?" Miss Tate asked.

"I don't know. I was going to speak to the mother last, since she probably knows the least of what happened that night. I only wanted to find out more about the victim."

"Let me do it," Miss Tate exclaimed. She looked more animated, the gray cast to her skin replaced by something resembling a healthier complexion. "I can speak to her. Ask whatever questions you think best."

Sebastian considered her offer. He didn't think that allowing Miss Tate to speak to Mrs. Paine would place her in any danger, and it would save him a trip to Holborn and give the grieving woman something to occupy her mind. The funeral was tomorrow. Once she buried Victor, the grief would take a different turn. It would be no less crippling, but it would be more passive in nature. There would be nothing left to do once the demands of sudden death were satisfied.

With the burial over, the deceased's room empty of their

belongings, and the friends and family returned to their own lives, the grief would eventually become a dull ache rather than an acute pain. It would settle in the chest and wrap itself around the heart, squeezing and bruising until one became so accustomed to it they were able to function almost normally. Some of those left behind, like Sebastian, needed a crutch in order to go on, but his burden was heavier than that of most. Miss Tate would grieve her brother for the rest of her days, but she wasn't the one who'd caused his death. She had nothing to reproach herself with and she could focus on the good memories and keep her brother alive that way.

"All right," Sebastian said. "You can speak to Mrs. Paine. All I want you to do is ask her to tell you what happened. Anything she can remember. No detail too small."

"How will I tell you what I have discovered?"

Sebastian was about to say that she could tell him after the funeral, but then realized how selfish that would be. "If I might call on you this evening," he said instead. Perhaps his presence, although brief, would help her get through the long hours.

"Yes," Miss Tate exclaimed, as if he'd thrown her a life preserver. "I will wait for you."

"I will try not to call too late."

"Anytime, Inspector. Sleep doesn't come easily these days."

"I know," he said under his breath. *Oh, I know*, he thought and drained the remainder of his pint. He tried to ignore the tremor in his hand as he set the tankard down. He hadn't had any tonic, but he might have to take a few sips if he hoped to get through the rest of the day.

Sebastian gave Miss Tate the address and walked her to the door. "Please, be careful, Miss Tate."

She nodded and offered him a shy smile. "I will be. Thank you, Inspector."

"Till tonight, then."

"Yes." And then she was gone.

THIRTY-SEVEN

Sebastian decided to start with Madame Lucille's, since it would be easier to gain admission before the doors opened to the brothel's well-heeled clientele. The address was in Pimlico, which wouldn't get the foot traffic an indiscriminate brothel would aspire to but would likely appeal to persons of quality who felt they were getting something a bit more desirable than they would at a less accredited establishment.

The three-story building bore a discreet plate that simply said "Lucille's." It wouldn't do to advertise what Lucille actually provided to those who need not concern themselves with her business. Given the establishment's reputation, Lucille didn't suffer for lack of custom. Sebastian knocked on the door and waited. No one came. He knocked again, louder this time. After what seemed an age, he finally heard footsteps and a woman of middle years opened the door. Given her ruddy completion, thinning hair, and abundant waist, Sebastian didn't think she was Madame Lucille. He held up his warrant card, and the woman squinted at it.

"What's it say?" she asked at last.

"Inspector Bell of Scotland Yard."

She looked genuinely surprised. "What do you want?"

"I need to speak to Polly Lawrence."

The woman shook her head, looking at him as if he were an overzealous teenage boy eager for his first sexual experience. "You can't talk to Polly without permission from Herself." Sebastian could practically hear the capital H in the form of address.

Although irritated to be thus rebuffed, he was pleased to hear that Polly was still alive and employed by Madame Lucille. If he had to pay his respects to the madame, then he would gladly do so.

"Then I would like to speak to Madame Lucille."

"She ain't receiving," the woman said. She made to close the door, but Sebastian's foot prevented her from shutting him out.

"I am an inspector of the police, madam," he said. "I will either speak to your mistress now or when I return with reinforcements and break down the door. I highly doubt Herself would prefer that. I only need a few minutes of her time."

The woman looked suitably cowed by this threat and opened the door to let him in. "Don't touch anything," she said, as if he was likely to shove a silver candlestick down his trousers.

"Just take me to Lucille," Sebastian barked, tired of this powerplay.

He was taken past several receiving rooms that were furnished in vibrant jewel colors. All the accents were gold and gave the rooms the appearance of royal chambers, the fashionable settees and heavy velvet curtains adding to the atmosphere of luxury. There were silver candelabras, bowls filled with scented flower petals, and tasteful paintings of nudes who all looked disturbingly young. Sebastian suspected that the nudes had been painted from live models and were quite recent.

The servant led Sebastian to a polished door at the end of the corridor and knocked.

"Go away," a petulant female voice replied.

"There's a policeman here to see you, ma'am."

"Don't let him in, Martha," the voice screeched.

"Too late," Sebastian said. "I'm coming in."

Madame Lucille appeared to have been resting before a busy night, her slight form arranged on a blue velvet chaise. Her face was pale, and her dark hair was worn in a modest plait. She wore a loose garment of pale blue silk, the collar and sleeves dripping ecru lace. Sebastian placed her in her late forties or early fifties, but this was a woman whose business was illusion, and he was in no doubt that, if he had met her a few hours later, she would have looked younger and more alluring through the use of artfully applied cosmetics and a flattering gown.

"How dare you barge in here?" Madame Lucille demanded as she sat up straighter.

"I have some questions regarding a complaint you made to Scotland Yard."

"You must be joking," Madame Lucille said. She looked genuinely amused. "I know there must be a backlog of cases, but this really takes the cake."

"Will you tell me what happened?" Sebastian asked. He saw no reason to strong-arm this woman. She'd broken no laws, as far as he knew.

Madame Lucille sat up, pushed her feet into dainty slippers, and walked over to a sideboard, where she reached for a decanter and poured herself a drink. She did not offer one to Sebastian before sitting back down.

"What do you wish to know?"

"Last year, you filed a complaint saying that one of your girls, Polly Lawrence, was kidnapped and raped."

Lucille let out a bark of laughter. "Good to know we can rely on our competent, caring police force," she said, shaking her head with disgust.

"I am sorry your complaint wasn't taken seriously at the time."

"Why would it be? As soon as that prick of a detective heard Polly was a whore, he tossed me out on my ear."

"Tell me everything you remember," Sebastian said. He took out his notebook and pencil and settled in a chair positioned across from the chaise.

Lucille nodded. "Polly was requested by a long-standing client—"

"Name," Sebastian interjected.

"I can't give you the name of a client. Anyway, she never saw him that night."

"I still need a name. Without it, I'm unable to investigate the case."

Lucille pursed her lips and gave him a baleful stare, then exhaled loudly. "He must never know you obtained it from me."

"You have my word."

"Wright."

"Thomas?"

The woman looked surprised. "No, Jonathan. I expect you know who I mean."

"I do. Standing client, is he?"

"We have many clients of his ilk who prefer that the girls come to them. That way, they can ensure their privacy."

"I take it Mr. Wright didn't ask Polly to come to his home."

"Of course not. He's married."

Sebastian couldn't help but wonder about the *honorable* Mr. Wright. Here was a man who was father to a likely murderer, secret source to a scandal-mongering journalist, and a closet convert whose newfound faith didn't preclude him paying for sex or selling government secrets. The whole thing reeked of hypocrisy, but it wasn't for Sebastian to judge the man without hearing his side of the story. There were men who did far worse things, and Sebastian had arrested a few of them.

"So, where was Polly to meet Mr. Wright?" he asked.

"Nowhere. He would collect her in his carriage and return her once he was satisfied."

"Can you elaborate on that?"

Another heavy sigh. "Even though I make sure my girls are clean, some gentlemen prefer not to risk the pox, Inspector. Mr. Wright never engaged in sexual congress with Polly. He preferred that she use her hands and mouth to pleasure him."

"How often did he see her?"

"Once a week."

"Did he ever bring anyone else with him?"

"Not that I know of."

"So, what happened that night?"

"It wasn't one of his usual nights. He always saw Polly during the week, but this was Saturday, All Hallows' Eve. I received a note saying Polly was to come out at ten o'clock. He'd be waiting in his carriage."

"Did you think it odd?"

"Not really. If the urge had come upon him and he was willing to pay, I wasn't about to question the change in schedule."

"What happened then?" Sebastian asked.

"Polly finished with her previous client and went out to meet Mr. Wright, as requested. A carriage drove up, she got in, and she didn't return until the small hours. She wore nothing but her smallclothes and was bloodied and bruised."

"Did she tell you what happened?"

"I think you had better ask her, Inspector. You can speak to her here. I don't want the other girls to hear any of this. It frightens them."

"Have they not heard it already?" Sebastian asked.

"I told them Polly was ill and kept her in isolation until the bruises began to fade. Once she was better, I told her never to speak of it again."

"Why?" Sebastian asked, although he could guess.

"Believe it or not, Inspector, I look out for my girls, and any client that abuses his privilege is not welcome to return. The girls weren't in any immediate danger, and I saw no reason to frighten them."

"What about Mr. Wright? Did he return?" Sebastian inquired.

"When Mr. Wright arrived on his usual day, I came out to see him, and we had a long chat. He swore that he had never written that note and had not seen Polly since the previous week. By that time, Polly was able to confirm that the man who collected her on Saturday night was not Jonathan Wright."

"Who was it?"

"She didn't know then, and she doesn't know now," Lucille said. "But you can ask her yourself. Shall I fetch her now?"

"Please," Sebastian replied, his hopes of putting a name to Adelaide's killer fading fast.

THIRTY-EIGHT

Polly Lawrence bore a striking resemblance to Adelaide Seaborne. She was fair, blue-eyed, and well proportioned. As John Ransome had predicted, she was young, no older than twenty-two, which meant that Lucille had been selling her since she was in her early teens, possibly even younger. Rage boiled within Sebastian, but he forced it down. Polly made her living by servicing countless men. She would be able to read his mood, as well as any change in expression, and he had no desire to upset her.

"Good afternoon, Polly," Sebastian said, using his most nonthreatening tone.

"Good afternoon."

Polly perched on the edge of the chaise and folded her hands in her lap. She was the picture of demure innocence, but Sebastian could sense her anxiety. She had no wish to talk about what had happened, and he knew he'd be stirring up painful memories.

"Polly, I'm Inspector Bell of Scotland Yard, and I need to ask you a few questions. Is that all right?" he asked gently.

"There's been another girl, hasn't there?" Polly asked.

"I don't know if the cases are related, but they might be."

"Is she badly hurt, this girl?"

"I'm afraid she's beyond earthly pain."

A sob tore from Polly's chest, and her eyes brimmed with tears. "I thought they were going to kill me. I really did."

"Can you tell me what happened the night you were abducted?"

Polly nodded but remained silent. Sebastian gave her time to compose herself and, after a long pause, she began to speak. "I went outside to meet Mr. Wright. He called regularly and was one of my favorite clients."

"Why was that?" Sebastian asked.

Polly smiled wistfully. "Because it was quick, and he was always appreciative. He usually gave me a crown. He said I should have something put by for when I was ready to leave this life."

"That's generous."

"It is. I was already paid for, so he didn't have to be nice to me."

"Did he always use the same carriage?" Sebastian asked.

"Yes, but then I suppose any black carriage looks much like the next in the dark."

"Was there anything different that night?"

Polly shook her head. "I wasn't really paying attention, but I thought the coachman looked younger. I didn't think anything of it though. A man in Mr. Wright's position can have more than one coachman, can't he?"

"Yes, I suppose he can. Who was inside when you got in?" Sebastian asked, inwardly praying that she would give him something he could use.

"I don't know," Polly replied. "The man wore a masquerade mask, but it wasn't the sort that only covers the eyes. It covered most of his face, except for the mouth and chin."

"What happened then?"

"He smiled and said, 'Hello, Polly.' I became frightened and reached for the door, but he grabbed me by the wrist. He said that Mr. Wright wanted to change things up a bit, and he'd been sent to fetch me. He told me not to be afraid. It was all just a little game." Polly shuddered at the memory. "He took out a flask and offered it to me. 'Here, have a sip of brandy,' he said. 'It will settle your nerves.' So I took a sip, and then another, and then this feeling came over me, like I was floating."

"What did the man do?"

"He kept talking to me, telling me not to be afraid and that we were going to have a wonderful time together."

"Where did he take you?"

"We drove for a while, but I couldn't be sure where we were. I couldn't seem to gather my wits about me. After a time, the carriage stopped, and he helped me out. I could barely walk, I felt so weak. And everything was strange. The trees were whispering to me, the clouds were pressing on my eyes, and the church was sinister and dark, looming above me. When we came inside, he took me down to the crypt. It had a low stone ceiling, and there were coffins and staring skulls. Only three candles were lit, and they threw eerie red light onto the ceiling and walls and made the skulls look like they were watching."

"Was anyone there?"

Polly nodded. "A group of men."

"How many?"

"About a dozen. They looked like devils, all dressed in black and their eyes glittering through the slits in the masks. I was terrified, but I couldn't find my voice or the strength to fight. They all seemed to be swaying and weaving in and out, as if I were fevered and my mind was playing tricks on me."

"I expect it was," Sebastian replied. "That man must have given you a large dose of opium."

Polly nodded. "The man who'd collected me pushed the flask into my hands and told me to drink. I didn't want to, but he held the flask to my lips and tried to pour the brandy into my mouth. Some spilled down my gown, so he said we had to get it off."

Tears slid down Polly's cheeks as she recounted what had happened next. "They tore my clothes from me and forced me onto the floor. They stood in a circle and chanted, but I couldn't make out the words. And then they watched as each man took a turn with me. One man bit my tit, and when I cried out some of them laughed."

"What happened when they were done?" Sebastian asked. He was so angry, he could barely keep his voice steady.

"One of the men—I think he was their leader—made a sign of the horns over me and said something like, 'Congratulations. You're now the bride of Hades,' and then he blew out the candles and they all left. He called me by some name I didn't recognize, but at that point I don't think I would have recognized my own name. I was sure I was dying, and I would breathe my last in that dark crypt, lying on the cold stone floor, bleeding into the stones."

"But you were able to get back," Sebastian prompted.

Polly nodded. "I don't know how long I lay there, but eventually I managed to get up and pull on my chemise. They had taken the rest of my clothes. For one terrifying moment, I thought they'd shut me in, and it would take days to die, but the door was unlocked. I made it outside and retched until I thought my innards would split, but vomiting helped to clear my head. I started walking and eventually made it back here."

"Polly, do you remember anything about the church?" Sebastian asked.

She shrugged. "It was big."

"Did it have a tower?"

Polly looked thoughtful. "Yes, with a weather vane. I saw it when the moon came out from behind the clouds."

"Can you describe it? Did it have any distinctive features?"

There were many buildings in London, not just churches, with weather vanes, and some of them were quite unique. There were ships, a fish at the fish market, a cow at Smithfield Market, a beaver, and even a grasshopper, atop the Stock Exchange. A unique ornament would make the church easier to find but, even if the weather vane didn't have any distinctive features, it would still help Sebastian to narrow down the possibilities.

"I don't remember anything special about it."

"Thank you, Polly."

"Does it matter?" she asked.

"It might."

It was only a hunch, and he didn't want to get ahead of himself, but Polly could be describing All Hallows by the Tower. It was one of the few churches that had both a weather vane and a crypt. And the name was unexpectedly appropriate.

"I'm very sorry for what happened to you," Sebastian said. "And I thank you for telling me. I just have a few more questions, and then you never have to speak of this again."

"Do you know who they were?" Polly asked before he had a chance to continue.

"No, but I intend to find out."

"How can you?"

"Everyone makes mistakes, especially when they think they are above the law."

Polly sighed. "What else do you need to know, Inspector?"

"Were there any animal parts in the crypt, that you could see?"

Polly gaped at him. "Animal parts?"

"Like entrails or organs."

"I didn't notice anything like that," Polly said.

"And the men, can you tell me anything about them?"

"They all wore masks and were dressed entirely in black. In

the candlelight, all I could make out was the bottom of their faces."

"Did you notice anything? Any unusual features?"

"A few had beards. One had fangs."

"Fangs?" Sebastian exclaimed.

Polly pointed to her own eyeteeth. "These teeth were long and pointed."

"Anything else? Doesn't matter how minor."

Polly suddenly smiled, but the smile was so sorrowful it nearly undid Sebastian. "The one who came to collect me had strange eyes. I only noticed it when he pulled me inside the crypt and the light fell on his face."

"How were his eyes different?"

"One was dark and the other like soft-boiled egg whites."

Sebastian permitted himself a small smile of his own. He could now connect Thomas Wright to the abduction and rape of Polly Lawrence and the murders of Adelaide Seaborne and Victor Tate.

"Thank you, Polly. You were a great help."

"Was I?" Polly asked, looking dubious.

"More than you know."

"Will you get them, then?"

"I will," Sebastian promised.

Polly stood and turned toward the door. "Thank you," she said.

"What for?"

"For listening and believing me. For a long time after, I thought that maybe I was losing my mind and I had imagined the whole thing. If not for the pain and the bruising, I would have believed it too."

"Have you seen Jonathan Wright since that night?" Sebastian asked.

Polly shook her head. "Madame Lucille sent another girl to him. I don't go outside. Not ever. I don't feel safe."

Sebastian wished he could reassure her, tell her that she was safe and nothing like this would ever happen again, but he couldn't. No woman was safe, especially a woman like Polly, who was viewed solely as a useful commodity whose life held little value. Sebastian didn't care to speculate, especially since it wasn't really relevant to the case, but Polly was so well spoken, he thought she might have come from a good family and been educated before life took a wrong turn.

THIRTY-NINE

It took Sebastian a long while to track down Hetty Cooper. He found her near Drury Lane, skulking in a doorway, after another prostitute pointed her out to him. He supposed it was just as well since, if he'd come this way earlier, she probably would not have been about her business yet. The prostitutes did not come out in full force until well after dark.

Like Polly, Hetty was young, but poverty and despair had left their mark on her pretty face. She was missing two teeth, and her hair was greasy and lank. She wore a gown of yellow silk, probably bought second- or even third-hand, and it showed signs of constant wear. The fabric was soiled, and the V-shaped bretelles were tattered. Limp bows hung from the pagoda sleeves, and the hem was covered in muck. Hetty turned her blue-eyed stare on Sebastian and tried to smile seductively. It came out as more of a grimace.

"Looking for a bit o' company, 'andsome? What's yer pleasure?" she purred.

"Hetty Cooper?" Sebastian asked, just to be sure.

She looked a bit taken aback but tried to cover up her suspicion with brazen flirting. "Know me by name, do ye? My reputation must precede me, and wif good reason. I always leave me customers well satisfied."

Sebastian could almost see the gears turning in her head as she wondered whether it would be wise to raise the price or if asking too much might see him off and she should stick to her usual rates.

"Hetty, I'm Inspector Bell of Scotland Yard." Sebastian showed her his warrant card, although he wasn't at all sure she could read.

Hetty balked. "What ye want wif me, then, Inspectah?"

"I only want to ask you a few questions. I'll pay you for your time."

"'Ow much?"

Sebastian held up a half crown, and Hetty's eyes fastened on it hungrily.

"All right, then, but only a few minutes, mind. Don't want to lose no paying punters on yer account."

It was too early in the day to hope for a steady stream of punters, but Hetty clearly had a talent for bargaining and self-promotion.

"Don't worry. I'll be quick," Sebastian promised.

Hetty snorted at that. She probably heard that a few times a night. "What ye want to know, then?"

"You filed a complaint with the police. You said you were kidnapped and raped."

Hetty's face tightened, and she clamped her teeth together at the unwelcome memory. Sebastian thought that, three years ago, Hetty had probably been very lovely and likely to catch the eye of someone who was accustomed to a higher class of prostitute, like Polly Lawrence.

"I don't want to talk 'bout it," Hetty said angrily.

"You want the coin, though," Sebastian replied.

She nodded.

"Hetty, I know it's painful, but I really need to know."

"Why? What's it matter now? Not like ye're going to catch them as done it."

"Another young woman was abducted. Only she was strangled and left to hang on a cross in Highgate Cemetery."

"I 'eard 'bout that," Hetty said, her expression thoughtful. "What makes ye think it's got anyfink to do wif what 'appened to me?"

"Maybe it doesn't, but I'd like to hear your story."

Hetty sighed. "It were awful. I still 'ave nightmares just thinking 'bout it."

"Tell me," Sebastian invited.

"I were just there," she said, pointing to a spot across the street. "Thought I'd find me some young swell as just come from the theater and were looking for a bit o' company. Anyways, this carriage drew up, and the door opened. The cove inside were nice-looking. Posh. 'E invited me inside. Said we'd go for a nice ride, and I'd be 'andsomely paid. So I got in."

Hetty seemed to fold in on herself, as if she could hardly bear to speak of that night.

"Then what happened?" Sebastian prompted.

"'E 'ad a flask. Black leather and silver," Hetty said dreamily. "It were lovely. 'Ad 'is initials on it too."

"Do you remember the initials?" Sebastian hurried to interject.

Hetty shook her head. "I don't know me letters." She drew in a shuddering breath and went on. "'E gave me a drink, and I took it. I thought it tasted funny-like and said so, but 'e just laughed and said I weren't used to fine brandy. 'Drink up,' 'e said. 'You'll get used to it.' So I did. The brandy made me feel like I were dreaming. It were peaceful, and I began to relax. The cove were saying something, but I could 'ardly understand. It was like I were not in me own body but floating above."

Sebastian nodded. Hetty had been given opium, just like Polly.

"'E brought me to a church. It were dark and creepy, and 'e laughed and said it were just a bit of fun for All Hallows. Said 'e always fancied getting sucked off in a church. I were too buggered on the brandy to argue, so we went inside. 'E pulled me along and down the steps."

"Into the crypt?"

Hetty nodded. "There were others there. Maybe a dozen, and all wearing black masks. I thought maybe I'd fallen asleep and were 'aving a nightmare, but, when they grabbed me and tore off me gown, it felt real enough then."

"Did they hurt you, Hetty?"

She nodded. "I'm used to taking many punters, one after another, but these men were rough, and cruel. They were all standing round, watching. And they were egging each other on."

"Can you tell me anything about their voices?" Sebastian asked.

"They was gentlemen. That I can tell ye for certain, and their clothes were of the finest cut."

"Did you see any animal parts?"

"Wha'?" Hetty asked, staring at him like he'd gone mad.

"Maybe pig entrails or hearts."

She shook her head. "Nothin' like that."

"What happened after they were done?"

"They blew out the candles and left me there, in the dark. I don't know 'ow long I lay there, but after a time I got up and found me way out. I stood there, in me shift, shivering and watching the sun come up. Never in all me life were I so 'appy to greet another day."

"Hetty, do you recall anything about the church?" Sebastian asked. She must have seen the church clearly if she had been outside at daybreak.

"It were All Hallows by the Tower," she said. "I didn't rightly know where I was during the night, but when I saw it by daylight I recognized it. That's when I decided to report them. I thought God had to have seen what they'd done. Well, if 'e did, 'e didn't bother to do nothin' 'bout it. The policeman laughed me outta the station. Said I were a filthy whore, and I should get along afore 'e locked me up and charged me with wasting police time. If 'e'd gave me a place to warm up and a meal, I wouldn't 'ave minded all that much," Hetty said plaintively. "'E did write it down, though, what I said. I reckon 'e were interested enough in me story to do that."

"Do you remember his name?"

"Nah," Hetty said. "But 'e were a thorny old git. A nice constable gave me a shilling on me way out. 'E felt sorry for me." Her eyes filled with tears. "There are kind people in the world. I always reminds meself of that."

"There are," Sebastian agreed. "Hetty, do you remember anything about the man who invited you into his carriage?"

"'E were young, handsome, and had lovely teeth."

"Did he have any deformities?"

Hetty looked surprised by the question. "No."

"Did he tell you his name?"

Hetty thought about it. "Yeah, 'e did. It were a strange name. 'Aden, mebbe."

"Haden? Are you sure?"

"No, but it were somethin' like that."

"Was it his Christian name or a surname?"

"I don't know. It were the only name 'e gave. Just said, 'Call me 'Aden.'"

"Did you ever see him again?"

Hetty shook her head. "I never go with anyone since that day. They can do their business right 'ere."

Sebastian handed Hetty the coin and smiled. "Thank you. I appreciate your help."

"Ye just gonna leave?" Hetty pouted. "Come on, Inspectah. I'll give ye a discount, seeing as 'ow ye overpaid for the information. I like me a 'andsome man. Always had a soft spot for a lovely smile." She held up the coin playfully and then sank it deep into her bodice.

"Thank you, Hetty, but I'm working."

"So am I," Hetty replied. "And I'm very good at me job."

"I'm sure you are," Sebastian said, and walked away.

FORTY

Once Gemma had delivered Victor's things to the undertaker and paid the balance for the funeral, she treated herself to a hot pie from a street vendor, then headed toward an omnibus stop. It was only as she walked down Bethnal Green Road that the significance of what Inspector Bell had said dawned on her, probably because just ahead she saw the familiar green and gold sign. Smith's Chemist Shop, which was owned by one Harriet Smith. She supposed it was possible that there was more than one Harriet Smith in London, but what were the chances?

Gemma knew Mrs. Smith. Not well, but enough to say good morning to if they passed each other in the street. Mrs. Smith had been widowed some years ago and had taken over the running of the shop, at least the business end of things. Gemma was sure that she knew as much as her husband had and could have managed splendidly on her own, but she had hired a young man to prepare the compounds and dispense medical advice, in order to retain those patrons who wouldn't trust a woman and would take their custom elsewhere.

Gemma had never needed to consult Mr. Wray, but she had visited the shop several times and had purchased items that she kept on hand in case of fever, severe headache, or indigestion. Mr. Wray recognized her immediately and smiled.

"Good afternoon, Miss Tate. How may I be of service today?" He didn't seem to realize that she was in mourning and Gemma was glad of it, since she didn't want to talk about Victor. Having to explain would only upset her.

"Good afternoon, Mr. Wray," Gemma replied crisply. "I was wondering if I might have a word with Mrs. Smith."

Mr. Wray gave her an understanding look. "Miss Tate, there's no need to be embarrassed. I assure you that I've heard it all and my only purpose is to alleviate your discomfort. If it would make you feel more comfortable, you can write down your complaint and I will furnish you with the appropriate remedy." He pushed a small writing pad toward Gemma and looked around for the pencil that had rolled some way down the counter.

Gemma sighed with impatience. The man seemed to think that she needed a cure for menstrual cramps or constipation. She smiled politely.

"Mr. Wray, I need to speak to Mrs. Smith regarding a personal matter."

"Of course. I do apologize. I thought—"

"It's quite all right. No harm done. Would you kindly fetch Mrs. Smith?"

Mr. Wray disappeared through a door behind the counter and returned a few moments later with Mrs. Smith. She was in her middle fifties but could easily pass for a much younger woman. Her hair had yet to go gray, her skin was surprisingly smooth, and her waist was as trim as that of a twenty-year-old.

"Good afternoon," Mrs. Smith said. "Mr. Wray says you wish to speak to me."

"Yes," Gemma replied. "If we could talk somewhere more private?"

"Please, come through here."

Mrs. Smith led Gemma to a small parlor at the back of the shop. It was prettily furnished with two chintz armchairs covered with lace antimacassars, a low table, and an oval rug. A painting of a pleasant country scene hung above the mantel and there were rose-colored poplin curtains at the window.

"This was my husband's sanctuary," Mrs. Smith said as she gestured for Gemma to take a seat. "He would ask me to mind the shop and have tea and cake while he read the paper. It was his favorite time of day."

"You must miss him very much," Gemma said.

Mrs. Smith nodded. "I do, but life goes on. And so will yours," she said, acknowledging Gemma's mourning attire. "I'm sorry for your loss, Miss Tate. Your brother, is it?"

"Yes. Thank you."

"How can I help?" Mrs. Smith asked when Gemma failed to explain the reason for her visit quickly enough.

"I believe you employ a maidservant named Saoirse Byrne?" Gemma began. She had never met Mrs. Smith's maid, but that wasn't uncommon. Their paths weren't likely to cross, especially since Gemma was a working woman herself.

A closed expression came over Mrs. Smith's face. "What of it, Miss Tate?"

"I was wondering if I might ask her a few questions."

"About?"

"An incident that took place a few years ago. In Vauxhall Gardens."

Mrs. Smith's reaction was one of instant displeasure, anger almost. "I think you had better explain yourself, Miss Tate."

Gemma realized how inappropriate her request must have sounded and admonished herself for not coming up with a more diplomatic explanation. For all she knew, Mrs. Smith knew nothing of what had happened to her maid and Gemma might get the young woman in serious trouble. Or she knew and thought it none of Gemma's business, which was the more likely scenario. Judging by Mrs. Smith's expression, Gemma had only a few moments before she would be asked to leave, so she plunged in, hoping the truth would tip the scales in her favor.

"Mrs. Smith, I believe my brother was murdered, and I have reason to think that what happened to your maid might have something to do with his death."

"How on earth could an attack on my maid, that happened several years ago, I might add, have anything to do with your brother's death?" Mrs. Smith demanded.

"My brother was the one who discovered the woman in Highgate," Gemma said and realized how half-baked her explanation sounded. "She may have been attacked by the same men," she added desperately.

"Based on what evidence, Miss Tate?"

Gemma didn't often get flustered, but Mrs. Smith was making her question the sanity of her errand. She clutched her reticule with both hands and stood, hoping she could still make a graceful exit.

"I'm sorry to have bothered you, Mrs. Smith. Good day."

"Sit down, Miss Tate," Mrs. Smith said and smiled, revealing two tiny dimples in her cheeks. "I can conceive of only two reasons for your visit. The first is that you're a silly woman who likes to invent conspiracy theories to bring some excitement into her day, but I don't believe that to be the case. The second is that you're in fact a very intelligent woman who's here for a good reason. I think you know something you don't wish to reveal. So, how about you tell me the truth and I will do the same."

Gemma lowered herself back into the seat and nodded. The attack on Saoirse Byrne might have nothing to do with the case but, now that she was here and she had the right person, she needed to find out for sure. At best, she'd learn something that could help Inspector Bell. At worst, she'd rule out a connection.

Gemma outlined the salient points and waited, hoping Mrs. Smith wouldn't change her mind and send her on her way.

"I see," Mrs. Smith said at last. "That's quite a story. I don't know that it necessarily points to the same men, but I will tell you what I know."

"Can I not speak to Miss Byrne?" Gemma tried. It would help to speak to the victim and learn anything she might remember of that night.

Mrs. Smith seemed to sink deeper into the armchair and her expression when she looked up at Gemma was one of deep sorrow. "Saoirse is dead, Miss Tate."

"Oh, I'm so sorry."

Mrs. Smith nodded and exhaled heavily. "I blame myself for what happened."

"Why? How could you be responsible for what happened?"

"Saoirse was a cousin on my mother's side. She had expressed a desire to come to England and I thought I would offer her a position. This way she wouldn't be alone in a strange place, and I would have domestic help and companionship in my widowhood. The reason I didn't tell anyone she was a relation was because there are those who would hold my Irish heritage, diluted though it may be, against me and withdraw their custom. People can be very unkind."

"Yes, I know," Gemma replied sadly.

"It was because Saoirse was my cousin that I gave her so much freedom. I didn't think she should have to join me in my mourning, so she sometimes went out."

"Who did she go with?" Gemma asked.

"She met a girl from Dublin at Covent Garden Market, and they became friends. On the night in question, the two of them had gone to Vauxhall Gardens, but became separated in the melee. When Saoirse couldn't locate her friend, she went in search of the exit and found herself alone in the Dark Walk. She saw a group of gentlemen and asked for directions."

Mrs. Smith's voice caught, and she went silent, her gaze straying toward the window while she tried to compose herself. "These were no gentlemen," she choked out at last. "They grabbed her and pushed her down on the ground. I don't need to tell you what happened next."

"No," Gemma replied, her heart squeezing with pity for the girl. She must have been terrified.

Gemma's mind was teeming with questions, but Mrs. Smith looked so distraught she had to give her the opportunity to tell the story in her own time, so she waited.

"I was beside myself when I saw Saoirse the following morning," Mrs. Smith finally said. "She was broken, and frightened to so much as go outside. I had convinced her to go to the police, thinking it might help her to feel better if the culprits were found, but the policeman who took her statement ridiculed her and made her feel grubby and worthless."

"I had much the same experience when I went to speak to them about Victor," Gemma said. "I was evicted from the police station."

Mrs. Smith nodded. "So you understand." She sighed heavily. "I don't think Saoirse would have gotten over what was done to her, but she would have learned to live with it. We all live with tragedy, don't we? Except that she found herself with child."

"Oh no," Gemma cried.

Mrs. Smith nodded. "I offered to give her something that would take care of the problem, but she couldn't do it. Being Catholic..." Her voice trailed off and she wiped the tears that slid down her cheeks. "She said it wasn't the child's fault and she would bring it up with love and acceptance."

"Did she die in childbirth?"

Mrs. Smith shook her head. "Saoirse decided to go back to Ireland, to her family. I begged her to tell her father that she was briefly married but was now widowed, but she couldn't bring herself to lie. She told him the truth of what happened. He beat her, berated her, and told her it was her fault, and she was a disgrace. He said the child would be given to an orphanage as soon as it was born. The next day Saoirse walked into a lake and condemned her soul to hell."

"How awful," Gemma cried. "She must have been in such torment."

Mrs. Smith nodded. "I should have been stricter with her. Should have forbidden her to go out in the evening, but I wanted her to see something of London and have a nice time while she was young enough to enjoy it."

"It wasn't your fault, Mrs. Smith," Gemma said.

"Maybe not, but I still feel responsible."

Gemma clasped her hands in her lap. She wanted to ask Mrs. Smith all manner of things but worried that the other woman would see her questions as intrusive in view of what had happened to her cousin.

"It's all right, Miss Tate. Go on and ask," Mrs. Smith said, obviously sensing Gemma's frustration. "I did promise that I would tell you the truth."

"Did Saoirse tell you anything about the men? Did she describe them?"

"She said that they were well-dressed and well-spoken."

"Did she see their faces?" Gemma asked.

"They wore silk masks over their eyes, and it was very dark. The Dark Walk was never well lit."

Gemma nodded. The poor girl must have been in a bad way. It was a wonder she managed to find her way home after what happened. There was nothing Mrs. Smith could tell Gemma that would either confirm or rule out a connection, and it was best that she left. She had obviously stirred up very painful memories and she was sorry for that.

"Thank you, Mrs. Smith. I'm sorry to have intruded on your grief," Gemma said, but Mrs. Smith didn't seem to hear her.

She said, "Saoirse did say something else. She had tried to tell the policeman who took her statement, but he dismissed it out of hand."

"What was it?" Gemma asked.

"The men spoke of appeasing the pagan gods through ritual sacrifice. And it was August the first. Lughnasadh."

"Lughnasadh?"

"It's a Gaelic festival that's celebrated in Ireland. Its origins are pagan."

"I see," Gemma said. All Hallows' Eve was also deeply rooted in pagan lore. "Did Saoirse hear anything else?" she went on. If the men had spoken, they might have unwittingly revealed something else.

"She heard several names mentioned as they egged each other on."

"What were they?" Gemma was at the edge of her seat, hoping for a real clue.

"Thomas. Peter. Also John. She said the one called Peter told her she was their bride, and it was her wedding night."

Gemma gritted her teeth. How cruel these men were, and how elusive. There were countless men named Thomas, Peter, and John. Still, relevant or not, she would tell Inspector Bell what she had learned and let him decide if it was useful.

"Thank you, Mrs. Smith. I appreciate your help."

Mrs. Smith escorted Gemma to the door. "I hope your inspector can find a way to make use of the information, but I can't see that he will make head or tail of this tale."

Gemma permitted herself a small smile. "He's a surprisingly clever man."

FORTY-ONE

Leaving Smith's, Gemma set off for Holborn. As she watched the streets go past through the grimy windows of the omnibus, she went over what Harriet Smith had told her. The more she thought about it, the more she believed that what happened to Saoirse Byrne was in some way relevant. And she also felt indescribably angry. Whether the men who attacked Saoirse were the same ones who'd assaulted Adelaide Seaborne remained to be seen, but the very fact that well-bred men could get away with attacking women without fear of retribution was maddening.

Saoirse Byrne was dead because of what was done to her, and so was Amelia Paine. Two lives lost with no consequences for those who had so carelessly destroyed them. No wonder Inspector Bell was so determined to find the perpetrators. He couldn't bear the injustice of it and needed to right the wrong, even if it was too late for the victims. And she was going to help him, Gemma vowed as she got off the omnibus.

It took time to find the correct address but, once she did, Gemma couldn't bring herself to walk up to the Paines' door. It wasn't that she was afraid to hear what Mrs. Paine had to say; it was that she felt guilty. Gemma was introspective enough to realize that she was dealing with her own pain by hiding behind the suffering of others and hated herself for it.

Inspector Bell would probably tell her that she was being unreasonable, but Gemma knew the truth of the matter. She had been the same after her parents died. That was probably the real reason she had volunteered to follow Florence Nightingale to Crimea. She had needed a purpose, and work to occupy all the endless hours a well-bred young lady was expected to fill without having anything real to do, especially while in mourning. There was only so much reading, letter-writing, solitary walks, and embroidery one could stomach, and without anyone to spend time with she had been lost. She had poured all her time and care into her patients, focusing on their pain instead of her own loneliness and grief. She had helped hundreds of men, but they had also helped her. They had given her a purpose and a place to channel her energy and feelings, and for that she was grateful.

And now, here she was, looking for renewed purpose and a place to siphon her grief. She doubted the conversation would help Mrs. Paine, but it would help Gemma. To speak to another woman of loss and grief would allow her to feel less alone. Perhaps Mrs. Paine would feel the same and welcome the chance to speak about her daughter. Finding her courage at last, Gemma walked up to the door and knocked, and hoped that the Paines still lived at this address.

The woman who opened the door was in her mid to late forties. She was slight and had a birdlike quality Gemma found endearing. Her ginger hair was scraped back into a tight bun, and her gown was unrelieved black. Either she had lost someone recently or she was still in deep mourning for her daughter. Mrs. Paine cocked her head to the side and studied Gemma for a moment, as if unsure if she had forgotten an appointment and should apologize for the oversight.

"Good afternoon," Gemma began. "My name is Gemma Tate. Am I addressing Mrs. Paine?"

"Yes," the woman replied, then her expression instantly hardened. "If you're collecting for some charity, I can't help you. I have no time for do-gooders or any coin to spare. I barely manage to scrape by as it is."

She began to shut the door, but Gemma hurried to forestall her. "I'm here about Amelia."

Mrs. Paine froze, her expression resembling a startled deer. "Amelia?" she whispered.

"Mrs. Paine, I'm sorry to disturb you, and I know this must be a painful subject, but I'm working with the police, and I was hoping I could ask you a few questions about your daughter."

"You're working with the police?" Mrs. Paine asked, her eyes widening in disbelief. "Well, now I've heard it all. What sort of fool do you take me for?"

"I'm not trying to dupe you," Gemma replied. "Have you seen the papers? The story about the young woman found in Highgate?"

Mrs. Paine nodded. "The Angel," she said bitterly. "No one called my Millie an angel. There were a few other names they had for her that I don't care to repeat." Her gaze narrowed. "Are you with a newspaper? Is this some dirty trick to get me to talk to a reporter?"

"I am not a reporter, but my brother was, and he was murdered after the woman's body was found. Victor had seen the suspect, you see," Gemma hurried to explain before Mrs. Paine could shut the door in her face.

"And now you're going to sell my story to the papers?" Mrs. Paine demanded, her voice shrill with indignation.

"No. I'm assisting Inspector Bell in his inquiries. He's interviewing other victims."

That got Mrs. Paine's attention. "Other victims?"

"There were two other young women who reported a similar attack. Both took place on All Hallows' Eve."

Mrs. Paine nodded. "A day I'll never forget."

"Please, may I come in?" Gemma asked. "This is not a conversation to have on the front step."

Mrs. Paine hesitated but finally stepped aside to allow Gemma inside. "Come into the parlor, then."

Gemma wasn't invited to take off her coat, so she didn't expect a long chat, but at least she was in the door. She hoped she could learn something, no matter how trivial.

"So who was she, this woman in Highgate?" Mrs. Paine asked once they were seated.

"Her name was Adelaide Seaborne," Gemma said. She had to be truthful if she expected Mrs. Paine to be candid in return. And Adelaide's name would be in the papers soon enough, so she wasn't betraying Inspector Bell's confidence.

"Adelaide Seaborne?" Mrs. Paine repeated.

"Yes. Did you know her?"

"No, but the name sounds familiar." Mrs. Paine looked pensive, as if she were trying to recall where she might have heard the name.

"Perhaps you'd seen the name in the society column," Gemma suggested.

"Yes, I must have," Mrs. Paine muttered, but she didn't look convinced.

"Can you tell me what happened to Amelia, Mrs. Paine?" Gemma asked gently.

Mrs. Paine nodded sadly. Despite her reticence, she seemed eager to talk about her daughter. "Millie was a good girl," she said. "A dutiful girl. She was so happy when she found the position at the milliner's. They needed someone to greet the customers and take down the orders, but they were going to train her up, teach her how to make hats. I've been widowed these fifteen years. I couldn't afford to pay for an apprenticeship, but this would have given Millie a start in life."

"It sounds like it was a very good opportunity, indeed," Gemma agreed.

"And it was. Millie contributed her wages to the household. She never kept anything back for herself. I told her, 'Millie, buy yourself something nice. You deserve it.' But she said, 'No, Mama. I have everything I need.' That's the kind of girl she was. Not a selfish bone in her body."

"What happened that day, Mrs. Paine?" Gemma asked gently.

"I don't know," Mrs. Paine said. Her pain was so raw, Gemma could feel its echo in her own heart. "Millie went to work as usual. When she didn't come home for supper, I became worried. I kept looking out the window, keeping watch for her. But she never came," she choked out. "I told myself there was some big order and Millie had to help get it ready in time, but the hours crawled by and there was no sign of her."

Mrs. Paine was openly crying now, her plain lawn handkerchief balled in her trembling hand. "In the morning, I went right over to Scotland Yard. I could have gone to the local station, but I wasn't taking any chances. I went straight to the top."

She wiped her streaming eyes and continued. "They were nice enough. Took down the details and told me to go home. It was about three hours later that a constable came by. A nice fellow, and very apologetic. He told me they had found a body that matched Millie's description and would I come to the mortuary with him to identify her." A desperate sob tore from Mrs. Paine's chest. "It was her. It was my precious girl. They covered her up to the chin, but I knew. I knew they were trying to hide what was done to her."

"I'm so sorry, Mrs. Paine," Gemma said.

Mrs. Paine nodded. "I'm sorry too. My Millie didn't deserve

that. She was always kind to everyone. She should have found a nice young man, married, and had a family of her own, and lived long enough to bounce grandchildren on her knee."

Mrs. Paine buried her face in the handkerchief, overcome by grief. She'd never see her daughter marry and would never bounce grandchildren on her own knee. Her only family and her future had been taken away from her in one fell swoop the day Amelia was taken.

"Mrs. Paine, was there anyone you can think of who might have wanted to hurt Amelia? Maybe someone she'd rejected or someone who'd been watching her?"

Mrs. Paine shook her head. "Millie never rejected anyone. Not in the way you think."

"So, there was nothing? Surely you must have gone over every detail, every word Millie had said. Was there no one she had mentioned? Perhaps one of the customers had made her uneasy."

"No. She never said anything like that. She enjoyed working with people. She had a knack for it."

Gemma sighed resignedly. She wasn't going to learn anything more from Mrs. Paine. She had just got up to leave when the other woman looked at her, her eyes puffy and her nose reddened with crying.

"She met her, you know."

"Met who?"

"The girl they found on All Saints' Day."

"Amelia had met Adelaide Seaborne?"

Mrs. Paine nodded. "She came into the shop one day. Something in the window caught her eye, and she wanted to have a closer look. That's how I know the name. Millie told me about her. I've only just remembered."

"Did they converse?" Gemma asked, leaning forward in her eagerness to hear more.

"Briefly. About the hat. Millie said Miss Seaborne was

beautiful, gracious, and wealthy. The perfect bride for any noble gentleman."

"Yes, I suppose she was," Gemma replied. Then a thought occurred to her. "Who was she with, Mrs. Paine?"

"With?"

"When she came into the shop. Surely she wasn't out walking by herself. Did she have her maid with her?"

"No. She was with a gentleman. Millie never mentioned his name."

"Did she describe him?" Gemma asked, desperate to learn something about the man.

Mrs. Paine stared into the distance as she tried to recall what her daughter had said. "He was older than Miss Seaborne and had dark hair and a pencil moustache. Millie said he was handsome, and ever so charming. He even paid her a compliment and thanked her for helping Miss Seaborne."

"When was this?"

"About a fortnight before Milli—" She couldn't manage to finish the sentence.

"Did Millie ever see this man again?" Gemma asked.

Mrs. Paine stared at her. "Where would she have seen him?"

"Perhaps he came into the shop again."

"Oh, no. Miss Seaborne changed her mind about the bonnet, and they left. That was the last she saw of either of them."

"Thank you, Mrs. Paine. I appreciate you talking to me."

Mrs. Paine smiled through the tears. "It's nice to be able to speak of her. Everyone is all sympathy and kindness at first, but then, after the funeral is done and time passes, no one wants to talk about the dead. They've moved on. I suppose that's the way of the world. Doesn't help anyone to dwell on these things. Too morbid. And if it could happen to my Millie, it could happen to anyone's child. People don't like to think such things. Reminds them how fragile life is. In the end, you're alone with your grief, and it's the one companion that never truly leaves you."

Gemma nodded. She understood too well how such loss transformed one's soul. "I'm sorry, Mrs. Paine."

"I'm sorry for your loss too, Miss Tate. But I suppose they'll catch the vile creature now."

"Why do you say that?"

Mrs. Paine gave Gemma a knowing look. "No one cares when a girl like my Millie is murdered, but when the daughter of a viscount is the victim, well, that's a different story altogether, isn't it."

Gemma couldn't argue with that, so she thanked Mrs. Paine again and left her to her memories. She was eager to share what she had learned with Inspector Bell.

FORTY-TWO

Sebastian pulled out his pocket watch and checked the time. If he hurried, it wouldn't be too late to call on Miss Tate, and he was eager to hear what she had learned from Mrs. Paine. Perhaps nothing at all, but it was nice to talk to someone and exchange ideas, and, since Miss Tate wasn't employed by the police service, he could theorize freely and not worry about the consequences. Helpful as Ransome had been, he was too ambitious not to seize a promising opportunity if it presented itself. He could put forth his own supposition to the superintendent and possibly even take over if Sebastian failed to solve the case quickly enough.

Miss Tate smiled when she opened the door, but the smile didn't reach her eyes. She looked tired, heartbreakingly fragile, and achingly melancholy.

"Please, come in, Inspector," she said, and held out a hand for his things.

Sebastian surrendered his coat and hat and followed her into the parlor. There was no dinner or a warm fire in the parlor tonight, only a cold room illuminated by a single lamp. Sebastian settled before the unlit hearth and watched as Miss Tate sank into the other chair.

"Miss Tate, are you quite all right?" he asked. It was a foolish question; he knew that, but he could hardly fail to acknowledge her sorry state.

"By this time tomorrow, Victor will be in the ground, and I will no longer have an excuse to put off real life."

"You are still in mourning," Sebastian reminded her, and she chuckled mirthlessly.

"Mourning is for those who can afford it, Inspector. I have to return to work, and look for new lodgings in my spare time. Life doesn't stop for death."

"No, it doesn't."

"Were you able to learn anything from the two women?"

"Nothing concrete, but I do have several more pieces to fit into this puzzle."

"And do they begin to form a picture?" Miss Tate asked.

"Both women were picked up by well-dressed young men. They invited them into their carriage and took them to a church, where their cronies waited in the undercroft. The men wore masks to disguise their identities, but their speech identified them as gentlemen. The man who came for Polly Lawrence arrived in place of Jonathan Wright and had one damaged eye. The man who solicited Hetty did not."

"So Polly was taken by Thomas Wright," Miss Tate concluded.

"I believe so. The two prostitutes were allowed to live, probably because the men didn't have anything to fear from them. No one would believe them and, even if they did, no judge or jury would ever take the word of a streetwalker over the word of a gentleman. Perhaps the other two victims presented more of a threat."

Miss Tate gave Sebastian a shy look. "I think I might have another piece of the puzzle for you, Inspector."

"Oh?"

"I spoke to Harriet Smith."

It took Sebastian a moment to recall who Harriet Smith was and how she fit into the investigation, but when he did he sat up straighter, his undivided attention on Miss Tate. "How did you locate her, Miss Tate?"

"It's quite a coincidence really, but Mrs. Smith owns a chemist's shop in Bethnal Green Road. We are acquainted."

"Why did you not say so before?" Sebastian demanded.

"I didn't realize," Miss Tate replied. "It was only when I saw the sign—"

"I see."

Sebastian wanted to chastise her for going behind his back and conducting her own investigation, but he couldn't help but be a little bit impressed by the intrepid Miss Tate. Besides, she was obviously all right, so no harm done, and he did want to hear what she had learned.

"And did you also speak to Saoirse Byrne?" he asked.

"Miss Byrne is dead."

Miss Tate relayed the details of the conversation, while Sebastian listened in silence, his anger and pity for Saoirse Byrne simmering just beneath the surface.

"The poor woman," he said once Miss Tate had finished. "She must have been absolutely desperate to resort to taking her own life."

"Yes," Miss Tate agreed. "What sort of parent drives their child to such despair?"

"The sort that's more concerned with his standing in the community than the well-being of their child," Sebastian replied. "Miss Byrne isn't the first daughter to be punished for the transgressions of others. The workhouses are full of women who put their faith in a man, in one way or another."

"I think there's a connection between what happened to Saoirse and the murder of Adelaide Seaborne," Miss Tate said.

Sebastian nodded. "So do I. I am sure there are more victims. I only wish I knew their names."

"And the dates must be significant. These men seem to strike on pre-Christian festival days."

"It would appear that they feel an affinity for the gods of old. Or maybe it's just a convenient story to justify their crimes, which is the more likely explanation. A sacrifice is always more noble than plain old murder. And a wedding to a deity sounds more romantic than rape," Sebastian replied.

"But if they worship the old ways, why take their victims to a church?"

"Maybe some perverse desire to anger God, or maybe because they didn't think they'd be disturbed and thought it a fitting setting for what they planned to do. I think I know exactly what church they used."

"You do?" Miss Tate exclaimed. "But there are hundreds of churches in London. How can you be certain?"

"This church is special," Sebastian said. "All Hallows by the Tower. It's the only church that has a weather vane, a crypt, and a name synonymous with the day the women were taken. I will visit the church tomorrow and see if I can find any evidence of Adelaide Seaborne's murder."

"It's been several days. Do you think there's anything left to find?"

"How often do they clean the crypt?"

"Valid point," Miss Tate agreed. She looked like she wanted to say something more but wasn't sure she should bring it up.

"What is it, Miss Tate?"

"The church is quite far from Highgate Cemetery and has its own graveyard. Why not leave the body there?"

"The men had a carriage at their disposal, and perhaps there was a particular reason the body was taken to Highgate," Sebastian said.

Miss Tate nodded. "And the body of Amelia Paine was taken to Kensal Green Cemetery. Also a good distance away, if she had been taken to the same church."

"Perhaps they wanted to ensure that we didn't connect the body to the crime scene."

"And what of the women themselves?"

"There doesn't appear to be a link between the four women, so perhaps they were selected randomly," Sebastian mused.

"I'm not so sure about that," Miss Tate said softly.

Sebastian waited for her to elaborate.

"Mrs. Paine happened to mention that Miss Seaborne came into the shop where Amelia worked. She was interested in a bonnet she had seen in the window."

Sebastian sat forward, fully alert.

"Do you think that's important?" Miss Tate asked.

"Could be," Sebastian replied. "Or it could mean nothing. The milliner is in Oxford Street. It's a central location where most fashionable ladies shop. Did Amelia say anything else?"

"Yes," Miss Tate supplied eagerly. "She was accompanied by a gentleman, who made a point of complimenting Amelia on the fine service she had provided. Mrs. Paine did not know the man's name, but Amelia had described him to her."

"What did he look like, this gentleman?"

"Amelia described him as handsome and charming. He had dark hair and a pencil moustache and was older than Adelaide."

"Is that so?" Sebastian asked, the gears in his mind immediately beginning to mesh.

It was a tenuous link, but it was a material connection between the victims and not to be ignored. And Sebastian could think of one suspect who wore a pencil moustache. Oliver Mayhew. Mayhew had an alibi, but alibis could be fabricated or bought, or even obtained by means of coercion. If Oliver Mayhew was in any way connected to the murders of Adelaide

Seaborne and Amelia Paine, Sebastian would have to find evidence and come at him with irrefutable proof, otherwise Mayhew would secure the services of the best lawyer money could buy and find a way to evade justice.

"What a sad coincidence," Miss Tate was saying. "Two lovely young women who couldn't have known that their lives would soon be cut short, possibly by the same man."

"There is something that might not be a coincidence, though," Sebastian replied. "Polly Lawrence remembers one of the men saying, 'You're now the bride of Hades,' which is very similar to what was said to Saoirse Byrne. And Hetty said that the man who invited her into the carriage called himself Haden, but she wasn't certain."

"Could be Hades. Hades abducted Persephone and took her to the Underworld to be his bride. Could this be some twisted version of the myth?"

"I don't know much about mythology, but the similar name does point to the same group of men. Perhaps Miss Paine was a test. They wanted to see if the police would follow up if they took a woman who was not a prostitute."

"Saoirse Byrne wasn't a prostitute," Miss Tate was quick to point out.

"No, but the men came upon her by chance. They knew nothing of who she was and, given that she was alone in the Dark Walk at night, they might have assumed she was looking for custom."

Miss Tate blushed and lowered her gaze. "Perhaps they wanted a virgin when they took Amelia Paine."

"That's what I was thinking," Sebastian said. "There was an investigation, but it was quickly abandoned. And no one bothered to follow up on the claims of the two surviving victims." An idea had come to him while they were conversing, and he was suddenly eager to be on his way. "I'm sorry, but I must leave you, Miss Tate. What time is the funeral tomorrow?"

"Two o'clock, but you don't have to come," Miss Tate protested. "You didn't even know Victor."

Sebastian smiled. "I know you," he said, and saw gratitude in her eyes.

FORTY-THREE

The evening was clear, the sky full of stars. Sebastian would have liked to walk, but time was of the essence, so he found a cab and gave the driver the address. When he arrived, he didn't go up to the front door but skirted around the building to the tradesmen's entrance. He thought the staff might be in the middle of dinner service, or, if the family liked to dine early, the staff might have finished serving and be having their own dinner.

A young footman opened the door and stared at Sebastian in obvious outrage. "It's a bit late to come calling," he said reproachfully.

Sebastian held up his warrant card. "I need to speak to the coachman."

"He's having his supper."

"This won't take long. Has the family already dined?"

"They have," the footman replied. "What of it?"

"How many were there to dinner this evening?"

"Just Mr. and Mrs. Wright. Why do you ask?"

"No reason."

The footman shrugged. "Wait here," he said, which was just

as well since Sebastian needed to speak to the coachman in private, not in the hall, where they would be surrounded by curious servants.

A few moments later, a man of about forty-five came out to greet him. He was of middling height and considerable width. His sizeable paunch strained the buttons of his waistcoat, and his cheeks rested atop a limp collar. A ring of fuzz that put Sebastian in mind of Caesar's laurels encircled his nearly bald head. The man didn't look too pleased to have his meal interrupted, but some things couldn't be helped. Sebastian showed him his warrant card, then asked him to step outside.

"What's this about, then?" the man asked. He tried to seem indifferent, but Sebastian thought he detected a note of nervousness.

"What's your name?"

"Barry Watkins."

"Mr. Watkins, I need to ask you a few questions."

"'Bout what?"

"A case I'm working on," Sebastian said casually.

"All right. What'd you need to know?"

"Does Thomas Wright have the use of the carriage?"

The coachman's eyes narrowed with suspicion, but to refuse to answer would be an admission in itself. "Yes, he does. What of it?"

"Did he take out the carriage on Sunday evening?"

The coachman nodded.

"And when he borrows the carriage, does he expect you to drive him?"

"That's not part of the deal," Barry Watkins replied. "He uses his own driver."

"So, he has a driver, but doesn't own a carriage," Sebastian stated just to be clear.

"That's correct."

"Have you met his driver? Is it always the same person?" Sebastian asked.

"Yeah, I met him. Don't know his name, though. We were never introduced. But he looked dodgy, if you know what I mean."

"I do. Can I see the carriage, Mr. Watkins?"

"You want to see Mr. Wright's carriage? What, now?"

"Yes, now. Can you get a lantern and show me?"

Barry Watkins sighed heavily; he must have realized he was likely to have to wait a good while to finish his supper. "Can't you come back in the morning?" he asked, a hopeful note creeping into his voice.

"I'm afraid not."

"Is Mr. Thomas in some sort of trouble?" Barry Watkins asked, now that the penny had dropped.

"No," Sebastian said soothingly. "I just want to make sure it wasn't your master's carriage that was involved in a fatal accident."

"I would've known if it was," the coachman said, clearly relieved. "It was in good repair when he brought it back on Monday," he hurried to add.

Mr. Watkins led Sebastian to the carriage house at the bottom of the yard and opened the door. The space was dark and smelled of leather, grease, and straw. The coachman walked over to a shelf, found a box of lucifer matches, and lit a lantern, then held it aloft until the carriage was enveloped in a pool of golden light. It was a landau with a black body and convertible roof. The roof was closed, the windows dark except for the pale reflection of the lantern. The carriage had a sinister, watchful air, as if it were a sentient being that wished to keep its secrets.

"May I have that?" Sebastian said, and reached for the lantern.

"You mean to look inside?" Mr. Watkins asked.

"I will leave it as I found it, Mr. Watkins. You have my word. Have you cleaned the interior since Monday?"

The coachman looked embarrassed. "Not as such," he confessed, then shrugged and handed over the lantern. He stood next to Sebastian, peering over his shoulder the entire time.

Sebastian didn't see anything incriminating right off, but, once he moved the lantern further in, he spotted several brown spots on the floor and a smudged stain on the tufted leather seat. He licked his finger, rubbed it against the stain, and was gratified when his fingertip came away red with blood. Someone had bled inside the carriage, but he had no proof it was Adelaide Seaborne.

Sebastian climbed in, set the lantern on the seat, and carefully examined the backrest. At first glance there was nothing to find, but then he spotted several long, fair hairs that had snagged on the buttons of the tufting closest to the far side of the carriage. He carefully pulled the hairs loose and pushed them into the pocket of his waistcoat.

"Do the Wrights use the carriage often?" Sebastian asked conversationally as he stepped out.

"Not so much anymore. Not since Mr. Thomas left home and Mr. Michael went off to Eton."

"And what color is Mrs. Wright's hair?" Sebastian asked.

Mr. Watkins looked mystified but answered dutifully. "Dark."

"Does she have a maid?"

"Yeah."

"What color is her hair?"

"Also dark."

"Are there any other women who ride in this carriage?"

"No. Why are you asking all these questions?"

"Just being thorough," Sebastian replied.

Both Mrs. Wright and her maid would wear bonnets when

riding in the carriage, as was only proper, but it was important to make certain the hair couldn't be theirs. Sebastian shut the carriage door, handed Watkins the lantern, and headed toward the double doors of the carriage house.

"So, this is not the carriage, then, that was in the accident?" Watkins asked as he caught up with Sebastian in the yard.

"No, I don't believe so."

"Oh, good. The master would be upset if his carriage was damaged."

"I'm sure he would."

It wasn't lost on Sebastian that Mr. Wright would be more upset about possible damage to the vehicle than the fact that someone had supposedly died. "It might be best if you don't mention the accident when you go back inside," he said.

"No harm done, so nothing to tell."

"Thank you, Mr. Watkins. You've been a great help."

The man shrugged and hurried toward the door.

By the time Sebastian got home, he was bone tired but knew he wouldn't be able to rest. Something had been niggling him since his conversation with Miss Tate and now he knew what it was. Oliver Mayhew wasn't the only suspect to favor a pencil moustache. There was someone else. Someone who now looked different but had been wearing just such a moustache in a photograph Sebastian had seen quite recently. He hadn't paid it any mind at the time, but now that minor detail had taken on a new meaning and could prove to be the final piece of the puzzle.

Sebastian was vibrating like a tuning fork, and his hands were shaking badly. He tossed his coat and hat onto the settee, then sank into a chair before the unlit hearth. The room was cold and damp, and he was hungry, but most of all he needed to relieve the jitteriness and quiet his racing mind. Desperate, he reached for the bottle of tonic, pulled out the stopper with his teeth, and took two long swallows. He promised himself he wouldn't buy another bottle, but he needed to get through tomorrow, and then he'd face his dependency head on.

He had begun to doze when Mrs. Poole arrived with a tray. Sebastian was surprised to find her at his door, since she didn't normally provide supper after hours, but the landlady must have taken pity on him, or hoped that he'd finally notice her and show his gratitude in a way that was more personal. Sebastian thanked her profusely, praised her kindness and thoughtfulness, accepted the tray, and wished her a good night. He wolfed down the cold chicken and boiled potatoes, then put the tray out into the corridor for Mrs. Poole to collect and locked the door. He undressed, turned out the lamp, and got into bed. The sheets were cold, and the springs groaned loudly when his weight settled into the mattress, but it felt good to lie still and close his eyes. Gustav jumped onto the bed and settled next to Sebastian.

Sebastian stroked the silky fur between the cat's ears and muttered, "Goodnight, old son," before falling into a deep sleep. He dreamed of dark, silent churches, cavernous crypts, and men wearing masks, their lips stretched into ugly smiles, their teeth unusually long, like fangs. Then the dream changed, and he was in a carriage. His body was slumped against the seat, his head knocking against the side as the carriage sped toward Highgate.

He woke sometime in the night, and in those few moments of consciousness he thought he felt Adelaide Seaborne's presence. She was trying to tell him something, but she was speaking in a foreign tongue. Greek, maybe. He didn't speak Greek, but he was certain she had just told him that she was the bride of Hades.

FORTY-FOUR

Friday, November 5

Sebastian was up early. His head felt like it was stuffed with cotton wool, his mouth was dry, and his extremities were stiff with cold. He washed and dressed quickly. When he bent to tie his boots, he noticed the corner of a page peeking out from beneath the woven hearthrug. He reached down, pulled out what was left of the paper, and let out a guffaw of laughter. Gustav had got hold of Sebastian's letter to the Pinkertons and had shredded it to ribbons. The culprit sat before Sebastian, looking at him with an expression of what could only be described as self-righteous smugness.

"I should punish you for this, you little rascal," Sebastian said. Predictably, Gustav did not reply, but did something with his shoulders that resembled a human shrug.

"I can write another one, you know."

Gustav tilted his head to the side and fixed his green gaze on Sebastian's face, as if waiting for him to come to a decision.

"You're probably right," Sebastian said as he knotted his tie. "Terrible idea. What would I do in America anyway?"

There were plenty of things he could do in America, but neither Colin Ramsey nor Miss Tate would be there, and he suddenly felt bereft at the thought of never seeing either of them again. It had been a long time since he had cared for anyone, and the feeling took him by surprise. He would invite Colin for a drink once the case was concluded, and he was sure he could find a reason to call on Miss Tate. If only to see how she was getting on. And he could always write another letter to Mr. Pinkerton if the situation called for it.

Completely unconcerned with Sebastian's emotional needs, Gustav walked over and nudged him with his nose. Sebastian made a mental note to buy him a nice fish on the way home and headed out. He didn't have time to wait for Mrs. Poole to make him breakfast. He'd buy a sausage roll and a mug of tea from a street vendor later, but first he had to get to the church.

The morning was misty and cold, smoke from a forest of chimneys drifted on the wind, and the briny tang of the Thames grew stronger as he neared the river. Fragments of his disturbing dream returned as he approached All Hallows by the Tower and took in the forbidding facade.

All Hallows was one of London's oldest churches. It had survived the Great Fire of 1666 and had been restored a number of times since. The assorted architects had each left their mark on the ancient building and, although the church was massive, it wasn't as beautiful or as welcoming as some of the other churches in London. As he stood before the arched doorway, Sebastian felt an odd reluctance to go inside, but he needed to examine the undercroft. He was certain he'd find what he was looking for, and the evidence would strengthen his case.

Despite the unhappy marriage of architecture styles, the interior boasted some lovely stained-glass windows, medieval statuary, and an intricately carved cover for the baptismal font, but Sebastian was not interested in any of these features. He found the stairs to the crypt and hurried down before anyone decided to inquire as to his purpose. He didn't think too many people went down to the undercroft, since there was nothing they could possibly wish to see, and had no desire to explain his reasons to some irritable clergyman.

The only light in the crypt came through the open door. Sebastian could make out the shapes of the stone coffins and an ancient archway, but the crypt was too dark to conduct a search. Several candles stood mounted on tall holders, and Sebastian looked around for something to light them with. He eventually found a box of matches discreetly hidden behind the base of a candleholder.

Striking a match, Sebastian lit two candles and took in the low-ceilinged space. It wasn't overly frightening, but he could imagine how terrifying the stone chamber might seem when crowded with masked men, their glittering eyes and cruel mouths lit only by candlelight. He reached for one of the candles and held it low to the floor. It didn't take long to find what he was looking for. Smears of dried blood were concentrated near the center of the room, and a few strands of golden hair were caught between the ancient stones. Another stain was level with where the head would be if the hair was indicative of Adelaide's position. If someone had no idea what had happened there, they'd never notice the hair, and the brown smudges could be explained away as dirt, but Sebastian knew precisely what they were. This was the place, and now he had the proof.

Carefully freeing the hair, Sebastian stowed it in his other pocket to keep it separate from the hair he had taken from the carriage. He then examined every inch of the crypt, in case Adelaide's clothes had been shoved behind one of the stone caskets or left in a dark corner. Finding nothing, he blew out the candles and hurried up the stone stairs, his steps echoing on the flagstone floor as he headed for the exit. The windows that had to be glorious when the sun was out were dull in the sullen light of the autumn morning, the interior dim and silent, the church strangely eerie.

When Sebastian arrived at Scotland Yard, he was glad to learn that Thomas Wright had been brought in not a quarter of an hour before and had made such a ruckus that he'd had to be cuffed and taken down to the cells.

"Should Constable Meadows bring him to an interview room?" Sergeant Woodward asked.

"Let him stew a few minutes longer," Sebastian said. "Is Lovell in?"

"Just arrived, and he's not in good spirits. I'd stay out of his way if I were you."

Sebastian nodded and headed directly to the superintendent's office.

Lovell folded the paper he was reading and shot Sebastian a baleful look. The headline screamed:

ANGEL UNAVENGED
Adelaide Seaborne's Killer Still At Large

"When I find out who leaked the victim's name to the press, I will personally see to it that the treacherous bastard spends the rest of his life in Coldbath Fields."

"I don't think anyone here fed the name to the press, sir," Sebastian replied.

"Oh? And what's your explanation for this monumental breach of confidentiality? I expect someone made a handsome profit."

"Is that Jacob Harrow's name in the byline?"

"It is. What of it?"

"I believe he knew all along who the victim was."

"And how would he know? Tell me that, Bell."

"Because he is acquainted with Thomas Wright and was present when Victor Tate was pushed beneath the wheels of the omnibus. He knows considerably more than you give him credit for."

"Which brings me to my next point," Lovell growled. "You had better have a good explanation for why an MP's son is locked in the cells, Bell. I know you believe he was involved, but let's be honest here. You don't have a shred of actual proof."

"Which is why I would like you to sit in on the interview, sir."

"So you can implicate me in your epic failure?" Lovell snapped.

"So that you can take credit for Wright's arrest."

Superintendent Lovell looked marginally mollified. "You have something?"

"I have something."

"Let's go, then."

FORTY-FIVE

Thomas Wright was fuming by the time he was brought into the interview room. He was red in the face and his hands were balled into fists, which he probably wasn't averse to swinging at Sebastian's head. Now that Sebastian was face to face with the man, he could see how startling his eyes were, the damaged one drawing the attention immediately. Although it was cloudy, there was a dark shadow where the pupil should be, while the other eye was black and glittering with fury.

"Unless you wish to be cuffed to the table, Mr. Wright, I suggest you calm down," Sebastian said.

"You ignorant baboon," Wright exclaimed. "How dare you have me dragged from my bed and hauled away in a police wagon for all the neighbors to see? When my father hears of this—"

"When your father hears of this, he will wish to distance himself from you in order to save what's left of his political career," Sebastian replied.

"I'll see you punished for this. And you," Wright bellowed, turning his rage onto the superintendent. "I know who you are. I've seen your photo in the papers. Enjoy your last day on the job, Superintendent. My father dines with Sir David Hawkins and the Home Secretary. He'll see that you never step foot in a police station again, not even as a bobby."

"Are you quite finished, Mr. Wright?" Sebastian asked.

Thomas Wright's anger seemed to have burned itself out, and he sat back, his malevolent gaze raking over Sebastian. Despite the deformity, he was still a good-looking man. He wore his dark hair parted on the side, the forelock carefully pomaded into place. His sideburns were neatly trimmed, and his clothes, although a bit disheveled at the moment, were of good quality and expertly tailored. He was lean and muscular, if not very tall, and his hands were elegant and long-fingered.

"Why am I here?" he demanded when Sebastian failed to state his case.

"A man fitting your description was seen near the body of Miss Adelaide Seaborne on the morning of the first of November. Not two hours later, you were present at the scene of an accident in the Strand that resulted in the death of Victor Tate. Incidentally, what happened to your eye, Mr. Wright?" Sebastian asked, both because he wanted to drive his point home and because he was genuinely curious.

"A childhood injury," Write retorted. "My brother accidentally poked me in the eye with a wooden sword. Not that it's any of your business."

"Still, your eyes do set you apart and make you quite memorable."

Thomas Wright let out a bark of laughter. "That's it? That's all you have?"

"That was just the opening volley."

"All right, then allow me to return fire, since you seem fond of military metaphors. I was nowhere near Highgate Cemetery, and I tried to help the unfortunate man who walked under the wheels of an omnibus. I did what I could for him."

"Well, aren't you the Good Samaritan," Sebastian replied calmly. "Very commendable."

"Are we finished now, Inspector?"

"Not quite."

"What else do you have?" Wright demanded.

Sebastian could feel Superintendent Lovell pulsating with tension. He would have asked the same question if he were of a mind to undermine his detective in front of a suspect.

"Mr. Wright, what year did you complete your studies at Oxford?" Sebastian asked, hoping Wright would correct him. He did.

"It was Cambridge, you idiot, and it was June 1855."

"Since June 1855, four women have been abducted on All Hallows' Eve. All were gang-raped. Two were strangled."

"What's that got to do with me?"

"One of the women was intimately known to your father. The man who came to collect her in your father's stead fits your description."

"Prove it," Wright challenged him with a self-satisfied smirk.

"Oh, I will," Sebastian went on. "You took her to All Hallows by the Tower and brought her down to the crypt, where your friends were waiting. They all wore masks, but even a mask can't hide everything." Sebastian fixed his gaze on the man's unseeing eye and was gratified to see his neck redden and the flush spread to his cheeks.

"I will not be made victim of your unfounded accusations," Wright exclaimed.

"But they are not unfounded, are they?" Sebastian continued. "On Sunday, you dined at your club, the Oxford and Cambridge Club in Pall Mall. You arrived just before seven and left at nine, according to the club's register. Your dinner companion was none other than your good friend, the Honorable George Seaborne," Sebastian announced, and felt the two men in the room stiffen.

"You then borrowed your father's carriage, which you used to collect Adelaide Seaborne, who believed she was to attend an All Hallows' séance. And I think I know just who invited her."

"It wasn't me," Thomas Wright screeched.

"No, it was her brother, who probably said he'd meet her there. Did George Seaborne ever attend a séance and tell his sister about it? Was that how he got her to agree?"

Thomas Wright nodded. "George and I attended a number of séances. I think he hoped his mother would come to him."

"And did she?" Sebastian asked, curious if George ever got what he'd come for.

"No, but another woman came the last time we went." Thomas Wright paled visibly, and Sebastian wondered if he knew exactly who the woman might have been. "She told George that his time was short."

"And did he believe her?"

"No. He found it amusing and proclaimed it to be a clever parlor trick."

"Did George tell Adelaide about his experience at the séance?" Lovell asked. "Was that why she had agreed to come?"

"He didn't tell her what the woman had said, but he did say that we were able to contact the dead. Adelaide was enthralled. She wanted to see an apparition for herself and thought All Hallows' Eve was the optimum time to try."

Thomas Wright sighed heavily. "Adelaide thought it would be spooky and fun and felt safe knowing that George would be there. And I think maybe she hoped that he'd be able to contact his mother. She knew it would bring him peace. She loved him," he added quietly.

Sebastian took a deep breath to tamp down his rage. Now wasn't the time to allow his feelings to show. He had to get Thomas Wright to admit to everything he had done, then use his leverage to coerce the man into betraying his friends.

"George Seaborne used to wear a moustache until quite recently, didn't he?" Sebastian asked. Thomas Wright stared at him, seemingly startled by the change in topic.

"Yes. How do you know that?"

"I saw an engagement portrait of George and his intended in Viscount Dalton's study."

Thomas Wright shrugged. "What of it? Is it a crime to change one's appearance?"

"No," Sebastian replied airily. "In fact, I think it's an improvement. That moustache made him look dodgy."

Thomas Wright smirked, clearly in agreement.

Sebastian could sense Superintendent Lovell's impatience but chose to ignore it. He couldn't afford to rush this. "Did you know that Amelia Paine and Adelaide Seaborne had met, Mr. Wright?" he asked instead.

"No." Thomas Wright was beginning to fidget and made an effort to still his hands, but he couldn't do anything about the mounting anxiety in his gaze.

"Oh yes," Sebastian continued conversationally. "She told her mother all about it. In fact, she had described the gentleman who had accompanied Miss Seaborne and said that he'd even paid her a compliment and thanked her for her excellent service. Handsome, charming, with dark hair and a pencil moustache." Sebastian paused to let that sink in, then continued. "At first, I thought perhaps she had been speaking of Oliver Mayhew, because he wears just such a moustache, but it wasn't him, was it, Mr. Wright?"

When Thomas Wright failed to reply, Sebastian continued. "It couldn't be Oliver Mayhew because Adelaide Seaborne was not yet out when Amelia Paine died. She didn't come out until the following year, so even if they were acquainted it would be most improper for the two of them to venture out alone. But shopping with one's brother is quite common. Miss Seaborne did not need a chaperone when out with George. She was quite safe."

Thomas Wright blanched, his panicked gaze sliding toward the door, so Sebastian went in for the kill. "George Seaborne had hand-picked Amelia Paine. Hadn't he? Just as he had chosen his sister. But it was you he'd sent to pick her up. Adelaide Seaborne wasn't afraid to get into your carriage. After all, she had no reason to think you would do anything to hurt her. You were one of her brother's bosom friends since university, and your father is a good friend to Viscount Dalton. Such a good friend that he gifted the viscount a beautiful and rather expensive edition of the Qur'an."

Thomas Wright's anxiety had been replaced by a white-faced mask of fear, but Sebastian was nowhere near finished.

"You took Adelaide Seaborne to All Hallows by the Tower, where she was raped by your friends. Was this some sort of All Hallows' ritual, Mr. Wright? Something you did every year? An All Hallows' prank? A pagan sacrifice? It seems that you and your friends were quite fond of pre-Christian ideology. The way I see it," Sebastian continued, his gaze never leaving Wright's pale face, "you started out with maidservants and prostitutes, then grew bolder when no one bothered to investigate their claims. But Amelia Paine had described the man she'd seen, and I expect Adelaide Seaborne put up more of a fight than you'd ever expected. I found blood and strands of her hair in both your father's carriage and the crypt at All Hallows by the Tower."

Sebastian took out the strands of hair from his pockets and laid them out on the table. "Shall we compare these to the hair on Miss Seaborne's corpse, or will you admit to your part in her death?"

"I didn't kill her," Thomas Wright choked out.

"You disposed of her body and then murdered the man who had seen your face."

Thomas Wright was white to the roots of his hair, his good eye darting in panic, like that of an animal that had just realized it was trapped and might have to chew off its own limb to free itself.

"I didn't kill either of them. I swear."

"And why should I believe you?" Sebastian asked. He could feel silent approval emanating from Lovell. The superintendent was probably already envisioning more flattering headlines and a possible commendation from the commissioner.

Thomas Wright had turned inward, his shoulders hunched and his head tucked into his body as if he could make himself smaller and less visible.

"Do you have any proof that you didn't kill either Adelaide Seaborne or Victor Tate?" Sebastian asked.

Wright shook his head.

"You will go down for this, son," Superintendent Lovell said. "This is your one chance to save yourself."

"There's no saving myself," Thomas Wright cried. "I'm finished, whether I tell you the truth or not."

"Now that's where you are wrong," Lovell said, adopting the gentle tone of a father talking to his son rather than a policeman browbeating a suspect. "If you're guilty of murder, you will hang. The other crimes carry a prison sentence."

"And you think that's so much better?" Thomas Wright challenged him. "To spend one's life in prison with the rest of London's scum?"

"So, you're ready to die on the scaffold?" Sebastian asked.

For all his bravado, Thomas Wright was clearly terrified, and Sebastian decided to press his advantage even further.

"I know what happened," Sebastian said. He was bluffing, but he needed to keep Thomas Wright talking if he hoped to get to the truth. "It was your loyal friend, George Seaborne, who killed both women, because they recognized him."

"Why would George kill his own sister?" Thomas Wright

asked, but Sebastian thought he was looking for a way to extricate himself. If he could prove George Seaborne hadn't been there, he could claim that he had been with George, and they would both have an alibi.

"Adelaide was his half-sister," Sebastian pointed out. "A half-sister he resented, who would receive a sizeable settlement upon her marriage, which was imminent."

Thomas Wright seemed to shrink further. "He'll think I told you that."

Superintendent Lovell sat up straighter, his attention fixed on the cowering man. He was no longer the loving father but the representative of the law who would push for the harshest penalty. "Mr. Wright, even if you didn't murder either woman or Mr. Tate, you're still guilty of abduction, rape, and willful abuse of a corpse. Likewise, you are an accessory to murder. The accused's willingness to cooperate and evidence of remorse can go some way toward mitigating the sentence. You might not be sentenced to life in prison, in which case you will still have a future once you're released."

A strangled cry tore from Thomas Wright's chest. "What do you need from me?" he rasped.

"For one, we need you to tell us who murdered Amelia Paine, Adelaide Seaborne, and Victor Tate. We will also need the names of your co-conspirators," Sebastian said.

Sebastian thought that if Thomas Wright could find a way to spontaneously combust, he would do so without a second thought; but, without a way to turn himself into a burn mark on the floor, he was trapped. Sebastian might not have irrefutable proof, but he had enough evidence to get a conviction, and Wright knew it. And the only way to reduce his sentence was to give up his friends.

"If I give you the list, will you keep my name out of it?" Thomas Wright asked, his gaze on Superintendent Lovell.

"Each one of those men chose to be there," Lovell said. "You are not responsible for their actions. Only your own."

"Still, I can't have them know it was me," Wright whined.

"They will think it was you regardless," Sebastian said. "There's a reason George Seaborne chose you to dispose of the corpse and follow Victor Tate. Your eye set you apart, and if you were seen, which you were, you would be the one they'd remember, and the one to take the blame."

Thomas Wright didn't bother to argue. He was intelligent enough to realize that this was the moment of truth, and he had to decide whether to sacrifice his own life to protect his friends or give them up in the hope that he might still have a future. "Will you speak to the judge on my behalf?" he pleaded, his gaze sliding between Superintendent Lovell and Sebastian.

"Why don't you draw up that list, and then we'll talk," Superintendent Lovell suggested placatingly.

"Can I do it down in the cells?"

"No, you will do it right here," Sebastian said. He couldn't take the chance of the man finding a way to top himself. "I'll get paper and a pen, shall I?"

Once the list was drawn up, Sebastian had his leverage, and he meant to extract every scrap of information he could to solidify his case against George Seaborne.

"Did George Seaborne murder his sister?" he asked.

Thomas Wright sank even lower in his chair and nodded without meeting Sebastian's gaze.

"And Victor Tate?"

"George pushed Victor Tate under the bus," Thomas Wright whispered. "It was easy, since there was a number of people getting off and on."

"That seems out of character," Sebastian observed. "George Seaborne doesn't strike me as someone who'd be willing to take such a risk."

"He wanted me to do it, but I refused."

"Surely he didn't kill Victor Tate to protect you," Sebastian taunted. "He's not that devoted a friend."

Thomas Wright shook his head. "He thought Victor Tate had spotted him at Highgate, and he wasn't about to take any chances. George didn't think anyone would question that Tate's death was an accident."

"Except that someone did," Sebastian said. If not for Gemma Tate's intuition, he wouldn't have had a hope of solving this case. "I don't have any further questions for Mr. Wright," he said, turning to Superintendent Lovell.

Lovell nodded agreement.

Once the charges were read, a sniveling Thomas Wright was taken down to the cells to await transportation to prison, while Sebastian and Superintendent Lovell returned to Lovell's office.

"I authorize you to arrest George Seaborne," Lovell said. "Once he's in custody, I will have the other men on the list discreetly picked up."

"Do I have your permission to use reasonable force?" Sebastian asked.

"Do what you must, Bell."

"Thank you, sir."

"Sebastian," Lovell said, finally permitting himself a small smile. "Well done, lad."

FORTY-SIX

Sebastian asked Constable Bryant and Constable Meadows to accompany him to Park Lane. They were young and, unlike some of the older men, who'd let themselves go over time, in fighting shape. Sebastian sat on the bench of the police wagon with Constable Meadows, while Constable Bryant was forced to ride inside, a condition he complained about bitterly until it started to rain. He quickly saw the benefit of staying out of the rain, and made the most of his dry ride by singing folk songs.

Lewis didn't bother to argue when they came to the front door. He had seen something in the grim lines of Sebastian's face and the stance of the two constables that awoke his instinct for self-preservation. A good butler acted as gatekeeper for the family, but even a well-trained man knew when to step aside. Lewis left the three men in the foyer while he went to summon George Seaborne, who looked as innocent as a newborn babe when he descended the stairs. He was dressed in a black suit, as befitted a man mourning his sister, but there was something feral in his face, a suppressed excitement, or maybe just an air of expectation. Perhaps he thought they'd come to tell the family they'd made an arrest.

Now that he could see George Seaborne clearly, Sebastian suspected that he had bullied Thomas Wright for years and wouldn't hesitate to implicate him if it came to it. There was a culture of bullying at most schools, and students who came from wealthy, noble families got away with acts of appalling cruelty against those who didn't have the courage or the support to stand up for themselves. Wright's injury set him apart and probably made him an even bigger target. He couldn't hope to beat someone like George Seaborne, so he had joined him instead.

"Inspector Bell, do you have news?" George asked airily.

"I do, Mr. Seaborne," Sebastian replied calmly. "But I think we should discuss my findings in a more formal setting."

George Seaborne looked stunned. "Meaning what, exactly?"

"Meaning that you are under arrest. I suggest you come quietly."

"And if I refuse?" All pretense at nonchalance instantly vanished. George Seaborne tensed, his eyes narrowing and his fingers gripping the banister tighter as he stared Sebastian down.

"Then I will have no choice but to bring you in by force."

George's gaze flitted about, searching for escape, but the closest way out was the front door, now blocked by the policemen. Sebastian supposed George could head the other way and attempt to escape through the conservatory or perhaps the French doors that led onto the terrace at the back of the house and the parkland beyond, but he wouldn't get very far. Outflanked and outnumbered, George Seaborne had little choice but to comply. He descended the last few steps slowly and stopped at the foot of the grand staircase, his gaze narrowed in thought, his hand on the polished railing. Something in his stance forewarned Sebastian that George wasn't ready to give himself up, and he braced himself for anything the other man might resort to. The two constables remained in place, awaiting orders, but, inexperienced as they were, they probably assumed George Seaborne would come quietly.

Whatever options George had been weighing in his mind, the scales must have tipped in favor of flight. He was clever enough to comprehend that Sebastian wouldn't be making an arrest unless the evidence was damning. He lunged sideways, heading toward a shallow alcove that contained an elegant occasional table topped by a statue, one of a pair, whose double occupied the alcove in the opposite wall. The statue was about a foot and a half tall, a bare-breasted nymph that might have been Venus or Aphrodite. Given the effort it took George to lift the thing, Sebastian belatedly realized that the statue was hewn of solid stone, probably marble, and made for a formidable weapon.

George didn't bother with the constables. To him they would be virtually invisible, brainless minions, just like the army of servants that saw to his daily needs. It was Sebastian he feared, and it was Sebastian he went for, roaring with rage and wielding the statue the way one would a club. George was aiming for Sebastian's head, probably hoping to bash his brains in and distract the constables long enough to escape, but Sebastian pirouetted out of the way, the statue missing his head by a hair's breadth. George nearly lost his balance but regained his equilibrium quickly and lunged again. His eyes were wild, his teeth bared, his hand grasping the base of the statue in a death grip.

It was clear that his goal wasn't to incapacitate or deter. He aimed to kill. The constables, who had frozen in the face of such naked aggression, remained rooted to the spot, leaving Sebastian without backup long enough to render him completely vulnerable. He saw the statue coming toward him, Aphrodite's head aiming for his own once again. He may have escaped harm had George Seaborne's arm arced downward, but George effortlessly changed the trajectory and swung his arm sideways. The toga-clad nymph crashed down on Sebastian's clavicle, and he thought he heard the crunch of shattered bone as he staggered backward, lost his balance, and landed heavily on the tiled floor.

Excruciating pain exploded behind his eyes, momentarily blinding him, and a wave of nausea assailed him as the impact of the blow reverberated through his upper body and rattled his teeth. His shoulder was on fire, and he wouldn't dare move it even if he were able to, for fear of the bones splintering and piercing the skin.

All Sebastian could make out was blurry shapes as he remained nearly paralyzed, his limbs refusing to obey. Unless he got out of the way the next blow would smash his skull, the impact splattering his brains all over the black-and-white floor. For a moment, he thought he heard Louisa's voice, urging him to save himself, but he knew it to be a figment of his imagination, the mind's response to physical trauma.

Gathering his wits about him despite the pain, Sebastian tried to scramble away, but George Seaborne loomed above him. His arms were raised as he gripped the statue with both hands like an axe, saliva dripping on Sebastian's face as if George were a rabid dog.

Sebastian shut his eyes, bracing for the blow that would finish him, but that blow never came. Constable Meadows, finally galvanized into action, tackled George Seaborne, letting out a bloodcurdling roar as he knocked him to the floor and wrenched the statue from his hands. Sebastian thought the constable would smash George Seaborne's skull, such was his fury, but he hurled the statue away, the nymph landing on the floor a few feet away with a loud crack that shattered the tiles. The neck, being the narrowest point, cracked, and the head rolled across the floor like a croquet ball, coming to rest near the front door.

When George pinned Constable Meadows down and tried

to strangle him, Constable Bryant finally got in on the action and brought his truncheon down heavily on George Seaborne's back and then his ribs. The blow forced George Seaborne to loosen his grip long enough for Constable Meadows to throw him off. George let forth a stream of obscenity as the two constables cuffed him and hauled him to his feet as if he were a sack of turnips. George threatened to kill them both, then swore he would be there to see them hang for assaulting the son of a viscount, but the constables weren't impressed with his threats.

Knowing himself to be safe at last, Sebastian shut his eyes and tried to breathe through the pain that radiated through his shoulder, neck, and chest, but his body's reaction overwhelmed him. He barely had enough time to turn his head before he emptied his guts onto the floor. The cool tiles felt good beneath his head, so he remained there, giving himself a moment before attempting to stand up. He could see the severed head of the statue out of the corner of his eye, and thanked God that she was the one to lose her head rather than him.

He sat up slowly and gingerly touched his collarbone. He could feel the jagged edge of a bone beneath his fingers, and applied pressure to minimize the damage as he attempted to get to his feet.

"Let me help," Constable Bryant offered. He pulled out his handkerchief and wiped Sebastian's mouth as if he were a child, then slid his arm beneath Sebastian's good arm and raised him to his feet. "You need a doctor," Constable Bryant proclaimed.

"Send for Mr. Ramsey. Ask him to meet me at Scotland Yard."

"Yes, sir," Constable Bryant said. "You heard him," he roared at Lewis. "Send someone to deliver a message."

"Yes, of course," Lewis replied. "I'll need the address."

Sebastian managed to mumble the address, and Lewis dispatched a footman who had been hovering near the stairs.

"I'll see you hang for this, you inbred halfwit," George

Seaborne screamed as Constable Meadows maneuvered him toward the door. "My father will—"

But he never finished the sentence. Viscount Dalton appeared at the top of the stairs, still dressed in his slippers and dressing gown. The viscount looked gaunt and hollow-eyed as he stared at his son and took in the soiled floor and the injured policeman. Lewis tried to speak, but the viscount waved him off as if he were a pesky fly.

"Papa," George cried shrilly. "Tell them to uncuff me."

"On what charge are you arresting my son, Inspector Bell?" the viscount asked, but there was no anger in his voice, only resignation, and sympathy for Sebastian's obvious pain.

"On a charge of murder, my lord," Sebastian replied.

He felt a little unsteady on his feet and wished he had something to hold on to. Since there was nothing nearby, he fixed his gaze on the viscount in order to keep the dizziness at bay. What he saw in the viscount's face wasn't shock but confirmation of what he must have suspected.

"Papa," George screeched again. "Surely you don't believe a word this cretin says. I am your son. Help me."

"I have no son," the viscount said, his voice carrying in the cavernous foyer.

That shut George up. He looked around wildly, probably thinking he might still rely on help from the staff, but none was forthcoming. Lewis stood silently by, his face frozen in horror. Sebastian had seen several parlormaids peek discreetly from the rooms they had been cleaning. One made a beeline for the puddle of vomit and began to clean it up using the brush and dustpan she had with her, her gaze straying to George with a mix of fear and grim satisfaction.

Sebastian's shoulder hurt like the devil, and pain pulsated through his entire left side and seemed to settle in his heart, but he'd be damned if he allowed someone else to question George Seaborne. Just then, Sebastian held all the cards, and Superintendent Lovell would not have enough information to charge the scoundrel. Sebastian followed the constables as they dragged a struggling George Seaborne outside and handed him into the police wagon.

"His lordship says you may use his carriage, on account of your injury," Lewis said as he followed them out. "I'll have it brought round."

Sebastian nodded. "Thank you." He was glad he wouldn't have to ride back with George Seaborne.

He watched as the police wagon pulled away, rattling down the cobblestone drive, and felt every jolt in his throbbing shoulder. He hoped the ride back in the carriage wouldn't be as torturous. The viscount's brougham came rolling from the carriage house, and Sebastian got in and settled on the plush seat. He leaned back and shut his eyes. As long as he didn't move, he could manage to keep the pain at bay.

FORTY-SEVEN

By the time he returned to Scotland Yard Sebastian felt marginally better, but Superintendent Lovell insisted that he be seen to by Colin Ramsey, who had just arrived, carrying his Gladstone bag and looking worried. It wasn't often that he had patients who were still breathing and could feel pain, so he took his duty to Sebastian very seriously.

"How bad is the pain?" he asked when he had settled Sebastian in one of the empty offices and was gently probing his shoulder.

"I think my collarbone is broken."

"That it is," Colin replied. "And I expect there's a fracture to the scapula as well."

"What can you do for it?" Sebastian asked.

Colin Ramsey shook his head. "All I can do is bandage your shoulder to keep the collarbone in place until it heals and give you something for the pain."

"I don't want any laudanum."

"I can give you a dose of morphine."

"A very small dose," Sebastian agreed. "I need to question George Seaborne."

"Think he did it?"

"I'm certain of it," Sebastian replied as Colin reached into his medical bag for a vial of morphine.

He set it aside, then took out a small case, opened it, and extracted a syringe, to which he fitted a needle.

"You're going to give me a shot?" Sebastian asked. He'd never had one before, and the sight of the long, sharp needle wasn't very reassuring.

"I'm going to administer the morphine directly to the affected area and hope that it helps to relieve some of the pain. You're going to be in agony tomorrow," he promised as he palpated Sebastian's shoulder with his fingertips, then chose a spot and pushed in the needle. It didn't hurt as badly as Sebastian had expected, but then, given the amount of pain he was feeling already, it was difficult to tell.

"You should start to feel relief within a few minutes."

"Thank you, Colin."

"My pleasure. After you finish with George Seaborne, I suggest you go home and take to your bed."

Sebastian shook his head. "Can't. I have to go to Victor Tate's funeral."

Colin nodded. "I'm going to come with you."

"I'll be all right."

"I would like to pay my respects to Miss Tate. A remarkable woman," Colin said dreamily.

"Don't go getting ideas," Sebastian said. He was only half joking, but he was gratified by Colin's startled expression.

"I know, she's in mourning, but I think she is in need of a friend," Colin said defensively.

"Couldn't we all?" Sebastian grumbled under his breath as he adjusted his shirt and attempted to fix the cravat.

"Let me do that." Colin Ramsey expertly tied the cravat, then helped Sebastian into his coat. "I'll be right here if you need more pain relief."

"I won't."

"So you say."

"Can I get you anything?" Sergeant Woodward asked before Sebastian entered the interview room. "You look dreadful."

Sebastian shook his head, and instantly regretted the action, since the movement sent a ripple of pain through his entire left side.

"George Seaborne will rue the day he ever laid eyes on you," Sergeant Woodward said under his breath.

"I hope so," Sebastian replied, and went in.

If George Seaborne had used the ride to Scotland Yard to consider his options and come up with a plan of defense, he'd come up short and had seemingly decided to play for sympathy. He was meek as a kitten, his eyes swimming with tears.

"I wasn't there when Addie died," he exclaimed. "I would have never allowed any harm to come to her. I loved her." He made a show of choking up with emotion.

Sebastian's gaze slid to George's cuffed hands, which were large and capable, the fingers powerful and blunt. Physically, he was a match to the killer.

"Mr. Seaborne, we know all about your All Hallows' Eve ritual and who was present. Why don't you tell us how it came into existence," Superintendent Lovell invited. There wasn't a trace of sympathy in either his bearing or his voice.

George Seaborne was wild-eyed, his gaze shifting from Superintendent Lovell to Sebastian and back now that he realized they knew more than he had first imagined.

"It was Thomas Wright," he cried. "His grandfather was a contemporary of Francis Dashwood and was one of the founding members of the Hellfire Club. He filled Thomas's head with stories of the club's past glories and bragged about the things they had done. And got away with," George added. "Thomas suggested we form our own club while we were at

Cambridge. We were all so sick of the endless rules and draconian morals that had been forced on us since birth. It was just an excuse to sow some wild oats."

George Seaborne looked to Superintendent Lovell, his pleading gaze all but saying, *Boys will be boys. Surely you understand.* Superintendent Lovell nailed Seaborne with an unforgiving stare and remained silent, giving Sebastian the floor.

"So being the elite group of intellectuals you believed yourselves to be, you decided to dress your true purpose in mysticism and cloak your activities in secrecy," Sebastian said. "That way, you didn't have to call what you got up to by more fitting names. Rape and murder. Tell us about this society, then, Mr. Seaborne."

The morphine was beginning to work and he felt more comfortable, and murderously angry with this jumped-up popinjay who thought he was above the law and could use people as playthings.

"We called ourselves the Sons of Hades and allowed only thirteen members at any given time to make the club seem more exclusive. All new members had to be vouched for by existing Sons and sworn to absolute secrecy."

This put Sebastian in mind of the Masons, but any secret society was based on similar principles: exclusion, secrecy, and covering for its members when they crossed the line, be it legal or moral.

"Was there an initiation ritual?" Sebastian asked.

George colored. "Well, yes, but it was nothing unlawful."

"What was it?"

"It varied from member to member," George muttered.

"I take it the ritual involved prostitutes?" Superintendent Lovell asked.

George nodded. "But none of them were harmed," he rushed to add.

"I suppose that depends on your definition of harm," Sebastian snapped.

"So, what did you do when you met?" Superintendent Lovell demanded. He could barely manage to keep the disgust out of his voice.

"We met once a month, usually in a private parlor of a local inn. We had a good supper, drank fine wine, and talked."

"And that was all?" Sebastian asked, his voice laced with disbelief.

George exhaled loudly. "We staged Greek orgies using prostitutes. Surely that's not illegal," he said petulantly.

"But dining, drinking, and fornicating wasn't enough, was it?" Lovell asked.

George shook his head. "It was Thomas's idea that we should offer up a sacrifice. He is quite taken with pagan rituals."

"What sort of sacrifice?" Sebastian probed.

"A young maiden taken at midsummer. A vestal virgin deflowered on All Hallows' Eve. Worshipping the gods of old. That sort of thing."

"Willing virgins are not easy to come by," Sebastian pointed out.

"We started with whores, choosing girls who were new to the profession. There was something intoxicatingly primal about taking those women in front of our friends. It made us brothers for life."

"Indeed. I take it you felt no remorse?" Superintendent Lovell inquired.

"Why should we have? They fuck for a living. What difference does it make if they fuck thirteen men in the course of a long night or one straight after another?"

"I expect they might have some objections if consulted," Sebastian said.

George shrugged, as if the very notion of these women having feelings had never occurred to him.

"So, you continued to meet after your Cambridge days?" Sebastian asked.

Seaborne nodded. "We did, but not as often. Life tends to get in the way of gentlemanly pursuits," he added with a smirk.

"When did you meet?" Lovell asked.

"At first, we gathered to mark the pagan festival days, but these last few years we only met on All Hallows' Eve. Peter White's brother is a curate at All Hallows by the Tower. We thought it was providence that we should meet there, given the name. The door is locked at night, but Harold White left the door open for us on All Hallows' Eve. That's how we got in."

"And every time you met you snatched some unsuspecting young woman?" Superintendent Lovell demanded.

"Only whores and maidservants," George replied with an air of infuriating superiority. It was as if the women they'd hurt weren't even human, just a means to an end that could be thrown away once the men were finished with them. Sebastian was sure that George Seaborne would not care about the child his friends had sired on Saoirse Byrne or the fact that she had died because of what they had done to her.

Most murderers paid for their sins at the gallows, but there were some for whom hanging was too good. They deserved to suffer the way they had made others suffer, their final moments on earth filled with agonizing pain and an unrepentant lack of mercy. There was only one man who had qualified for such a fate in the past, but Sebastian was beginning to think that George Seaborne might be another.

"How did you graduate from rape to murder?" Superintendent Lovell asked, interrupting Sebastian's morbid thoughts.

George stared mutely at the scarred wooden desk, his jaw working as he tried to figure out how to extricate himself from a charge of murder.

"I think I can answer that, sir," Sebastian said, and turned to George. "You met Amelia Paine when you visited the milliner's shop where she worked. You took a fancy to her and thought you could get away with taking her. You'd done it before and didn't think anyone would look into her claims too strenuously, Amelia being your social inferior. So you waited for her to finish work on October thirty-first, then offered her a ride home. She recognized you, was flattered by the attention, and accepted the ride. I expect you offered her some brandy laced with opium, then took her to the church. Perhaps you never intended to kill her, but she threatened to report you to the police, and you panicked. So you strangled her and left her body on the other side of town, just to make certain no connection could be made to All Hallows by the Tower or your bosom companions."

"I didn't strangle her. It was Peter White. She wouldn't stop screaming."

"But you did strangle your sister after you had invited her to join you for an All Hallows' séance with your friends. You had it all planned. Adelaide was flattered to be included and probably thought it exciting to be sworn to secrecy. She was to sneak out after dinner and make her way to the carriage that would be waiting for her."

"Why would I kill Addie?" George cried.

"Because killing her would protect your inheritance," Sebastian replied.

"It was never about the money. And I never meant for her to die," George exploded. "I only wanted to ruin her so no decent man would marry her."

"Why?" Superintendent Lovell exclaimed. "She was your sister."

"Because I hated her!" George Seaborne roared.

"What had that poor girl ever done to you?"

"Adelaide replaced me in my father's affections, just as her mother had destroyed my mother. My father got that whore with child while my mother was ill, recovering from yet another stillbirth. Mother was improving, and then suddenly she was gone. Just like that. I always suspected foul play. It's easy enough to get rid of a wife that's no longer fit for purpose."

For a moment George looked like a heartbroken little boy, but the expression was immediately replaced by bitterness and anger. "I never expected my father to marry his mistress, but I expect my stepmother is really talented between the sheets. Or maybe she knew the truth about my mother's death, and this was a way for my father to keep her quiet. Anyway, I despised Adelaide from the day she was born, but I never saw her as a threat, not until I realized how well she might marry."

"You were afraid your sister would outrank you?" Sebastian taunted.

George Seaborne looked away, but not before Sebastian noticed the panic in his gaze. That was it, the reason Adelaide had had to die, or one of them. George couldn't bear the thought that the sister he despised would rise above him and become a marchioness while he remained plain Mr. Seaborne until his father finally died, which wouldn't happen for years yet, possibly decades.

"So, you had hoped to disgrace your sister and claim her dowry as a consolation prize when she failed to marry," Superintendent Lovell said.

George shot them a look of pure vitriol. "You just don't get it, do you? It wasn't about the money or the rank, although the thought of her as a marchioness did sting somewhat. I wanted to hurt my father and his worthless whore. I wanted to destroy their little darling and watch them suffer. And once my father was dead, I would cut her off without a farthing, regardless of what he had stipulated in his will."

"So why did you encourage Adelaide to accept David Parker?" Superintendent Lovell asked. "He isn't a marquis, but his family is wealthy and influential."

George sighed and shook his head, as if he couldn't believe how thick Lovell was being. "If Adelaide married Parker against my father's wishes, he would have cut her off, and that would have served my purpose just as well. I wanted her gone. Erased from our lives. Cut off from my father. But dear Addie wasn't about to forsake her position and go off to America. She wanted Father's blessing, and she meant to have her portion. That was when I realized I had to come up with a new plan, one that would destroy her so utterly there would be no coming back."

"So you had your friends rape your sister?" Sebastian ground out. "Did they not object? Surely some of them had met her and had perhaps even held her in high regard."

Seaborne shrugged. "Most of my friends understand the importance of pedigree and the bonds of loyalty. A few needed to be persuaded."

"In other words, you blackmailed them into doing your bidding," Sebastian said.

"I prefer persuaded."

"Was Thomas Wright one of the men who needed to be coerced?" Lovell asked.

George smiled wolfishly. "Thomas has his uses."

"Because of his eye?"

The smile grew more satisfied until George must have realized it was just that miscalculation on his part that was responsible for his arrest. A man with a less memorable visage might have been the key to getting away with murder.

"Did you ravage your sister as well?" Superintendent Lovell asked.

"What kind of monster do you take me for?" George cried. Neither man replied. "Anyway, once the opium wore off, she fought like a tiger, and tore off my mask when I tried to restrain her. Once she knew I was there, there was no going back. She would tell Father."

"So you beat her head against the stone floor and strangled her, then had your flunky, who would do anything to remain in your good graces, take the body to Highgate in his father's carriage and mount her on a cross while you watched. The purpose being that there would be no doubt that Adelaide was dead, and your father wouldn't waste endless time and resources searching for her."

George nodded again.

"Why the pig's heart?" Superintendent Lovell asked. "Was it to emphasize her lack of *pedigree*?" Lovell emphasized the word and made it sound like an affliction. At this stage, he probably had more regard for a farm animal than for the man seated before him.

"The pig's heart was meant to serve a dual purpose," Sebastian interjected before Seaborne could reply. "Mr. Seaborne detested his father's valet and wanted to frame him for the murder. He thought that a pig's heart used to desecrate his sister's body would point the finger at someone who saw the entrails of a pig as the worst possible insult. He also resented his father's interest in the Islamic religion and feared that the viscount wouldn't stop at reading the Qur'an. He'd heard of several well-respected Englishmen who converted to Islam after time spent in India and Turkey. One such individual was the viscount's good friend, Jonathan Wright, who practiced in secret since he feared losing his position in Parliament should the truth come out. Mr. Seaborne feared that his father might be tempted to do the same, especially once he lost his beloved daughter." Sebastian fixed Seaborne with a hard look. "I would hazard a guess that your father was aware of your feelings on the subject."

George Seaborne hunched his shoulders and stared at his cuffed wrists.

"To hang the heart of a pig around Adelaide's neck must

have come like a flash of inspiration, meant as an added insult to your father. Both your and Thomas Wright's fathers, in fact—but it was that oversight that led your father to suspect you. Once he heard about the heart, he realized that his daughter's killing had been neither random nor spontaneous. It had been quite premeditated, and the killer could be his own son or the son of his close friend. I expect he prayed to any God that would listen that he was wrong, but, when we arrived to take you into custody this morning, he knew that the only reason we'd barge into the residence of a viscount and take his son was if we had proof of his involvement."

"I only wanted to get rid of that sanctimonious heathen and teach my father a lesson," George cried. "He was so fascinated by all that codswallop. I was afraid he'd disgrace the family and turn us into pariahs."

"Ironic that the disgrace proved to be you," Sebastian said.

"A lesson your father will never forget," Superintendent Lovell agreed.

Sebastian was satisfied that George Seaborne would be charged with the murder of his sister, but there was one more charge he needed to bring.

"You accompanied Thomas Wright to Highgate and watched from afar as he mounted Adelaide on the cross. You couldn't bear to miss seeing your sister disgraced and wanted to ensure that Thomas Wright followed your instructions to the letter. That was when you saw Victor Tate. Mr. Tate had seen Thomas Wright, and you couldn't be sure that he hadn't seen you as well. If he had, he might have been able to identify you from society photos or make the connection once the victim was identified.

"Deciding not to risk it, you followed Mr. Tate, waited until he summoned a constable and made his report, all the while hoping that he would mention Thomas Wright's damaged eye, then boarded the same omnibus while Thomas Wright followed in the carriage. You weren't as discreet as you had thought because Victor realized he was being followed. He even made a note of it in his notebook. When he got off the omnibus, you got off behind him and pushed him just as the omnibus began to move. He didn't stand a chance. The wheels rolled right over him. You waited in the carriage while Thomas Wright pretended to help the victim in an effort to make certain he was dead. You couldn't afford any witnesses, in case the crime was attributed to you. And no one would be able to state that Thomas Wright was on the same omnibus, since he wasn't there."

"How?" George choked out. "How did you figure it all out?"

"You're not as clever as you imagine yourself to be, Mr. Seaborne," Sebastian replied. "Mr. Harrow of the *Daily Telegraph* happened to be acquainted with Thomas Wright and was able to identify him as the man he saw at the scene of the accident. That in itself meant little, since there was nothing to tie Thomas Wright to either murder, but Victor Tate had mentioned Mr. Wright's deformity in his notes, and, when I called at your club, there was your name in the register, right above Thomas Wright's, on October the thirty-first. The concierge was happy to confirm that you are good friends and dine together often, sometimes with other university chums. The rest was easy enough to figure out once I had a clearer idea of what I was looking for."

Sebastian pulled out his watch and consulted the time. "I'm sorry, sir, but I must get to a funeral. Would you like to do the honors?"

"It will be my pleasure," Superintendent Lovell said. "George Seaborne, I hereby charge you with two counts of murder, abduction, rape, interference with human remains, and the attempted murder of a police officer. You will be transported to Newgate Prison, where you will await trial. Take him down," he called out to Constable Meadows, who was waiting outside. "And arrest Peter White."

He turned to Sebastian. "Take a few days, Bell. You'll need to see to that shoulder."

"Yes, sir," Sebastian replied, and headed for the door.

FORTY-EIGHT

Sebastian and Colin Ramsey made it to Highgate Cemetery just in time for the funeral. The undertakers' carriage was already there, a modest conveyance for those who didn't have the luxury of ordering extravagant catafalques and black-plumed horses. The coffin was also plain, one step above a pine box. Sebastian and Colin joined the small knot of mourners by the yawning grave. Jacob Harrow and two other men, presumably colleagues, stood to the right of Miss Tate, and a woman dressed as a nurse beneath her dark cape stood to her left. There was another gentleman, dark-haired and well dressed, standing just behind Miss Tate.

Miss Tate looked concerned when she took in Sebastian's appearance, but there wasn't time to ask for an explanation.

"Shall we begin?" the vicar asked, and Miss Tate nodded her consent.

She didn't weep during the service, and only the tension in her shoulders and the pallor of her veiled face spoke to her grief. Afterward, she thanked everyone for coming and introduced Sebastian and Colin to her employer, Mr. Gadd, and her friend, Miss Lydia Morton. Within a few minutes everyone was gone, including Colin Ramsey, who had a fresh corpse awaiting his attention. That left Sebastian and Miss Tate alone.

"The killer is in custody, Miss Tate."

She looked up at him, her gaze clear and focused. "George Seaborne."

It wasn't a question but a statement of fact, and Sebastian couldn't help but smile. If they would allow women into the police service, he thought Gemma Tate might make quite a name for herself.

"Yes."

"What will happen to him?"

"I expect he'll hang," Sebastian replied.

"And if the judge decides to forgo the death penalty?"

"He will still spend the remainder of his days in prison, or possibly get sent down to Botany Bay, which from what I hear can be a fate worse than death."

Miss Tate nodded. "It's his father I feel sorry for. To lose both children, and in such an awful way. At least if George Seaborne had died in Crimea, the viscount could have said that his son was a hero. All he can say now is that his son was a remorseless killer. Do you think he knew?"

"I think that perhaps he had suspected, but no father wants to think the boy he loves is capable of murder."

"We're all capable of murder," Miss Tate said quietly. "Only sometimes the murder is praised and sometimes it's punished."

She was no doubt referring to the carnage she'd seen in Crimea, and Sebastian couldn't help but wonder just how deep a scar such an experience left on a person's heart and mind.

Miss Tate looked up at him, her gaze warm with concern. "Are you in a lot of pain?"

Sebastian nodded. "George Seaborne wasn't going to go down without a fight."

"I'm sorry you're hurt, but I thank God you're alive and that Mr. Ramsey is looking after you. Is there anything I can do?"

"I'll be all right," Sebastian hurried to reassure her.

"I can help in other ways," she said softly, her gaze caressing his face.

"I'm sure I don't know what you mean, Miss Tate." Sebastian thought he might be blushing. What on earth was she offering?

"I think you formed a dependency on opium after your wife died. There's no shame in it, Inspector. Grief and self-blame are not easy to live with."

Sebastian nodded. Gemma Tate was too perceptive for her own good. Or maybe his. "I mean to break the habit."

"I can help. Mr. Gadd has offered to give me another week off, fully paid. He's still hoping I will accept his offer. I can come by and look after you."

Sebastian chuckled. "No women allowed," he said, quoting Mrs. Poole.

"I'm not a woman," Miss Tate replied with an ironic grin. "I am a nurse. I can wear my uniform if that will pacify your landlady."

"Think of your reputation, Miss Tate," Sebastian said, but he would welcome her help, and he longed for her company.

"I'll take my chances," Miss Tate said. "My reputation is not uppermost in my mind just now. May I call on you tomorrow?"

Sebastian opened his mouth to refuse, to assure her that he could manage on his own, but he couldn't bring himself to lie. "Yes," he said.

"Then perhaps you had better call me Gemma," she said with a small smile. "We are about to spend a lot more time together."

"Gemma," he said softly, and, as he looked down at her upturned face, he knew that this woman had the power to save him.

EPILOGUE

December 1858

Sebastian made a mug of tea and settled at his desk, ready to dive into paperwork. Superintendent Lovell had kept him on light duties since he'd returned to work a week ago, but he didn't mind. His shoulder was on the mend, he hadn't gone anywhere near Mr. Wu's opium den in well over a month, and the time he'd spent with Gemma Tate had been a balm to his soul. He still missed Louisa and thought of her every day, or more accurately every hour of every day, but the weight he carried was just a little bit lighter, and his guilt a little less visceral.

Christmas was around the corner, and he hoped that this year he wouldn't be spending it alone. Besides, he'd received the best present a man could hope for. George Seaborne had been found guilty on all counts and was to be hanged in the new year. Thomas Wright and the remaining Sons of Hades were all headed to prison, except for Peter White, who would be joining George Seaborne on the scaffold. It was the best outcome Sebastian could have wished for, and he was glad.

He took a sip of his tea, then nodded as Superintendent

Lovell walked into the office, his expression one of extreme irritation.

"Everything all right, sir?" Sebastian asked.

"A man was hanged from Traitors' Gate. With a meat hook. A passing boatman spotted the body and reported it to a constable. I assume you're ready to get back to work?"

"You assume correctly, sir."

Lovell smiled. "Good man. This is just the sort of thing newspapermen live for. Don't give them any reason to rake the Yard over the coals, Bell."

"You can count on me, sir," Sebastian replied.

He grabbed his coat and hat and was out the door before Superintendent Lovell could come up with any more admonitions. He couldn't wait to get started on a new case.

A LETTER FROM THE AUTHOR

Huge thanks for reading *The Highgate Cemetery Murder*; I hope you were hooked on the case as Sebastian and Gemma struggled to get justice for Addie and Victor. Their adventures will continue. If you want to join other readers in hearing all about my new releases and bonus content, you can sign up for my newsletter!

www.stormpublishing.co/irina-shapiro

If you enjoyed this book and could spare a few moments to leave a review, that would be hugely appreciated. Even a short review can make all the difference in encouraging a reader to discover my books for the first time. Thank you so much!

Thanks again for being part of this amazing journey with me and I hope you'll stay in touch—I have so many more stories and ideas to entertain you with!

Irina

irinashapiroauthor.com

facebook.com/IrinaShapiro2
x.com/IrinaShapiro2
instagram.com/irina_shapiro_author

Printed in Great Britain
by Amazon